MARK LAGES

SCOWL

THE
BONAPARTE INTERVIEWS

authorHOUSE®

AuthorHouse™
1663 Liberty Drive
Bloomington, IN 47403
www.authorhouse.com
Phone: 1 (800) 839-8640

Published by AuthorHouse 04/17/2019

ISBN: 978-1-7283-0882-1 (sc)
ISBN: 978-1-7283-0883-8 (e)

Library of Congress Control Number: 2019904559

INTRODUCTION

The following compilation of Scowl interviews spans forty-four years, and although I am talking to the same man over and over, the interviews cover a wide variety of topics. Since Scowl has never been shy or at a loss for words, a lot of editing was required to make everything fit into a concise book that would be short enough to entice readers, yet long enough to say what I thought the book should say. Also, some redundant interviews were dropped completely, but you will be pleased to learn that some interviews in this book have never been published before and are just now seeing the light of day. All the interviews are presented in chronological order, beginning in August 1957, the same month and year that *American Bandstand* hit the ABC television network. The interviews end in 2001, just a few months prior to the September 11 attack on the World Trade Center. Prior to each interview, I offer some insights and background for each conversation I had with Scowl. I've tried my best to make this book flow like a single cohesive story, like a biography told through the subject's answers to my questions. I don't think you'll have to be a diehard fan of Scowl to appreciate this book, and fan or not, I think you'll enjoy reading this anthology as much as I've enjoyed putting it together. So, without any further ado, make some popcorn, buckle your seat belts, hold on to your hats, and let the games begin.

Learn more at:
www.marklages.com

The First Interview

—•—

I n order to completely comprehend the meteoric rise of the white-hot, guitar-playing phenomenon known to the world as Scowl, you really had to be there. You had to be living in America in the fifties, in tune with this great *Ozzie and Harriet* and *American Bandstand*–crazed country. As a wet-behind-the-ears arts and entertainment journalist, I was right there, with my finger on the pulse of it all. My name is Ralph Bonaparte. When Scowl made his first appearance on *The Ed Sullivan Show* in the spring of 1957, I was twenty-six years old and working at the *Los Angeles Times*. It was my first job after having graduated college, and let's just say I happened to be at the right place at the right time, standing with a rabid crowd of other reporters covering Scowl's performance. It was my first interview with Scowl that put me on the map as a journalist, and I'll always be grateful for the opportunity. Many reporters tried to gain favor with the popular songwriter and singer. He was a bona fide American sensation. He could make the young girls lose their minds and scream like crazy. He was the latest and greatest in a recent wave of popular young stars to burst onto the music scene in the fifties, and everyone wanted a piece of him. But it was me. I was the one he picked out of the group for his first interview.

I have always wondered why he selected me rather than one of the more influential and established reporters. I mean, he could've had his choice of anyone. We were all willing, able, and scrambling to cut a deal with him. I heard he'd been offered unimaginable amounts of money and promises for cover photo shoots in high-circulation magazines, and what red-blooded teenager would turn down money and the promise of more and more fame for an interview with a young nobody like Ralph Bonaparte? Why he picked me out has always been a mystery to me. Perhaps he felt someone as young as me would be better suited to relate to his nubile followers, and perhaps he didn't trust the older reporters. Or perhaps he saw something in my eyes, like I was the sort of person he felt he could confide in. Or maybe he just felt sorry for me standing there without a chance in hell, my notepad and pencil in hand, overshadowed by older and more experienced press men.

"Hey, you there," he said, pointing at me, "come with me."

"Me?" I asked, and he nodded his head and walked away. Like a dumb puppy dog following its new master, I followed right behind him, and we climbed into his black Cadillac limousine. We drove and talked all the way to his hotel in Beverly Hills, and when we were done, he stepped out and had the limo driver take me back to my car at the concert venue. You know, I've asked him several different times why he chose me that evening, and he always evades the question. Maybe there was no real reason. Who knows? He either jokes around about something unrelated, changes the subject, or just tells me to move on to my next question.

Like I've said, to understand how Scowl burst on the popular music scene, you have to understand the fifties in America. It was a glorious and remarkable time, and I honestly don't think there has ever been, nor will there ever be, another decade quite like it. It was a clean-cut, butch-waxed, black-and-white TV, Coca-Cola-powered age of innocence and optimism, an age of malt shops, jukeboxes, souped-up hot rods, and rollicking dance hops. It was all things that were clean, happy, and pure. I don't know how else to describe it. I know it all sounds too good to be true, but things were different back then. Moms were stay-at-home moms, and dads were working-stiff dads. Gays were all still in their closets. Walt Disney opened the doors to Disneyland, and Mickey and Minnie Mouse romped about on cartoons on their TV clubhouse and became household words. Marilyn Monroe was in her twenties, untouched by the demons that would later corrupt and kill her. Dwight Eisenhower was our television-friendly president, and his God-fearing wisdom was unquestioned. He informed the nation he would send a handful of unarmed advisors to Vietnam to keep the Communists from threatening our red-white-and-blue way of life, and we all believed in him. His heart was always in the right place. He raised the minimum wage from seventy-five cents to a dollar (wow, a whole dollar!). He built the interstates and brought us and all our shiny, American-made automobiles closer together. One nation under God! But

2

you have to think television to understand how Scowl became such a sensation. Television was the means, for while Lucy was giving birth to little Ricky and while Fess Parker entertained us as Davy Crockett in a silly coonskin cap, the stage was being set for a completely different kind of idol—a rebellious troubadour, a scowling, guitar-strumming bard, a strange-looking teenager who would set fire to the hearts and souls of America's youth. They had heard him on the radio, but when he finally appeared on *The Ed Sullivan Show,* he entered our living rooms and became more than just a guitar and a voice. The kids went crazy over him. He turned the fifties upside down and inside out with his gravelly voice, his catchy song lyrics, and his unorthodox dance moves. Because of his perpetual sneer, they all called him Scowl.

So who exactly was this boy? Where did he come from, what were his parents like, what did he eat for dinner, and what was his favorite color? Everyone in America—and I mean everyone—wanted to know more about him. When Scowl invited me into his limo that evening after the concert, I knew I was on the brink of something big, something much more important than any other story or person I'd ever covered, perhaps more important than anything I would ever do in the future. In the limo, Scowl reached for a crystal decanter and poured himself a half glass of whiskey. He asked if I wanted any, and I shook my head.

"Aren't you too young to be drinking?" I asked.

He just laughed at my question. "I'm Scowl," he said. "Haven't you been paying attention? I can do any damn thing I want to do." And he was probably right. Men three times his age were duking it out for the chance to be a part of his inner circle. Everyone wanted to be with this boy, and no one was about to deny him anything. He was a star, and that was undeniable. And stars get their way. "You know, there are a lot of other reporters who would give their right arm to be sitting with me now," he said, sipping his whiskey. "But I handpicked you. You want to make a name for yourself? You want an interview with me? Well, my good man, now you've got it. Just be sure not to go too easy with the questions. I don't want anyone kissing my rear end. Don't be afraid of me. If you're up-front and honest with me, I'll be the same back. But you've got to promise to be a straight shooter." Scowl stared at me, sizing me up, wondering what I was going to say.

"I can do that," I said.

"Fine, fine, fine," Scowl replied. "Then we have an understanding. Now go ahead and start your interview. Ask me anything you like." He reached for a comb from his back pocket to comb his wavy hair, and that was precisely how my first conversation with Scowl began. I racked my brain for something intelligent to ask him while he drank his whiskey and gazed out the window. The date was August 17, 1957. I will never forget the date. Not ever. In a way, it was a birthday. It was the birthday of a relationship that would last for decades.

———— ⊶⊷ ————

You asked me to interview you this evening here in your limousine. Is there a reason why you picked me over all the other reporters?

No, ask me another question.

Okay, how do you think the concert went tonight?

I think it went great. I didn't get all cockamamie nervous and didn't forget any of the words to my songs. I hate when I forget the lyrics. The boys all played their best, and the audience was outstanding. I'd be happy if every concert went this well.

Do you ever get nervous before concerts?

Once in a while I get the jitters. Not very often, but once in a while. And sometimes I'll make a mistake. Of course, with all the girls shouting and screaming, it's hard to tell when I make a mistake.

Does all the screaming bother you?

Sometimes I wish the girls would tone it down a notch, especially during certain songs. Great Scott, I wonder sometimes if they can even hear anything I'm doing onstage. I mean, it's all about the music, isn't it? That's really what I am, a musician. I'd like to be known for my music above all else. If it makes the girls scream, then so be it, but I'd like them to listen.

Some critics have said it's your trademark sneer and crazy dance moves the girls come to see—that you're just an idol and that your music is irrelevant.

They're just critics. That's what they do. They like to criticize. It's kind of a crappy way to make a living, but that's what they do.

So you don't agree with them?

They're not giving my fans enough credit. And they're not giving me enough credit. I'll bet a lot of them are envious. Envy makes people say odd things.

Where did you learn to dance?

Dance? Is that what you call it? I guess it's just something that comes natural to me. I move the way the music makes me feel. If it looks different from anything you've seen, it's because my music is so different. I'm not like other performers because my music is so unique. No one's heard anything like it, not ever, not even me. Heck, sometimes I surprise myself.

What makes your music so unique?

It has to do with the way I was raised.

What's so special about how you were raised?

It's no secret that my dad was a butcher and my mother was a homemaker. They were as on-the-level and pure middle class as Ward and June Cleaver. But they had something special in mind when it came to raising me. They never tried to mold me into anything ordinary. They taught me the world was a wide and wonderful place that was filled with promise and opportunity. They always recognized my creativity. When I showed a desire to draw, they bought me a ton of crayons, charcoals, and pastels. When I showed an inclination to write, they bought me a brand-new typewriter and reams of paper. When I showed an interest in music, they came home with an acoustic guitar and had a piano installed in the front room. They never had me take music lessons of any kind; rather, they wanted me to explore and fend for myself. And, of course, I was influenced by other popular musicians who were selling music at the time, but my sound came largely from my own creative juices. I think I have my parents to thank for all this.

Are your parents fans of your music?

I wouldn't say they're fans. I'm not really sure they understand it. But they're happy I'm doing what I like to do. They're proud of my independence. And they're proud of my success. Dad says, "I don't really get it, but you must be doing something right."

Did you parents have any musical talent?

Dad sang in the church choir when he was my age. I've heard him try to sing solo as an adult, and he's not very good. He sings off-key, and I always feel kind of bad for him. I don't think he realizes what a crappy singer he is. That's about it for him. Mom never did anything musically to speak of. I had an uncle in Louisiana who played the trombone for a little Dixieland band, but I never heard him play. I saw he was interviewed recently by a magazine reporter, and he said he didn't care for my music. Most adults don't care for what I do.

Tell me about the money. What's it like to be such a moneymaker, to have access to so much cash at the age of nineteen?

Great Scott, it's fantabulous.

Can you tell me any good stories?

Well, I guess all your readers know about the house in Beverly Hills I bought for my parents. And I guess they know about the new Cadillac I bought for Mom. But here's a story your readers may not know anything about, the day I rented an entire movie theater in Culver City to see *Rebel Without a Cause.* I've always been a big James Dean fan, but the last time I tried to go to a movie, I was swarmed by crazy girls who recognized me. It was a disaster, and I had to leave before the movie even started. So rather than go through that ordeal again, I rented out a movie theater. I brought along a couple friends, and we had the entire place to ourselves. The proprietor made a batch of popcorn just for us, and we watched *Rebel Without a Cause* without any interruptions. It was an expensive day, but I could easily afford it, and it was worth every penny. I think when Dean died in Salinas, we lost a true national treasure.

Did you know some people have called you the new James Dean?

I know it's meant as a compliment, but it's kind of a dumb comparison. He was an actor, and I'm a musician. I don't want to be thought of as an actor, or a writer, or as an artist. I want to be known for my music.

What do you think of people calling you Scowl? Does the nickname bother you?

It doesn't bother me. It's just a nickname, and they don't matter much. Listen, I know I have a kind of sneer on my face. I don't do it on purpose. It's just the way I look. You can even see it in my baby pictures. It's kind of funny.

What's your real name?

It's Arnold Simon Kruse. My parents named me after my grandfather, my father's father. His name was Arnold. I understand that he was a character. He fancied himself as an inventor, but I don't think he really invented anything that anyone uses. Just before he died, he was working on a perpetual motion machine. I don't know where Mom and Dad got my middle name. I think they just liked the sound of it.

There's a rumor that you're having your name legally changed to Scowl. Is there any truth to this?

I was thinking of it. No one ever uses my full name anymore. Everyone just calls me Scowl, so I may as well get the name changed.

Speaking of names, there's a rumor about one of the names you used in your songs. They say your hit "Dear Cindy" is actually about a girl by the name of Cindy Lou Jacobsen, a girl you used to date in high school. Is this true? Is the song about her?

No, the two Cindy's are unrelated. Yes, one is a real girl I dated, and the other is just a name I used to write a song. Picking names in my songs is an arbitrary process. I just choose the name that feels right for the sound of the song. In this song I was actually looking for a name that rhymed with windy. Then I changed the lyrics so that the word windy was no longer in the song, and I guess I could've changed the name of the girl, but I didn't. Cindy it was. Sometimes people draw parallels between my songs and my personal life that don't exist. It can be annoying. I now realize I should've used a name other than Cindy, but when I wrote that song, I wasn't famous, and I had no idea that people would be reading so much into it. Live and learn, I guess.

Do you still see Cindy Jacobsen? Do the two of you still talk?

I haven't spoken to Cindy for several years. I heard several reporters have tried to interview her, but that her dad told them to leave her alone. I don't think her dad wants her to become known as the girl who dated Scowl. I don't think he'd consider it a compliment. Many adults have the wrong idea about me. They think just because I'm a performer that I'm a bad influence, that perhaps I'm even a little bit evil—you know, like I sold my soul to the devil for fame and fortune. I've heard there's a lot of talk about the way I dance when I sing, the way it seems to imitate some primitive African rituals, the way it seems so sexually suggestive. I can only tell these people that I move the way my music makes me feel, that I'm not trying to lure their children into any dark or bad place. Music is just music. Great Scott, these people just need to calm down.

I have one last question for you. There are many parents out there saying your performances and your kind of music are unchristian. So I need to ask you straight up, do you believe in Christ?

I've gone to church every Sunday for as far back as I can remember. I still go to church. My mother and father taught me to love Jesus Christ and let him into my heart. Like all of us in the world, I'm a sinner, but I'm also a God-fearing Christian. I always have been, and I always will be faithful. Don't believe everything you read about Scowl in the news. I'm not the anti-Christ. I'm not a bad person. There are a lot of lies being spread out there about me and my music. Well, maybe I shouldn't call them lies. Maybe I should just call them misunderstandings.

MAYBELLENE

— • —

My first interview with Scowl was a great success. It was printed in the entertainment section of the Sunday edition of the *Los Angeles Times,* and sales of the paper that weekend were off the charts. Not only were people talking about Scowl and the interview, but now they were talking about me, Ralph Bonaparte, the young reporter who wrote the article. They wanted to know how this neophyte journalist had been able to secure the interview of the year. I appeared on several news shows, and I was the subject of interviews myself. Everyone wanted me to tell them more about Scowl (which I wasn't really able to do). Just because I had done the interview with Scowl, they now thought I was some sort of rock 'n' roll and Scowl expert. A month after the interview, I received a handwritten letter from Scowl in the mail, complimenting me and thanking me for "a job well done" on the interview. "I knew you were the right person for the task," he wrote. "This coming October I'll be on board for a second interview. I'm giving you notice now, so you'll have plenty time to prepare and compose some better questions. The public is demanding information about me, and you're the person I choose to provide it. I'm going to have Bobby call you to arrange for a time and place." The Bobby he was referring to was none other than Bobby Breen, Scowl's manager and right-hand man. Back then, everything having anything to do with Scowl went directly through Bobby Breen. He was the thirty-four-year-old business guru behind the pop star, Scowl's sole chief executive officer, concert coordinator, product development expert, marketing manager, and advertising department all rolled into one five-foot ten, blond-haired, buck-toothed package. I was looking forward to hearing from him. Just the fact that I would be talking to him made me feel important, knowing my name was now in Bobby's Rolodex.

When Bobby finally called, I was working on a story about a singer named Jeffrey Sparks who was rising quickly in popularity at some LA clubs. But he was absolutely nothing compared to Scowl, and I dropped everything having to do with poor Jeffrey after Bobby called. I wanted to prepare myself for the upcoming interview. Scowl wanted to meet with me the first week in October in a private room at the Beverly Wilshire. He was on tour and would only be in town for a couple days. I worked like a darn dog to get ready for this second interview, listening to all Scowl's 45s over and over on the phonograph in my small apartment. I read every newspaper and magazine story about him I could get my hands on. I read the *Los Angeles Times* from cover to cover each morning, making myself familiar with current events, hoping to find some topical questions I could ask. I'd ask what he thought of Martin Luther King, Jr., and how he felt about Althea Gibson winning her title at Wimbledon? Did he read Senator John Kennedy's Pulitzer Prize-winning book *Profiles in Courage?* Did he have an opinion on the crazy underground nuclear tests being done in Nevada? How did he feel about the attention being paid to Alan Freed's radio show, about how respected psychologists were now tying rock 'n' roll music and culture to "medieval types of spontaneous lunacy" and "prehistoric rhythmic trances"? Seriously, you can't make this crap up. There were so many different questions to ask, I now wondered just how much time Bobby Breen was going to give me with his famous nineteen-year-old star. Would I have a half hour, a full hour, even a couple hours? Would I be able to keep asking questions until I ran out of things to ask? I called Bobby Breen and asked him about the time issue, and he told me I could have just an hour of Scowl's time. "Don't go over an hour," he warned. "If you go over, you might not be asked back." I was glad I called. Now I had something to work with, and I listed my most pressing questions on a sheet of paper and borrowed a tape recorder from the equipment room at the *Los Angeles Times*. I was ready for the interview with Scowl. I couldn't have been more ready.

In our last interview my closing question was about Christ, and you responded that you were a believer. Now I have to ask you, do you think God has had

anything to do with your remarkable success? Do you think he has special plans for you?

My good man, I think God has some special plans for each and every one of us. If we observe carefully, we'll know precisely what to do, we'll know where we're going, and we'll learn how to best get there. But we have to pay attention. God's a very busy man, and he hasn't got time to spoon-feed each of us the information we need to follow along with his wishes. I've had people ask me if I really believe I deserve all this fame and wealth. They wonder if I should be squandering money on Cadillacs, Rolex watches, four-fireplace homes. They ask if I should be renting an entire theater just to watch a new James Dean movie with a couple of friends. Can this sort of self-indulgence really be a part of God's divine plan? The very idea seems crazy to them. Well, what they don't understand is that fame and fortune are only a very small part of the equation. What is really important about me is my music. I believe this in my heart of hearts. I reach out and touch people with my music and with my lyrics, and I make the world a better place. If you listen to my songs, I mean really listen, you'll understand what I'm talking about. I believe Jesus Christ is speaking through me, helping others understand the world they live in. Through my music they're finding joy, accepting sorrow, and becoming better human beings. I am only a little over five feet tall, and you can rightly call me a runt, and to many adults I seem like a pesky fly they ought to swat. But sometimes big things come in small packages. And I am a big thing. Great Scott, make no mistake about it. You can't tune in a radio station today without hearing one of my songs, and you can't open up a newspaper or magazine without reading about my life. I'm everywhere, and it's no accident.

Tell me more about your music. I'm interested in your politics. Your song "Freedom Rings" has been described as a call for racial equality. In the song you say, "Someday a Negro will be our president." Did you really mean to say that?

Yes, I meant to say that.

Don't you think it's a little naïve? Or a maybe just a little farfetched?

Not at all. I specifically said someday. I didn't say today, or tomorrow, or the day right after that. I said someday, and I believe someday a man won't be judged by the color of his skin. I think it's a part of God's plan for us to treat one another as fellow human beings. That knucklehead Strom

Thurmond can talk until he's blue in the face, but it isn't going to stop progress. It's inevitable.

You realize this is the sort of thing that will hurt your record sales in the South?

I sell plenty of records. Selling lots of records has never been a problem for me.

No, I suppose not.

I keep telling you and everyone else that it's not all about fame and fortune. It's not about selling millions of records so I can get even richer. Sure, I get a kick out of having money and selling lots of records, but it's all about the music. You have to pay attention to the music. For me, the music is everything.

Can I ask you about another song? Tell me about "Ode to Rachael." What does this song mean?

What do you think it means?

I've heard a couple different interpretations. On its surface, it seems to be a story about a girl who falls in love and marries the boy of her dreams, only to have the marriage torn apart by friends and family. But I've also heard it interpreted to mean that Rachael was a colored girl who married a white boy, and her marriage was torn apart because no one accepted their interracial union. Who exactly are you talking to here? Are you really condoning interracial marriage? Who should be listening to this song?

Everyone should listen to my songs.

But who is your target audience?

The world is my target audience. I want everyone on the planet to listen to my music. Just because my music is popular with young people, just because girls scream when I sing, and just because a lot of teenagers buy my records, it doesn't mean my music was written solely for them. My music is for everyone, of every age, of every color, of every religion, and of every nationality.

Are you aware that Leonard Bernstein called you a fake?

He's entitled to his opinion.

You don't have anything to say in response?

No.

Don't you want to defend yourself?

My good man, what the heck do I care what a putz like Leonard

Bernstein thinks? What do I care what any naysayer thinks? I write my music from the heart. I know what I'm doing.

Is it true you bought you mom another Cadillac?

Yes, that's true. She now has two of them. One's red and the other is blue. I'm going to buy her a white one soon, and she'll then be red, white, and blue, just like an American flag. Great Scott! What could be more patriotic than that? Some people say I'm un-American, but they don't know what they're talking about. I'm as American as apple pie and baseball. When I cut my finger, I bleed Coca Cola. When I take the stage, the communists run for cover. I'm Chairman Mao's worst nightmare.

But can you understand how some people like Bernstein label you as a fake? On one hand you're trying to show a social conscience, and on the other you're buying your mom Cadillacs? Don't you see a contradiction here?

A contradiction?

Shouldn't you be doing something more constructive with your money?

What could be more constructive than pleasing your own mother? If more people took good care of their moms, the world would be a better place. I'm certain of this. And besides, people expect me to be extravagant. They'd be disappointed if I didn't buy my mom cars and a big house in Beverly Hills. They'd wonder what the heck was wrong with me, hoarding all my cash. They wouldn't have anything to fantasize about, and people live out their fantasies through my behavior. They wonder to themselves what they'd do with all this money, if only they were me. I'm just making the fantasy real for them, giving them something to dream about, living up to their expectations. What a dull world this would be if there weren't a few prodigal people like me.

That's not the answer I expected.

I promised that if you asked me honest questions, I'd give you honest answers. That's what I'm doing here. I'm just telling it like it is. So what's your next question?

What do you think of Marilyn Monroe?

Now this is interesting.

What do you mean?

We've gone from Negroes running for US president to a putz like Leonard Bernstein to Cadillacs and now to Marilyn Monroe in just a handful of questions. Was this your plan?

I have a lot of questions here on my list. I'm just trying to get through them all.

I think Marilyn just turned thirty, or maybe she is about to turn thirty. She's a very lovely woman, and she's become very popular. But you know, she seems too weak and vulnerable to me. I think she's headed for trouble. She seems like the kind of girl Hollywood will chew up and spit out. Does she appear that way to you? Whenever I see this woman in a movie, she seems like a schoolgirl trapped in a grown woman's body, like she'd probably be better off as a tomboy, walking around in overalls and pigtails. Her straps are always falling from her shoulders and her high heels are always falling from her feet. Doesn't she always look like her clothes are about to come off? I don't know, but there's something about this woman that makes me very uneasy, like she's headed with her eyes closed toward some kind of awful tragedy.

How about Elvis Presley?

I won't discuss my competition. It's bad luck. He seems like a nice guy. That's all I'll say.

So what do you think of the underground nuclear testing they're about to do in Nevada?

Are you familiar with my song "Atomic Genie"? I wrote it shortly after seeing *Them* at the drive-in in my hometown. Did you see *Them?* What a great flick! You must know something about this crazy movie, about the giant ants that attack the good people of New Mexico following the government's nuclear testing. In the movie the scientist says profoundly that "the atomic genie has been let out of the bottle." I liked that line, and that's where I got the idea for my song title. Are we going to be attacked by giant ants? Who the heck knows? I don't think we really understand all the repercussions of playing around with atomic energy. And why do we need to keep making bigger and bigger bombs? Pretty soon we're going to have enough of these bombs to destroy the entire world and the moon a hundred times over, and then what will we do? All it takes is for some dumbbell trigger-happy leader to get the ball rolling, starting up a great nuclear war. Have you ever listened to "Atomic Genie"? If you listen to the lyrics, you'll know exactly how I feel about it. Giant insects eating people? That's just the beginning.

I've listened to "Atomic Genie," and it's an intriguing piece of songwriting.

In fact, I've listened to all your songs, and I've come to like them a lot. So I say we now drop the current events and get back to the music. They say much of your unique sound comes not just from your unique voice, but from your band. When did you first meet the boys in the band, and how exactly did you put the band together?

It wasn't unusual for kids to join up and play in rock 'n' roll bands when I was younger. When I was seventeen, there was a group of boys who played around the block from my parents' house. They called themselves the Epics, and I'd heard them playing several times. There was Terry on the drums and Alan on the bass guitar. Richard played lead guitar, and Trevor blew the saxophone. Trevor could blow that saxophone like there was no tomorrow. They used to play in Trevor's garage, opening up the door so everyone in the neighborhood could hear. They played a lot of Chuck Berry tunes back then, and I would sit in Trevor's driveway with the other kids, listening to the music. Richard was the lead singer, but while the instrumentals and backup voice harmonies were pretty good, Richard's voice left a lot to be desired. He just wasn't a great lead singer. I approached the boys one afternoon and asked if they wanted a new singer, and they asked who I had in mind. "Why, me, of course," I said. They all looked at one another, and then they decided to give me shot at it. They played Chuck Berry's "Maybellene," and I grabbed the microphone and sang my dang heart out. Great Scott, do you know how it is when something sounds so perfect that it's obviously just meant to be? My voice meshed perfect with the boys' instruments, and we all knew right then and there that we had stumbled onto something very special, a sound other kids would want to hear. I joined up with the Epics, and my good man, the rest is history. I soon began writing songs for our band, and kids from all over the neighborhood would come to hear us play. And that's when we met up with Bobby Breen. One of the kids in the neighborhood knew Bobby's parents, so one thing led to another, and Bobby came to hear us play. He told us he wanted to be our manager. He said he could get us gigs and that maybe he could even get us a recording deal. Bobby was in the business, managing some other bands in Southern California. We trusted him and believed in his abilities. He seemed to know what he was talking about. So just two years later, here I am, one of the most popular rock singing stars in the country. I tell you, it all happened so fast that it just doesn't seem

way. There's really nothing I can do about it, and there's bound to be a little friction. It's never escalated so that we have had to worry about him leaving. Not yet, anyway.

When did people first begin to call you Scowl?

My uncle Teddy gave me the nickname years ago. He used to laugh and say I always looked like I was scowling. At first, I didn't like being called Scowl, but as time went by, the name sort of caught on. My dad was calling me Scowl, and then there were my friends. Bless her maternal heart, Mom has always called me Arnold. She still calls me Arnold to this day. On the day we first met, Bobby asked me my name, and I told him it was Arnold Simon Kruse. He said *that* name had to go. "No one's going to buy a record cut by someone named Arnold Simon Kruse." Then Richard said everyone called me Scowl. "That's perfect," he said. "From now on *everyone's* going to call you Scowl. Kids all over the world are going to be climbing all over one another in record stores and spending their parents' hard-earned money to buy Scowl's records." Some things, whether you like it or not, just happen. I guess it was inevitable. So I was Scowl.

Did you ever thank your uncle for giving you the nickname?

I did tell him it was his fault. He thinks it's all hilarious. "Just let me know if I can be of further help," he told me.

Everyone will want to know, and I've got to ask, do you have a girlfriend? Is there an important girl in your life?

Great Scott, are you kidding me? I have thousands of them, or haven't you heard. They all want to marry me. Even little ten- and eleven-year-olds. They all say they love me. They write me letters and tell me how they can't live without me.

I guess it'll be difficult to pick one out.

It will be impossible. I don't know if I'll ever be able to settle down with a girl.

Does anyone in the band besides Alan have a steady girlfriend?

No.

Do you stay in touch with any of your old high school buddies?

I'm on the road ten months out of the year. I don't really see any old friends. I've heard some of them called my parents' house looking for me, but I've never returned their calls. Between writing new songs and performing old ones, I don't have time for anything else. I'm like a slave to this business. Bobby and the band are my only friends, and honestly, I think they're the only friends I need.

I have one last question. If you were to be granted a single wish for anything in the world, what would you wish for?

Just one wish? Well, I'd wish for these days to go on forever, from now until the day I die. I wouldn't change a thing in my life. You know, I really blessed. Have you ever listened to the lyrics of my song "Everything I Want"? It's on my *Hopscotch* album. I think it's the third track on the second side. Now that song's all about me. I truly have everything I want.

THE PLANE CRASH

———•·•———

My second interview with Scowl was even more popular than the first. The *Los Angeles Times* published the interview in three installments to help them sell more papers. Scowl was now more popular than ever, and he was suddenly selling more records than any other popular artist, even more than good old Elvis. I began to get calls from the managers of other singers, hoping I would do interviews with them. Everyone suddenly wanted to be interrogated by Ralph Bonaparte, and the *Los Angeles Times* gave me a handsome raise. I received a letter from Scowl telling me again what a great job he thought I'd done and thanking me for my efforts. He said he'd call me soon to schedule another interview, but I didn't hear from him for nearly two years. Scowl continued to write new songs and pump out best-selling records. He was competing with the likes of the Everly Brothers, the Kingston Trio, and Little Richard. And of course, there was Elvis. These were great years for Scowl. Meanwhile, life in America was rolling forward toward the sixties. The Giants moved to San Francisco, and the Dodgers moved to LA. IBM sold its millionth electric typewriter. Hula-Hoops hit the market, and the public was swishing its hips and whirling twenty-five million of the stupid things around their waists. America was a wonderful place to live, and Scowl was at the apex. Then it happened, like an ominous portent. Buddy Holly and his friends died in their fateful plane crash on February 3, 1959. I got a call from Scowl a week after the accident, and he said the crash had made him realize just how fragile life was, and how precious time was, and how he was due for another interview. We set up a meeting for the following week at his Brentwood home, and I showed up with my tape recorder and list of questions. The drapes inside the house were drawn, and it was ominously dark. We sat on Scowl's front room sofa. He was now only twenty-one, but he looked like he'd aged ten years.

It's great to see you again, Scowl. It's been nearly two years since our last meeting. You called and told me you were deeply affected by the recent plane crash involving Buddy Holly, Richie Valens, and J. P. Richardson. Is there anything you specifically wanted to say about this tragedy to your fans?

I just want to say life is short. I don't know what else to say. Great Scott, life is so confoundedly short. It's an illusion, isn't it? I mean, when you're young, you feel like you're invincible, like your young life will go on forever. It's one of the great things about being young, knowing that you have your whole life ahead of you, knowing that death isn't on your doorstep. Heck, death isn't even in your neighborhood. He isn't even in your town. Then something like this happens to people you know, and you realize that death isn't so far away after all. You can feel him breathing down your back. A plane crash. A car wreck. A terminal cancer diagnosis.

Where were you when you got the news?

I was sitting here at my home. I was working on a new song about a boy who was remembering a girl from his past, wondering what it would be like if they ran into each other. Then Bobby called me with the awful news. It completely broke my concentration. He told me what happened, and I couldn't believe my ears. All that kept going through my mind was how amazingly fast a life can end. And then I realized something. I realized I was sitting in my house wearing nothing but a bathrobe and slippers in the middle of the day. I was all alone, and it seemed like I didn't have a friend in the world. I kept imagining God when it came my time to meet him, when my life was over. He was saying, "Where are your friends, Scowl? Where are all your friends?"

What else did Bobby say to you?

That was it. He gave me the news, and I hung up the phone. There's something terribly lonely about death, isn't there? The way it just shuts off the lights. I used to think we all went to heaven, but heaven is just so much bunk, isn't it? I won't be meeting God when I die. Now when I think of people dying, I think of them suddenly floating out in space, no oxygen, no gravity, no sounds or smells, just millions of pinprick stars representing all the other lonely souls who were once among the living, once laughing, working, breathing, coughing, sneezing, itching, and scratching. Oh, there was a terrible, cold loneliness about this vision, and thinking of it made me shudder. I mean, I really shuddered. I now realized I had no one in my life. I mean, I had my mom and dad, and I had Bobby and the boys in the band, but I didn't have a girl I could call my own. I had no life partner, nobody to share my days and nights with. I had no one who could keep my bed warm at night, and no one I could wake with in the morning. It occurred to me how ironic it was that this twenty-one-year-old musical sensation with a million or so female fans was so remarkably alone. I may as well have died in that plane crash.

Did you know any of the three victims personally?

Buddy Holly and I met briefly at a party given by Alan Freed. I never met the other two.

It sounds like this accident has affected you profoundly.

Yes, it's very upsetting.

You said heaven is bunk. Do you actually believe this? Are you having second thoughts about your own faith in Christianity?

Don't you ever wonder about this? When you think of heaven, aren't you immediately inclined to look upward? And when someone asks you where heaven is, don't you point up toward the clouds? But wait, when you're in Russia and you're asked the very same question, and when you point upward, you're actually pointing toward the opposite direction. How can heaven be in two opposite directions? Or are we saying God has a separate heaven for Russians than he does for all us Americans? If you're an American visiting Russia and you die, does your soul go up to Russian heaven where you won't like the food or be able to speak the language, or does the soul make a U-turn and go around the world so it can get into American heaven? And where exactly *is* heaven? Why haven't astronomers been able to see it with their powerful modern telescopes? I mean, seriously, they can see things that hover in space light years away, but so far there are no pictures of the pearly gates. Oh, I still believe in God, and I believe in the teachings of Christ, but I'm just not so keen on heaven as being an actual place.

Are you still going to church?

I have to admit I don't go as often as I should. I spend so much time on the road that it isn't feasible, and when I'm finally home, I'm so exhausted on Sundays that I just want to stay indoors and read a good book or magazine or watch TV.

You like to read?

Yes, I read quite a bit. I didn't used to read. It's something I'm doing more of now.

Are there any books you've read recently that you'd like to share with your fans?

I recently finished *Walden* by Henry Thoreau. It's a book everyone ought to pick up and read. It isn't like any other book I've known. It was written in the seventeenth century about this guy's life in the wilderness back east. He builds himself a small makeshift cabin and lives there alone for two years. The book describes his life in this natural setting, but most importantly it tells of all the different thoughts that go through his head. The book made me want to do something similar, leaving my own celebrity lifestyle behind and making due in a wilderness, growing my own food, hunting animals, and chopping firewood. Maybe I would keep a journal of all the things I thought about, the same way Thoreau did. I could bring an acoustic guitar along with me and write some music. I would let my hair and beard grow out, and I'd bathe just once a week in a pond, without any soap or shampoo. I'd like to believe I could be self-sufficient like this, that I could swing it. I think nowadays people are too dependent on one another, too specialized, and too addicted to modern-day comforts. Then I think to myself, would I really want to live in a dirty old cabin in the woods, among all the bugs and other vermin, shivering in the cold and sweating in the summer, without access to well-stocked grocery stores, hospitals, televisions, clean sheets, and indoor bathrooms? Thoreau's primitive lifestyle is fun to read about in a book, but I'm not sure I'd really want to try it out for myself. I like my big house here in Brentwood. I like my closet full of clothes, and I enjoy being able to click on the TV when I have nothing better to do. I enjoy sitting on my sofa, reading a good book in the evening, drinking a cup of tea or coffee. And there's nothing quite like being able to get up in the middle of the night and go to the kitchen for a snack, or to put on some warm, clean clothes right out of the electric dryer, or to wash up in a hot shower after a long day. No, I don't think I'd actually like to live like Thoreau, but I do like reading about him. That's the great thing about books—you can read and learn about how others have lived without ever actually having to do without all the conveniences you've grown used to.

Have you ever thought of being a writer?

Well, obviously, I do write lyrics for my songs. But I suppose you're referring now to writing something like a full-length novel. I have some ideas for a few books, but I don't think I have what it takes to work so long on one project. My song lyrics only require a few days, where a book requires months, maybe even years. I don't think I have the stamina for that.

I heard you were called by the noted biographer Harry Peters to write a book about you.

Yes, can you believe it? He called me last Wednesday to propose the project. I'm only twenty-one and already this guy wants to write my biography. I told him to forget about it. I told him my life had just started, and I hung up the phone. Some people seem to think I've done all I'll ever do and that my life has peaked. It's frustrating, being seen this way. I have a long way to go before I'll ever call it a day. I have so much left to live for and so much more to accomplish. I'm barely into chapter one of my life and already this guy wanted to write a book. He should've known better.

Besides your songwriting and performing, what other projects do you have in the pipeline?

Well, I swore I'd never do this, but it looks like I'll be in a movie. Me? An actor? Kind of funny, isn't it? I was approached by the producer Bill Atherton several months ago, and he wants me to be featured in a movie about a love story between a young motorcycle gang ruffian and a high school cheerleader. I'm supposed to play a Marlon Brando-type guy with a leather jacket and greasy jeans who meets this girl on the boardwalk in Santa Cruz while hanging out on a Saturday afternoon. The girl is with her friends and runs into the motorcycle guy after she rides the merry-go-round. They literally bump into each other in front of a cotton candy stand, and it's love at first sight. Later she brings the boy home to meet her family, and her parents become obsessed with breaking up the relationship. I have to play a bad boy, but he has this good side to him. The idea is that I've got myself trapped in this lifestyle of hanging around with motorcycle kids, when really all I want is a normal life with a wholesome girl, and I become torn between my ne'er-do-well motorcycle friends and this sweet and squeaky-clean high school student. I've never pictured myself as a movie actor, but I think I could do a good job playing this role. I can relate so well to this character. I know exactly what it's like to be trapped in a certain persona, unable to live a normal life, unable to just meet a nice girl and get to know her. Do you think I have any acting ability, or do you think I'm just fooling myself? I'm so used to being on stage, to having people watch me, expecting me to perform. Bill Atherton says I'm a natural for the part. He says their trying to get Nicholas Ray to direct the film, the same guy who directed *Rebel Without a Cause.* Can you imagine this? You know, I didn't want to be in movies, but I'm thinking this might be a great step for me. I can take Brando's role in *The Wild One* to the next level. I mean, Brando was great, but there's always room for improvement, right? They haven't come up with a title for the movie.

Do they have any idea who they'll cast as the high school girl?

Bill says they're talking to Natalie Wood. Can you imagine acting opposite Natalie Wood? Great Scott, like a dream come true! I think they're also talking to a girl named Audrey Wheeler. Natalie is a possibility if Ray directs the film, since he's already worked with her. But Bill says he likes Audrey Wheeler, that she's relatively unknown but perfect for the part.

When will the movie go into production?

I don't know yet. And I haven't even said yes to the role. I'm still thinking about it.

Let's say you agree to it. Will shooting this movie interfere with your performing and songwriting?

It probably will. But Bill thinks my fans are ready to see me in pictures. "It's the next logical step," he said. He said he might even have me perform a few songs. He isn't sure about this yet. He doesn't want the picture to be a musical. Bobby thinks this is a great opportunity, and the boys in the band said they wouldn't mind taking some time off from touring. Going from town to town is exhausting. Seriously, it seems like we've been on the road forever. I asked my mom and dad about this, and both of them liked the idea of me being a movie star.

Speaking of your mom and dad, how have they been?

They're fantabulous. No kidding, they couldn't be any better. With all the money I've been making, neither of them has to work, but Dad still works at the old butcher shop. He likes to keep busy. I guess carving up dead animals is in his blood. And Mom has her hands full with all her charities. When they heard about the plane crash, and when I told them how I felt about it, they both said doing this interview was a good idea. They said it would be good for me to get my feelings off my chest, to spend some time with you. They said whenever you publish one of our interviews, it seems to lift my spirits. It energizes me and gives me a more positive outlook on life. Do you remember our last meeting? I said that I had everything I wanted in life. I need to take my own words to heart. I need to appreciate what I have. It's true that I sometimes I get off track and forget how really great things are for me. Sometimes I wish things were different when I should be so grateful for what I have.

But you still wish you had a partner?

A partner?

A young woman like you described earlier, who you can share your life with?

Yes, I still wish I had her. I wish I could find a girl.

Are you giving up on it? You haven't sounded too optimistic.

Oh no, I'm not giving up. I'm just not sure how to go about finding her. I'm like the man stranded at sea in a little lifeboat, dying of thirst. I'm surrounded by this huge body of water, but unable to drink from it. It's an odd sort of irony, to be surrounded by all these girls but to also be unable to get to know even one of them. Maybe I should start a competition. I could solicit biographies and photographs from all my female fans, having them send them in, asking them to tell me why they should be my girl. I could have someone I trust go through them all and pick the most promising submissions. Heck, I could have you do it. You could narrow the group down to ten, and I could then invite each of them to my home for dinner. I could interview them and then pick one lucky girl to be mine, and mine forever. What do you think? Are you up to the task? I'm kidding, of course, but now that I think about it, maybe it's not such a crazy idea after all. I haven't come up with a better one.

Motorcycle Kid

—•—

After publishing the plane crash interview in the *LA Times*, the newspaper was overwhelmed with letters from Scowl's female fans. They misinterpreted his fanciful scheme to solicit girls as an actual request, and thousands sent in their photographs and bios. When I called Scowl and told him about the problem, he laughed out loud. "What do you want me to do with all these letters?" I asked, and Scowl said, "I don't want to look at them. Go ahead and destroy them." It was strange for me, charged with destroying all these letters, discarding the hopes and dreams of thousands of sincere Scowl fans. It was a little sad to think they believed they actually had a shot at winning over Scowl's heart. I couldn't believe they had misread the interview, that they had put so much time and effort into this bogus contest.

Six months following the interview, shooting started on the Bill Atherton film. Of course, Scowl was given the leading role. It was decided that Audrey Wheeler would play the girl. Atherton was unable to get Nicholas Ray as the director, so he chose a relatively unknown director by the name of Gabriel Sanchez. Sanchez had several black-and-white, low-budget horror films under his belt and was hoping to break into the youth market with this film. The title of the film would be *Motorcycle Kid,* and Atherton figured they could shoot the film, edit it, and have the whole thing ready for release in just a few months. I received a call from Scowl near to the end of shooting, and he said he had an announcement to make. He wanted me to drop everything I was doing and swing by the studios for a quick interview. When I arrived, I found Scowl in his trailer, between shoots and reading a book. He was seated on a sofa with his feet up on the coffee table, his hair plastered back and dressed in greasy blue jeans and a leather jacket.

I understand you're about done with the shoot. So tell me what it's it like being a movie star.

It's a gas.

You called and said you had an important announcement to make. Do you want to make it now?

Ask me some questions first. Ask me something about the movie.

Okay, how do you like acting? Is it anything like you thought it would be?

It's everything I thought it would be, and yet it's not at all what I expected. Being in front of cameras is something I'm used to and something I love, but I never realized how much I depended on my music. I've relied on my music as a crutch. When I'm in front of the camera as an actor, I have no band to back me up, no thumping bass or pounding drums or twanging guitars. It's just me and the lights and cameras and all my memorized lines of dialogue. The words sound so bare. My voice sounds so utterly naked. At first, it's the strangest sensation, but then slowly but surely you get used to it. Now I feel like a veteran, like I'm ready to sign up for my next movie. I talked to Bill, and he has several ideas in the works.

How do you like working for Gabriel Sanchez?

He's been terrific. He's a little younger than I thought he would be, but he's very knowledgeable. Did you know he was the director of *Bloody Birthday?* That was one of my favorite movies when I was in high school. He told me something interesting about the fake blood used in that film. Do you remember the scene where Judy cut into the birthday cake and blood squirted out from the incision? Did you know the fake blood wasn't even red, that it was just black India ink? They filled several balloons with ink and stuck them inside the cake. They don't have to use red blood in black-and-white movies. Black ink works just fine. Don't you find that interesting?

That was one Sanchez's biggest box-office hits. What other movies did he make? I'm not that familiar with his work.

He also filmed *Death on Blood River* and *The Bloody Creature*. Both those films were very popular when I was in high school. But *Bloody*

Birthday is the one I really remember. That was one of April Lancaster's first movies. I don't think she's doing horror movies anymore, but I had such a big crush on her back then.

Has Sanchez been helping you with your acting?

He's been a lifesaver. He helped me to express myself without my music. At first, it didn't seem like it would be possible. And he taught me to tap into my emotions without being too self-conscious. Most importantly, he got me to stop listening to myself as I spoke. I had a real problem with it, listening to my own voice. I would hear the words as they left my mouth, and it would distort all my perceptions, sort of like the feedback you get when you play a guitar too close to the amplifier. You can't be too self-conscious while you're acting. You just have to let yourself perform naturally, to go with the flow, to roll through the words of your dialogue without listening to yourself talk. It's a lot easier said than done, but once you get the hang of it, it's a lot of fun. It allows you to actually *be* your character, rather than just playing a character. It allows you to be a real actor.

Tell me about the character in the movie. What's he like? Is he similar to you?

His name is Tommy Bright. He's in a motorcycle gang, but he's misunderstood. He isn't like the other boys in the gang. Everyone thinks he's a bad seed, evil in a way, but deep inside he just wants to be like everyone else, to be loved and respected. And more than anything he wants to make this young girl his. She represents all that is right with the world, and he has fallen deeply in love with her and everything she stands for. He is similar to me, isn't he? I mean, how many parents would describe me as a bad seed, even as evil? I don't know how I earned this sort of reputation. All I've ever tried to do is perform my music, and my music comes from my heart. How could that be a bad thing? Yet I seem to bring out the worst in adults. I make them uncomfortable and suspicious. I cause them to keep their daughters from me. Seriously, I'm one of the most misunderstood men in America. Did you read about the preacher who recently held a record-burning party at his church in Alabama? He asked for all the teenagers in his community to bring their Scowl records with them to throw into the fire? Did you read about this? Why do I bring out so much animosity in adults? Like Tommy Bright, I am misunderstood.

Like any other red-blooded American kid, all I'm looking for is some love and respect from others. I'm not looking to hurt anyone, yet for all the trouble I seem to cause, I may as well be just another member of Tommy's motorcycle gang.

Will you be doing any singing in the movie?

I will only perform the theme song, "Motorcycle Kid." I wrote the song specifically for the movie, and I sing it during the beginning of the film. But the film isn't a musical. It's just a regular movie.

How has it been acting opposite Audrey Wheeler?

Audrey is the reason I asked you to come over for this interview. Audrey, Audrey, Audrey. Lovely, fair, brown-eyed, charming, leading-lady Audrey. One-in-a-million Audrey. Heart-of-gold Audrey. I'm here to tell you that I've fallen in love with her.

You've fallen in love with Audrey Wheeler?

The two of us are going to be married. I proposed to her last week, and she accepted. Great Scott, she said yes! I called her dad and asked if it was okay with him, and he gave me the green light. We haven't set a date for the wedding yet, but we'll be announcing it soon. I wanted you to be the first to know.

I'm stunned. How did this all happen?

Just like in the movie, it was love at first sight. I knew she was for me the minute I laid eyes on her, and she said she felt the same way about me. If when you see this movie in the theaters, you see sparks flying between us, it's because those sparks were actually flying. We are the real thing, the two of us. I have finally found my soul mate, and her name is Audrey Wheeler. She is soon to be the wife of Scowl. She will be packing up her things and moving into my house in Brentwood, and I've never been happier.

HERE COMES NANCY KIMBALL

—•◦•—

T
he wedding was held in the spring of 1960. It was a quiet event held
in Hawaii on the garden island of Kauai, and only a few close friends
and relatives were invited. The ceremony was performed with little fanfare.
During this same year, the Lakers moved from Minneapolis to LA, and
John Kennedy was nominated to run for president. I wasn't invited to
Scowl's wedding, and I didn't hear from him again until fourteen months
after he and Audrey tied the knot.

By the summer of 1961, Kennedy had been elected. Clark Gable had
died of a heart attack, and four hundred Green Berets were being sent to
help in Vietnam. Scowl had written and recorded a handful of love songs
over the past year that he packaged into an album and dedicated to his
new bride. The album was titled *For Audrey*. It's probably true that all his
female fans were sorely disappointed that he'd been married, but the union
didn't seem to stop them from buying his records. He was still one of the
country's top recording artists, and his sales showed no signs of waning.
He started filming his second movie, again with director Gabriel Sanchez.
This time he would be starring opposite female singing sensation Judy
Prout. The first movie had been a huge financial success, and producer
Bill Atherton proclaimed to the press that a new star had been born. He
promised the public a string of Scowl movies to come, and Scowl seemed
on board with this. I was busy at the time working on an article for the
LA Times all about Ernest Hemingway's death when I took the call from
Scowl at my office. He was ready for another interview and invited me to
join him for lunch at the Brown Derby in Hollywood. I brought along my

tape recorder and wondered what Scowl had on his mind. What intriguing piece of news did he want me to break to the newspaper-reading public?

First let me congratulate you on your marriage. I haven't heard from you since the ceremony. So, tell me, how's married life treating you?

Fantabulous. Life couldn't be better.

I don't suppose I need to tell you that you broke a lot of hearts.

They'll get over it.

How's work going on your latest movie?

It's great. I'm loving every minute of it. Lights, cameras, action, right? I never thought I'd like acting as much as I do. It agrees with me. It gives me a creative outlet I never experienced with my singing and songwriting. I was a little disappointed that they didn't cast Audrey in the movie, but I trust Bill knows what he's doing.

So what's next for Scowl? Is there anything surprising on your horizon?

I'm glad you asked. It's the reason I asked for this interview. I've decided to write a book.

We've talked about this before. I believe you said you didn't have the stamina to write an entire book. Has something changed your mind?

I've been reading a lot lately between my shoots on the movie set, and I got to thinking that I could really do just as good or even much better than the authors I've been reading. You know, I've always been a writer, what with my song lyrics, and I decided I ought to take the leap and give myself a shot at writing a full-length novel. There's so much going on in the world, and I have so much to say. I'm bursting at the seams with ideas. The older I get, the bigger and more wonderful the world seems to get, and the more inspired I feel.

Your fans have been criticized by some for shunning literature, as being the television generation. Do you really think they'll be interested in turning off their TVs to read a book?

Yes, if it's written by me.

What will this book be about?

I was always told if you're going to go through the trouble to write, you ought to start with something you know well. So I'm thinking of writing a story about an all-American girl around the age of sixteen who lives with her doctor father and homemaker mother in a quiet, all-American suburban neighborhood. Her name is Nancy Kimball, and she has fallen head over heels in love with a teenage singing star. She's never met this boy in person, but she owns all his records and thinks she knows him better than he knows himself. She listens to his deeply personal music over and over in her bedroom, and she develops this bond with him, this infatuation that she knows can only be satisfied by meeting up with the singing star. So she runs away from home and hunts him down, finding him in his mansion where he lives with his parents in LA. She lies about her age and gets a job as a waitress in town. She rents a small apartment and then stalks his every move for months, keeping a written journal describing what she sees. Things finally come to a head when she decides to come out in the open for a face-to-face with her true love. Every one of her hopes and dreams comes down to the success of this meeting. It is all she's longed for her entire young life. I mean, everything is in the balance. She rings the doorbell to the house, and when the boy answers the door, she is standing on the porch, all hundred and ten pounds of her, her heart beating into her throat and her underarms sopping wet with perspiration. "My name is Nancy Kimball," she says.

What happens after that?

I don't know yet. That's as far as I've gotten with it. What do you think?

I think I'd like to know what happens.

You'll have to read the book.

Have you started work on this book, or is it still just an idea?

I'm on chapter three.

When do you expect to be done?

I have no idea. I've never written a book before. So far, the process of writing has been pretty easy, but I may get writer's block, or some other project may come up and require my time. It's just something I've been working on, something I've recently wanted to do. Audrey has been encouraging me to complete this project, and she says I ought to be a writer. She thinks I have a natural talent, and I do, don't I? Look at all my song lyrics. I do have a way with words.

How is Audrey?

She's doing great. She's been auditioning for movie roles recently, but she hasn't landed a part. I tell her to keep trying, that everyone knows how talented she is, that the right role will come along. It just takes a lot of perseverance.

Do you two intend on having children?

Oh God, no, that isn't in our plans. It's nowhere on the horizon. We have our careers to think of. Did you hear that Alan and Alice were married?

Yes, I heard. Your bass player. How is marriage treating him?

They had a baby girl last year.

I wasn't aware of that.

Here's the thing. Alan told me how everyone told him a baby would change his life. He said the baby has changed his life all right, but not in the way he thought. He said he figured when people said a baby would change his life that they were referring to some great spiritual awakening, some transformation deep in his soul, some great light that would shine down on him. What they didn't tell him was how a baby would actually *change* his life. Wow, was he ever surprised. You're not married yet, are you?

No, I'm not married.

All I can say is, "Beware of women who want to have children." Alice wanted to have a baby with Alan right after they were married, and Alan says his whole life now revolves around their daughter, around spoon-feeding her and putting her to bed and making sure she has the right toys to play with and changing diapers and keeping things out of her mouth and buying the right baby furniture and babyproofing the house and doing everything possible to keep the little critter from crying. He says he's never been so exhausted. He can barely find the time to work on his music, and he said he might have to back out of our next tour, that I should probably be looking for someone to replace him. He doesn't want to be away from his daughter, and he doesn't think Alice will be able to handle the baby on her own. I can't imagine having that kind of drag on my life when I'm only in my twenties. I've got too many other things I want to do. What do you think? Do you think I'm being selfish? Alice told Alan she thinks I'm selfish, but I think I'm being realistic.

How does Audrey feel about this?

She feels the same as me.

I think most women want to have children. Do you think Audrey might change her mind?

Listen, I'd make a lousy father, and I know it. And Audrey knows it. I wasn't put on this earth to look after a little slobber-and-poop monster. I was put on this earth first and foremost to be an artist. Whether it's my music, my acting, or my writing, I was put here to be a creative force. My success proves this, doesn't it? Do you think God would make me such a tremendous success if he thought I needed to be a father, if he thought I didn't have a great gift to share with the rest of the world? Did you know the *Wall Street Journal* recently ranked me as the number one income-producing entertainment artist in America? Can you imagine that? When Bill Atherton told the press a new star was born, he knew what he was talking about. I may sound like I'm bragging, but I have the Midas touch. I've never failed at anything in my life. Leonard Bernstein should be eating his words, after calling me a fake. A fake indeed! Do you remember when he called me that? Why, I'm as real and significant as it gets. The world's going to grow tired of *West Side Story*, even if it did star Natalie Wood. But no one will ever grow tired of Scowl.

THE CAFÉ ON SUNSET

When Scowl's second movie, *Young Rebel*, hit the theaters, it was another big success. It didn't attract the same box-office receipts as his first movie, but it did very well. It certainly did well enough for Bill Atherton to begin work on a third film. He put his screenwriters to work while Scowl took some time off and worked on his book about Nancy Kimball. One afternoon in June, I received a call from Bobby Breen saying Scowl was ready for another interview. Less than a year had passed since our previous meeting at the Brown Derby. In that time, I had quit my job at the *LA Times* and was working as a freelancer on a book about the infamous plane crash of 1959. When Bobby called, I figured Scowl had finally finished his book and was going to use our interview to announce it to the public. Even though I no longer worked at the *LA Times*, I knew they'd publish any interview I had with Scowl. He was still very newsworthy.

Little did I know the bombshell Scowl was about to drop on me. Bobby set up a meeting for us at a small café on Sunset Boulevard, and when I arrived, Scowl was wearing the strangest disguise. He was dressed up in a pair of baggy jeans and a threadbare Harvard University sweatshirt. His hair was unkempt, like he'd driven to the café with his head sticking out the car window, and he wore a fake beard and sunglasses. It was actually comical, the lengths Scowl now had to go in order to keep his identity secret. Per Bobby's orders, I didn't bring my tape recorder; instead, I took notes using pencil and paper. It was slow going, and Scowl whispered to me the entire time so that I felt like we were spies exchanging classified government secrets over croissant sandwiches and coffee. To this day, it makes me laugh to think about it.

I presume we're here to discuss your book.

My book?

The book about the girl who chases down the teenage singer? I think her name was Nancy Kimball.

Oh, the book has been completed. I wrapped up the final draft a month ago. And I decided on a title. It's going to be called *The Life and Times of Nancy Kimball.* It's at the publishing house now.

When will it hit the shelves?

It should be available at bookstores in three or four months. It still needs to be edited.

Isn't that why we're here today?

No, no, it's something quite different. I wanted to meet with you concerning another matter.

And that would be?

Do you remember years ago, I told you if you asked me honest questions, that I'd give you honest answers? Do you remember that?

Yes, I remember.

Have I let you down yet?

Not that I'm aware of.

Then ask me about Audrey.

What would you like me to ask?

I'll leave that up to you.

Are the two of you having difficulties?

No, it's not really that.

Is her family having some sort of trouble?

Her family is fine. In fact, they couldn't be better. Her parents are coming to visit this week.

Are you having trouble getting along with them?

No, we're all fine. Everyone is getting along fine.

Is Audrey having trouble with your parents?

No, that isn't it either. What kind of journalist are you? Do I have to draw you a diagram? You need to ask me the right question.

I don't know what else to ask. Did Audrey land a part in a movie? Does she now have to work on location in some other town or in a foreign country? Are you worried that you'll miss her, that you won't know what to do without her?

You're getting colder.

I give up.

I thought you were good at this.

You're going to have to give me something more to go on. And why are we whispering? We're the only customers in this café.

Do you remember when I told you about Alan and Alice, about how they just had a baby girl, and about how Alan thought he'd have to leave the band for a while? He said he couldn't travel on tour knowing that his kid needed him. He also thought Alice would need him to help her raise the kid. He thought they'd both be needing him. Wouldn't you think it'd be nice to be needed like that?

Yes, I think that'd be nice. But I still don't know what you're driving at. Did something happen to Alan?

Do you know how old I am?

I think you're twenty-three.

Actually, I'm now twenty-four. To someone who's older than me, I probably seem like a kid. And I guess they'd be right. I am just that. I've got such a long way to go in my life. You're not that much older than me, are you? Do you ever stop to think how young you actually are, how many years you have left to live? I mean, in the scope of it all, we're barely out of puberty, aren't we? But have you ever noticed how fast everyone wants us to grow up? Why is that? I don't mean as in acting more mature, or displaying good manners, or going to bed at a reasonable hour, but growing up as in taking on responsibility. And I'm not talking about the good kind of responsibility, the kind that gets you somewhere. I mean the sort that locks you down. It's this persistent demand to grow up, to become one of them, to trudge through life like my poor father, forever making sacrifices for the well-being of his family. You know I take care of my parents financially, right? Neither of them has to work at all, yet my father labors away at that ridiculous butcher store every day. He can't help himself. He's like a zombie in a horror movie, with stiff arms and legs, stumbling like a thoughtless stick figure to work every day at the crack of dawn, carving up meat for his customers. He doesn't know any better, and you know what? He doesn't want to know any better. Why are people so inclined to be slaves, handing over their freedom so willingly for such a pitiful existence, making this lifetime pact with responsibility? What is it about our independence that makes us so ready to give it up? I don't mean just give it up for a month or so, but give it up for the rest of our lives. Am I making any sense to you? I don't want to do this. I don't want to let go of my youth. Great Scott, I want to stay young forever. I mean, not young literally, but young at heart. Young and free and moving forward.

I still don't understand.

Audrey's pregnant. We found out yesterday. I'm going to be a father.

You're kidding, right?

I wish I was.

A New Baby Boy

O ne thing the public always liked about my interviews with Scowl was his candor. He always said exactly what he had on his mind. But the pregnancy interview did not go over well with his fans. His wife was pregnant, and most people who read the interview were outraged at his distaste over the prospect of becoming a father. "The poor child," they said, and they had a good point. It was wrong to bring a baby into the world who wouldn't be loved unconditionally by both parents. Scowl seemed to care more about his own adolescent freedom than he did about the welfare of his own coming flesh and blood, and to most people this attitude was awful. In addition to the unpopular interview, his book, *The Life and Times of Nancy Kimball*, was on bookstore shelves across the country, and the book was getting some horrible reviews. One critic wrote, "If any girls are still screaming after this, they are likely screaming in agony. The book tortures even the most optimistic reader, one painful page at a time." I read *Nancy Kimball* from cover to cover. It wasn't as bad as the critics made it out to be, but it wasn't exactly engaging either. It read like a story written by youth lacking in insight, someone who had convinced himself he should write even though he had nothing important to write about. Scowl should have stuck to his music and his movies. Scowl was now on movie number three, and at least this appeared to be going well. This third film was again being produced by Bill Atherton and directed by Gabriel Sanchez. The movie was a tale of a boy who loved to surf, who lived by the ocean, and who met the girl of his dreams at a rock 'n' roll beach party. The part of Scowl's movie girlfriend was being played this time by teenage star Anita Joslin.

As if things weren't going bad enough, everyone was talking about Scowl and Anita Joslin. As Audrey suffered through the discomfort of pregnancy, rumors abounded that Scowl was having an affair with Anita. The two were often seen together on and off the movie set. Scowl and Anita both denied the rumors, but the gossip continued right up until the day Audrey gave birth. The child was a healthy eight-pound, two-ounce boy. They said Scowl held and rocked the baby in his arms right after it was born. He seemed to have had a change of heart about being a father, and he took an immediate liking to the healthy infant. He and Audrey named the child Roger Simon Kruse, after Scowl's dad. The press had a field day with the event, and Scowl handed out big Cuban cigars to all the reporters at the hospital. Scowl called me that same afternoon to give me the promising news. He asked if I could meet him at the hospital the following day, and I agreed to come. Audrey was still recuperating while the hospital staff vacated a room down the hall for the Scowl and me. Scowl sat back on one of the empty beds. I turned on my tape recorder and began the interview.

So how does it feel to be a father?

I think I might like it.

Did the baby inherit your trademark sneer?

It's hard to tell. At this point, his lips don't seem to have any sort of exact expression. The baby just sort of sits there and drools.

Did you name him Scowl Jr.?

No, we named him Roger Simon Kruse.

And how is Audrey holding up?

She's doing fine. You can visit her when we're done. She'd probably like to see you.

So how's life been treating you? You were a little concerned about things the last time we spoke. You were worried about the responsibility of caring for a child. Are you now feeling up to it?

Life is good. Audrey and I are looking forward to raising our little boy. Something inside me has changed as I've lived with Audrey through her pregnancy. I've been working on a new collection of songs about my future life as a father. Most of the songs have been inspired by my own father, the way he raised me, the sacrifices he made so that I could be a successful artist. Audrey and I want to provide the same sort of nurturing environment for our own son, an environment in which he can grow into his own, to find his own way in the world. I'll always be grateful to my own parents for the way they brought me up. My way of saying thank you to them will be to bestow the same sort of encouragement to our own son. There's no telling what the little guy will want to be when he grows up. He may want to be a popular singer like his father, or a talented actor like his mother, or a politician like John F. Kennedy, or a businessman, or a doctor, or even an attorney. It's such a big world out there; there is such a wonderful spectrum of possibilities. Having a son is such a marvelous and eye-opening opportunity. We're being allowed by God to create our own little breathing and speaking human being. He'll grow up to take his place in our society. He'll make a difference, large or small, loud or subdued, but he'll make a difference all the same. Of all the things I've created over my life, I think Roger Simon will be the flagship. I think he'll be my most amazing creation of all. There's just no telling what will happen.

Are you prepared for the way this little boy will change your life?

I'm ready for anything.

I hate to ask this, but how have you and Audrey been dealing with all the gossip about your alleged affair with Anita Joslin? This must have been difficult to handle during Audrey's pregnancy.

Anita has been a very good friend. I'll admit that we became very close during the filming of our movie, but that was the extent of it. There was no fooling around, nothing like the press implied. Anita taught me that my family is everything, that my place in the world was with my loved ones. She was very supportive. I've explained all this to Audrey, and she understands it. Besides, Audrey doesn't believe everything she reads in the papers. No offense, but newspapers often spread unfounded lies, lies they know to be lies, especially about celebrities. Audrey and I are used to it, having both lived under the spotlight for so many years, and it's one of the reasons I insist on doing these interviews with you, to set the record straight. You've always treated me squarely, and I've never shied away from the truth.

So your affair with Anita didn't happen?

It didn't happen.

Will you be going on tour again anytime soon?

My latest album should be released in a couple months, but I'm not sure we'll be touring. I'm just not sure we can get the band together. Alan and Alice just had another baby six months ago, and they've got their hands full. It was difficult enough getting him away from his wife and kids to help me with my album. And now that I'm a father, I'll have my own hands full with Roger Simon. And that's not all. My lead guitarist Richard has been working on his own solo album. It's something he's always wanted to do, and he may be touring with his own band. I think Richard is calling the new band The Grapevine, but I don't know how he came up with the name. Then there's Trevor. He'll be putting down his saxophone and getting married this summer, and he'll want to go on his honeymoon. I think they're planning to go to the south of France for a couple of months. And Terry has moved back east, still a crazy as ever. He's been at Timothy Leary's Millbrook estate for over a month now. God knows what he's doing there or when he'll be back. I have no idea if he'll even want to play the drums for us again. We've been trying to reach Terry, but he doesn't return our calls.

It sounds like everyone's busy.

Yes, they are.

Have you ever thought of starting up a new band?

Yes, I've thought about it. I mean, nothing in life lasts forever, and there are lots of talented musicians out there. But it seems a shame to see all the boys in our band going their separate ways.

Have you heard of the Beatles?

Yes, of course I've heard of them. They're a British band. I hear they're very popular. I've heard some of their songs.

So what do you think of them?

I think I've told you before that I don't like to discuss my competition. It's bad luck.

What did you think of Marilyn Monroe's suicide?

It didn't surprise me at all. I told you before that I expected something awful to happen. She was just a girl playing around with the big kids, and she got hurt. She didn't actually kill herself. No, you can go and call it a suicide if you want, but they did all the killing. They beat her into submission, and they probably don't even know what they did. What a waste.

In The Misfits, *Clark Gable said to her, "You're the saddest girl I ever saw."*

I think it's a classic line.

Tell me about the reviews you received for The Life and Times of Nancy Kimball. *Are you disappointed your book didn't sell better than it did?*

Yes, I'm disappointed.

Why did you choose Nancy Kimball as your main character? Why not a boy? Your critics said you lacked insight into the character's life.

I never really thought about it. I suppose it was because I was fascinated by all these girls.

By all these girls, you mean your fans?

Yes, I mean my fans. I mean the girls who buy all my albums, the girls who tack my pictures up on their bedroom walls. I'm talking about the girls who scream at my concerts and write me letters by the thousands. Who are these creatures? They are the daughters of loving husbands and wives, the granddaughters of World War veterans and sweet little old ladies, the nubile products of our churches, schools, and communities. They follow me in droves, and you can't imagine what it's like to be someone like me, an idol, a Pied Piper, a preposterous focal point. These girls are so young. They're so hopelessly naïve and bent on reaching out for something they can never have. You're right to say this interests me. It interests me a lot because it is my life, my sustenance, and none of it makes any sense.

Are you having second thoughts about your career? You once told me God has plans for all of us. Are you having trouble figuring out his reason for all your success as a recording artist? Or maybe your success as an actor? Or maybe even your lack of success as a writer?

God has his reasons for everything.

But you're wondering.

Sure, I'm wondering. It's my job to wonder. Like I told you before, God doesn't have time to spoon-feed his plans to us. We've constantly got to keep our eyes open and our minds in gear. It's up to us to figure things out for ourselves.

Have you been going to church lately?

Unfortunately, no.

How do you stay in touch with God?

You know, I pray a lot. Every night before I go to bed, I set aside time to pray to God. I admit my sins and ask for forgiveness. I ask for his help in understanding his plans for me. I then ask him to look out for my wife and parents. I ask him to look out for my friends. And now I ask him to look after my newborn son, to keep him healthy, to help us lead him in the right direction. It's really the best I can do. I don't have time to go to church every Sunday, and I think God understands this, that I'm very busy. When I was a kid, our preacher used to say idle hands are the devil's workshop, and my hands are never idle. There's no devil in my immediate future. I'm always doing something.

Do you think you'll write another book?

That's a good question. You know, I enjoyed writing *Nancy Kimball*. I really did. It might be true I didn't do a terrific job developing Nancy's character, and that could be the result of my novice writing skills. But maybe the book wasn't well received because it didn't have a happy ending. I think that disturbed a lot of people.

You certainly didn't end the story on a happy note.

No, I didn't. And I've thought about this a lot. I really think people want happy endings to their stories. In fact, I think they require them. The real world is already filled with too many disappointments as it is. We don't need to be reminded of them. We don't need to be reading about them. If I decide to write another book, you can expect it to have a happy ending.

Are you familiar with Jason Trumbo?

Yes, I'm aware of him.

He was one of the critics who wrote most harshly about your book. Among other things, he said, "Scowl is nothing more or less than yesterday's latest fad." Do you have anything to say in response?

I'm here to stay.

That's it?

What more do you want me to say? I don't care what Leonard Bernstein says, and I don't care what Jason Trumbo says. I don't plan on going anywhere. Scowl will always be around, and he'll always be relevant. Like the inventor of the abacus said to his peers a long, long time ago, you can count on it.

BURYING THE PRESIDENT

———•———

When John F. Kennedy was assassinated, it turned the world on its ear. It was such a shocking, bloody event. Even those who didn't like the man were appalled and saddened. Scowl had always been an active Kennedy supporter, and he had campaigned for him when Kennedy was running for president. The Kennedy campaign staff thought Scowl would be helpful in attracting younger voters, and they even produced a TV ad featuring him. Kennedy sent Scowl a handwritten letter thanking him for his support, and Scowl kept the framed letter on his living room wall. The day that Kennedy was killed, Scowl called me at home. He sounded so horribly distraught, and I wasn't sure whether he was calling to be interviewed or if he just wanted vent his frustration. I recorded our telephone conversation without telling him what I was doing. I plugged in my tape recorder and hooked it up to the phone.

———❧———

This Goddamn country is going to hell in a handbasket. There's no turning back.

Things certainly seem to be going badly.

When a president can't drive down a public street to greet to his supporters without getting shot in the head, there's something seriously wrong with this place. I'm thinking of moving up to Canada. I'm thinking of getting the hell out of here.

You're not really serious about this, are you? Moving to Canada?

I'm not sure I can take this country anymore. There's too much violence and too much hatred. People don't want to get along. All these idiots go to church every Sunday, yet it's a frighteningly unchristian place. We've become a nation of hypocrites.

But it could be worse.

Could it? I think it's actually getting worse every day. The sky isn't clearing at all. It's growing darker, and the clouds are heavier and more threatening. There's a horrible storm on the horizon, and I can feel its chill in my bones. When Kennedy was first elected, I thought it was a great day for America. It was to be four great years of hope and promise. I thought the sun would lift itself by its own bootstraps and shine down on everyone. It really all seemed so inspiring, seeing this great man become our president. But what the heck is happening? It's not good, not at all good.

They say it's always darkest before the light. Do you think this might be true?

I say it's just getting darker, period, and that it's going to get even darker. Think about it. Lyndon Johnson will now be taking the wheel. Texas killed Kennedy, and now Texas will be taking over. It's a travesty.

What do you plan to do? I mean, besides moving to Canada?

I don't know.

Is there something you like to say to your fans, something that you'd like to see them say or do?

I'm not sure there's anything to be done. Our great leader has been assassinated. He wasn't just libeled or scandalized, but actually killed. Don't you realize how serious this is? We go about our daily lives like nothing is wrong with this country, and someone ups and kills our president. It's like we're all doomed. I feel like we're all aboard the Titanic, laughing, eating, and dancing our lives away, completely unaware of the awful fate that lies ahead.

Like a ship of fools?

Exactly.

They say music can move people. Perhaps you can help with your music.

I'm no longer that naïve. I might have thought that way several years ago, but certainly not today. Do you want to know what music actually is? It's a catchy beat for tapping your fingers on the steering wheel when you're stuck in traffic. It's something to dance to when you're out with a date. No one cares about the lyrics. They mouth the words to my songs like they know what they're saying, but the words themselves mean nothing. Lyrics are like word-ghosts. They're of no more significance than the notes blown by a mockingbird in a tree. Half of the time people don't even know the words, and they just hum along to the melodies. Do you really think I'm able to change anything in our world by writing a dumb song? I'm the most popular recording artist in America, and I have about as much influence on our society as an ant. I'm talking about real influence. Sure, I can sway the public on the style of sunglasses they purchase, or the flavor of soda they drink, or the brand of cigarettes they smoke. But when it comes to truly important matters, like how we treat one another as human beings, or how we respect one another's differences, I really have no influence at all. People just want to be people, and people are people. We envy, hate, and lie to one another. We insult one another. We stab one another in the back for a few bucks. We scheme and maim and kill. There is no other animal on earth that is as despicable as human being. And now we're killing our own leaders. Soon they'll bury Kennedy in some lonely grave, and along with his body they'll be burying the hopes and dreams of our nation, our last vestiges of aspiration, our chance to be something great and admirable. I hate what has become of this country, but there's nothing I can do about it. I am powerless.

I think others would be surprised to hear you say this, that you're powerless. Do you really believe this? Don't we all have some power?

No, we don't.

So where does that leave someone like me?

What do you mean?

I mean, if you're powerless, what does that mean for an everyday journalist like me? Am I even more powerless than powerless? Am I completely ineffectual?

I'm sorry if this disturbs you, but I don't know how else to say it. I think most of us are just victims. I think we're like shards of shells stranded on a desolate beach. We go nowhere under our own power, always at the mercy of the ocean's strength. We're worn smooth by the gritty sand and bleached colorless by the sun, and there's nothing we can do about it. I know it's a bleak view of things, but it's the truth. I'm just telling it like it is.

I'd prefer to think there's something I can do. I'd like to think I have some influence.

So would I. But I know better. I'm only twenty-five, and already I've seen too much.

SAN FRANCISCO

— •●• —

I asked Scowl if I could publish our phone conversation regarding the Kennedy assassination, but he said he didn't want it made public. He said he was upset at the time and probably said some things he didn't mean. To tell you the truth, I didn't think he'd said much to worry about, and I asked him to read the transcript. I mailed it to him, but I don't think he ever looked at it. And he never got back to me. Although it wasn't published at the time, I've included the conversation it in this book because it marked a pivotal time in Scowl's life. It was the time when he became fed up. Yes, really fed up. Right up to the top of his head. It was just a few months later that he decided to drop out, literally disappearing from the public eye. Much to the surprise of everyone, he fired Billy Breen and the rest of his staff. He called Bill Atherton and Gabriel Sanchez told them he wouldn't be making any more movies. Then leaving Audrey and his one-year-old son behind in Brentwood, he moved to the Haight-Ashbury district in San Francisco and bought an old, dilapidated Victorian house. Because his face was still so well-known, he very seldom ventured outside the house. He holed up in this place with his guitar and disillusionment. He befriended an intimate group of odd characters who became his new entourage, and he cut himself off from the outside world. Well, more or less.

What a strange and unlikely group people he decided to associate himself with. In this odd entourage was his new bodyguard, a man who apparently had no last name and was simply called Frank. He was a massive six-foot-five giant of a man who looked like he could break a phone pole over his knee with ease. Frank was one of the few people in the district who didn't either drink lots of alcohol or smoke marijuana. He kept a sober eye on Scowl's front door, allowing only certain visitors to enter, keeping away curious fans and the news reporters who occasionally came by. There were rumors about the famous people allowed to drop in on Scowl. Timothy Leary was said to have paid several visits to the house. Allen Ginsberg supposedly stopped by, and so did Ken Kesey and friends. Many up-and-coming musicians paid their respects, including Jerry Garcia, Jim Morrison, and Paul Kantner.

Frank stood faithfully at his post, seeing to it that Scowl wasn't bothered by undesirables. Also living in the house was Kevin "The Mouth" Smalley, a fast-talking hustler who went out on the streets and procured Scowl's illicit drugs from local Haight-Ashbury dealers. Kevin spent most of his free time in the house in front of the TV, smoking marijuana and drinking beer. There was also Ernest Jackson, who was known to the group simply as Dragon, and there was a young runaway girl named Claudia Jenkins. Claudia was a seventeen-year-old poet from New York who sometimes helped Scowl with his lyrics. I'm not sure of all the names of the rest of Scowl's new group of comrades, but there were others. I think a total of ten people were living in the house.

When I received a call from Scowl, I was surprised. Seriously, I didn't think he was going to contact me again. I knew he'd left his wife and child, and I'd heard he moved to San Francisco. But that was about it. He was no longer in the news, and he hadn't recorded any music. I should probably clarify what happened. I didn't actually receive the call from Scowl himself. I received the call from the kid they called Dragon. He told me Scowl wanted to meet with me as soon as possible, and he gave me the address of the Victorian house. He said I didn't need to call before coming, that I should just swing by and Frank would let me in the door when I gave him my name. "Be sure to bring a driver's license with you," Dragon said. "Frank will check your ID to make sure you are you." It sounded so bizarre, but I was intrigued. I wanted to visit right away. I was married now, and my wife, Julia, wasn't thrilled about me going all the way to San Francisco, especially to the Haight-Ashbury district, which was home to some very strange people. "How will I know you'll be okay?" she asked, and I told her I trusted Scowl. "Scowl is a lot of things," I explained, "but he's not dangerous. In all the years I've known him, he's never put me in harm's way."

I drove to San Francisco the next day and arrived in the early afternoon.

I found a place to park my car and stepped up to the front door of the house. When I knocked, the door opened. There in the doorway was big Frank, all three hundred twenty pounds of him. "What's your name?" he asked. When I told him my name, he checked my ID and then let me in the house. It was like nothing I'd ever seen in my life—colorful plastic beads hanging in the doorways, psychedelic posters thumbtacked to the walls, weird fake flowers in vases, and rickety shelves filled with rows of poetry and books and classics. The kitchen counters were stacked high with unwashed dishes, and black flies buzzed around them. There were old magazines and newspapers all over the floors. The place was a housekeeper's nightmare. When we reached the front room, I found Scowl seated Indian style in the middle of the dirty floor. His hair was long and oily, and he had a thick, untrimmed beard. In his lap was his old acoustic guitar, which he strummed, mumbling some desultory lyrics. He looked up at me, and despite the beard that covered much of his face, I recognized that famous Scowl sneer. His eyes opened wide, and he jumped up from the floor to greet me.

"Ralph!" he exclaimed. "I'm so glad you came. We've got so much to catch up on." Just a little over a year had passed since I last saw Scowl, since we last talked about the Kennedy assassination. It was weird how much things had changed so much over such a short period of time. It was like night and day, this transformation. If it wasn't for the iconic sneer, I probably would never have guessed that this was him. I cleared some newspapers out of the way and sat down on the floor. I had brought along my tape recorder, and I asked him if he minded that I use it. "Be my guest," he said cheerfully. Oddly enough, the tape recorder seemed to put him at ease. I seemed to be his only connection to the past, Ralph Bonaparte the reporter and his trusty little tape recorder, a past that now seemed like eons ago. We immediately began to talk.

So, Scowl, how've you been?

Fantabulous! Or should I say groovy. I've been just groovy, my good man.

This house is a far cry from your Brentwood home.

Isn't it, though?

So much seems to have changed with you. I don't even know where to begin. How's Audrey doing? How's your son, Roger?

I don't know. I haven't talked to Audrey for months. I haven't tried to call her, and she can't reach me. I don't have a phone here. When we need to make a call, we use the public phone down the street.

You don't have a phone?

I tell you there's nothing worse than constantly being interrupted by a ringing phone. Today's telephone is the scourge of the twentieth century, a real bother. You want my advice? Do away with your phone, Ralph. Its absence will provide you with peace of mind, and you won't believe the difference it'll make in your life.

So what have you been up to?

It must seem strange to you.

What do you mean?

I mean, my living here like this, with this beard and long hair, in this house with all these strange furnishings and assorted human characters.

It's certainly different.

I've been on a journey, my good man, a long and fascinating journey.

A journey to where?

To my very being. To deep in the center of my soul. I've been finding myself.

And what have you found?

I found a young man who was lost at sea, drifting into the horizon. I've been at the mercy of ocean currents, going nowhere. How many years do you think I've been lost like this? How many years did I waste? I was searching for something I had locked inside but never knew existed. I was trying to find myself but was failing miserably. I was looking in all those places society tells us to look, and I was being taken for a ride. I was being brainwashed and misled. This is the great joke our society plays on us, for none of the places I looked held anything I sought. They were only illusions. Life is filled with illusions, Ralph. It is a great carnival mirror maze, hundreds and thousands of blinking images, reflections, and confusing shadows. Worst of all is the illusion of power. How many times did I think I had real power? Great Scott, I thought I ruled all. I thought I controlled the hearts and minds of the girls, the radio airwaves, the pages of your middle-class newspaper. I thought I was master of the universe. Remember I told you I had the Midas touch, that I couldn't fail, not even if I tried? But after the assassination, I felt completely powerless. Like I told you back then, I discovered that things that really mattered were completely out of my purview. I was not the master of all I surveyed. In fact, I was the master of nothing. Like Bernstein said, I was a fake. I was empty and lonely, as vacuous and trite as a bad character in a poorly written book. That's why my own book was such a flop. Don't you see? Great Scott, I couldn't breathe life into poor Nancy Kimball any more than I could breathe life into myself.

Actually, there's been a new interest in your book. Since you disappeared from the scene, there's been a growing curiosity about Scowl.

I suppose absence might make the heart grow fonder. It's funny, isn't it?

Do you have any interest in returning to the public eye? Do you have any interest in producing a new record? Are you still interested in music?

I told you years ago that my music was everything, and I meant it. To me, my music still is everything. It's not the same sort of music I used to write when I was younger, but it's my music. And, yes, I've been thinking of putting out a new album. That's one of the reasons I brought you here, to stir up some interest.

Have you talked to Bobby?

Bobby and I have nothing to talk about.

Do you have a new manager?

I don't need a manager. I can manage myself.

Tell me more about your music. What's different about it? Do you think you can compete with new groups like the Beatles?

Listen, the Beatles hijacked my screaming fans. I'll never have those girls back, but that's fine with me. I don't plan to compete with the likes of them or any of their wannabe contemporaries. My fans are more grown up, and I think they'll relate to something different. I'm not a teenager anymore, not even in my early twenties. While I'm still young, I've lived a lot of life for a guy my age, and I have a lot to say about the world. There's a place for me in the music business—not the place I used to hold, but a place for a new kind of artist, a more mature artist, an artist who knows who he is.

Have you been following the music scene? A lot of bands are starting up these days.

Oh yes, there are a lot of them.

You'll have a lot of competition. What makes you think anyone will pay attention to you?

Because I'm Scowl.

Will that be enough?

Since when wasn't it? It's always enough just to be Scowl.

Listen, I'd like to know more about the place Scowl now lives in. Tell me more about your life here. How long have you lived in this house?

It's been a little over a year. I bought it at a foreclosure sale.

How many other people live here with you?

Nine or ten, maybe. I've lost track. You can ask Frank if you really want to know. He keeps tabs on that kind of stuff.

And Frank is your bodyguard?

I like to think of him as my doorman. When I first moved in here, I had a lot of curious visitors and reporters knocking on the door to see me. I guess it's one of the drawbacks of being famous. It's a lot better now than it used to be, but I still need to keep Frank at the door. I am Scowl, and you never know who'll want to get in.

Do you follow current events these days?

Yes, more or less.

What do you think of Martin Luther King Jr. winning the Nobel Peace Prize?

I think he deserved it. I take my hat off to the man. There's so much violence in the world today, it's just nice to see someone get his point across without a gun or an axe handle.

What do you think of Vietnam?

I think it's getting out of hand. I think the country is getting involved in something that isn't any of our business. We seem to be itching for violence, and to what end? I've never seen a country so hell-bent on fighting every adversary it imagines. Sometimes I think we'd be a lot better off just leaving our enemies alone and minding our own business. All this violence is a terrible waste of time, money, and lives. But then you've got guys like Barry Goldwater saying things like, "We cannot allow the American flag to be shot at anywhere on earth if we are to retain our respect and prestige." Is he kidding? You mean as a kid I should have gotten in a fistfight with every kid who ever hurled a rock or insult my way? I would have spent my whole childhood fighting. It's ridiculous, this combative mentality, this chip-on-the-shoulder attitude our country's leaders seem to be encouraging. You know, Martin Luther King Jr. has the right idea. Nonviolence is the key. Only from a stance of peace and nonviolence can good things can happen. Make love, not war, man. Isn't that what they like to say these days? That's the kind of philosophy I believe in.

Did you vote the last election?

The choice was Johnson versus Goldwater. Wow, and no I didn't vote. There was no choice. It was canned spinach versus sauerkraut, and I don't like either of them.

What do you think of Johnson's recent pledge to create a Great Society?

Bah! Great Scott, he's a gun-slinging cowboy and a war monger. That's how he'll go down in history. This Great Society is a scam.

Is there anyone you would actually like to see become president, in the next election maybe?

How about Peter Sellers? Did you see Sellers in his most recent roles? Have you seen *Dr. Strangelove?* I think Sellers would make in excellent commander in chief. Do you remember the war room? My favorite scene is where George C. Scott and the Russian ambassador fall into a scuffle and President Sellers says, "Gentlemen, you can't fight in here. This is the war room." I laughed so loud, everyone in the theater was staring at me. God, that was hilarious. So, yes, let's vote for Peter Sellers. Or maybe he's a Brit. Oh, well, whatever.

Is Dr. Strangelove *the best movie you've gone to recently?*

Yes, I liked it a lot. I also liked *The Pink Panther.* I guess you could call me a Peter Sellers fan. I seem to like his movies.

How about books? Have you read any interesting books lately?

I just got done reading *Don Quixote.* It's one of the funniest things I've read in years. I know scholars like to attribute all sorts of complicated meanings to the story, such as it being an attack on the Catholic church, or as it being a work of radical nihilism and anarchy, whatever that means, but I see the story as a comedy. It's a comedy plain and simple. It's truly a funny book, and I think everyone ought to read it. When Don Quixote asks a lowly innkeeper to dub him a knight, or when he fights for the honor of his imaginary Dulcinea, or when he attacks those iconic monster windmills, you just can't help but laugh your head off. It's so nice to know that people from the seventeenth century had such a great sense of humor. Cervantes was a terrific comedic writer. When you read history books, you always have the impression that the characters from our past are so dreadfully serious. We forget people were and always have been laughable human beings, just like they are today. You know who would make a great Don Quixote? Peter Sellers would be perfect for the role. I don't know who you would get to play Sancho Panza, maybe someone like Ernest Borgnine. Ernie would be good. But Peter Sellers would make a great leading man.

Do you have any desire to make movies again?

I would consider making movies again, but only if they were something more interesting than what I was doing before. The three movies I made were really just for kids. I'd like to act in something deep, something that had some meat on its bones. I really enjoyed the acting I did, and I'd like to be approached for some serious roles. Maybe some producer or director will see something in my acting persona other than the boy-meets-girl characters I used to play.

Sir Chester Hatfield said, "There's nothing more disappointing than the performance I gave, and nothing more promising than the performance I'm about to give."

I like that quote. It says a lot. Although I haven't got a clue who Chester Hatfield is.

Do you ever plan on reconnecting with Audrey and your son?

I don't know.

You don't talk to her anymore at all?

Audrey doesn't understand me. She doesn't understand my rejection of the old Scowl, the Scowl who didn't know himself, the Scowl who was lost. She wants me to cut my hair, dress like a square, and live back in our house in Brentwood. She never did understand why I wanted to move up here to San Francisco. She has everything she needs in Los Angeles. She has her beauty parlor, the babysitters, her Lincoln Continental, all the clothing stores on Rodeo Drive. She thinks I'm crazy. When I first moved up here, she tried to get me to see a psychiatrist. Can you imagine that? She thought I was mentally ill. You know, when Kennedy was shot, everything changed for me. But I sure as heck wasn't mentally ill. I just realized I'd been getting nowhere, that I had to search for the real me. I needed to find the truth, no matter the cost, no matter who I had to leave. I still love Audrey, and

I love my son. I'm sorry that I had to leave them behind. But it wouldn't have done either of them any good for me to be hanging around in my bathrobe and being miserable. I would've made their lives miserable. It would have been a bad situation.

Do you still talk to your parents?

I haven't talked to Mom or Dad for quite some time, but I think they're siding with Audrey. They want me to come home. My dad told Audrey that this San Francisco thing I've been wasting my time with is just a phase, that I'll be returning soon. I wish he wouldn't get her hopes up like this, because he's wrong. I'm happy with my new life here. I feel like a butterfly who's just broken out of its chrysalis.

I have one last question. If you were to sum up your future in just a few short words, what would you say?

I'd say don't count me out.

DULCINEA

---◦---

T he great surge in rock 'n' roll music during the sixties meant that
producers (and people calling themselves such) were scrambling like
crazy to get a piece of the growing market. Because Scowl had already
made a name for himself, he had no trouble getting signed up with a
legitimate and well-respected record label. His first recording was the
single "My Child" a touching tune that he wrote about a mother saying
goodbye to her only son who was leaving for duty in Vietnam. The song
was a resounding success with both critics and fans. Jason Trumbo, once
so critical of Scowl, wrote surprisingly that, "This new sound and message
comes through loud and clear. Scowl has decided to take life in earnest and
is now hitting his stride as a true artist." You couldn't turn on the radio
without hearing the song. Gone was the great familiar sounds of the old
band. The music that accompanied Scowl's voice was now being provided
by a group of musicians Scowl met at a night club in San Francisco who
called themselves the Jetliners. Scowl talked them into playing with him,
and he had a list of new songs he'd written just for them and himself. And
they were catching on. Many of the new songs were hits right out of the
starting gate. His album with the group was finally released and included
all his recent work. It was titled *The Return of Scowl* and was nearly
outselling the Beatles' *Rubber Soul*.

In the meantime, Scowl fell in love with that runaway poet from New
York I told you about, the one who had been living for the past year in his
Haight-Ashbury house. They were with each other constantly. Claudia
Jenkins was now eighteen, legally old enough to be Scowl's girlfriend in
public. When Audrey caught wind of the affair, she packed her belongings
and moved out of the Brentwood house to her parents' home in Laguna
Beach. She also took their son with her. She filed for a divorce on June

12, 1965, and Scowl received the papers five days later. He received a letter from Audrey telling him she'd moved out, and that was when Scowl decided to return home, not to Audrey, but to the Brentwood house.

When he moved back with Claudia, he also brought the Jetliners with him. With the money they were making from appearances and recordings, the band members were all able to buy homes in LA. Then Claudia and Scowl decided to give Brentwood house a name, and they called it Dulcinea, named after the legendary love of Don Quixote's life. "Elvis has Graceland," Scowl told reporters, "But I have my Dulcinea." During this time, I was doing unrelated research for a book I was writing about Bob Dylan. Everyone wanted to know who Dylan was. Everyone was curious about his musical roots, his rumored relationship with Woody Guthrie, and how such a fresh talent seemed to rise from nowhere. I was thirty-four years old, and had established myself as a respected rock historian and critic. But I was still best known for my exclusive interviews with Scowl. With his resurgence, I was again in the spotlight, and in the fall of 1965, Scowl called me for another interview. "To heck with Bob Dylan," he said. He wanted me to come to Dulcinea to discuss his new love life, and he said he had news that would make it worth my while.

Remember I told you about Frank? When I arrived at Scowl's front door in Brentwood, Frank let me into the house. He looked like he'd lost some weight since I last saw him, but not much. "Follow me," he said, and he led me into the front room. There on one of the sofas sat Scowl, his guitar in his lap and a cup of hot chamomile tea on the coffee table. A slender stick of jasmine incense burned from the fireplace mantel, and the drapes were wide open so we could see the colorful flowers and healthy trees in the backyard. Scowl was scribbling some notes on a piece of paper, presumably writing another song. "Scowl," I said, "It's good to see you again." He smiled and set down his guitar. "Get out your tape recorder," he said. "I'll fill you in."

You said you had some news about your love life.

Yes, I did. Some wonderful news, my good man. It'll curl your toes.

Are you going to tell me what it is, or are you going make me play twenty questions?

First, ask me about this guitar.

Okay, tell me about your guitar.

I bought it at a Beverly Hills auction last month. I don't even want to tell you what I paid for it. Great Scott, I almost didn't get it. Some idiot kept upping the price on me. I think he finally realized I wasn't going to let him outbid me, so he gave up. They say the guitar once belonged to Danny Cedrone. Do you know who Danny is? He was with Bill Haley and the Comets when they recorded *Rock Around the Clock* in 1954. I was just sixteen at the time, just beginning to find my voice. Man, if only this guitar could talk, the stories I bet it could tell us. Do you believe in ghosts? I've done some reading, and they say that ghosts can inhabit inanimate objects such as closets, tables, and chests, so I say, why not guitars? So, tell me, do you think Danny's musical spirit might be living in this instrument? The strings are all new, but the body and neck are all original. I wonder if Danny's in here. I've been using this guitar to compose several new songs, and I swear it feels like Danny is talking to me, leading me from one chord to the next, making my fingers move up and down the neck and frets in the most amazing ways. I think I'm going to call my next album *Danny's Tunes*. It will be a compilation of all the songs I've composed using this old guitar.

What else have you been up to, I mean besides writing music? You said you had some interesting news about your love life.

I've been offered a part in another movie.

Who offered it?

I got a call from Joseph Crabtree. Have you ever heard of him?

I think so.

He's an up-and-coming director. He has a few films under his belt, and he wants me to audition for the role of a young drug addict who's been admitted by his parents to a mental hospital. Do you think I can play a crazy person? I told Crabtree I had plenty of experience with drugs, but that I didn't use them anymore, and that I had no real experience with being crazy. He said he thought I'd be perfect for the part, and he arranged for me to audition next week. Why do you suppose he thinks I'd be so perfect for the part? Do you think I come across as a drug addict, or as some kind of a kook? I'm really beginning to wonder what this guy sees in me. Of course, I asked Claudia what she thought, and she said I ought to try to get the part. She says a movie would do wonders for my record sales and popularity. When I asked her about me playing the role of a crazy person, she said it would actually do me good for the public to think I was a little crazy. She says crazy people are loveable. "Just look at your hero, Don Quixote," she said. "He was as crazy as they come."

So are you going to audition?

I think I will.

Anything else new in your life?

I'm thinking of writing another book.

Another novel?

Sales of *Nancy Kimball* have picked up ever since the release of my last album. My publisher called and asked me if I wanted to write again. I told him I'd think about it. He thinks I'm marketable.

Do you have any ideas?

I was playing this guitar, and I got to thinking that maybe I could write a story about some other famous musician, say a jazz trumpet player who for whatever reason falls on hard times and pawns his instrument. The trumpet stays in the pawnshop window for months, and in the meantime, the musician dies. Some guy finally comes into the pawn shop and buys the trumpet for his kid. It's to be a birthday gift. The kid unwraps the present, picks it up, and begins to blow. Low and behold, he plays the trumpet like a pro, and everyone is amazed at the boy's amazing talent. It's magic how this kid suddenly knows what he's doing, and that could be the title of the novel, *The Magic Trumpet.* What do you think? Do you think that title would catch on? Weeks and months go by, and no one can believe the kid's ability. He quickly becomes famous and starts his own band; he cuts albums and fills auditoriums with standing-room-only crowds. He's all over the radio, and he appears on TV. Everyone wants to see the fantabulous boy and his magic horn, until one night after a concert, he accidentally leaves the trumpet on the roof of his father's car as they are leaving the venue. The dad drives off, and the trumpet tumbles from the roof and into the street. A truck runs over it, leaving the destroyed trumpet in its wake. I imagine it's raining the whole time. Can you picture the rain? The camera zooms in on the soaking wet trumpet, and it is flattened beyond repair. When the dad and son realize they've left the trumpet behind, they turn around the car. The boy jumps out and picks up his damaged trumpet, sobbing. The dad buys the kid a new horn the next day from a music shop, but it isn't the same. When the boy lifts the instrument to his lips, nothing comes out but garbled, useless noise. He's now unable to play anything. I'm not sure what happens next. I'd like to think the boy suddenly realizes it was *him* playing the trumpet all along. Maybe the dad tricks him into thinking he's repaired the old trumpet, when in fact he's just bought him a similar one. When the boy blows into the similar trumpet, thinking it's the original, he's able to play the music again. It proves the talent was actually his. I don't know exactly if this is the ending I want, but however the story turns out, it'll be happy. You can count on that. If I learned anything writing my last book, I learned to write a happy ending.

That could be an interesting story.

I have other ones.

So what's the story about your love life? You still haven't told me that. What was the news you wanted me to break?

I'm married.

I thought you were divorced.

I divorced Audrey, my good man. Now I'm married to Claudia.

When did this happen?

Last week. Claudia and I drove to Las Vegas. We got married in one of those walk-in chapels. No one knows about it yet. Just you.

Where is Claudia now?

She's downtown somewhere, buying some things for the house.

Do her parents know about the marriage?

No one knows except us. And you.

Do you want this published?

Yes, as soon as possible. Tell all your readers about it. Tell them Scowl is married again, and now he wants the whole world to know. He wants to stand on the rooftops and shout it out.

It sounds like she's made you happy.

You have no idea. She's my love, inspiration, and the driving force behind all my recent success. Dante had his Beatrice, and Cyrano had Roxane. I now have Claudia. She is everything that's right with the world.

Do you plan on having children?

I told you before that I'm a lousy father. I've gone that route, but my heart just isn't in it. I don't have what it takes. You can ask Audrey about that. No, it will just be the two of us, Scowl and Claudia. The two of us will be living here at Dulcinea for the rest of our natural-born lives. Until death do us part, just like we promised each other.

THE GRIM REAPER

I didn't talk to Scowl again for over a year. We were brought back together in the winter of 1966 following the death of Terry, the drummer in the old band. He died at the young age of thirty, asphyxiated by his own vomit after drinking and drugging all night with friends. Scowl called me the evening after he learned of the tragedy. He didn't necessarily want a formal interview, but he wanted me to publish his thoughts. So, after calling him, I hooked up my recorder to the phone and we talked. Several times Scowl began to cry while he was talking, but for the most part he maintained his composure. I remember that I was still in shock. Thirty was way too young of an age for anyone to up and die, no matter how reckless they may have been or how closely they lived on the edge. Terry's death took me completely by surprise. Seriously, when I was first told about it, it was like having the wind knocked out of me.

Both of us just learned about Terry. I understand you want to say some words about him.

Yes, some words. I would never have become what I am today without Terry and the other boys. I remember when I first saw Terry in the band, he was amazing. I remember when they called the band the Epics. They used to play in Trevor's garage in the evenings and on weekend afternoons. It seems like only yesterday. God, how quickly time goes by, right? I was just a nobody then. I auditioned to play with their band, and I stood up to the microphone and sang "Maybellene." That day I'll never forget, not in a million years. For Scowl, that's when it all started, when I sang "Maybellene."

Have you talked with Terry's dad?

I spoke to him just an hour ago. He's devastated. He thought his son was turning his life around. He told me he couldn't believe the way Terry died.

When's the last time you spoke to Terry?

It was about six months ago. He had called me in the evening, and he sounded like he was doing great. He didn't sound like he'd been drinking or taking any drugs. He said he'd met a girl named Rebecca and that they were thinking of moving in together. He said Rebecca had a three-year-old son and that he liked the boy. He said the kid needed a father figure, that he was going to clean up his act and try to behave.

Everyone I've talked to about Terry thought he was in the process of a major turnaround.

That's the impression I had.

I haven't interviewed Rebecca yet. Have you talked to her at all?

I don't know her, and I haven't called her.

Have you talked to any of the other guys in the band? I'd like to know what they have to say.

I talked to Alan. He was extremely upset. He was completely beside himself. Alan doesn't often show much emotion, but I think Terry's death really knocked the crap out of him. I think in retrospect, all of us wish we'd done more to help Terry clean up his act. He lived his life like he played his drums, fearlessly and like a madman. Alan said Terry called a few weeks ago and told him the same things that he told me, that he'd met Rebecca and was settling down. Alan said that he honestly thought Terry had turned a corner, that he was in a much better place. But I guess he wasn't. Jesus, now that I look back, we should've done more to help. We should've paid closer attention to our friend, and we should've stepped forward and interfered.

Is there anything else you'd like to say?

I think Terry's death is only going to be the first of many you're going to hear about. Rock 'n' roll is becoming a crazy, evil culture, and Terry isn't going to be its only victim. I think other young men and women are headed down the same road, the way things are going. As you probably already know, I've been filming a new movie that's directed by Joseph Crabtree. It's about a young man who becomes addicted to drugs and alcohol, and in the story his parents have him committed. Drugs and alcohol have become a real problem these days, and the movie has a message. I think today's kids are watching and idolizing all these rock 'n' roll stars drinking to excess and taking drugs, and they think the behavior is okay. And being so young, the kids think they're indestructible. But they're not. We're all fair game, and the Grim Reaper would love to get his hands on each and every one of us, especially the kids. As far as he's concerned, the younger the better. He is an evil, evil man.

Wasn't there a time when you were taking drugs?

Yes, but those days are over. I haven't touched that stuff for two years.

What do you do instead?

There are so many things to do. I read, and I write my music. If I'm lucky, I act in movies, but I always keep myself busy. They say idle hands are the devil's workshop, and they're right. People today need to stay busy, and they need to get their kicks out of the sober joy of living each day to its fullest, not out of provoking the Grim Reaper.

What do you say to all those kids out there who aren't listening to you? What do you say to the kids who say you don't know what you're talking about?

I say your days are numbered. I hate to say it, but it's so true, isn't it? I say, what the heck is wrong with you people? Open your eyes! And if you can't see you're headed down the wrong road, say your goodbyes. Say goodbye to your loved ones, your mom, dad, sisters, and brothers. Say goodbye to big blue skies and warm summer days. Say so long to your friends, aunts, uncles, and cousins. Wave goodbye to your dreams. The Grim Reaper is standing right behind you, breathing steam and sharpening the blade of his scythe, and when he calls out your name, there will be no turning back. Think your invincible? Great Scott, can't you see how he's laughing at you?

HOWDY

———— •●• ————

S cowl's Grim Reaper interview wasn't much of a hit with the youth in America. In the months that followed the talk we had, he wrote and released "Goodbye Friend," a touching song about Terry's life and death, about how alcohol and drugs had taken his beloved drummer's life, but the song didn't do well. No one wanted to hear any more about the tragedy. When his movie *Asylum* came out at the theaters, the film was popular with older adults, but young moviegoers didn't care for it. They weren't in the mood to be lectured about the evils of drugs and alcohol, especially when they were having such a blast getting high. And getting high was now more popular than baseball. Forget Micky Mantle and Willie Mays, now the kids had Timothy Leary, Jim Morrison, and John Lennon. Thanks to the popularity of drugs, Scowl was twenty-nine years old and in danger of becoming irrelevant. Claudia and Scowl spent months brainstorming the matter, trying to decide where they ought to take Scowl's career. I wasn't privy to any of their talks, but I knew Scowl was worried. I also knew that Scowl would come up with a plan, well, because he was Scowl, and because despite his feigned indifference, he was addicted to the trappings and thrills of fame. It's just like they say, where there's a will there's always a way, and with Scowl there was always a will. It was something you could count on. Time marched by, and it would take two years for Scowl to figure the puzzle out.

In the meantime, life in America rolled forward like a loose cannon. Musical artists like Janis Joplin, Jefferson Airplane, and Jimi Hendrix exploded on the scene and were taking the rock 'n' roll world by storm. The Vietnam War was raging, killing hundreds of thousands of human beings to prevent them from being communists. And Muhammad Ali was stripped of his boxing title for refusing to take part in the genocide. It seemed like everyone was now turning against the war, including Walter Cronkite. The country was clawing and growling at one another like a bag full of angry cats. Race relations were still a mess, and Detroit had the worst race riot in US history, leaving thirty-eight people dead and whole sections of the city smoldering in charred ruins. Then thousands of America's kids flocked to San Francisco for the Summer of Love (some crazy season of love, right?), and President Johnson stunned the nation by saying he wouldn't run for a second term. Finally, and perhaps worst of all, Martin Luther King Jr. and Bobby Kennedy were both gunned down. And the patriots shouted, "America, love it or leave it." It was beyond belief. These were such weird and violent years, yet during all of this turmoil and in this fertile ground for songwriting, there wasn't the slightest peep out of Scowl. He remained quietly watching everything unfold on his TV, safe and sound at Dulcinea, wearing his old bathrobe and slippers, drinking tea, and writing songs that he wasn't recording. It was spring of 1969 when he finally gave me a ring, and honestly, I was surprised to get the call.

"I'm going to change everything," he told me. "I now know exactly what I'm going to do. I'm going to slip into hibernation. In a way, everything will stay the same, but really everything is going to change." I had absolutely no idea what he was talking about. At this time Julia and I were expecting our second child. Our first was a boy we named Carter Evan Bonaparte, and he was now one year old. I was now thirty-eight and still working as a freelance writer based in Los Angeles. I had six published books to my name, and my articles appeared in national periodicals and local papers. But I hadn't published an interview with Scowl for quite some time. I'd be lying if I said I wasn't curious to find out what Scowl was up to. I set up a date to meet Scowl in Brentwood later that week and showed up at Dulcinea with my tape recorder in hand. Frank let me in through the gates. He led me to the front room where Scowl stood near the fireplace, waiting. He was dressed in jeans and boots, with a cowboy hat atop his head. He removed the hat and smiled at me, reaching for a handshake. It was funny. He still had that trademark sneer on his face; it looked different with Western garb, but it also somehow looked appropriate.

What's the story with the Western clothing? Are you a cowboy now?

It's the new me. Do you like it?

I'm not quite sure.

I'm a country music artist.

Since when?

Since Claudia and I decided this was the only way for me to go. Now go ahead and ask me your questions. I'm sure you have questions.

I'm not sure where to begin.

Ask me about black bears.

Okay, I'll bite. Tell me what you know about black bears.

They hibernate.

I'm aware of that.

Do you know much about hibernation? When winter rolls around, the bears curl up into a hollow log or cave, and they go into a deep sleep. Well, they don't actually sleep. They hibernate.

So what do you know about hibernation?

It's different from what most people think. Most of your readers probably think when bears hibernate, they simply close their eyes and snooze the winter away, sawing logs and living off their stored fat. But it's a lot more complicated than that. They're actually quite busy. They lower their body temperatures twelve degrees below normal to insulate themselves from the cold. The temperature outside can drop as low as twenty below, but the bears are able to survive. Can you imagine that? Twenty below? And they lower their body temperatures? I mean, wouldn't you think they'd want their body temperatures to be up higher, like wrapping themselves in an electric blanket? But no. They lower their temperatures, and you know what? No one knows how they do this. No one knows exactly what triggers this physiological activity. Their heartbeats slow down to as few as eight beats per minute, and they cut their metabolic rates in half. They stay in perfect water balance without having a drop of water to drink. Have you ever wondered how bears relieve themselves while hibernating, how they piss and poop? They can go a hundred days without pissing or pooping at all.

This is interesting. But I'm curious, what does any of this have to do with you?

Because this is what I'm going to do. I'm going to hibernate. I'm going to roll up in a ball and wait for spring. I'm going to roll up in a ball and make my living playing country music to mainstream America. I refuse to take part in this rock 'n' roll winter. I don't want any part of it. I don't want to see my friends die. And more will die. You can count on it. I'm switching to a world that isn't dominated by kids enamored with marijuana, LSD, cocaine, and heroin. Just like when I first started out in this business, I'll be aiming for the bull's-eye, for the heart and soul of this wonderful, moral, and wholesome country. When I first started writing my songs, rock 'n' roll was about youth, America, and apple pie. It was about love, joy, and heartbreak, not about taking illicit drugs and destroying lives. Pardon my French, but fuck all this stuff. That's how I feel. There's not a soul on this planet who can change my mind.

You don't like today's rock music?

No, I don't.

Do you feel left out?

I feel disgusted.

Do you think you'll be able to break into the country music scene? Won't it be difficult?

I've already arrived. I've been flying back and forth with Claudia between LA and Nashville for months, and the right people there have been meeting with us and hearing my music. I've signed with a new record label, and they're producing a couple songs that will be on the airwaves any day. They say they like what I'm doing, and they agree with where I'm going. Their marketing people think they can make my new sound catch on. They like me, Ralph. Great Scott, they like everything about me. Claudia has been acting as my manager, and she's brought a whole new level of energy to my affairs. She's so young and full of life. I've put my future in her very capable hands, and she seems to be making the right things happen. I owe a lot to Claudia.

Is this one of the reasons you called me for this interview, to tell the public about your sudden foray into country music?

Yes, that's right.

What are some of the songs you've recorded?

I have a ballad coming out titled "Jimmie Joe," and a bluesy number being released that is titled "A Young Man's Pain." We're also working on a duet with Tammy Wynette that should be released later this year. It's our own rendition of Tom Paxton's "The Last Thing on My Mind." My producer thinks the duet will be a hit, and everyone who's involved with this recording thinks we have a winner.

Do you see yourself ever returning to rock?

Only when winter's over.

When do you think that will be?

It could be a long, long time.

Can I ask you some more personal questions?

Ask any question you'd like. I've always told you to be tough on me. Personal questions are not a problem.

Have you been in touch with Audrey?

I heard she remarried, but I haven't had the chance to talk to her about it. We haven't talked since I moved down from San Francisco. I heard she married a real estate developer named Jeff Albright and that she moved into his gigantic house in Newport Beach. I heard they enjoyed a fantabulous wedding in the guy's large backyard, but I wasn't invited to it. But I wish her all the best. She was once the light of my life, and I still do care about her.

Have you talked to your son at all?

No, I haven't.

Do you know how old he is?

He's going to turn six this month.

How about your parents? How are they doing?

They're getting older. Dad stopped working at the butcher shop, and Mom has slowed down. Claudia and I had them over to Dulcinea the other night for dinner, and we had a good time talking about old times. Dad told Claudia stories about me she'd never heard. At first Mom and Dad weren't too happy about me marrying Claudia, but I think they're warming up to her. They once thought of her as a home-wrecker, but now they're beginning to just see her as my wife. And they're very excited about this country music thing. They've always been big country fans.

What's going to happen to the Jetliners?

They're on their own.

Are there any hard feelings?

Listen, I catapulted them to fame when I asked them to join me in San Francisco, when I moved them to LA. I think they're grateful for that. And it's not like I didn't give them a chance. I asked them if they wanted to try playing country music, but they said no. I think they'll do fine. They just need to find a new singer, and there are lots of good singers out there. They'll find someone. I think they'll be fine.

Do you have a new band?

No, I've just been playing with studio musicians. I have no plans to join up with a band.

What about movies? Have you had any movie offers recently? You've received a lot of critical acclaim for your role in Asylum.

The critics liked that movie. And I've received some other offers, but nothing that interests me. I'm looking for a role as a cowboy or country music singer, something more in line with my new career path. No one seems to be offering me those kinds of roles. I don't know if those kinds of roles are available. Maybe after my new songs are released, they'll begin to see me and decide to cast me in an appropriate film. In the meantime, I've been busy with my music, and I haven't really had time to act.

And I suppose we won't be seeing any books from you?

Not in the immediate future.

When we first met, you told me the music was everything. You told me to listen to your music. Is your music still everything?

It is everything.

Even this new country genre?

Let me tell you something about the way I was raised. I think we've discussed this subject before. My parents never told me exactly what to do with my life, and they never tried to force me into any sort of profession. They exposed me to as many different paths as possible and let me pick my own. Do you know how to tell if someone is left- or right-handed?

How can you tell?

You throw something at them and see which hand they use to catch it. That's exactly what my parents did. They threw all this stuff at me and looked to see what I raised my hands to catch. Right off the bat, I grabbed for music. From a very early age, I've liked to sing and compose songs. I liked a lot of other things, but music was my passion. A person needs a passion in life, a thread of light that runs through all their life events. It's like any great work of art—a theme is essential. Without a backbone, we can't stand, walk, or run. Without the burning sun, the earth turns cold and dies. I can't tell you how many people inhabit this world without a serious fervor for anything, without a primary purpose for living. They stumble from one day to the next without any direction. I'm one of the lucky ones. Maybe it's because of the way I was raised, or maybe it's because I'm lucky. Maybe God decided to give me a break. But for me it all comes down to my music. So now you're asking if country music is right for me. You want to know if it's just another fad. Is Scowl jumping from one popularity contest to another? Has he completely lost his mind? I can tell you that I know exactly what I'm doing. I didn't leave rock 'n' roll. It left me. If you really listen to all the music I've written over the years, you'll understand. Just listen to it. Then you won't need to ask me any more questions about it.

Do you think your fans will be disappointed?

Fans are people. They come in all shapes and sizes. Sure, I'll lose some of my old fans, but I think I'll also gain new ones. I think I'll always be selling records, because that's what Scowl does. He sells lots and lots of records.

Don't you ever wonder about all this?

What do you mean?

Do you ever wonder whether you're really headed in the right direction? Haven't you ever looked back on something in the end and wished you'd done it differently?

Never.

Not even on occasion?

Listen, everything we do in our lives and everything that happens to us is for a reason. It's all for God's greater cause. And God doesn't make mistakes. Don't ever let anyone tell you otherwise.

So if you fail at this country music venture, you'll be okay with it?

I'll be okay with it.

But you don't think you'll fail, do you?

Let's just say it's highly unlikely.

THE CASH BOX

———————•◦•———————

S cowl was right. His venture into the all-American world of country music was an enormous success. Critics loved his new sound, and the public couldn't dig deep enough into their pockets to buy his records. His fan base was now older and less hip, and he was no longer just performing for immature sons and daughters; he was also performing for their parents. He watched with interest as the Smothers Brothers were given the boot, as Sharon Tate was stabbed until she died, and as Ted Kennedy got a slap on the wrist for drowning Mary Jo Kopechne, but he didn't sing about any of these things. He concentrated instead on everyday life. He was Norman Rockwell with a guitar, and there was a huge market for his simplistic music, a burgeoning population of record buyers who longed for the America that used to be before the sixties got a hold of it. People needed relief, and Scowl delivered it. Of course, he had his critics and enemies. Activist Jerry Rubin called Scowl's music "cow shit on vinyl," and the academic Theodore Roszak called it "a hackneyed haven for anti-intellectuals." But President Nixon praised the rock-turned-country singer during one of his press conferences, saying, "At a time when so many are intent on tearing things down, this talented young man has been willing to step forward and remind us of what is good and right with this great nation."

Maybe you liked Scowl, and maybe you didn't. But his record sales were healthy, and the guy was rolling in money. That you could not deny. He was invited to all the right Hollywood and Nashville parties, and he won loads of awards for his songwriting and singing. He appeared on the TV talk shows, and he did a few commercials for breakfast cereals, shampoos, and cars. He even took time out of his busy schedule to speak at the graduation ceremony for his old high school in Arcadia. Yes, his life was moving forward magnificently. Unknown to him, however, was the fact that his father had been diagnosed with colon cancer. No one wanted to upset Scowl's applecart, and so he wasn't told about the diagnosis until late. Neither of his parents wanted him worrying or taking time from his busy schedule. They were both thrilled to see their son doing so well. Scowl was finally told about his father when he had to go to the hospital, when the problem could no longer be ignored. The doctors told Scowl his dad had only a short time to live, and eight days later, on May 20, 1970, the man passed away. I read about it in the newspaper, and I thought of calling Scowl for an interview. But knowing how much he loved his father and knowing how upset he would be, I waited for him to come to me. Several months passed before I finally got a call from Claudia saying Scowl wanted to meet. I asked her how he was doing, and she said about as well as could be expected. She said Scowl's mom was taking the tragic loss especially hard, and his mom's state of mind bothered Scowl more than his own grief. Claudia told me to come to Dulcinea the following week, and I showed up with my tape recorder. Frank let me in the front door, and I found Scowl seated at the kitchen table, drinking a cup of tea and watching the kitchen TV. He clicked the set off and motioned for me to sit down. He looked awful. His hair was a mess, and he hadn't shaved for days.

∞∞∞

It's been a while since we last talked. How are you holding up?

I'm doing better than I look.

I was sorry to hear about your father. How's your mom doing?

She's hanging in there.

Is there anything special you'd like to talk about today?

I do want to say something about my dad. Over the past few weeks, I've thought a lot about what I'd say to you about him. I have so many great memories. Do you have any memories of your own father that really stand out? I don't mean that just stand out, but that shine brighter than any others. I'm talking about the kind of memories you've found yourself turning over and over in your head at night. Whenever I think of all the money I'm making, I think back to when I was twelve, when I lived with my family in our house in Arcadia. I went through a phase when I resented my dad. It wasn't him personally that I resented, but rather it was his lot in life. The resentment made me feel so guilty. As a butcher he didn't make much money, and my mom stayed at home, so there was no second income to make things easier. I remember some years were very lean, and it seemed we had barely enough to get by. We always had food on the table and clothes on our backs, but we didn't have many of the things other families had. We didn't go on vacations and often couldn't afford dental work. We didn't eat at restaurants or go to any movies. I had a friend who lived across the street from us named Mike, and his family was in the same boat. His dad was a car mechanic at the Chevrolet dealership. Mike's father was one of the dealership's top mechanics, but the job paid little. You'd think he would've made more. One day Mike and I decided to take matters in our hands. It was a dumb decision, but it seemed to make sense at the time. We were young and naïve, and we didn't think we'd ever get caught.

Get caught doing what?

During those years, Arcadia was a relatively small and close-knit town. Everyone knew everyone, and we all talked about one another, especially at night during dinner. I remember Dad used to talk about Mr. Jeffries, who owned the town's movie theater. The man lived over the theater in a small two-bedroom apartment with his wife, and Dad said every morning that Mr. Jeffries would come downstairs to collect his cash box from the ticket kiosk. He'd take the box up to his living room and log it all into his ledger. This meant the money was sitting unguarded in the kiosk all night, just begging to be stolen. Dad and several others tried to convince Mr. Jeffries to take the cash upstairs at the end of each evening rather than the following morning, but Mr. Jeffries always told them the same thing, that he had the situation under control. His employee Doris minded the business at night so he could turn in early. He didn't want to wake in the middle of a good night's sleep just to run downstairs and grab a damn box. "I've been doing it this way for years," he said. "Never had a problem with it." Well, he never had any problem with it until Mike and I came along.

What did you do?

Mike and I hatched this devious plan. Since we knew Mr. Jeffries left his money in the kiosk during the night, we decided rob the cash box. We'd sneak out of our houses after everyone else had gone to bed, and we'd walk downtown to the theater. We'd use a crowbar to open the kiosk door and use the same crowbar to open the cash drawer. We figured between walking to and from the theater and taking the money, the entire operation would take about an hour. So, when the night finally came, we tied bandannas over our faces like a couple of stagecoach robbers in a Western movie. The bandannas were just in case someone saw us. Obviously, we didn't want to be recognized. We also wore gloves so we wouldn't leave any fingerprints. We took no chances. When we arrived at the theater, Mike pried open the kiosk door, and it popped right open like it wasn't even locked. He then went to work on the cash drawer, which was a little more difficult to open. While working on the cash drawer, Mike dropped the crowbar and it made a loud sound when it hit the tile floor. It woke up Mr. Jeffries, who immediately came downstairs with a flashlight. "I got it!" Mike said, pulling the cash box out. "Hold on, you two," Mr. Jeffries said. He was now just twenty feet from us, and the beam from his flashlight shone directly on our faces. Mike's bandanna was still intact, but mine had slipped loose. "Let's go!" I shouted, and the two of us ran off. "Did he see you?" Mike asked, noticing my loose bandanna. "I think he did," I said.

So what happened?

Mr. Jeffries saw me all right. He called the police and told them about the burglary. Thirty minutes later Officer Munson showed up at my parents' house. Munson and my dad were friends. They were on the same bowling team and sometimes they played poker with a group of other men on Saturday nights over at Chester Avery's house. I had an ear pressed against my bedroom door as I listened to Dad and Munson talking. I felt like my heart was going to beat its way right out of my chest. I heard Munson tell Dad about the burglary at the theater, and he said Mr. Jeffries thought he might have recognized me. "When did this all take place?" my dad asked, and Munson told him. Then my dad said, "It couldn't have been my son. I was up late tonight at the very same time this burglary took place. I was having trouble sleeping and went to the kitchen to make a sandwich. I walked past my son's bedroom and looked in on him, and trust me, he was sound asleep." Then Munson said, "Well, hell, that's good enough for me. I'm sorry if I disturbed you. I'll tell Jeffries he was mistaken." And that was that. I was off the hook, and I never heard another thing about it.

Your dad never brought it up?

My father never brought it up at all. Not ever. He saved my miserable hide and never said a thing about it. I can't imagine what would have happened to him if they'd figured out he lied. He would have been humiliated, and there might have even been legal repercussions. We never talked about it, and I never had the chance to thank him. I really don't know what he was thinking. Maybe he thought my conscience would get the best of me, that it would be punishment enough. Or maybe he understood my frustration over our financial situation. Maybe he felt guilty that he wasn't able to be a better provider, so maybe he felt like the robbery was partly his fault. He never did scold me, and he never asked me to return the money. I've run the events of that evening over in my head a thousand times, and I'm still not sure what happened.

Why do you suppose this memory is so important to you? Why does it keep playing in your head?

I think it's because it was the first time I saw what a father is willing to do for his son. My dad lied without even weighing his options. He wanted to protect me. When he was on his hospital bed during his final days, I asked him about that night, if he remembered it. He said, "Oh sure, I remember it. You would've got in a lot of trouble. You and Mike. I guess I felt I had to do something. If you were a father, you'd understand." I reminded him that I was a father, that I had a seven-year-old son, and he said, "Oh, you have a son, but you're not a father." He just stared at me sternly, and I changed the subject. I seemed to be upsetting him.

Maybe that's why this memory haunts you. Are you wishing you were closer to your own son?

I suppose that's possible.

Do you ever talk to him?

I send him birthday cards every year. That's about it. I'm not sure Audrey really wants me talking to him.

Have you ever asked her about it?

No, I haven't.

What have your parents said about this?

Both of them tried to get me to contact the boy. Mom used to bother me often, but more recently she's left me alone. Now I kind of wish she'd kept after me. I might have done something about it if she hadn't dropped the issue. But you know, I don't remember ever telling anyone I would make a good father, and I made no promises. Don't you find it ironic that

I would have such a great father, yet been such a lousy one myself? Maybe Alan's wife was right when she said I was selfish. Maybe I'm selfish. Maybe that's the long and short of it.

None of us is perfect.

Let's change subjects. I've said all I want to say about my dad. Ask me about something else.

Okay, I heard you were offered another movie role by Joseph Crabtree. Do you have any interest in it? I heard he wrote the part specifically for you.

Joseph said he liked my work so much in *Asylum* that he wanted to direct me in another film. He said he decided to write a new screenplay. He read our last interview and understood that I was looking for a certain kind of Western character. He said the screenplay was written with my new persona in mind, that it's the story of a young man from Wyoming who's volunteered to serve in Vietnam. I told Joseph I wasn't interested in a political agenda, but he said the movie was more a love story than it was any sort of statement about the war. I asked Joseph to send the screenplay, that I'd take a look at it. My music writing has been a little flat lately, and I figure a movie might be just the thing to keep me going. I received the script last week, and I've been reading it over. I won't tell you the details, but I will tell you that it looks promising. I have always liked acting. This project could be very good for me.

I take it there'll be an actress opposite you. Any idea who it will be?

No, we haven't discussed it.

Will any of your music be in the movie?

Joseph said I could write and sing the title song. But there won't be any other music by me.

What's the name of the movie?

Right now, it's called *Faraway Places*, but that title could change. It depends on the producers.

"Faraway Places" sounds like a good title for a song.

Yes, it does.

When I talked to Claudia on the phone last week, she said you were writing a farewell song to your father. How's that coming?

It's been hard. I don't want to write something dark and depressing. I want the song to be joyful and very optimistic because that's the way my father was. I'm trying not to dwell on the fact that he's left a giant hole in our lives. I want to celebrate his fifty-eight years of life, but it isn't easy when you're grieving. Perhaps it will take some time, and maybe I need to let a few more months pass. When Dad died, it really took the wind out of my sails. I wish they'd told me about his cancer sooner. There's so much I wanted to say, and it just seemed like the final week wasn't enough. Have you ever known that someone you love is about to die? It's a very difficult thing. You want to say so much, but given the chance to speak, you seem to come up with so little.

BRUSHSTROKES

—•—

S cowl stayed in touch with me off and on for the next year. He went
ahead with his second Crabtree film. The producers made some minor
changes to the screenplay, but they didn't change the title. During the early
days of filming, Scowl wrote the title song, "Faraway Places." He called me
and performed it over the phone, and I said I liked it. It was actually quite
good. It sounded more like a popular ballad than a country tune, but I
didn't tell him that. Also, during the shooting, he did a lot of reading. He
was into the classics now and sped through Plato's dialogues in a couple
weeks. He got a big kick out of Plato. But the most interesting thing Scowl
spent time on between shoots wasn't his songwriting or reading. It was his
painting. He hired an art teacher to come down from Santa Barbara and
give him daily painting lessons in his trailer. Scowl told me he was learning
to paint portraits, and he said he felt he had a real feel for the craft, that he
couldn't wait for me to see his work. He said he planned on showing the
work in Los Angeles just as soon as he was done with the movie. When
the movie was just about finished, with only about a couple weeks left to
go, Scowl called me for an interview. He wanted to discuss his artwork,
to generate some public interest in it. I didn't mind being used this way.
It was nothing new for Scowl to use our interviews to promote himself.
Regardless, he always had some interesting things to say.

When I walked into his trailer, I was taken completely by surprise.
The place was filled wall-to-wall with his crazy portraits. I didn't know
quite what to say. Some of the paintings resembled human faces, but most
of them were so abstract that they could have been paintings of about
anything. The place reeked of oils and turpentine, giving me an immediate
dull headache. I have to be honest. The paintings looked like they'd been
done by a six-year-old. Scowl said his art teacher told him the paintings

had a lot of promise. I guessed I just didn't know much about modern art. So maybe it was my own ignorance that made me want to laugh out loud. This particular collection of forty-two portraits is well-known in the art world today, but back then it was the about silliest thing I'd ever seen. Like I said, I don't know much about art, so I guess I should keep my mouth shut. I turned on my tape recorder, and we started the interview.

What do you think?

It looks like you've been busy.

But what do you think of them all? Have you ever seen anything like this?

I truly can't say I have.

There are forty-two of them. They're each titled by a number, in the order they were painted. Number One is the first one I painted and Number Forty-Two is the last one. Pick any one of them out, my good man, and I'll tell you the story behind it.

How about this one?

Number Twenty-Eight. This is my fourteenth portrait of Claudia. Can you see her fiery green eyes? She was very angry on the day I painted this. I left the kitchen door open when I drove off to work that morning, and one of Claudia's favorite cats got outside. The cat's name is Dolly, a calico named after Dolly Parton, and Claudia had searched high and low for her. She couldn't find the cat anywhere. She called our neighbors, but no one had seen it. She then drove all the way over here to the movie set just to storm into my trailer and tell me about what I'd done, to tell me how mad she was. She said she felt like kicking me. I told her to take a seat, right over there on that stool. That's where I have all my subjects sit. "Now hold that feeling," I said to her, and as Claudia sat there fuming, I got out my oils and went to work. Can you see the flames burning in her eyes? Can you see the furrow in her brow? Can you feel all her frustration and anger? It reaches out and grabs you, doesn't it? This is one of my favorite portraits of Claudia because she so seldom gets this mad at me. Whenever I look at this portrait, it makes me think of her and those stupid cats. People love each other, sure, but I think in this country they love their dumb pets more. I haven't been able to figure this out. Do you know what I'm talking about?

Have you ever been to Mexico? It's a lot different down there. They treat animals like animals, but up here in America we treat our animals better than we treat our own children.

What happened to Dolly?

She was waiting at the front door when Claudia arrived home. I was off the hook.

That's good to know.

Go ahead and pick another portrait.

Okay, how about this?

Number Thirty-Two. That's an interesting choice you just made. It's a portrait of Mrs. Driscoll. She's the gal in charge of the wardrobe here. She provides all our costumes for the movie, makes sure they fit just right, and makes sure they're where they ought to be. She says she's been doing this for over thirty years, and I believe her because she's very good at what she does. I'd guess she's now about sixty. She has such an interesting face, those wrinkles and age spots, and those eyes. What she must have seen over the years through those marvelous eyes. Think of the stars she's dressed. Think of the stars she's worked for. She likes telling the story about George Raft, about how they had a torrid love affair back in 1942 when they were filming *Background to Danger.* She tells about how she met Bugsy Siegel through Raft, and how she was later invited to the opening of the Flamingo in Las Vegas. She says she didn't go to the opening, but she still has the paper invitation in her scrapbook along with a thousand other mementos. People like Mrs. Driscoll intrigue me. They are an integral part of the movies, yet they aren't. There are stars, directors, and producers who are in the spotlight, and then there are people like Mrs. Driscoll, always busy doing this and that, attending to the needs of others. Do you think I've captured the real Mrs. Driscoll in this portrait? Can you see her proximity to fame? She is so close to being famous in a way, yet light-years away from it.

What about this painting? Who's this supposed to be?

Ah, Number Thirty-Nine. That would be you.

This is supposed to be me?

I used a photograph from one of your books to go by. This is one of the few portraits I did without having the subject pose in person.

I'm having a difficulty seeing myself.

That's because you're not an artist, my good man. You never have been an artist. Sure, artists fascinate you, but I think you're confused by them. It's odd, isn't it? You're in the dark, yet you're somehow qualified to explain to the public all you see and hear about the subjects of your books and articles. I think you've become one of my most interesting portraits of all, the writer who doesn't understand life's secrets yet feels compelled to purvey them to the public. The most notable feature of your portrait isn't your eyes, or nose, or ears, but it's your mouth, that place where you do all your talking. You talk and talk and talk. That's what you do. That's what we're doing now, talking about my artwork, talking about my oil paintings. I can tell from the look on your face that you're utterly confused by my artwork, that my portraits make no sense to you. Will you tell your readers that Scowl's gone mad? No, I think you know better than this. You've always been straight with me, and I think you'll publish my words exactly as spoken. And when you publish this interview, here's what I'd like your readers to walk away with. I'd like them to know that Scowl is genuine. He's the real deal. He's as honest as Abraham Lincoln and as serious as a war.

Why did you choose me?

Why did I choose you for this portrait?

No, why did you choose me to be your interviewer? It's been fourteen years since you picked me out from a group of perfectly capable journalists. You've had me do all your interviews ever since, and I've never heard you complain about me. If I'm really so much in the dark as you say, why did you single me out?

Who do all these portraits remind you of?

I'm not sure what you mean.

Who am I like? I know I knew nothing about art when I started painting, but Cynthia says my work reminds her of a couple famous painters. Can you guess who they are?

Who's Cynthia?

She's my art teacher. She says I'm a cross between Rembrandt and Jackson Pollock.

I see the Pollock.

You know about Jackson Pollock? I didn't even know who Pollock was until I started working with Cynthia, until she made the comparison.

I bought some artbooks that have plates of his work. I've read up on him over the past few weeks. Very interesting guy. Very interesting, indeed. He said, "It doesn't make much difference how the paint is put on, so long as something has been said." I think Pollock would've liked my portraits. What do you think? I think they have a lot to say. They speak to you, don't they? Can you hear them all talking?

Seriously, I don't see how anyone can get a word in edgewise.

Isn't that the truth?

NOSEDIVE

W hen Crabtree had finished filming *Faraway Places,* Scowl collected the canvasses from his trailer and moved them to a rented space downtown Los Angeles. He opened a gallery in the space for his forty-two paintings. Then he got the word out to art lovers, and the showing was an immediate hit. I'm not sure that his country music fans really cared about or understood the work, but the art world adored it. Never underestimate the power of celebrity when it comes to the tastes of art lovers. They are celebrity crazy more than they'll ever let on. Many of them were talking about my interview with Scowl in the *LA Times,* and their only complaint about the interview was that it was too short. They wanted to know more. Sydney Axelrod, a friend of mine and art critic for the *LA Times,* wrote, "Scowl's portraits show an unwavering empathy and love for his subjects that none of today's painters can match. His gallery is a must-see for all enthusiasts." It seemed once again that Scowl had the Midas touch. Everything he touched turned to gold. The paintings were fetching unheard-of prices, and it seemed collectors who deemed themselves important wanted to own one of these remarkable portraits. When asked if he had plans to do more of them, Scowl said forty-two was his limit. This drove the prices even higher, and every one of the paintings was sold within a month.

Just a short time after the paintings went on display, *Faraway Places* made it to the theaters. Some critics who were hoping for an antiwar message called the film trite, but the public loved it. It did well at the box office, and already Crabtree was working on another screenplay for Scowl to read. Things couldn't have been going any better for Scowl and Claudia. They were firing on all cylinders, roaring forward. Trouble didn't come until the fall of 1971, when Claudia was diagnosed with breast cancer.

It was unusual for someone her age to get the deadly disease, but after struggling like a trooper to survive, she passed away in January 1972. I called several times to offer my condolences, but Scowl never returned any of my calls. I didn't hear a word from him. He was apparently in no mood for an interview.

This would prove to be one of the darkest times in my friend's life. In addition to Claudia dying, his mother passed away from a sudden stroke just a few months later. His family had vanished. He had no one to inspire him and no one to hold him up. There was no one to manage all of his affairs, no one to share a bed with, and no one to offer sage words of advice. They were all gone, all of them. When I first read the reports of Scowl's drinking, I didn't believe them. I thought they were just unfounded rumors. I knew how he felt about drugs and alcohol. But reports kept coming in, and the stories became more numerous until they simply couldn't be ignored. There were scuffles with cops, a couple of drunk driving arrests, and some violent incidents with reporters and photographers. One night, Scowl got drunk and drove down to Newport Beach to see his son and Audrey. He caused a horrible scene there, and Audrey's husband had to call the police. Then something strange happened. The stories stopped coming in. There was nothing in the news about Scowl at all. He had holed himself up in Dulcinea, out of the public eye. Frank and his team of bodyguards kept everyone away while their boss watched TV and drank himself into oblivion. From the day Claudia died, two years had passed, and Scowl's world had completely fallen apart.

It was Joseph Crabtree who finally got through to him. Crabtree knew of a private group of alcoholic actors and directors who held clandestine AA meetings at one another's homes. Crabtree talked to Frank, and the two of them got together one day and convinced Scowl to join the group. In his recent memoir, Crabtree wrote, "Scowl was at the end of his rope. I'd never seen a man so completely beaten and without hope. He was too far gone to even cry. He was devoid of any emotion, and there was just nothing left of the man. Frank and I talked to Scowl for hours, and it was like he couldn't hear us. Our mouths were moving, but nothing was registering. And then it happened. Scowl was drinking a Scotch and water at the time, and he set the drink down on the coffee table. He said, 'Okay, I'll do it.' It was that simple.

I called one of my friends in the AA group, and they arranged to have a meeting held at Dulcinea that evening."

Scowl met his new group of friends, and he seemed to like them. He would continue to attend their meetings for months. One of them gave Scowl his own AA book, and Scowl read it several times. He worked his steps and stayed off the booze. He ate the right foods and began to exercise. He did this for six months before he finally picked up the phone and called me. I honestly didn't think I'd ever hear from him again. When he called, he sounded happy and lucid, and I was so glad he called. He asked me how my family was, and I said we were all doing fine. I told him Julia was now working part time as an assistant editor for a small publishing house, and I was working on a book of stories about the Rolling Stones. I told him Carter was now six years old and that Pamela was already five. He couldn't believe that my kids were so much older. He said, "It seems like they were babies the last time we talked." I asked if he was calling for an interview, and he said he didn't want to interrupt my work. When I told him that he wouldn't be interrupting, he said, "In that case, meet me at Dulcinea tomorrow afternoon. I'll tell Frank to expect you. We have a lot to talk about."

I understand you're now in AA. How does it feel? Are they helping you?

I never thought I'd be one of *those* people, but it's been right for me. It's a great group of people. They saved my life.

I've been told you're attending meetings with some rich and famous people. Can you tell me about any of them? Who are they? What are their stories. Any names I would recognize?

I can't tell you anything. No, it's called AA for a reason. We need to be able to participate anonymously. We only go by first names, although everyone knows who each other is. It's tough when your famous, trying to find any anonymity. Can you imagine if a person like me stepped into a run-of-the-mill AA meeting? It would be a disaster. Word would get out to the public, and people would show up just to hear me talk and just to look at me there. They would be gawking at me, hanging on my every pitiful word. Reporters and photographers would elbow their way into the meeting. Those who really needed help would have to go elsewhere.

It would be a three-ring circus. You know, some things are very difficult when you're well-known, and getting sober is one of those things. I was lucky that Crabtree knew about the private meetings. Those meetings saved my life.

Was it a life-and-death situation?

Do you know anyone who had a serious drinking problem? I mean, intimately?

Actually, no.

Alcohol abuse is always a life-and-death situation.

How much were you drinking?

I didn't keep track.

Did you get the shakes?

Yes, at times.

Did you ever get DTs?

Listen, these physical symptoms you're talking about play a very minor role. In fact, physical symptoms are almost irrelevant. It is what alcohol does to your life and spirit that really hurts. It drives a vile sword into your very heart and soul. It consumes and corrupts you and sends you spinning out of control and into a terrible fog. You find yourself humiliated on a daily basis, and you learn to despise and shame yourself. You do things you wouldn't ordinarily do, and you associate with people you ordinarily wouldn't have anything to do with. You look at yourself in the mirror, and as God is my witness, you can't believe the face looking back at you. You've become a new person, and now you're now one of the doomed. And you can suddenly see the Grim Reaper standing behind you, looking over your shoulder, that cold, evil, and soul-snatching Grim Reaper! There are clouds of his evil breath steaming up the mirror, and there is a knee-weakening glint from the blade of his scythe. Yes, everyone now hates you, and you despise them all back. It seems your life had come to an end, so you drink more alcohol. You're searching for that feeling you were once able to summon up so easily, but now the good feeling doesn't come, no matter how much you drink. More booze only brings more pain, more misery, and lots of self-loathing. Then it begins to burn like a hot poison in your veins, yet you can't stop consuming it. You are trapped in a vicious circle. You feel like there's no way out.

It sounds horrible.

It *was* horrible.

You never used to drink much. Did you start drinking heavily just because you lost Claudia?

I think that's obvious.

You've always spoken out against abusing alcohol. Why would you turn to it in such a time of despair?

I don't know. I suppose it was because I just needed a relief from all the pain and loneliness I was feeling. I tried to do other things, but nothing was working. I tried writing songs, but everything I wrote came out so terribly sad. I tried reading several books, but I just couldn't concentrate. I even tried my hand at painting, but nothing I painted took my mind off Claudia. Then one afternoon I sent Frank to the store to buy us a bottle of Scotch, and I opened it up when he got home. I poured a good stiff drink and swallowed it. My heart turned warm, and I found for a moment that the booze gave me a sense of relief, a rush of euphoria. I suppose that's how it is for a lot of people, the booze giving relief at first. But then it turns on you. It betrays you and becomes your enemy. It hates every bone in your body, and it brings you into the fiery den of the devil himself.

Do you think alcohol is evil?

Yes, I do.

Even in moderation?

Yes, even in moderation. There is nothing good about it. It has no redeeming value.

I heard while you were drinking that you drove down to Newport to see Audrey and your son, Roger, and that Audrey's husband called the police. What happened that night? Did you get to see Roger?

I was afraid you'd ask me about this. Listen, I've tried to piece together what happened, but much of it is a blur. I was sitting in my kitchen that afternoon, drinking my Scotch straight from the bottle, getting ready to go out on the town. I didn't have plans to go anywhere special. I just wanted to get out of the house. Then it occurred to me that I really ought to visit my son. I remembered how Mom used to plead with me to see the boy. "He needs you," she used to say. "He needs love from his real father." I can't tell you how many times she begged me, but her words just rolled off my back. I knew as far as love went, the boy had all he needed from his mom and his stepdad, and building his hopes up for any kind of normal relationship with me would only be a cruel thing to do. Why tease the boy with the hope that he would have his real father when everyone knew it would never happen? But on this night, my head was swimming with booze, and I felt a sudden longing to see the child in person. I imagined how he would be so excited to see me, how he'd run up and hug me and call me dad. He was now nine years old, old enough to understand the importance of meeting his flesh-and-blood father. I brought my half-full whiskey bottle with me, and I drove toward Newport to see my son.

You were drinking and driving?

I did it all the time.

What happened when you arrived at Audrey's?

This is where the story gets hazy. When I arrived, I had finished off the bottle of Scotch, and I was teetering on the edge of a blackout. Do you know very much about blackouts?

Not really.

Most people think of blackouts as simply being unable to remember, but they are really much more than that. They are altered states in an altered state. Does this make any sense to you? The person is drunk, which is one state, but then on top of that he is thinking and acting in a whole unrelated state. He's no longer himself. He's actually another person, like a person in a dream. It's like there is an alien creature occupying his body and mind, using his arms and legs and head as its own. I first learned about this creature one night while driving my car home from a bar in Beverly Hills. I had a lot to drink, and I blacked out while I was driving. One moment I was cruising along Wilshire, and the next thing I knew I was parking my car in my garage. It was like I had lived fifteen minutes without living them. Who had been driving my car? Who had their foot on the accelerator? Who'd been listening to my car radio and breathing my air? It was the creature. It had taken over all of my motor and intellectual functions so that I had absolutely no control over my life. I was lucky that it had the good sense to drive me home that night. We could've ended up anywhere. Hell, we could've wound up in Upstate New York or Tijuana or somewhere in Canada. That is what a blackout is. It's much more than just a matter of losing a few memories. Great Scott, it's like a bizarre Ray Bradbury science fiction story. I didn't like it at all. I really hated it. I had a lot of blackouts while I was drinking, and I didn't like any of them.

So what happened in Newport Beach?

I remember arriving in town, and I remember driving to Audrey's home. Beyond that I don't recall much of anything until I suddenly woke up in a jail cell. The creature had taken over my body that night. It rang the doorbell and yelled at Audrey, and I saw my son. I made such a horrible scene that Audrey's husband had to call the police. The officers handcuffed me and brought me back to the station to be locked up until I was sober. When I snapped out of my blackout, I was right in the middle of talking to one of the officers. I had no idea what I'd been talking about. I stopped midsentence and said, "What am I doing here?" The cop was patient, and he filled me in on what I'd done. It was like he was telling me about someone else.

So you don't remember seeing your son?

I don't remember seeing him at all. I don't remember anything I said to him. I couldn't even tell you what he looked like. I feel so terrible about it. It breaks my heart that Roger had to see me in that state. He'll never know who I am. My friends in AA think I ought to go back down to Newport and apologize, to make amends. I'd like to do this, but I'm not sure Audrey or Roger will even want to see me, let alone hear anything I have to say.

What's the most important thing you've learned in AA?

I've learned a lot of things in AA, but I guess most importantly I learned I now had two problems to deal with, each mutually exclusive of the other. I learned on one hand I still hadn't come to terms with Claudia's death. On the other hand, I had this raging addiction to alcohol to contend with. I had to solve the alcohol problem before I could even begin to address the loss of Claudia, and trust me, it wasn't easy. Despite all the problems the alcohol had caused me, I still felt a ridiculous desire to drink. AA taught me to turn my cravings over to God. At first this was very difficult, for I was angry at God. I was furious he had taken away the love of my life, and I no longer trusted him. But I had to have faith that everything in this world happens for a good reason, no matter how wrong it may seem at the time. I knew this was true, but I didn't feel it. When I finally made the leap of faith and let go of my anger, turning my life back over to God, that's when my desire to drink stopped. It was like God had yanked it right out of my psyche. God now held me in his loving arms. He answered my prayers and assured me everything is as it should be. God, and only God, is the shining key to sobriety. In AA they like to call it a higher power, but don't let them fool you. It's God they're talking about. It's all about God, as in the Bible, as in our father who art in heaven.

So have you been able to accept Claudia's death?

I'm working on it.

But life is getting back to normal?

It's getting closer.

Have you been writing any songs?

No, I've stayed away from music. I don't feel like writing or performing.

Are you reading?

I've been reading parts of the Bible.

How about your artwork? Have you picked up a paintbrush at all?

No, I haven't.

Besides going to AA meetings and church, what have you been doing with all your time?

I've been working with Joseph on a screenplay for another movie we might make. He's been coming over to Dulcinea a lot lately.

Does this story have a title?

We're thinking of calling it *Crossroads*. That's the working title.

Can I ask what it's about?

It's kind of about everything we've been talking about this afternoon. It's the story of a famous writer named Noel Handy who crashes his car into a tree and loses his wife in the accident. He turns to alcohol to assuage his guilt and loss, but he finds himself suffering the same way I did. He hits the bottle. He has run-ins with the police and altercations with strangers. He drinks himself deeper and deeper into his insanity. When he hits rock bottom, he finally joins an AA group as I did. Through the group he tackles his addiction and gradually learns to accept life on life's terms. Joseph thinks the story will be a big hit so long as we tone down the God angle, and he thinks my own personal experiences will make the movie seem more real to the audience. He also says I'm not the only person with harrowing experiences like this, that there will be many people in the country who can relate. And he says the fact that everyone knows who I am will make the tale all the more compelling. It'll be kind of like a true story, except about a fictional character. I've enjoyed working on this screenplay so far, and I hope Joseph is right about the movie being successful. I really don't need it to bomb. I've had enough disappointments over the past few years to last me a lifetime. This screenplay has been a terrific catharsis, a way to release my pent-up emotions and unload all my recent experiences.

Whose idea was it to write the screenplay?

It was Joseph's.

Do you intend to play the lead role?

That's the plan.

Audrey was interviewed in the LA Times *briefly last month. She said she was glad to hear you were getting your life back together.*

Yes, I read that. It was good to hear.

I'm sorry if I already asked you this, but do you think you'll ever visit with Audrey or you son again, if only to apologize?

I don't know. Like I said, the members of our group think I ought to see them and try to make amends. It's one of the twelve steps in AA.

How old is Roger now?

He's eleven. In a couple years he'll be a teenager. It's sad to think I've gone on so many years without him being in my life, without me getting to know him. I still send him birthday cards.

I have to be honest, you still seem a little down to me. When do you think you'll be your old self?

I wouldn't really say I'm down. I'm just tired. I've been through a lot. Trust me when I say the old Scowl will be back. I know what the public wants, and my story is for sure going to have a happy ending.

THE PROPOSAL

———— •◦• ————

*C*rossroads was a hit with critics and the public. It was distributed to the theaters in June 1975, and as you may recall, it was nominated for three Academy Awards. It was up for best screenplay, best picture, and Scowl was up for best actor. This was the same year that the Vietnam War ended, the same year that prison sentences were handed out to Watergate defendants, and the same year that Sony VCRs appeared in American homes. The Academy Awards came and went, and unfortunately it also became the same year that *One Flew Over the Cuckoo's Nest* walked away with the wins. There were many who felt Scowl should have beat Nicholson for best actor. But regardless of the outcome, Scowl was now an actor to be reckoned with. Noted film critic Jonathon Scott said, "Never has there been a more heartfelt portrayal of an alcoholic. Scowl's acting is a true inspiration, and his performance will be remembered for years."

Scowl was now thirty-seven years old. No longer was he just an adolescent heartthrob with a sneer and strange way of dancing. Those crazy days were long gone. He was now an adult, a thoughtful man with much to offer to his fans. He relished his recent success in Hollywood, and perhaps more than anything, he now cherished his friendship with Joseph Crabtree. He wasn't shy about telling people that Crabtree had saved his life, and they began work on yet another movie. They were writing a screenplay about a misfit who stalks and assassinates a president. The plan was to have Scowl play the misfit and to have Jack Lemmon play the president. The idea for the movie was inspired by the recent attempts on Gerald Ford's life, and the main character was to be a man named Willie Wade, a thirty-five-year-old unemployed construction worker with a handgun and a radical agenda. The movie's purpose was to show just how vulnerable the country was. It was a thriller with a point to it, and the working title was *The Strange Case of Willie Wade*.

While they worked on the script for *Willie Wade*, Scowl spent a lot of time at Joseph's home. The Crabtree family had taken Scowl in as one of their own, and he often stayed for dinner and watched old movies on TV with them at night. The Crabtrees had a son and a daughter. Their son, Miles, was twenty-three and just out of college. He lived in San Francisco, working in the financial district where he was learning the ins and outs of the money game. The daughter, Jennifer, was twenty-one and was enrolled in UCLA's film school. She was still living at home, and she was often in the house when Scowl visited. I suppose it was inevitable that young Jennifer would develop a crush on her father's favorite actor. She was interested in filmmaking, and he was a genuine Academy Award nominee. At first Scowl didn't pay the girl much mind, figuring her to be too young for him, not taking her interest in him very seriously. But as time went by, Scowl began to take notice of the girl. He looked forward to his visits at the Crabtrees' house, not just to work on the movie script with Joseph, but to see Jennifer. Then one thing led to another, and he mustered up the courage to admit his interest in the girl and ask Joseph if it was okay for him to take her out on a date. Joseph said yes, and that was all he needed to hear. When Scowl finally called me for an interview, I had a pretty good idea what he wanted to talk about. I suspected that he'd fallen for Jennifer. Of course, there were rumors, and usually where there's smoke, there's fire. We met at that same Sunset Boulevard café where we met fourteen years ago when Scowl announced that Audrey was pregnant, except this time he had no disguise. A few people recognized him and asked for autographs, but for the most part they didn't bother us. Scowl wanted me to tell the world that he was in love again, but that was not all. He said there was a lot more to it. Much more to it, as a matter of fact, and as you will soon see. Always with a flair for drama, he would save the best part for last.

Do you know why I called you for this interview?

I have a suspicion.

Before we get into it, I need to clear the air about something. The buzz around town is that Joseph and I are going to film a movie that's about the assassination of a president. Have you heard about this project?

I've heard about it.

Well, I need you to tell my fans that the movie is off. For me, anyway.

What do you mean it's off?

I've decided to stop working on the project. Joseph can go ahead with the movie using some other actor to play the lead, but I've made a decision not to take any part in it. I decided it wasn't for me.

What changed your mind?

Happy endings, my good man.

That's it?

The other afternoon we had a meeting about the movie, and that night I woke in a cold sweat. I realized there was no way to write this story with a happy ending. In order for the movie to get its point across, the president would have to be killed. There was simply no way around it. If the attempt on the president's life was stopped or failed somehow, and everyone in the story lived happily ever after, the movie would lose its purpose, and no one would learn anything. But I made a promise to myself ever since writing *Nancy Kimball* that I would never again get myself involved in a story that didn't have a happy ending. This is a promise I made to myself and a promise I made to my fans.

Does Joseph know about this?

Yes, I told him. I think he gets it. He said he was disappointed, but I think he understands. He said we could work on something else together in the future. He thought maybe a comedy would be appropriate, and I liked this idea. I've never acted in a comedy before.

Do you have any ideas for a comedy?

No, I don't.

I'm surprised you backed out of a Crabtree movie, but I guess you're doing what you think is right.

Yes, it's right. It's right for me. If there's any one thing I've learned over the years, it's that life is short, and we must take advantage of every chance we have to do what's right for us. There's no time to waste doing anything else. Heck, any day I could be taken deathly ill, or I could die in a car accident or plane crash, or I could slip and fall and break my neck. I read in the paper about an attorney in Los Angeles who slipped on a wet floor in a lavatory, hit his head on the urinal, and died hours later. Just like that, the guy was dead. The poor guy was just trying to take a pee, and now he's dead. They said he was in his thirties, that he had his whole life ahead of him. We're only given so much time, and we ought to give life our best shot. And for me, this best shot means acting in the sort of movies that are right for me. So what do I want? I want people to watch my films and step out of the theater believing that there is a lot of good in the human race. I want them to feel that hope does spring eternal. When people look back on my body of work as an artist, I want it to bring a smile to their faces and ignite joy in their hearts. Life is a great and wonderful gift if you treat it well, if you take proper care of it, if you love and respect it. This is if, and only if, you make every effort to do the right things.

I remember when Nancy Kimball *first hit the bookstore shelves how you fretted over the public's reaction to its unhappy ending. You said it was a mistake. Yet, in recent years, critics have lauded the story's realism. Are you saying the critics are wrong?*

Real is as we choose.

Meaning?

Meaning, the critics are wrong. Every work of fiction is in the author's hands. The storyline is as real as the author wants to make it. The author is all-powerful, like a god. Great Scott, just think of it! He alone has the power to raise his characters high toward the heavens or twist them and send them down into the depths of despair. He can make them cuss, swear, and spit out their dialogue, or he can have them speak with a civil and loving tongue. It's all up to him. He can fashion them as ugly and mean-spirited as the devil himself or sculpt them to be divine as the Virgin Mary. It is all up to the author and his intent. I happen to think an author has a responsibility to treat his characters well, like they're friends, like they're a part of his family. You know, if you love and care for your characters, you'll look out for their best interests. And if you're looking out for them, you'll show them how to grow and blossom rather than let them die on the vine. When I wrote *Nancy Kimball,* I let my characters down. It was my job to help Nancy Kimball find fulfilment, and I dropped the ball. I failed her miserably, and that's all I'm trying to say. It didn't have to happen that way, and I don't want it to happen again.

That's interesting. Have you given any thought to writing another book?

I've thought about it, and I have a few ideas. But I'd need a good chunk of time to do it, and time's a little scarce for me right now. I've been busy with other things. There just aren't enough hours in the day.

What's a typical day in the life of Scowl like? Can you walk me through it?

Well, I wake up at eight. I exercise and then eat breakfast. I like to eat cereal for breakfast, usually a bowl of Lucky Charms or Captain Crunch. I then spend the rest of the morning answering my fan mail. I don't have a manager or any writers, so I spend a lot of time on this. I like to at least make some effort to write my fans back. I don't answer all the letters that I receive, and I don't write long responses, but I like to send notes and comments to let them know I care. I wouldn't be anywhere without my fans. I'm constantly aware of this. By noon it's time for me to eat lunch, and I make a sandwich, usually a ham and cheese. I wash the sandwich down with a glass of milk and put on my jeans and a T-shirt. Afternoons are my creative periods, and lately I've been working on my music. I brew myself a cup of tea and sit alone in the front room with my guitar. I'm planning to release a new album later this year, a compilation of love songs. Some of the music will be love songs I've already recorded but arranged a little differently. But the rest of the album will be filled with the new material I've just written, inspired by my latest love. I need to tell the world about this new love. I want everyone to know about her.

And you're referring to Jennifer Crabtree?

Yes, I am. And yes, all the rumors are true.

Is she the reason for this interview?

Listen, I was smitten by Audrey, and I was head-over-heels in love with Claudia. Nothing will ever lessen the feelings I had for those two women, but Jen is something altogether different and very special. I feel like she's my light at the end of the tunnel, my silver lining, my warm spring day. She is such a lovely creature. She's so young and enthusiastic, yet she is wise beyond her years. Never have I enjoyed talking to anyone as much as I enjoy talking to Jen. Sometimes we just sit and chat for hours, and sometimes I'll just stare at her quietly, dumbfounded by her beauty. After everything that has happened in my life, it's hard to believe we found each other.

You certainly sound in love.

Yes, I'm in love.

What do you and Jen talk about?

We talk about everything under the sun. We talk about current events, music, and art. We talk about our pasts and try to guess our futures. We talk about what we had for dinner, or the last book we read, or about our favorite movies. You name it, we talk about it.

Can you name one of your favorite movies? I don't think I've ever asked you this before.

You'd probably expect me to name some famous film like *Casablanca, Giant,* or *On the Waterfront,* which are all great movies. I mean, there are a ton of great movies I could name, but one of my favorites is a little-known Hal Ashby film called *Harold and Maude.* Have you ever seen this film? It was a disappointment at the box office. Not a lot of people paid to see it, but I think it's one of the all-time great films. Claudia and I went to see the movie at the theater when it first came out, and I remember we both couldn't believe what we'd seen. When I brought this movie up to Jen, it turned out to be one of her favorites too. Joseph took her to see it when she was only sixteen, but she fell in love with the film. Like Claudia and me, she was mesmerized by the way Ashby was able to aim such an improbable and sad love story toward such a joyous and happy ending. I really admired Ashby for this.

Again with the happy endings.

Yes, again.

I don't have any more questions. Is there anything else you'd like to say?

Yes, as a matter of fact there is. I'd like to end this interview with a question.

What's your question?

The question isn't for you. The question is for Jen, who I know will be reading this interview.

Well, go ahead.

Jen, my darling, will you marry me?

Anything else?

No, I think that will do it.

A New Priority

⸻•⸻

The proposal interview appeared in *People Weekly* just five days after I met with Scowl, and his fans loved it. They were thrilled he had opened his heart in public and made everyone a part of his personal life. And they were also dying to know Jennifer's answer to his question. She did of course say yes, and the wedding date was set for June 1976. Joseph Crabtree was asked what he thought of the engagement, and he said he couldn't imagine having a better son-in-law or a better husband for his daughter. In the meantime, Scowl's new album was released. It was at first going to be called *Love Songs,* but Scowl changed his mind about the title. He decided this might be too feminine for his male fans, so he renamed the album after one of the tracks, "Arrow through My Heart." It wasn't a country album, nor did it sound much like rock 'n' roll. I guess you'd say it fell somewhere in between. The album didn't sell as well as many of Scowl's other records, but it sold enough to be considered a financial success. Meanwhile, Scowl and Jennifer tied the knot in a gala Hollywood invite-everyone-you-know wedding ceremony held at the Crabtree estate, and after the wedding they enjoyed a long, romantic honeymoon in the Caribbean. When they finally packed up their things and flew back to the States, Jennifer moved into Dulcinea, and I don't remember ever seeing Scowl happier.

Scowl was now thirty-eight. He was changing, and his priorities were maturing. He called to talk to me, to set up another interview, and we talked for an hour or two on the phone. He spent a lot of the time talking about his childhood. He was obsessed with his relationship with his parents. He didn't tell stories about things that had gone wrong or about any disappointments; rather, he recalled how good things were when he was a kid and how much happiness he'd experienced growing up with his parents in their small house in Arcadia. I think I knew Scowl pretty well, and I could tell exactly where he was headed. He was telling me how his life was going to be different. He no longer just wanted to be a movie star, or an idol, or a songwriter, or a singer, or a stage performer. He wanted something much more meaningful. He told me he wanted to be a father. His own dad had always told him over and over how the greatest joy of his life had been raising Scowl, watching him grow from a clueless child into a mature, kind, and successful adult. "Unless you have a boy of your own, you'll probably never understand how happy you've made me," his dad said when he married Audrey. "I hope you experience the same joy. There's nothing in the world like a man being a dad. You can forget travelling around the world in eighty days, and forget being crowned the king of a country, and forget flying to the moon or Mars in a rocket ship. Fatherhood is without a doubt the penultimate achievement and experience for any man living on the face of this earth, whether he be tall or short, rich or poor, thin or thick, north or south. There's absolutely nothing anywhere in this big world that surpasses it."

At thirty-eight, Scowl had everything a man could ask for—money, fame, and the girl. He had everything except for this fatherhood thing. He did have Roger, of course, but Roger didn't really count. Scowl hardly knew the boy, and that ship had sailed years ago. What Scowl wanted now was a *real* son, a boy he could call his own, not a boy being raised by an ex-wife and a real estate developer in Orange County. Fortunately for Scowl, Jennifer was on the exact same page; they set out to start a family of their own. Scowl would hear the great news in September 1976, and that's when he called me for this interview. He was thrilled to death and wanted to share the good news with everyone.

So what's on your mind?

Do you have good childhood memories?

I suppose I do.

I love my childhood memories. When I was in the third grade, it was 1946. That's the year I first showed a real interest in music. I remember what I used to do. I would sing out loud in the shower stall as though I was onstage, as though I was performing in front of hundreds of adoring fans. I had a favorite song back then. I would sing "To Each His Own," pretending my own big band was playing in the background, and I'd hold my plastic comb to my mouth like it was a microphone. That song was a huge hit that year, and I knew every line by heart. I learned lots of other songs later on and even began making up some of my own. Dad took notice of my interest in music, and when I turned nine, he brought home an acoustic guitar for my birthday. It was like magic, the sounds that came out of that great and glorious instrument. Then I remember hearing Mom and Dad talking about me one night while they were in the kitchen. They thought I was asleep in my room, but I was listening from the shadows of the hallway and heard every word they said. Dad wanted to buy me a piano. He said I obviously had musical talent and that I needed a piano, that all great musicians had pianos to compose songs. Mom was for this idea, but then they couldn't figure out where they'd get the money. Mom said they were barely paying their bills as it was, and a piano was an expensive purchase. That's when Dad proposed working evenings. He heard there was a night watchman job opening at the Santa Anita racetrack, and he applied for the position. And he was hired. Sadly, I guess, I didn't see much of my dad during those months. He'd come home after putting in his time at the butcher shop, get a few hours of sleep, and then he'd change into his uniform. Off he'd go to the night job, coming home early the next morning, having breakfast with us, changing clothes again, and driving to the butcher shop. I was just a kid, and I didn't really appreciate the sacrifice my dad was making for me. I just thought he was doing what all dads did. And then it happened.

What happened?

One night while Dad was at the racetrack, a group of burglars arrived at the main building. By the time my dad saw them, it was too late. One of the men clobbered my dad in the face with the butt of his gun, and they tied him up and went about their business. They made their way to the accounting office, found the safe, and worked on opening it. In the meantime, Dad was able to get himself free, and he found a phone to call the police. When the cops got there, the burglars were in the accounting office, still fiddling with the safe. The burglars were captured and arrested, and the story was in the local paper. You should have seen my father's face the day after. They had split his cheek wide open, and he had to have thirty stitches. The skin all around his cheek was as purple as a plum, and his eye was a little swollen. He looked like a boxer who'd just survived a great fifteen-round brawl, and I thought my dad's wounded face was the coolest thing I'd ever seen. Everyone in our community knew about what my dad did, and for several weeks he was a hero. I was proud of him, and I brought some friends to the butcher shop after school to show off his face.

What did your dad think of bringing all your friends to see him?

I think he loved it. He had them all circle around, and he told them every exciting detail of the robbery, probably embellishing the story. You know, like W. C. Fields in *The Bank Dick.*

Did you get your piano?

I did. They gave it to me for Christmas. I knew it was coming, but I acted surprised.

Which instrument did you end up using most often to compose your songs? Was it the guitar or the piano?

I think the guitar was a lot easier to play. It was so simple, six strings as opposed to eighty-eight keys. It was easy to strum chords and sing along. But I used the piano too. I don't think either of them was any more useful to me than the other. And believe it or not, I still have that same piano. I moved it here from my parents' house when Mom passed away. It's in one of the guest rooms if you ever want to see it. It hasn't been tuned or played for years, but I've kept it.

Your father was a remarkable man.

Yes, he was. He was only a humble butcher, yet he was so much more. He was my biggest cheerleader and supporter. Whenever told him I thought I couldn't do something, he'd set me straight. He never wavered in his confidence, and I don't think there was anything he wouldn't do to help me along. Are you familiar with the writer Tom Wolfe? He's calling our current times the "me decade." If my father got wind of this, he'd probably turn over in his grave. Jen and I have talked about this subject, how all people these days seem to care about is themselves. Adults no longer care about their children, and children don't care about their parents, and parents don't care about each other. Did you know three out of five marriages these days end in divorce, and that one in five children are living in a one-parent home? I think this whole movement started in the sixties, with its obsession to find ourselves. Now all we care about *is* ourselves. It's a sad state of affairs. You know, I would really like to be like my dad, putting others first and making sacrifices. It's funny, but I'm just now discovering things my father knew intuitively. There was never a doubt in his mind. The man was amazing. He understood just what it meant to be a man and exactly what it meant to be a father.

So does this mean you'll be reaching out to your son, Roger?

No, Roger doesn't need me. He has Audrey and his real estate stepfather to love him and care for him. It would be wrong for me to interfere. I've accepted the situation for what it is. I've moved on.

But moved on to what?

The here and now.

What does that mean?

It means Jen and I are starting our own family. Jen's going to be a mother, and I'm going to be a father. We just went to the doctor and found out that Jen is pregnant. If it's a boy, we're going to name him Alex, and if it's a girl, we're going to name her Alexandra. To be honest, I haven't been this excited about anything for years. I feel like a million bucks, like I've made a breakthrough, and I can't wait for this little human being to pop out of Jen and call me dad. Me, a dad. I'll do anything for this kid. It'll want for nothing. I'll work as a night watchman if that's what it takes. I'll do everything and anything.

AN ANGRY FAN

———— •⦿• ————

Everyone was now talking about Scowl becoming a brand-new father. Joseph was excited about becoming a granddad, and Jennifer's mom was equally thrilled. But the excitement went way beyond the immediate family. They were discussing the topic on TV talk shows, and there were updates on the nightly news. Most of the public opinion was positive, and Hollywood was abuzz. Even Las Vegas was in on the action. They were taking bets on whether the baby would be a boy or a girl, and thousands of gamblers were putting down their wagers. There was one person, however, who did not take the news so well. Her name was Lynette Ann Bauer. She was a thirty-nine-year-old longtime fan of Scowl, one of those crazy girls who used to scream and cry at his concerts when he was a teenage phenom. Now, even as an adult, Lynette was still obsessed. She lived alone, and she lived in a dream world. The walls of her Torrance house were covered with Scowl movie and concert posters. There were stacks of shoeboxes filled with photographs taken by Lynette while she'd been stalking Scowl over the years, and there were several scrapbooks filled with newspaper and magazine clippings about Scowl. It was kind of bizarre, and this woman would prove to be a problem. In fact, she would prove to be a huge problem.

On December 3, 1976, Lynette drove to Dulcinea in her little Toyota. Using a ladder that she untied from the hood, she climbed over the brick wall that surrounded the property and carried a container of gasoline to the rear of the house. Scowl and Jennifer were gone at the time. They were at a friend's beach house for the weekend, not due to return until the following day. The only person looking after Dulcinea was Frank, and he was keeping an eye on the front yard. That's where the nuts usually came in, over the gate and up to the front door.

Apparently, the rear door to the home was unlocked, and Lynette let herself in. Splashing the walls, floor, and furniture with gasoline, she started up a roaring fire with the strike of a match. She then fled the scene and sped away in her car. Within minutes the rear of the home was engulfed in flames, and by the time Frank noticed what was happening and called 911, there was nothing he could really do. He went to the side yard and turned on a hose, spraying water into the fire, but it was pointless. It was so hot that the water evaporated before it even hit the flames. By the time the fire trucks arrived, the entire house was burning. The firemen did what they could with their fire hoses, but it was no use. And by early morning, Dulcinea lay in smoldering ashes, a complete loss, a wet pile of charred lumber and burnt possessions. When Scowl and Jennifer returned to the house, a throng of reporters tried to get their comments, but they didn't have anything to say. They were in complete shock. Their home had been burned to the ground.

Lynette would not get away with it. A neighbor who lived a few houses down saw the smoke and then saw Lynette climbing over the wall and getting into her car. She wrote down Lynette's license plate and gave it to the police, and patrolmen found Lynette that same night at a restaurant not far from Brentwood, eating dinner as though nothing had happened. They brought her in for questioning and compared her fingerprints to those left on the gas can behind the house. When the prints matched, they charged her with the crime. She didn't have a chance. She was given a fair and speedy trial and found guilty. When it came time for her sentencing, Scowl came to the courtroom and asked the judge if he could speak before they sent the woman off to prison. The judge allowed Scowl to talk, but to the surprise of everyone, Scowl did not demand a long sentence for the lady. Instead, he asked that the judge have her committed to a mental hospital for treatment and care and possible rehabilitation. He said clearly the woman was not in her right mind when she set the fire and that she obviously didn't know right from wrong. Scowl argued that if anyone's opinion should carry weight in this matter, it should be his, being that it was his home that had been destroyed. The judge said against his better judgment he would honor with Scowl's wishes, and the woman was sent to Everdale Hospital. Lynette's parents were interviewed on TV, and they thanked Scowl. When the news reporters tried to contact Scowl to get his comments, he told them the only person he would talk to was me, so it appeared we were about to do another interview. We didn't actually meet until weeks following the trial. We met at the dining room table of the Crabtrees' house while everyone else was gone; the others had left the house so we could be alone. Scowl wanted it this way. He didn't want the others there, distracting him. Scowl asked if I wanted a cup of tea, and I said yes just to be polite. The truth is, I don't even like tea. I then turned on my recorder.

⚬⚬⚬

I haven't talked to you since the fire. I was very sorry to hear about Dulcinea.

Fortunately, no one was hurt.

Do you plan to rebuild?

We're working on it. We have an architect drawing up plans for the new house. His name is Chester Bryant, and perhaps you've heard of him. It'll be another five months before we have the drawings ready. There'll be a couple months of bidding, and we're being told to allow a couple years for construction.

Where are you staying in the meantime?

We're staying here with Jen's parents.

How's that working out?

The Crabtrees are magnificent people. They're very accommodating, and we get along well. In the meantime, Jen and I are looked for a place to lease. It looks like we won't be moving back to Dulcinea for some time.

What's it like to lose your home to a fire?

It's devastating. I don't think there are any words that really describe it. It's true what they say, that you don't appreciate what you have until it's gone. And I'm not just talking about the valuable things we lost; I'm talking about everyday items like a favorite coffee mug, or a pen you liked, or a pair of comfortable shoes. It's all just gone, all of it, every little bit of life's minutia. It's like having your identity ripped right off of your bones. Every detail of your life has been erased from the blackboard in one fell swoop. You find yourself reaching for things that are gone, looking into mirrors that don't exist, walking into former rooms that are not there. It's really hard to fathom, the way these past images stay in your mind, all the things you once had. It's a lot like losing a loved one. Have you ever lost someone very close to you? During the first few months, you find yourself about to talk to them, or about pick up the phone and call them. You expect to see the person any minute, walking from around a corner or from behind a door. But the person never materializes. He or she is just gone, and gone forever. It's all so hard to reconcile. It doesn't seem real.

Tell me something about the new house you're building. Will it be like the old one, or are you going to do things differently?

The new house will be quite different.

Will it be bigger?

It will be about twice the size. It's going to have a lot of things the old house didn't. It'll be a definite improvement.

Will it be the same architectural style?

It will be an English Tudor, just like the old one.

Tell me about some of the different things the new house will have.

It will have a wing just for our child. There will be a kid's bedroom, of course, and a play room with all the latest books, games, and toys, and an entertainment room with a TV, stereo, and video games for when it's older. Our new house will also have a movie theater, a billiard room, and a bowling alley.

A bowling alley?

It'll be just a couple of lanes.

I didn't know you bowled.

I don't bowl. I just thought it'd be cool to have a bowling alley. Once when I was performing in Wisconsin, I heard about some rich guy who had a bowling alley in his house. I thought it sounded awesome

Anything else?

Yes, of course. I'll have a recording studio. I've always wanted a studio in my home. I'll be able to produce records from my house, just like Elvis. It'll be a dream come true.

It sounds like there are some advantages to having your home burn down.

We're trying to make the best of it by adding these improvements. Of course, there are things we'll never be able to replace. The piano my dad bought me when I was a kid is now history. My Danny Cedrone guitar is gone, and so are all my photographs, scrapbooks, and memorabilia. A lot of the things we lost in the fire are irreplaceable. But there's nothing I can do. I keep telling myself that God has a reason behind everything.

I don't have to know what the reason is; I just have to have faith that the reason is a good one.

Tell me more about Lynette Ann Bauer. There are rumors you visited her at Everdale Hospital. Are those rumors true?

Yes, I visited several times.

Is there something you hope to gain?

I'm just trying to help out. She's a troubled woman, and someone needs to make an effort to help her.

Have you talked with her doctors?

Only briefly.

What's your take on this woman? Why do you think she burned your house down?

I wish I could give a good answer. Ever since writing *Nancy Kimball*, I've tried to understand the mind-set of my more extreme fans. You have no idea what it's like to have these people obsess over you like this. They just need to realize that I'm a human being too. What am I but a sack of bones, some organs, and several quarts of blood? I'm just another person who breathes in oxygen and blows out carbon dioxide. I sneeze, cough, hiccup, fart, and burp just like the rest of you. I laugh when I'm happy and cry when I'm sad. My forehead perspires when I exert myself, and my underarms sometimes itch like crazy. I am no different from anyone else in this world. So why is there this focus on me? It's a mental illness, this idolatry, this fervent belief in something that isn't. Great Scott, this woman burned my entire house down! Did she think we were inside? Did she plan on burning us to death along with the house? I guess we'll never really know for sure. In all my years as a performer, I've never understood these kinds of fans. I tried to understand them when I wrote *Nancy Kimball*, but I don't think I even scratched the surface. Women who are like Lynette fascinate me. I don't hate her. I feel sorry for her. I feel that just by me being me, maybe I have ruined her life.

Surely you don't hold yourself responsible.

To a certain extent, I must.

Tell me, besides working with your architect, do you have anything else in the works? The last time we talked you were working on your new album. That album has been released, so what's next for you?

Jen is due to have the baby in June. I'm sure that will keep us busy.

And besides that?

Joseph has a screenplay for a comedy. I've read it, and it's funny. I laughed out loud at a few of the gags. If this movie is made, I'll play a pair of twin brothers, one who is a grocery store manager who lives a frugal and moral life with his soccer-mom wife and three kids in a home in the burbs. His twin brother, on the other hand, is a hedge fund manager who lives downtown LA in a high-rise penthouse apartment. This brother is the opposite of the first brother. He is single and rich. He entertains one woman after the other and spends money like it's going out of style. The brothers get together for lunch one day and decide they've had enough of their lives. The twins come up with an idea. They decide to switch places. The hedge fund manager moves into his brother's suburban home, and the grocery store manager takes over the big penthouse apartment. The screenplay is very well written, and there are a lot of good laughs. At the end, the brothers get together and decide they want their old lives back. I'm not sure this story is that original, but it's very well written. The dialogue is a lot of fun, and I'd enjoy the challenge of playing twins.

Any idea who else will be in the movie?

No, not really.

Do you think your fans will like seeing you in a comedy?

Yes, my fans will like it.

Charlie Chaplin called comedy "a sad business." Would you agree with that?

Charlie Chaplin was an idiot.

Who's your all-time favorite comic?

That's easy. It would be W. C. Fields. I hate that he had to drink so much, but I love his work as a comic. Have you seen his pictures? I think he's one of the funniest men who ever lived.

I heard a story about Fields when I was in college, that during his last days when he was on his deathbed, he had a friend bring him a Bible. Fields opened the book, and his friend said, "I didn't know you read the Bible." Fields looked up smiling and said, "I'm looking for loopholes."

I wonder if Fields ever had fans like I do, back when he was alive. I don't think he did. He was probably lucky that way.

THE PLAYBOY INTERVIEW

———— •◦• ————

On June 29, 1977, Jennifer gave birth to Alex Joseph Kruse. It was in all the papers and gossip magazines, and most of Scowl's fans were elated. Jennifer and Scowl had leased a house in Beverly Hills, and the drawings for Dulcinea were done. The construction bidding was complete, and they had selected a contractor. According to the contractor, the project would be completed by February 1979. In the meantime, Jennifer stopped her studies at UCLA to take care of the baby, and Scowl started work on the new comedy with Jennifer's father. The name of the film would be *The LA Switch*. Scowl was the only well-known actor starring in the film. Crabtree didn't want Scowl to be overshadowed by other big names, nor did he want to have to pay for them. About halfway through filming, one of Crabtree's marketing associates called me to arrange an interview with Scowl that Crabtree wanted to see published in *Playboy*. Everyone who was anyone was being interviewed in *Playboy* those days. It was the cool thing to do, and even Jimmy Carter did an interview in the magazine. Crabtree thought the timing of this interview would be perfect to promote *LA Switch* to the public. When I spoke with Crabtree's marketing guy, I was told Crabtree wanted to make the interview a retrospective of Scowl's life. When Scowl and I discussed this idea, he said he was too young for a eulogy. "I'm not another Elvis Presley," he complained. I tried to put a positive spin on the idea and told Scowl that the interview would simply remind people of how he got where he was today. I told him I thought his fans would be interested. Scowl seemed okay with the interview appearing in *Playboy*, but he vehemently refused to participate in a retrospective. He said he'd come up with something better. Then he told me to show up at his house with my tape recorder. Scowl was ready, but I didn't know what we were supposed to be talking about, nor did I know what kind of questions I should ask. I decided to start things off with a question about Elvis and his recent death.

———— ⬗⬗⬗ ————

I guess the first thing I ought to ask you is about Elvis Presley's recent passing. Any thoughts you'd like to share?

So rock 'n' roll took another life. That's about the long and short of it, isn't it? His life didn't end well. Not for him, and not for his fans. Died on a damn toilet, trying to go to the bathroom. His bloated body at the end of its rock 'n' roll rope? Imagine that. But let's talk about something else.

What do you want to talk about?

Are you familiar with Plato's dialogues?

Yes, I read them back in college.

So I take it that you know something about Socrates' dialectic method?

Yes, I know a little about it. But it's been a while since I studied anything having to do with ancient Greek philosophy.

Listen, I'm going to make this interview easy for you. You won't have to come up with a single question. I'm going to ask the questions, and you're going to provide me with answers. I'll be interviewing you for a change. At first it will seem like we're learning something about you, but we'll actually be learning about me. Are you ready for this?

I guess so.

Do you go to church?

Yes, I go to church.

Do you believe in the Bible?

Yes. I mean, not always literally, but I do believe generally in what it has to say.

It is a good source of truth, of rules to live by, and it teaches us some important lessons in morality.

Yes, I'd agree with that.

Do you think human beings are different from the animals that populate our world?

They are similar in many ways, but yes, they are quite different.

Would you compare yourself to an elephant?

No, not really.

To a giraffe?

No, I guess not.

Have you ever seen a lion smoking a cigar or a pipe?

No, obviously not.

Or an alligator reading a newspaper?

No, of course not.

Aside from some physiological similarities, wouldn't you say humans and animals are really completely different from each other?

Yes, I guess that's a fair statement.

Have you ever talked to an animal?

I talk to my cat every once and a while.

And what exactly do you have to say to your cat?

I ask her how she's doing, or I'll ask her if she's hungry. Sometimes when I'm watching TV, I'll say something like, "Can you believe that?" or "Did you hear what that guy just said?" It's just friendly conversation. I don't actually expect her to answer.

Does your cat ever respond?

Sometimes she meows.

Do you think your cat actually understood you, or is she just meowing, just making noise in response to the sound of your voice?

I think she might be trying to talk. But, of course, cats can't talk.

If you put a typewriter in front of your cat and put in a sheet of blank paper, would she be able to type her thoughts for you?

No, of course not.

A cat could press down on any key with its paw, couldn't it?

I suppose it could.

But it wouldn't even occur to her to use the typewriter this way, would it? A cat doesn't understand the purpose of a typewriter. Isn't that an accurate statement?

Yes, that's accurate.

Does your cat do math? Does she own a slide rule?

Nope, of course not.

Have you ever seen your cat try to drive a car?

Ha, no, never.

Has your cat ever doodled on paper while she was bored? Has she ever used a paper clip or a stapler? Has she ever laughed at a dirty joke?

I'd say none of the above.

Yet sometimes you feel inclined to talk to her? I'm still wondering why you do this.

I guess it is sort of pointless. I guess I'm just talking in general, sort of to myself, and not actually talking to my cat.

Does your cat wear clothes?

No, she doesn't.

When Adam and Eve were in Eden, do you suppose they were wearing any clothes? I mean, before they bit into that apple, weren't they stark naked?

Yes, I think they were.

They were naked, just like your cat?

Yes, they were naked.

Do you have any children?

You know I do. I have two kids.

Do you have any daughters?

I have one daughter. Her name is Pamela.

How old is Pamela?

She's now eight.

Does she wear clothes, or does she run around naked like your cat?

She wears clothes of course.

Do you love Pamela?

Of course I do. She's my daughter.

Do you ever talk to her?

I talk to her all the time.

And she responds to you?

Sure, she responds to me.

If you put a typewriter in front of her, she'd be able to figure out a way to make it work? She could type you a message if she wanted?

Yes, she could do that.

And yet she's just a kid.

Yes, she's just a kid.

Will you love her any less twelve or thirteen years from now? Say when she's in her late teens or early twenties, will you still love her?

I'll love her just the same.

So your love isn't dependent on her being a child? You'll love Pamela as a young woman the same as a little girl?

Yes, I will.

It's my understanding that you plan to sell this interview to *Playboy*. Is that true?

Yes, that's true.

Are you aware of my feelings about that magazine?

No, not really.

Do you believe in first impressions?

I'm not sure what you mean.

Do you believe first impressions are important?

I suppose they are.

If you were an alien visiting earth from outer space, and you were hiding in the bushes looking through a pair of binoculars, what would be your first impression? What clue would tell you that there was a difference between human beings and other animals?

I don't know.

Wouldn't it be their clothes?

I guess that makes sense.

Wouldn't humans be the only creatures wearing clothes? Can you think of a single animal that puts on clothing in public, that spends money on shirts, pants, dresses, shoes, hats, and belts? The clothing would be a dead giveaway, wouldn't it?

Well, I suppose it would be.

How would you define prostitution?

Are we going somewhere with all these questions? You seem to be jumping from one subject to another. I'm not sure what you're trying to get out of me.

I told you you'd learn something about me, didn't I? We're not here to learn about you. We're here to learn about Scowl, no?

Yes, that's right.

Then answer my questions. Tell me, how would you define prostitution?

I'd say it was performing sexual acts for financial compensation.

Would that include any sexual act?

Yes, I suppose it would include any sexual act.

Does one actually have to touch another in order for his or her act to qualify as sexual?

I've never really thought about it.

Is talking to someone in a sexually suggestive way a sexual act?

You mean just talking?

It could be sexual, right?

Yes, I suppose it could be sexual.

And isn't talking an act?

Yes, it's an act.

Both of us were just kids once, no?

Yes, we were both kids.

When you were a kid, would you ever expect a young girl to just walk up to you and remove her clothes?

No, I'd say not.

That would be pretty strange, wouldn't it?

Yes, that'd be strange.

Do you remember Marilyn Monroe?

Yes, of course I do.

Do you remember when I told you that something about her bothered me, that she was a tragedy waiting to happen, that she was like a little girl trapped in a big girl's body?

Yes, I remember something like that.

Didn't she pose for *Playboy*?

Yes, she did.

When I lived in Haight-Ashbury years ago, people were talking about a sexual revolution. People still talk about it today. Have you thought much about this subject?

Not really.

What do you suppose it means? What does it actually suggest? Does a sexual revolution imply we're all supposed to have sex with one another just for the sake of having sex?

I guess I don't know.

When I was sixteen, I had a crush on a girl who was a year older than me named Karen. My hormones were raging at that age, and I couldn't get the image of this lovely girl out of my mind. Great Scott, she was so beautiful. She had a sweet, round face like a Renaissance angel and a pair of bright blue eyes that made my knees weak. Her lips were full and rose-petal red. I think she wore some eye makeup. I'm not sure about the makeup, since I don't know that much about makeup, but her eyes were so lovely and perfect, she had to be using something. She had these amazing eyelashes that fluttered like butterfly wings when she laughed. And she had the most perfect teeth; they were pure white and had a wonderful shape to them. All I could think of for weeks was what it would be like to kiss this girl, to have her warm rose-petal mouth touching my own. I imagined that her kisses tasted like honey. And I haven't even told you about her body. She had a lovely figure, and she always dressed nicely, the way young girls dressed those days. I remember being in love with all her clothes. I was crazy about everything she wore, her blouses, sweaters, skirts, and shoes. She wore a heart-shaped silver locket around her neck, but I don't know whose picture was in it. The locket lay just above her chest. She was never sunburned, but always tan from sitting in the sunlight on the school's front lawn for lunch each day. I used to sit nearby and watch her eat. I was absolutely obsessed with this girl. She was perfect just the way she was. If you'd asked me what would make her any better, I would have told you she didn't need to change a thing. Did you look at *Playboys* when you were in high school?

I guess I did.

My friends and I certainly looked at our share of *Playboy* magazines over the years. Yes, we looked at plenty of them. We'd look at the naked girls, comparing them to one another, examining their unclothed bodies. But I can tell you now, looking back to those years, I can't recall a single one of those girls the way I can remember Karen. I don't remember what their faces looked like or even what their bodies looked like. But Karen, well, that's a totally different story. I remember everything about Karen. If you gave me a pencil and piece of paper, I could draw her for you in vivid detail, right down to the silver heart-shaped locket, right down to those fluttering eyelashes. She never removed her sweater for me, never unclasped her bra, never hiked up her skirt, yet she's been permanently etched in my psyche.

I'm not sure what you're driving at.

Toward the end of the school year, I finally got up the nerve to ask Karen out. We went to a movie. I don't recall which one. We went out in my dad's car, and I took her home when the movie was over. We stood on her porch for a minute, talking, and then I leaned for a goodnight kiss. When our lips touched, I imagined fireworks bursting in the sky, and I saw a zillion pinprick stars twinkling for eternity. When we were done with the kiss, I opened my eyes, and I looked at Karen. She was smiling at me. It was amazing.

Did you ask her out again?

We went out together until the beginning of summer.

Then what happened?

Her family moved to Arizona. That was the last I ever saw of her. But even to this day, I can remember her like it was yesterday.

What does this have to do with anything? What are you driving at?

It has everything to do with everything. Did you ever have a crush on a girl?

I suppose I did.

What kind of life do you imagine for your daughter, Pamela? Do you hope she'll meet some nice boy? Do you see her courting boyfriends, enjoying their company? Do you ever picture her getting her first goodnight kiss on the porch of your house? Can you visualize some lovesick boy having a crush on her? What exactly to you imagine for your daughter?

I imagine only good things for her.

What do you think of masturbation?

Pardon me?

What are your thoughts on masturbation?

I guess it's something people do.

Does the subject embarrass you?

Yes, a little.

This interview is for *Playboy*, isn't it? Aren't we allowed to discuss this sort of thing?

Yes, I suppose it's appropriate.

What do you suppose most men do with their *Playboys*? Do they just sit on the sofa and read the interviews, or do they open them up in privacy of their bathrooms to fantasize about having sex with other men's daughters? Which do you suppose it is?

I've never really thought about it.

Have you ever noticed that people who smoke marijuana never talk about where their stash comes from? As long as they've got it, they seem to be satisfied.

I suppose that's true.

Take your average pot-smoking teenager. To this kid, marijuana is a harmless and pleasant pastime. He lights up a joint and inhales. He feels high and may turn on some music. Or perhaps he'll hang out with friends, joking and laughing. He's feeling all warm and fuzzy in his euphoria, and everything seems right with the world. He might enjoy a creative urge to draw a picture, or maybe he'll strum a song on his guitar. Or he might just feel like kicking back and pondering life. But whatever he finds himself doing, he never bothers to contemplate the source of the weed he's been smoking. It's grown and harvested by criminals, the dregs of society. It's not like marijuana comes from some mom-and-pop corner market. So why doesn't the kid care where his weed came from?

I don't know.

Don't you find it curious?

Yes, I suppose it is.

What are you going to do when some kid comes calling for your daughter? Are you going to going to let him walk away with her?

I don't know.

Won't you want to know something about the kid?

Sure, of course.

Won't you want to talk to him?

I think it goes without saying.

Shouldn't you get your wife involved? Don't you want to know what she thinks?

Yes, I think so.

It's a big deal, isn't it?

Yes, it's a big deal. It's a very big deal. I care about my daughter.

You should care about her. I agree with you. Beware of wolves dressed up like sheep. Listen, I'm no Socrates, but I think I've made my point.

Made what point?

I've said all I wanted to say, and this interview is over. We're done here.

CAT POOP

—•◦•—

The *Playboy* interview was never published. *Playboy* didn't get it, and didn't like it, and so they didn't print it. I never sent it to anyone else. I'm including it in this collection of interviews only because I think it says a lot about Scowl. He took me by surprise that day. I thought it was amusing that a man who was once considered to be such a bad influence on America's young women was now so much on their side. When Crabtree read this interview, he just shook his head. He said, "Scowl is right. Of course, he's right. I should never have asked him to do a damn interview for *Playboy*. Honestly, I don't know what I was thinking."

I spent the next year working on a book about Elvis Presley's final days while Scowl and Crabtree completed the filming of *Switch*. When the movie was released, it was an immediate hit. The film received lukewarm reviews from critics, but the public loved it. It amazed me how easily Scowl had made the transformation from a serious actor to a comic. My wife, Julia, went with me to see the movie, and she thought it was hilarious. Several friends of mine also went to see it, and they thought the same. I called Scowl in the fall of 1978 to congratulate him on the success of the project, but he wasn't available. I left a message for him to call me, but he didn't return my call. I not only wanted to say congratulations, but I also wanted to know what his next venture would be. He always seemed to have something interesting in the works, and I was hoping to find out what it was. When Scowl finally did call, the date was November 8. It was the evening of the day that Norman Rockwell passed away. Scowl heard about Rockwell's death on the evening news, and he wanted to talk about it. He didn't sound outrageously upset, but he was obviously sad that the famous painter was gone. "He was one of a kind, a real American treasure," Scowl told me. "We need to do an interview in his honor. Can you meet tomorrow evening? There are things I need to say." Of course, I said yes, and I went to his house.

It's been a year since we last met. I think you wanted to discuss Norman Rockwell?

I wanted to do an interview in his honor.

What do you know about him?

I know he was born in Manhattan. Don't you find that odd, given all the rural and small-town settings in his paintings?

I guess that's odd.

You know, he did most of his work for the covers of *The Saturday Evening Post.* He started working for them early in the twentieth century, when there were still horse-drawn cabs on the streets of New York. Ernest Hemingway was just a teenager working for the *Kansas City Star,* and F. Scott Fitzgerald was still busy cramming for tests at Princeton. Rockwell was eighty-four when he finally died. People like to say he was an illustrator, but I think he was a true artist. I'd put any of his work up against the contemporaries of his time; in fact, I'd say his work was better. It had a special decency, something that's sadly lacking in modern art. Decency is so important. I think it used to be this country's heart and soul. You can look high and low in the art world these days, my good man, but you'll have a very hard time finding decency.

Would you describe your own endeavors as decent?

Yes, I'd like to think of them that way. Within certain circles, however, my decency makes me rather unpopular.

I wouldn't describe you as unpopular.

Maybe unpopular isn't the right word. Of course, I'm quite popular. Perhaps I should say shallow. Some critics have described me as shallow, and I think it's because I'm always searching for a happy ending. Each of Rockwell's paintings seems to have a happy ending, doesn't it? No one these days appreciates the happy ending, at least not the critics. For some reason, cynicism evokes a more positive response from them, as if an artist is obligated to bring forth life's bitter disappointments rather than its joys. I don't know why this is. I've never understood this point of view. I'd buy a Norman Rockwell painting any day of the week rather than some dreary work by someone such as Edward Hopper. In fact, I wish I had a Rockwell hanging right now on a wall in my home. I'd look at it every morning before starting my day, just to put me in the right frame of mind. I'd be inspired by it. It would make me smile, and I'd be proud to be an American.

They say Rockwell only painted utopias.

Do you really think so? I actually think he painted realities. I just think there are those who'd like to skew reality with their own pessimism. Does life imitate art, or does art imitate life? It's an age-old question. I say it's a little of both, that they imitate each other. I say Rockwell's paintings not only described life in this country as he saw it, but inspired us to continue on in the same vein. The key to Rockwell's paintings is the great inspiration they ignite. It's all about inspiration, pure and simple. An average work of art conveys a certain point of view to its audience, but a great work of art actually inspires us. Rockwell's paintings were all great works of art. They inspired us to carry on with living in a world chock full of love and good humor. I think Rockwell truly cared for the characters he painted, and I think you can see this in every stroke of his brush. There is nothing utopian or shallow about this and certainly nothing to be ashamed of.

Which is your favorite Rockwell work?

I think they're all great, every one of them.

Do you think he's one of the greatest painters of the twentieth century?

Without a doubt.

Up there with Pablo Picasso?

Right up there with Pablo.

Have you ever thought of painting again?

I've thought about it. But I've decided to start work on something else.

Can you tell us what that is?

I'm writing another book.

That surprises me, considering the disappointing sales of Nancy Kimball.

I've learned a lot since then.

What's this book going to be about?

Do you remember when I told you my book idea about the dad who buys his son a trumpet at a pawn shop? Well, I've decided to go ahead with this story, except I've made some changes. The story will be about an electric guitar, not a trumpet. I thought this would make the story more current for younger audiences. The electric guitar will be pawned by a very talented rock 'n' roll musician who falls on hard times and then dies of a heroin overdose. A father buys the guitar for his young son, and the boy quickly learns to play it. The spirit of the dead musician is in the guitar, and the boy becomes a rock virtuoso overnight. The boy tours with his band all over the world, bringing crowds to their feet. Then one night while packing up their equipment, the boy leaves the guitar on the ground. One of the band's moving trucks backs over the guitar, crushing it. At first the boy thinks he'll never be able to play again, his magical guitar having been destroyed. But there's a remarkable twist, and the story has a sweet and happy ending.

So what happens?

You'll have to read the book.

But what's the twist?

If I told you that now, it would ruin the ending for you. I'm not telling anyone the ending. I'm not even telling Jen. It's a complete secret.

Your publishers will know.

Of course, they will. But the public needs a reason to buy the book, and if I reveal the end to you now, and you blab it to everyone, they'll no longer have that reason. I want to give everyone something to look forward to.

How far are you along?

I just completed the outline. I'm now working on the first chapter. If nothing comes up to distract me, I should be done by summer.

Do you have a title?

I'm calling it *Bill's Guitar*. Bill is the name of the guy who originally pawned the guitar, and he's the spirit in the instrument. I'm thinking if this makes a good book, it could make an even better movie. Of course, I'm too old the play the lead. Maybe I could play the father or Bill. I ran this movie idea by Joseph without telling him the ending, and he thought it had potential. And so does Jen. She thinks it's a great idea.

How is Jen doing? How's the baby?

Life is definitely different. Having a child is not at all like I expected. What were your kids like? This kid is an absolute terror. He's in the pantry dumping my cereal all over the floor, and while I'm cleaning up that mess, he's got the knife drawer open in the kitchen and he's removing the cutlery.

God knows how he doesn't slice himself open. I put the knives back into the drawer, and while I'm doing this, he's got the cabinet door under the sink open, looking for the dish soap. Nothing three feet off the floor is safe from this child. We've had to move and rearrange everything on all the lower shelves. When he isn't attacking our shelves, he'd going after the cats. They come to him expecting to be petted, and he grabs them by their tails. He likes hearing them hiss and growl. It makes him laugh. And worse than this, he goes after their litter boxes, removing chunks of cat poop and putting them in his mouth. I tell you, it's really disgusting. We try to get him out of the house into the fresh air, and we take him for walks in his stroller. He has a stuffed bear that he has to take everywhere with him, but he always drops it when we go on these walks. He does this when we're not looking. Then he'll cry because he's missing the bear, and we'll have to backtrack until we find it. Once on our way back, we saw that a loose Labrador had snagged the stuffed bear, and I had to chase the stupid dog all over the neighborhood until I got it to stop. When I got the bear out of the Labrador's mouth, I brought it back to Jen and Alex. It was sopping wet with dog saliva, and Jen stuffed it in the compartment under the stroller so she could throw it in the washer when we got home. She didn't want Alex to have it until she washed it, and he cried all the way back to the house. I was thinking that if the cat poop hadn't already killed the kid, I doubted a little dog saliva would do much damage. But when it comes to Alex, Jen's the boss.

At least you live in a nice neighborhood, a place where you can take Alex on walks.

It isn't Brentwood, but it's nice. Most the people are friendly, and they're used to seeing famous people, so no one really bothers us.

How's Dulcinea coming?

I was just over there yesterday. It's close to being finished, and the contractor thinks he'll only be a couple weeks over his original schedule.

Is it turning out as you hoped?

It's been a long haul, but yes, I'm happy with the way it's turning out. You know, I never knew how much work goes into building a house. You couldn't pay me enough to be a building contractor. This guy we hired says he's only thirty-five, but he looks like he's fifty. His face is weathered, and he's about forty pounds overweight. I think he hits the bottle when he goes home, because when I see him in the morning, he always looks like he has a terrific hangover. You've never heard anyone with such a loud voice in all your life. Even when he's just a foot or so away from you, he shouts like you're clear across the property. I think after listening to power tools and hammering his whole adult life, he's losing his hearing. I think that's why he shouts all the time. I've talked to some of our neighbors, and they say they can hear him barking at his employees all day long, and I apologized. Fortunately, our contractor doesn't cuss much, or all this yelling could be a real problem. Have you had much experience with paint colors? They're painting the outside of the house now, and we're on the fourth combination of colors. They ask us to pick from an assortment of tiny paint samples, but the colors never look the same once they go up on the walls. Jen asked the architect to help us choose, but he told us he's color-blind. Can you imagine that? I think we hired the only color-blind architect in all of Los Angeles. What were the odds?

It sounds like you've had your hands full.

I'm not complaining. The house is going to be great. And I love my life, and I love my family.

You have a kid who eats cat poop, a Labrador running around with his stuffed bear, and a color-blind architect working on your house—your life sounds like a Norman Rockwell painting.

It does, doesn't it? Yes, I like the sound of that. What can I say? I like the man.

THE OPEN HOUSE

The new and improved Dulcinea was completed and furnished in February 1979, and Scowl and Jen held an open house to celebrate. It was a gala event, and a lot of different people were invited. I came to the party with Julia; this was the first time Julia met Scowl in person. Richard and Alan from the old band were there, as was Bobby Breen. There were several of the Jetliners and some friends of theirs I didn't recognize. Jen's parents showed up of course, and so did the crazy color-blind architect and his charming wife. Scowl's book publisher, his current music producer, and his art teacher from Santa Barbara were also there. I'd guess there were over a hundred people milling around in the spacious house, drinking punch, eating hors d'oeuvres, and peering into all the rooms. Scowl pulled me aside toward the end of the evening and asked me to come to his study. "Did you happen to bring your tape recorder with you?" he asked. I said no, that I didn't think we'd be doing an interview. "I want to do one right now," he said. "Here, you can use mine. You can take the cassette home with you when we're done." I set my glass of punch on Scowl's desk and reached for the tape recorder he'd removed from his desk drawer. "I'll need to tell my wife what I'm doing," I said. "She's going to wonder where I am." Scowl said not to worry about it because Jen was already telling her.

Go ahead and ask a question.

So how does it feel to be back at Dulcinea? How long has it been, over two years?

It's been way too long.

Are you happy with the new home?

I couldn't be happier.

We've stepped away from your party for this interview. So, tell me, what's on your mind?

Remember I told you everything happens for a reason, that God has his plans for each of us?

Yes, I remember that.

Do you remember Lynette?

Yes, she the one who set fire to your house.

Did you know I'm still visiting her at Everdale, that I now see her once a week?

I didn't know that.

We've become good friends. You know, she's told me a lot about her life. Do you know I'm the only one who comes to visit her? Her mother died last year, and her sister moved to Tennessee. If it wasn't for me, she'd have no one coming to see her. She'd be locked up in Everdale and completely on her own. Do you remember the concert where you and I first met, when I invited you for a ride in my limo?

Yes, I remember. You never did tell me why you picked me that night.

Did you know Lynette was at that concert? She was one of those hysterical girls in the audience. She was only a teenager then, but her parents let her come to the concert with a group of friends. In all these years, I don't think I've ever met any of the girls who went to those concerts, not in person. I've answered lots of fan mail from them, but I've never met any of them face-to-face. It's a shame when you think about it, this invisible wall I've had to build between me and my fans, the way I've kept them out of my life. It's a shame, but it's been a necessity. When Lynette and I first started talking, she told me about her college days. She was a student at UCLA. She wanted to be a writer and was majoring in English. She said ever since seeing me at that concert, she was deeply in love with me. She said she knew it was love because I was all she could think about. She saw my face everywhere she went and heard my music playing in her head. At night she dreamed about me, and during her spare time she would listen to my records and read magazine and newspaper articles about me. She says she read the first interview we did in the *LA Times* over and over, until she knew every single word by heart. This became a serious obsession, so serious that she eventually had to drop out of college, no longer able to concentrate on her studies. She packed up her things and moved back to her hometown of Torrance, where she got a job at a donut shop. She moved into a little house and has lived in the same place ever since. Up until the night of the fire, she's worked at that same donut shop, seven days a week, eight hours a day, and no one ever suspected her of being obsessed with me. She made no friends, and she had no romantic interests, so obviously, there was no one to keep an eye on her. In her spare time, she wrote up a storm, and she told me she completed sixteen full-length novels since dropping out of college. The stories all had me cast as the main character, all of them being about my remarkable heroics. She said there's one story about me being a fireman who saves a dozen children from a burning apartment, and there's another story about me being a brave army sergeant in Vietnam, and yet another about me piloting a crippled 747 and all its passengers to safety by landing the plane on a freeway.

Has she ever tried to get the novels published?

She said she used to send them out but that they were always rejected and sent back. She finally stopped sending them. And now get this. She now believes that when she dies, the manuscripts are going to be discovered by someone going through her things. She thinks they'll be bought and published posthumously, that she'll be famous. I know it sounds crazy, but I believe she actually thinks this is going to happen.

She told you this?

Yes. I think she's made some progress since burning our house down, but she still has some powerful delusions. Her doctors told me some of her days are better than others. I guess she sent me all kinds of fan mail over the years, but I don't remember any of it. I get a lot of fan mail and only read a few of the letters each morning. I just don't have time to read and respond to every letter that I get, and I throw a lot of the letters away. Her letters must've been in the batches that I tossed. If I'd read her some of her letters, I would've learned that she thought the two of us were going to get married. This was right after Claudia died. Lynette went on a diet to lose weight, wanting to look her best for our wedding ceremony. After she lost the weight, she visited four or five of bridal shops, trying on wedding dresses. She spent hours upon hours stalking me, getting to know all my routines and tracking me. She was scheming on a way the two of us could meet face-to-face, but she never did get up the nerve to approach me. When I finally married Jen, she was furious. She hated my new bride and everything she stood for. When Lynette read our interview announcing that Jen was pregnant, she finally snapped. She told me she read the interview over and over and couldn't believe what was happening. Then, in a fit of rage, she purchased a five-gallon can of gasoline, strapped a ladder to the hood of her car, and as they say, the rest is history. She burned down my house.

I still don't understand why you continue to visit this woman.

It's the least I can do.

Why would you feel obligated to do anything?

Did I ever tell you how I met Claudia?

No, I don't think you did.

Before I met her, Claudia lived in Queens, New York, with her parents. Her father was a machinist, and her mother was a housewife. Claudia said her parents got along fine during the first years of their marriage, but as time moved on, the father developed a terrible drinking problem. By the time Claudia was a teenager, he was drunk every day. He spent a good chunk of the family's income on booze and prostitutes, and often they'd have trouble paying rent, buying groceries, or keeping up with the utility bills. Claudia said several times the electricity was shut off. She didn't mind the financial problems so much as she minded all the drinking. When her father came home at night, he could be belligerent and violent. His breath would stink of cheap whiskey. He'd toss Claudia's mom around, smacking her with the back of his hand, telling her how useless she was. It was a miserable life for a young girl, but she learned to put up with it. That is, until the night she finally ran away. That night, her mom left to take care of the grandma who had fallen ill. Her mother said she'd be back the next day. Claudia's father came home drunk and found his daughter alone in the house. The father wasn't angry that the mom was gone; in fact, he was perversely excited. Claudia said when he looked at her, he had the strangest look in his eyes, like a lion looks at prey, and she instinctively ran to her bedroom for safety. Her father threw open the door and cornered her in the room, throwing her down on the bed. He crawled on top of her, still stinking of whiskey, and his face was now nose to nose with hers. He kissed her and was expecting her to kiss him back. She could feel his erection through his pants, and she reached to her nightstand for the lamp. When she had the lamp in her grasp, she brought it down atop of his head, and he groaned in pain and rolled off her. She got up and ran out of the room as quickly as she could. When she looked back, her father was on the bed unconscious. Claudia had to think fast. She knew what she had to do, and she ran to the closet and grabbed one of the suitcases. She packed her things and ran out of the house. She then ran to the nearest highway and stuck her thumb out for a ride, getting into the first car that stopped. At the time she had no idea where she was going or what she was going to do. She was penniless and distraught. But she would figure something out. Through the kindness of a few strangers and a bit of good fortune, she managed to survive day by day. One thing led to another, and six weeks later she found herself on the streets of Haight-Ashbury. When I first discovered her, she had found her way into my garage and was curled up like a cat, sleeping in a corner on the floor. I woke her, and I invited her up into my house. I fed her and took care of her. I listened to her remarkable story, and I read some of the poetry she had been writing. The rest is history. I fell madly in love with her.

Why are you telling me this?

Only to tell you how grateful I was to her father. I've always wanted to thank him from the bottom of my heart.

You wanted to thank him?

Yes, for abusing Claudia.

That makes no sense.

I told you before that everything happens in life for a reason. Every event is a thread in God's tapestry. If Claudia's father hadn't forced himself on her that awful night, she would never have run away from home. She never would have traveled clear across the continent to Haight Ashbury, and I'd never have found her hiding away in my garage. I owed everything to that man. I'm glad he was who he was. If we ever meet in person, I will gladly shake his hand and be his friend. If he needs money, I'll loan it to him. If he needs help, I will give it to him. If he wants free tickets to my next concert, I'll see that he gets them. Front row seats. I'll even throw in a parking pass.

Are you serious about this?

Yes, I'm quite serious.

So I suppose this brings us back to Lynette.

Yes, and it also brings us back to this open house, to this party, and to this wonderful new house.

How so?

None of these people would be here now drinking punch, eating hors d'oeuvres, and making small talk if it weren't for my friend Lynette. She made everything possible. None of this would've happened without her. Everything you now see around you is because of her, and I will forever be indebted to this woman.

I guess that's one way of looking at it.

If you have faith in God, it's the only way to see it. And I do have faith in God. Everything happens for a good reason. Everything that happens is a part of his supreme plan. When you finally see the world this way, you see the world as God has made it. Suddenly everything comes into focus, and you see the ups and downs of life not as ups and downs, but simply as many reflections and shadows that are all a part of one another, all working together to form a single glorious vision. You lose your hatred, envy, anger, and insatiable need for vengeance. The bad makes the good and the good makes the bad. The sour makes sweet, and the cold makes warm, and the poor makes rich, and all the evil in the world stirs up the sublime. I believe in God. I believe God knows exactly what he's doing. Faith is the key to life. It's all about faith.

SCOWL'S SONS

—•—

During the months following Scowl's open house at Dulcinea, he worked on his book. He also recorded a new album in his home studio, an album that was nothing like his previous recordings. It was a joyful collection of children's songs recorded just for kids, and it included "Old MacDonald," "Row Your Boat," "O Susanna," and many other childhood favorites. The project started as something fun to do with Alex while Scowl took breaks from his writing, but it evolved into an actual commercial album. He figured many of his fans were now parents, and he thought they'd enjoy having something to play to their kids. He was right about this, and the album sold like crazy. The cover featured a photograph of Scowl and young Alex working in the music studio, sitting on a stool with Alex seated happily on Scowl's lap. Alex's youthful and out-of-tune voice was featured on several of the songs.

I talked to Scowl the summer the album was released, and he updated me on his life. He said he was about half done with *Bill's Guitar*. Work on the children's album had interfered with his writing time, but now he was finally able to work on the book without being distracted. Barring any more interruptions, he expected the book to arrive on bookstore shelves in fall of 1979. He told me he was a little nervous. Not only were people reading less these days, but his previous attempt at writing had been such a disappointment. He said Jen had been reading the story as he wrote it, and she was constantly encouraging him. But Scowl still had fears about the project. Comparing acting to writing, he told me, "It's one thing to act and speak another person's dialogue from a screenplay, but it's wholly another to create your own story. It's such a raw and challenging endeavor. It's you, the scenes, the plot, and a handful of characters holed up in the same room for months on end. I'll be glad when the book is done, but I'm not sure I ever want to do this again."

I was now forty-eight. My son, Carter, was eleven, and my daughter, Pamela, was ten. It's amazing how quickly your children grow up. In just a few short years, my kids were no longer little snot-nosed, grass-stained kids. They were about to enter junior high, about to enter puberty, and in just a few years, they would be asking to drive my car. I was still happily married to Julia, who was still working at her part-time job at her publishing house. My career was chugging along nicely, but despite all the books and magazine articles I'd written, I was still best known for my interviews with Scowl. Everyone associated my name with his. When I met people at parties and social events, they would always ask, "Aren't you that writer guy who always interviews Scowl?" And I'd always say, "Yes, that's me." It was the end of summer, when our kids were preparing for the start of school, that I got a call from Scowl asking for another interview. I asked him if we would talk about his new book, and he said no, that he wanted to talk about his sons.

Jen and I were talking about this the other day, that children are amazing little creatures.

Yes, they are.

Do you know what Alex calls me?

No, I don't.

He calls me Poppa. Where do you suppose he got that from? No one around here calls anyone Poppa.

Maybe he got it from watching TV.

I suppose that's possible.

So how do you like being a father?

I'm loving it. I love it so much it makes me very sad.

Why would it make you sad?

It's knowing that these days can't last forever, that Alex is going to grow up, that eventually he'll be getting married and having children of his own. I feel like I'm about to miss everything. If I don't pay close attention, these years are going to pass me by.

The time does go fast.

It was only yesterday that we brought Alex home from the hospital. He was all wrapped up in his warm cotton blanket like a little Indian papoose, and he'd make the weirdest sounds. I'd listen to him while he was in his crib at night, tossing, turning, and gurgling like a baby hippopotamus. I used to get up in the middle of the night and go into his room. I'd just stand there staring at this perfect little human being, wondering how I could possibly have ever have shunned being a father. I'd count his toes and then I'd count his fingers. His little eyes would open for a moment, and he'd look at me wondering who the heck I was. Then he'd close his eyes and fall asleep. He was the most amazing little thing I'd ever seen. Now he's already two years old. I feel like I've been travelling in a time machine.

A time machine?

The years are just whizzing by.

It can feel that way.

I called Audrey the other day.

What did you say to her?

I wanted to know what our Roger was like when he was a baby. I asked her if he made strange sounds at night like Alex, or if he was quiet. I wanted to know if he woke up wanting to be fed, or if he waited politely until morning. Audrey was very kind, and she answered all my questions. But I could tell she didn't understand why I was calling. Why was I calling? In my own way, I was really asking her about something else.

What were you asking?

I was asking if she thought Roger might ever want to know me.

Why didn't you just ask her?

I don't know.

Maybe you were feeling guilty. Or maybe it's a touchy subject. Or maybe after all these years, you feel that it's inappropriate to ask.

Yes, that's probably all true. You know, I did what I felt was right at the time, leaving Audrey and Roger in Brentwood while I went to San Francisco. I wouldn't have made a good father, and I knew it. I wouldn't have had my heart in it, and there were so many other things I needed to do. But now that I look back, what the heck did I really accomplish? What did I need to do? What was more important than spending time with my own son, comforting him, teaching him, and loving him? I skipped out on the greatest and most significant opportunity ever to come my way so that I could live in a house full of long-haired hippies. I meditated and did yoga and listened to music. Big deal, right? We smoked weed and dropped psilocybin and LSD, hallucinating, laughing, acting like idiots, all in the name of finding ourselves. So what exactly did I find? Looking back, it now all seems so absurd. The only good thing to come out of those days was Claudia.

You were younger then. Young people need to find their way.

I was a fool.

Did you ever get around to asking Audrey if Roger would want to see you?

No, but I plan to call her back.

What will you say?

I'm going to ask her how Roger's doing.

How old is he?

He's sixteen. He's old enough to drive a car. In two years, he'll be old enough to vote.

Do you know anything about him?

I know what I've heard from others. People have told me that he reminds them of me. They say the two of us look a lot alike. I've heard he likes to play the guitar and that he also likes to sing. I remember how Audrey and I were going to raise him much the same way I was raised. We were going to throw all sorts of possibilities his way and see what he raised his hands to catch. Maybe he would be a musician, or maybe a great painter. Or maybe he'd want to be a doctor, a lawyer, or a butcher like my dad. There was no telling, right? But we'd leave the choice up to Roger. I've sometimes wondered how Roger was actually raised, and I've wondered about just what kind of man his stepfather is. I mean, I know Audrey loves the boy, but how could a strange man like her second husband love him the way I could have? I've thought about this a lot, especially recently.

What do you know about Roger's stepfather?

I know next to nothing. What the heck was wrong with me? Don't you think it's been irresponsible of me to allow my own flesh and blood to be raised by a complete stranger? I really wonder about the decisions I've made.

Hindsight is twenty-twenty.

Did you know my mother kept photo albums filled with pictures from the day I was born up until the day she died? The albums used to be up in our attic, before that fire destroyed them. Sometimes I would go up there to look at them. I'd sit there looking at the pictures, remembering all those days gone by. There was the time I was throwing snowballs at Dad during our winter visit to Big Bear, and those hot summer days in Arcadia when my friends and I would play in the sprinklers. There were photos from the weekend we visited San Juan Capistrano, when Dad sprained his ankle walking through the mission gardens, and there were also some shots of me singing with the old band in Trevor's garage. But as I recall, there were almost no photos of Roger. It's very depressing, being reminded of your failures, and sometimes I'm actually glad we lost all those photo albums in the fire.

But you now have Alex.

Yes, I have Alex.

Perhaps God is giving you a chance to redeem yourself?

I like looking at it that way. That's exactly what Jen says when I bring it up to her.

So how has Jen been doing?

She's great as usual. She always has such a positive attitude, and it does me a lot of good just being around her. She was trying to choose between being a stay-at-home mom or going back to UCLA to continue with her studies at film school, and she decided to stay home. I'm happy with her decision. Since I now work out of the house, it seems I'm with her all the time. We see a lot of each other, and that's the way it should be. We belong together.

Is the book almost done?

Yes, it's nearly completed, and I'm really enjoying myself. At first it was a little difficult, but now I'm totally in the swing of it. Every day I can't wait to jump back into the story and lose myself in the details. I like to watch as the story unfolds. Writing is such an amazing art form. You can't stand it up against a wall, or hang it up in a museum, or listen to it in your car, or watch it in a theater. No, you have to sit down and read through the entire thing from beginning to end. While most art forms can be appreciated rather quickly, in a matter of minutes, writing requires a big investment of time. And you can't let your reader down. No one wants to spend hours and hours reading a book only to be disappointed. There's an unwritten promise a writer makes to the reader, that he will make every possible effort to create a book that is compelling, that he will keep the reader's attention, and that he won't disappoint at the end of the story. It's a promise the writer has to take very seriously, otherwise he will lose his fans and his future books will go unread. I think there's nothing sadder than an unread book. Think of all that effort and work, and no audience.

Have you reached the twist yet?

I'm almost there.

Still keeping it a secret?

Yes, absolutely.

What do you think you'll do after the book is done? Do you have any projects planned?

Joseph said he might start another movie, and he asked if I was ready to get involved. He said it's difficult finding decent screenplays, but he now has a couple that sound interesting.

How about your music?

I'm always working on my music.

BILL'S GUITAR

———————— •◦• ————————

*B*ill's Guitar hit the bookstores in November 1979, just in time for the Christmas shopping season. The book wasn't a best seller, but it was popular with Scowl's fans. Since it sold relatively well, the publisher considered it a mild success. Readers liked Scowl's writing style, simple and to the point. Critics said his dialogue felt real and that it flowed nicely, and they said the twist at the end of the story was very clever. It was a far greater triumph than *Nancy Kimball*, and when I talked to Scowl about the book, he seemed happy with the all feedback he was getting. Yet I could tell he still had some reservations about writing, and I doubted he would do it again. "I worked a lot harder on this book than I ever worked on any one song," he told me. "It's funny how something I spent so many hours on would be such a tepid success, when something like a song, which sometimes takes me only a day to write, can create such a splash." I asked Scowl what he was going to do next, and he said he was working with Crabtree to turn *Bill's Guitar* into a screenplay. Crabtree was sure that the story would make a terrific movie. It was Crabtree's brilliant idea to have Scowl play the father and to have Scowl's son, Roger, play the son. "I don't know if the kid can act," Crabtree said. "But this idea of having your real-life son play your son in the movie might be just the sort of gimmick that makes this movie a hit. We'd need to have the kid audition, of course, and we'd have to get the idea cleared through Audrey."

Was it a good idea? A bad idea? Who knew? The kid had to have some talent, after all, he was Scowl's flesh and blood. Before Scowl knew what was happening, Crabtree called Audrey and ran the idea past her. Since Roger was still a minor, she would have to be on board. She told Crabtree she would think about it. Crabtree then asked Scowl to call and convince her this was a great idea. He said, "Tell her that it would be a golden opportunity for you to finally get to know your son. I think she's always wanted the two of you to be closer to each other." Scowl called me, wanting to get my opinion. I told him I didn't know Audrey or Roger very well and that I was probably the wrong person to ask. But I did say it sounded promising. The boy was now sixteen and would be seventeen by the time Crabtree started filming. Neither Scowl nor Roger was getting any younger, and I knew there was a void in Scowl's psyche caused by the years he missed with the boy, a void he'd be wise to fill. This set up seemed like the perfect way to do it.

In March 1980, the screenplay for *Bill's Guitar* was finished, and Crabtree began the process of casting. Scowl was able to talk Audrey into letting Roger audition. Roger was very excited, not so much because he would be working alongside his father, but more because he had this chance to be the leading actor in a movie. The audition went well, and Crabtree saw potential in the boy. Roger would require some professional coaching, but the overall idea now seemed plausible. Within weeks, Crabtree was able to get Audrey's final stamp of approval, and filming started in summer. About halfway through the production, Crabtree started promoting the film. He touted the father-son acting duo and the opportunity everyone would have to see Scowl's son for the first time. Crabtree also thought it would be useful for me to interview Scowl, and we met on the set in Scowl's trailer.

So we meet again at a movie set in your trailer. Do you remember the last time we did this?

It was when we were filming *Faraway Places,* when I painted all those crazy portraits.

Any plans to paint during this film?

No, not yet.

How does it feel to be starring in a movie with your son? How are you two getting along?

Except for the actual film shoots, I hardly ever see him. They have him very busy with his acting coach. The kid has a lot to learn.

How about meals? Do you dine with him?

He's always eats his meals with the younger kids on the set. He doesn't seem interested in eating with his old man. In fact, he doesn't seem interested in doing anything with me.

Tell me about his acting ability. How's he doing? What do you think the public is going to think of his performance?

I think he's a natural. A sort of diamond in the rough. He memorizes all his lines like a pro, and his delivery is getting better and better. I think the public is going to fall in love.

Like a chip off the old block?

Something like that.

Do you think he'll warm up to you in the weeks to come?

I don't know.

He can't ignore you forever.

I can remember when I was his age. The last person I wanted to spend time with was my father. I can remember my sixteenth birthday. We went down to the local Department of Motor Vehicles to get my driver's license. Mom took me down in the morning, and by noon I was a licensed driver. My friends and I made plans; I was going to drive all of us to Santa Monica, and we were going to hang out at the beach. It was a perfect summer day, and it would be the ideal way for me to celebrate my independence. That's exactly what having a license meant to me—it was all about independence. I could gas up and go wherever I wanted. I could drive all the way to Tijuana, to the mountains in Big Bear, or to the beaches in Santa Monica. All of Southern California was at my disposal. I remember getting ready. I put on my swimming trunks in my bedroom and grabbed a couple towels from the linen closet in the hall. As I made my way to the kitchen to grab a soda for the road, my dad appeared from around the corner. "Where are you going?" he asked. He seemed to be surprised that I was ready for the beach since I hadn't told him anything about it. I told him where I was going, and he said, "Gee, your mom and I thought it'd be fun for the three of us to drive to Laguna this afternoon. We thought we'd grab a birthday dinner at one of the restaurants there and check out some of the art galleries." I told Dad I'd made other plans, that I needed to use the car so my friends and I could go. Dad got this odd look on his face, like he was about to cry. It was like I'd just punched him in the stomach. I had no idea what was going on. But why in the world would I opt to drive with my parents when I could go to the beach with friends? I was absolutely clueless. It wasn't until just a few days ago, during the filming of this movie, that I came to understand what happened that afternoon. My father knew he was losing me, and the feeling was just beginning to sink in. I was no longer his little shadow. I had my own plans, friends, a license to drive, and I was now much more interested in being with my buddies than I was in driving to Laguna with Mom and him. I mean, art galleries? He had to be kidding, right? My dad placed the car keys in my hand, and I ran outside. I hopped in the car, cranked up the radio, and sped away to get my friends. I had no idea what had just happened or what I'd just done to my dad. Like I said, I was clueless.

Did you and your dad ever talk about that day? I mean, later on.

No, we never talked about it. There would have been no reason for my dad to bring it up.

Do you think Roger is looking for his independence?

Oh, yes.

And you're okay with this?

Yes, it's okay. I'm not going to complain. It's just too bad about the timing.

I see what you mean.

Some relationships just aren't meant to be. Don't you think that's true?

I don't know.

I'll tell you another story. This isn't a true story. It's something I concocted. During my senior year in high school, I wrote a short story for my English class about a boy named Charlie. He was a senior in school, and he had a girlfriend named Melinda. He and Melinda had been going together for over a year, and everything was going fine for the couple until he discovered Nanette Fabray. Perhaps you remember Nanette Fabray? She was Sid Caesar's comedic TV partner on *Caesar's Hour.*

Yes, I remember the show.

Well, never mind that she was a person on TV. Charlie fell hard for Nanette, and he began writing fan letters to her every day. I picked Nanette for this story because at the time I wrote the story I had sort of a crush on her myself. She was funny and attractive, and she was an older woman. When I was a kid, older women like Nanette seemed especially sexy. This guy Charlie sends Nanette all his fan letters, but she never responds. In these letters he pours his heart out, telling her how much he loves her. He tells her how if the two of them could meet he's sure she would feel the same. He sends pictures of himself, writes page after page of poetry, and even does a clumsy pen and ink drawing of her face. This infatuation grows into a full-blown obsession, and he completely loses interest in his high school sweetheart. Melinda senses Charlie's distance, and she reaches out to other boys. She begins dating a kid named Henry, and one thing leads to another so that she gives Charlie back his ring and goes steady with Henry instead. And Charlie is suddenly left on his own. Right before these kids graduate, Charlie hears the news that Nanette is marrying the president of one of the show's commercial sponsors. Of course, I made this part up about the sponsor. Nanette never did get engaged to one of the show's sponsors, but the engagement was necessary to make my story work. Charlie is devastated by her decision, and he comes crashing back to reality, only to find that his girl Melinda is now happy with Henry. Charlie pleads his case, but Melinda wants nothing to do with him. And that was the end of my story. I think the teacher gave me a C. I figured the story was worth a B.

Why have you always been so interested in performers and their fans?

I don't know. I guess the story I wrote was sort of prophetic. Who knew that I'd soon have my own obsessive fans? I guess it's funny.

It's not unlike the Nancy Kimball *story. The stories end badly for both of your main characters.*

Yes, I guess they do.

So why tell me now about Charlie?

Only to point out what I said, that some relationships are just not meant to be. We can hope, pray, scheme, and maneuver, but sometimes things just won't work out, no matter what we do, no matter how hard we try. It might be right what they say, that one is often better off leaving well enough alone. Isn't that what they say? I'm not sure I'll ever be that close to Roger. It might not be in the cards, and I might just be seventeen years too late.

You once told me you weren't a quitter.

I'm not a quitter.

Aren't you going to keep trying?

Oh, knowing me, I'm sure I will. Yes, I'm sure I will, but I'm also a realist.

THE DEBACLE

———— •❦• ————

W hen *Bill's Guitar* was released to theaters, there was a lot of
anticipation. Everyone figured they'd get a solid performance
from Scowl, but no one was quite sure about Roger. Who exactly was
this seventeen-year-old who looked a little like his dad? Did he inherit his
father's acting talents, and could the kid really stand on his own two feet?
The reviews from critics were the first sign of a problem. Roger's portrayal
of the boy in the movie was blasted by one critic as "ten percent Scowl,
and ninety percent chimpanzee" and by another as "indisputable proof
that acting talent is not hereditary." Word quickly got out that the movie
was a flop, not because of Scowl, but because of his son. Some audiences
actually booed in the theaters, walking out, and the film was soon being
called the "worst movie of the year." Audrey was horrified at the reaction
to her son's performance, and she blamed Scowl for talking her into letting
Roger take part in the project. I tried to call Scowl soon after the film
was released, but he didn't return my calls. Meanwhile, the situation
spun out of control. Moviegoers were piling it on, and the film was being
ridiculed by everyone. And Scowl? Not only had he failed to make a of
father-son connection with Roger, but he'd led him right into a public tar
and feathering. The kid was finished. This was surely to be Roger's last
stint as a Hollywood actor, and Scowl's dreams for his son were completely
shattered. I really wanted to talk to him, to offer support as a friend, but
like I said, he wouldn't call me back.

In the meantime, Scowl was on the phone every day with Audrey,
trying to figure out how to deal with their disillusioned and humiliated
son. He was due to return to high school to finish his last semester, but
he refused to go. Nothing Audrey said seemed to help, and when Scowl
tried to talk to him, the boy became even angrier. Roger blamed the entire

debacle on his father. He said it was all Scowl's fault—the bad movie reviews, the booing fans, and the pitiful box-office receipts. He even blamed Scowl for the story, which he complained (wrongly) was a large part of the problem. When Scowl finally did call me for an interview, a year had passed. When I talked to Scowl on the phone, he said nothing about Roger or the film. He wanted to get together with me, so we met at Dulcinea shortly after Christmas.

—❦—

Is there anything specific you'd like to talk about this afternoon?

Ask me anything.

How are Jen and Alex?

They're both doing great. Did you know Alex is five? Can you believe it? I think the last time we spoke, Alex was only three. I told you before that raising a kid was like climbing into a time machine. It seems like only yesterday that I was watching him sleep in his crib, and now he's already a walking, talking boy.

Five is a great age.

He has trouble pronouncing words. Did your kids have difficulty with this?

Yes, a little.

A helicopter is a *hellihopper,* and strawberries are *strawbabies.* When we're eating spaghetti, he says, "Pass the pascetti."

He'll grow out of that.

It's such a shame.

What's a shame?

It's a shame he has to grow up at all. Adults are louts compared to kids. It's like comparing puppies to full-grown, mangy dogs. You just want your dog to stay a puppy forever.

Did you have a good Christmas?

Everything went fine. I think we all got what we wanted, and Alex told his first lie.

He told a lie?

Jen and I were sitting in bed reading before going to sleep, when Alex came into the room crying. He was holding his left hand, and one of his fingers was bright red with blood. It was a good-size cut, not big enough to require stitches, but deep enough to cause a lot of bleeding. Jen took Alex into the bathroom to dress the wound. When she was done, she brought Alex back, and I interrogated him. "What happened?" I asked. "How'd you cut your finger?" Alex swore he cut his finger on the lid to the wicker hamper in his bedroom. Jen and I went to his room and removed the wicker lid, examining it carefully, looking it over, feeling both sides with our fingers. For the life of us, we couldn't find anything on the lid that might have caused Alex to cut his finger. "Are you sure this is where you cut your finger?" Jen asked. "You need to tell us the truth. We need to know how you cut yourself so we can keep it from happening again." Alex had this incredibly guilty look on his face, like he was hiding something, like he was telling us a lie. "Come on," I said. "Out with it. How'd you really cut your finger?" Alex lowered his head and led us slowly to the front room. He took us to the back of the Christmas tree and showed us a shattered glass ornament on the floor. Alex had been playing with the tree, broken the ornament, and cut his finger on it.

That was his first lie?

It's the first we know about. Don't you think it's a riot that he would lie like that? Even at the young age of five, the human mind decides telling a lie is better than telling the truth. Lying comes so naturally to us, even at an early age.

You haven't told me much about Jen. What's she been doing with her time? What a typical day like in the life of Jen?

You should probably ask her instead of me. It's not like I'm not attached to her. I do know she gets up early, about an hour before Alex and me, and while we're sleeping, she makes breakfast and coffee and she straightens up the house. We have a maid who does the housecleaning, but Jen still likes to tidy up. She likes to keep things clean and orderly. Alex and I are awake by eight, and the two of us eat breakfast with Jen. By eight-thirty, Jen is helping Alex pick out his clothes, and she takes him to preschool. She gets back at about nine-thirty and helps me with my fan mail. She reads through the letters and decides which I should respond to. Sometimes she writes the replies, but I always do the actual handwriting myself.

Tell me about some of this fan mail. What are your fans like? What do they have to say?

My fans are all over the map. I have older fans who have liked me since the fifties, and I have younger fans who have just discovered me. I have male fans just as I have female fans. You might be surprised at the number of male fans I have. All these fans write about all kinds of things—about their relationships, about their friends and family, about my music, and about my movies and books. I get a lot of fan-written songs they want me to perform. They think they've written the greatest song for me yet. I've received thousands of them. Most disturbing are the letters from fans like Lynette, who are obsessed with me to the point of it being unhealthy. Can you imagine the sort of pressure this puts on me? Ever since the trouble we had with Lynette, I take these letters seriously. I always answer my most obsessive fans, and I try to talk them down from the ledge. I try to infuse some reality into their lives, gently but firmly. I turn the worst letters over to the police.

To the police?

What would you do with them?

I don't know. I guess I've never really thought about it.

You haven't asked me anything about my music.

No, I haven't.

I'm working on two new albums. One will be all about trains. Did you know Alex is crazy about trains? He makes trains in his wing of the house by placing all his stuffed animals into rows. He has an awful lot of stuffed animals, and he always makes his favorite bear the locomotive. We bought him several picture books and videos about trains, and he spends hours looking at them. Last summer we took a trip up to Alaska, and we rode an old Yukon train through White Pass and into Canada, and Alex was in awe. On that trip I wondered how many songs have been written all about trains. I figured there were probably a lot, certainly enough to fill an album. I figured the album would have broad appeal, not just to train buffs. I mean, who doesn't love trains? They're as all-American and inspirational as any Norman Rockwell magazine cover. I've already completed a few of the tracks, and I like how they're turning out. One of my favorites is a country version of Steve Goodman's *City of New Orleans* that I recorded with a little-known bluegrass band I discovered a couple years ago. The Arlo Guthrie version will always be a classic, but I think my take on the song will find a lot of fans.

What's your other album?

The second album will be a collection of Christmas tunes. I was listening to the radio, and I noticed how many musicians have produced Christmas recordings. There are a ton of them, but there's never anything from Scowl. It's time I tackled the holiday season. My new album will include all the family favorites, recorded here in my home studio. The title of the album will be *Christmas with Scowl,* and we'll release it right before the holidays next year. I expect it to be a big seller.

It sounds like you're busy.

There's never a moment's rest. I've told you there are no idle hands in the Scowl household.

I haven't asked you anything about Bill's Guitar. I realize it's probably a sore subject, but everyone's going to want to know, and so I have to ask, what's your take on all that happened?

I suppose you're talking about the movie, and not the book?

Yes, I'm asking about the movie.

I've thought about it a lot.

Do you think the movie was as bad as everyone made it out to be?

I'm the wrong person to ask. There's something your readers should know about Roger and me. We've never been close over the years, but I've always loved him. A parent can't help but love his child. And when a parent sees his child perform in front of others, whether as a musician, athlete, dancer, or even as an actor, the parent probably sees what he wants to see. What they say about love being blind is truer than ever when it comes to your children. When I watched my son Roger filming his scenes for *Bill's Guitar,* memorizing his lines, working with his acting coach, following Joseph's instructions, I couldn't have been any prouder. I thought Roger nailed every scene. I thought when the movie hit the theaters that he'd take the world by storm. I thought the public would see what I saw—a wonderful young man, an up-and-coming movie actor who took his craft seriously and put on the performance of his young life. I've watched the movie over and over since it was released, and to this day all I can see before my eyes is my beloved son. You know, when all the complaints about the movie came in, I was really taken aback. It was all so hurtful. Every bad thing written and said about my son was like a blow to me. There's nothing more upsetting than seeing someone you love being attacked the way Roger was attacked.

Are you angry at your fans?

I'm angry at myself.

Why is that?

Do you love your children?

Yes, I do.

Would you ever do anything to hurt them?

No, of course not.

I set my son up for disaster. If anyone should've seen the impending disaster, it should have been me. I've been in the spotlight my entire adult life. I know what critics are like, and I know how brutal the public can be. It was like shoving my own son into a barn full of dry hay and throwing in a match. I'm not sure he'll ever get over it. I'm not sure the wounds will ever heal.

How is Roger doing now?

After this happened, he refused to go back to school. He wouldn't even leave the house. Audrey had to hire a tutor to homeschool him for the rest of the year. He's now done with his schooling, but I'm not sure what he plans to do. I don't know if he's going to college or if he's going to get a job. He won't talk to me, and Audrey asked me to stop calling. My plans were a complete bust. I was a lousy father to begin with and an even lousier father in the aftermath. You can't imagine how much it hurts to know that the boy now wants nothing to do with me. It's sad beyond words.

If Roger is reading this interview, is there anything you'd like to say?

Nothing except that I love him. That's all I can say. That's all I have left to offer.

CHRISTMAS WITH SCOWL

T he year was still 1982. My interview with Scowl about the *Bill's Guitar* fiasco was widely read and well received. Although his fans and critics had rejected Roger's acting performance, Scowl didn't shoot back at them vindictively. He seemed willing to take the entire weight of the event on his shoulders. In our interview he not only took ownership of the situation, but he also opened his heart to his fans about his love for his son. I think everyone felt a little guilty for what had happened. When his *Trains* album was released late summer, it was a smashing success. It seemed to be just the sort of effort the public was looking for. And meanwhile, life went on. Mark David Chapman began his second year in Attica for killing John Lennon, and Ronald Reagan was serving his second year as president. *E.T. the Extra-Terrestrial*, *Tootsie*, and *First Blood* dominated the box office, and the world's fair opened in Knoxville. They asked Scowl to perform one of his train songs during the fair's opening ceremony. How many years had it been since I first interviewed Scowl, since he was a nineteen-year-old rock 'n' roll heartthrob performing for throngs of screaming girls? Did I really understand him? Did I really have a grip on what it was that made this man tick? He had been called a fake, and he had been called a fad. Yet here he was in living color, performing at the world's fair, still a darling of the general public. When November arrived, he was ready to promote his Christmas album, and he called me for an interview. I arrived at Dulcinea two days later, eager to ask my questions.

———— ❧ ————

You must be pleased with the terrific success of Trains. *Did you think it would get this kind of reception from so many people?*

I had a feeling.

You still seem to have a finger on the pulse of the buying public.

It's more than that.

You ought to be proud.

No, I ought to be grateful.

Grateful for what?

I ought to be grateful for the way this album turned out. I ought to be grateful for all the people in my life, my family and friends, all the musicians who worked with me, and all my fans. And, of course, I should be grateful to my fantabulous God.

There's no room in there for a little pride?

Not really. Not if I want to be honest.

Do you think of yourself as an inspiration? Something like Norman Rockwell?

I'd like to think that.

And you're not proud of this?

No, not really. Like I said, I'm grateful.

Do you intentionally try to be inspirational?

Yes, I think it's important.

Your fans seem to agree with you.

Well, I am my fans.

Pardon me?

I am my fans. And they are me. I'm talking about all of them. From the most casual, once-in-a-while listener to the most rabid devotee, I am my fans. We live on the same planet, cry the same tears, and breathe the same air. We are in all of this together.

I've never heard you describe your fans quite this way. Is this something new?

Just a realization. Have you ever practiced what they call Transcendental Meditation?

No, I haven't.

You ought to try it. When I was in San Francisco, I was visited by Maharishi Mahesh Yogi. Do you remember this nut? He traveled around the globe rubbing elbows with all sorts of famous people, teaching them to meditate, and at my request he spent a couple days sitting Indian style in my front room. We brought him lots of flowers, food, and even some cash in exchange for his expertise. He's the one who assigned me my own mantra, and he taught me to free my mind. I recently started to meditate again, to calm myself after the *Bill's Guitar* fiasco. Do you want to know what I now see when I meditate? It's strange, but it's true. When I meditate, I do not become one with the universe. No, I am at one with my fans. This is my life. My fans are my identity and priority. They are me.

Doesn't this concern you?

No, why would it?

Aren't you afraid of losing your identity?

I don't think you understand what I'm saying. Listen, let me try to explain. Your son's name is Carter, right?

Yes, his name is Carter.

How old is he now?

He's fourteen.

He's very important to you, no?

Of course, he's very important to me.

Do you want Carter to love you? Do you want him to appreciate all the things you do?

Yes, I think that's fair to say.

Do you feel the tug?

What do you mean by tug?

The way Carter tugs at your heartstrings. Don't you think it's amazing how children are able do this? You're not romantically in love with them like you might be with your wife, but still they tug at your heartstrings with such undeniable strength. You feel them next to you. In fact, they actually are you. They are in your blood and under your skin. Your life revolves around them, around their spirit and well-being. You work and try to provide a good home for them, and you try to raise them to be good and kind adults. When they cry it saddens you, and when they laugh it brightens your day. Am I on the mark here? Does this describe the way you feel about Carter?

I'd have to say yes.

So are you any less of a person because of your son? Less of a person because of this love?

No, I'm not.

You're actually a better person because of him, isn't that true?

Yes, I think that's true.

You're a better person. You've become one with him without losing your identity. In fact, your identity has become stronger, deeper, and more mature. And the more you give of yourself, the more you gain. This is true of fans as it is of a son. It's a simple concept, and I think I've known it intuitively all my life. But now I know it like I know my own name.

What about fans like Lynette Ann Bauer? Are you at one with them?

Yes, I'm one with all of them. Did you know I still visit Lynette?

No, I didn't.

I see her once a month.

How's she doing?

She's still delusional. She doesn't seem to be making any progress, but I think my visits make her incarceration at Everdale more tolerable. She thinks we're married now and that we have several children together. She thinks I'm taking care of the children at Dulcinea, waiting for the doctors to set her free. She always says it won't be long, but the way things are going, I doubt she'll ever be freed. I think she's going to spend the rest of her life in that place, and it makes me sad. Recently she's been pulling her hair. Her doctor has a name for this, but I forget what they call it. She yanks her hair out, not in big chunks, but little by little, a few strands a time. Her hair is getting thin as a result, and it makes her appear even more disturbed than she is. When you ask if Lynette is a part of me, or is me, I have to answer yes. Her upsetting behavior is as much a part of me as the blood that runs through my arteries and veins. I can't ignore her, and I can't pretend she doesn't exist. Every month I go to see her, to see me. I do this because I love her just like I would love any other fan. She's a human being, and she's deserving of my time.

Most people won't understand this.

God put Lynette on this planet for a reason, and God doesn't make mistakes. I guess that's the only explanation that I need.

I think we've veered off track with this talk about your fans. We still haven't discussed your Christmas album, and that was the reason for this interview.

The album will be released next week.

Any surprises to look out for?

There are three duets. One is a version of "Silent Night" I sing with Ray Charles. I think you'll be hearing a lot of this one on the radio. It's really something special.

What are the others?

You'll have to buy the album to see. But I will also tell you that I rounded up some of the boys from our original band to back up a few of the songs. Alan plays bass on "White Christmas" and "The Christmas Song," and Richard plays guitar on "Frosty the Snowman."

How about Trevor and his saxophone?

Trevor hasn't played the saxophone for years. He lives down in Irvine, where he started a high-tech company. He finally got his degree in electrical engineering from Stanford and started up this company with his father using the money he made as a musician. He's raking in more money now than he did when he played for me, and he's living in Newport Beach not far from Audrey's house. He sends me a Christmas card every year and calls once and a while to touch base. We keep say we're going to get together for lunch or dinner, but it never happens. If you remember, he got married back when the band was breaking up, and he's still married to the same gal. They have one kid, a boy, who's now seventeen, and I think he's interested in political science. They plan on sending him to Stanford next year.

How about Alan?

Alan is still married to Alice. I'm not sure of the ages of their two kids. Until the Christmas album, the two of us haven't been in touch. Alan told me he's working on and off for Fender Guitars as some sort of consultant. He doesn't really need the money, but he likes to keep himself busy in the industry. He's also been floating around from band to band, doing guest gigs. I think you can hear him playing bass on a couple Eric Clapton albums, as well as on several of Richard's recent efforts.

How is Richard doing?

As you know, Richard has kept in the public eye. His Grapevine group was fantabulously successful, and his solo albums have done very well. Like Alan, we haven't really kept in touch, but when I called and asked him to join me for the Christmas album, he seemed surprised and pleased. Of all of us, I think he had the most musical talent back when we were just beginning. His guitar playing was essential to my early rise. We had a lot of fun together at Dulcinea recording "Frosty the Snowman," and I think our fans are going to be impressed. It'll be like nothing they've ever heard.

Who sings on the "Frosty" track?

Why, me, of course. What would be the point of buying a Scowl album if you didn't get to hear him sing?

THE WOLVES

I n late spring of 1983, Joseph Crabtree came to Scowl with another idea for a movie. This time he wanted to remake the popular 1934 film *The Thin Man*. The original starred William Powell and Myrna Loy as Nick and Nora Charles, where Nick was a hard-drinking retired private detective and Nora was a wealthy heiress. Nick and Nora try to settle down to lead a calm married life, but they are pulled into a whodunit involving the disappearance of a friend named Clyde Wynant. For years the film has been a fan favorite, and Crabtree now had visions of Scowl playing the clue-seeking leading man, while having Maria Barringer play Nora. Crabtree had always wanted to direct Maria, and he saw *The Thin Man* as the perfect opportunity. The idea came to him in the middle of the night in a dream. He dreamt that pairing Maria with Scowl would put him back on the map, something he needed badly after having failed so miserably with *Bill's Guitar*. The day after he had the dream, Crabtree called Scowl and described his vision. At first Scowl was reticent, and he told Crabtree he would need time to think about it. Scowl obtained a copy of the film and watched it in his home theater. He tried over and over to imagine himself acting with Maria, playing the clever detective and Maria's husband. Perhaps he'd have to grow a William Powell mustache for the part, and he tried to picture it. He called and asked my opinion, not on the mustache, but on the entire project. He said the more he thought about it, the more he could picture himself playing the character. "What do you think about this?" he asked. "Do you think old Crabtree has lost his mind, or is this idea a stroke of genius?" I really didn't know what to say. I didn't like it when Scowl asked for my opinion on career decisions. The last time he'd asked for my opinion on a movie role it concerned whether or not to use Roger in *Bill's Guitar,* and at the time I thought that was a good idea. I was clearly not the right person to ask, so I told Scowl I preferred not to give an opinion. But as it turned out, it didn't really matter since his mind was already made up. He called Crabtree the next day and told him yes, and now all Crabtree had to do was get Maria on board. It was the beginning of summer when Scowl contacted me again and asked for an interview. He said he had good news about the film and wanted to discuss it with me. He wouldn't tell me over the phone whether Maria had actually said yes, but he seemed so excited that I assumed she had agreed to everything.

Tell me about The Thin Man. *Is it a go?*

Yes, it's a go. We're going to do it, my good man. We're set to begin filming this fall.

Was Crabtree able to get Maria Barringer?

We'll get to that later. First let's talk about the screenplay. It was written by John Holliday, the same guy who wrote the script for *The LA Twins.* I love the way this guy writes my parts. I won't have to change a single line. It's like he gets right into my head, and I think he's one of the best comedy writers today.

Is The Thin Man *going to be a comedy?*

It's sort of a comedy-whodunit. It's a lot like the original movie, except with some changes that will make it more current.

What kind of changes?

To begin with, Nick Charles won't be wearing his thin mustache. I bounced the idea of the mustache off Joseph, and he said no way. He said if I wore a mustache, I'd look like some sort of sleazy Columbian cocaine smuggler, not a loveable private eye. He said working around my sneer was going to be difficult enough without having to deal with a mustache. There's a small committee of experts who've been working with Joseph on the way I'll look. They say they're going to cut my hair short and neat, like I'm some hotshot Wall Street stockbroker, and they're going to dress me in sport jackets, like Paul Drake in those Perry Mason shows on TV. In fact, I'll look a lot like Paul Drake, except I'll be shorter and not so broad shouldered.

Will the story be set in the thirties, or will it be set in current times?

It will be set in the thirties. It will be the same great story as the original movie, except for some minor differences. For example, Nick won't be a heavy drinker. In the original movie, Nick was quite the lush, always on the prowl for a drink. I told Joseph I wouldn't act in the movie if our Nick drank a lot, that it wasn't the kind of image I wanted to project to my fans.

What other changes are there?

The storyline will be the same, but the end is going to be different. There will be a surprising conclusion, a twist to the ending of the original movie. Holliday came up with the idea, and I think it's ingenious. He said we'd need something to set the new movie apart from the old, and this ending will do it. I can just hear the jaws hitting the floor. Audiences will really be astonished at how everything shakes out.

I don't suppose you'd like to give us a clue now as to how the story ends?

Nope. No way.

Is Maria going to play Nora Charles?

I'll get to that in a minute. First, I need to make something clear about the film's title. When I first told Jen about this movie idea, she said she wasn't sure if I struck her as an actor people would identify as a thin man. They might see me as slender, but not so much a thin man. She said when you call someone a thin man, you imply the person is both thin and relatively tall, just like William Powell. When I brought this up to Joseph, he said this was a hurdle we were going to have to jump. This problem had nothing to do with me, but it had to do with the movie's title. People have always misinterpreted this title. In fact, the thin man wasn't William Powell; he was actually Clyde Wynant, the man Nick and Nora were trying to find. Most people don't know this. Most people think William Powell was the thin man.

What else can you tell me about the film?

Did you hear that Joseph originally wanted to shoot the film in black and white? That's what they were saying. They said Joseph wanted to stay true to the original, and he loves black-and-white movies. But his fellow producers talked him out of it. They convinced him that the public these days wouldn't stand for a black-and-white movie, and I have a feeling they're right. Black-and-white movies just don't draw big crowds at the box office. So Joseph is going to do the opposite; he's going to make the film exceedingly colorful. The film will be full of brilliant colors pulled from every band in the rainbow, like an old Technicolor movie, like the *Wizard of Oz*. Joseph says it's going to be a feast for the eyes.

It sounds intriguing.

America needs a movie like this. Do you know what I mean by this? There'll be no cynicism. No illicit drugs, or gratuitous violence, or steamy sex scenes. This will be a tribute to the eighties, the real eighties, the Ronald Reagan eighties, the way things should be. It will be a clean, fun, and light-hearted story. I really think this movie has a chance to be a great success. I think this is the kind of thing people in American want to see.

Jason Trumbo recently wrote there's no need to remake this movie, that the original Thin Man *stands just fine as it is.*

I think he's wrong. If ever there was time to revisit the classics of Hollywood, this is it. The public is tired of the modern swill they're being fed. They're yearning for something like this. Honestly, I think people will flock to see it.

Having someone like Marie Barringer play the role of Nora Charles will certainly help draw moviegoers. So, I'll ask you again, is she in the movie?

She made several demands of Joseph, and he had a hard time with some of them.

What sort of demands?

Money for one. She wants an awful lot of money.

Is Joseph going to give in to her?

She also wants some changes made to Nora's character. She wants the Nora in this movie to be an English heiress, not an American heiress. Maria has been learning to speak with an English accent for the past year, hoping to act in an English role, and she wants to show off her accent.

That seems workable.

She also wants Nora to be college educated, a bright and hardworking woman who is successful in her own right. She doesn't want Nora to be a flippant rich girl living off a trust fund. She suggested Joseph make her an English girl who moved to America and graduated from Harvard Law School. She wants her to be a successful attorney, and her idea was that Nora and Nick met while working on a murder case together.

So what did Joseph have to say about all this?

He went for all of it.

So I take it Maria is in the movie?

Yes, she'll play the role.

This should be interesting.

Yes, don't you think?

Do you mind if I change the subject for a moment? I'd like to ask you a few questions about your son Roger.

Okay, go ahead.

There was an article in People *about Roger a couple months ago.*

Yes, I'm familiar with it.

They say Roger is now living on the streets in San Francisco, apparently doing odd jobs and begging for money, barely getting by. They implied he has a serious problem with drugs. They say they tried to interview Roger, but he wouldn't talk to them. Do you know if any of this report is true?

Yes, the report is true.

Isn't there anything you or Audrey can do?

We've tried everything. Audrey and I have talked with him over and over. We've tried to get him to go visit a psychiatrist, but he's refused. I've gone up to the city several times to see what I could do. The boy is consumed with hate. He hates Audrey and me for getting him involved in *Bill's Guitar*, and he hates the world for their reaction to the movie. It has brought him down, eating away at him, destroying his life. I know he was laughed at, humiliated, and rejected and that his self-worth was ripped away and stomped on mercilessly. And I don't blame him for feeling bad, but he's let it get the best of him. He needs to pick himself up and dust himself off. He needs to put this in his rearview mirror. Most importantly, he needs to stop feeding the wrong wolf.

The wrong wolf?

My dad used to tell me a Cherokee legend about wolves when I was young, whenever I felt angry. I wrote the story down on a sheet of paper and I took it to Roger, handing it to him and telling him to read it. I told him to read the legend every morning, that it might help him to see things more clearly. The story is about a Cherokee grandfather who is talking to his grandson. He tells the boy there is a fight going on inside of him, a fight between two wolves. One wolf is anger and hate. The other wolf is love and happiness. The grandfather says the same fight is going on inside of everyone. The boy thinks about this for a moment and asks, "Which wolf will win?" The grandfather replies, "The one you feed." It's a good story, no? I gave the paper to Roger hoping he would take the time to read it, hoping he would take the message to heart. I have no idea if he's even bothered to look at it. For all I know, he just wiped his nose with it and threw it away.

There must be something else you can do.

At this point, it's up to Roger. I've done all that I can. I can't very well step into his shoes and take the walk for him. He's an adult. It breaks my heart, but what more can I do?

Do you feel guilty for any of this?

Oh, yes. I'm quite guilty. I don't just feel guilty. I am guilty.

It must be terribly frustrating.

You have no idea.

Don't you find it ironic that you're now involved with The Thin Man, *such a colorful and carefree comedy, while your son is suffering so?*

It isn't really ironic. It's just life. Bad things happen all the time, and we have to learn to grin and bear them. It's like they always say on the stage: the show must go on. Sure, it's a cliché, but it's a very profound one. We can't stop with world from spinning every time we run into a problem. I know I've been criticized for rose-colored glasses, but when people take these jabs at me, I think they're missing the point. I know life can be bad. I know terrible things happen in the world. I know people can be cruel, mean, greedy, careless, evil, and violent. I am not blind, and I don't think I'm naïve. But here's what I also think. I think, yes, the show must go on. We need to feed the good wolf every chance we get. We need to let the bad wolf go hungry. Or we're all doomed.

CAPTAIN AHAB

—•◦•—

S cowl's ability to judge his audience was uncanny. Just as he predicted, *The Thin Man* was a huge success. It seemed to be just the sort of movie the public was longing for, and there were stories of people seeing the movie two, even three times. They couldn't get enough of it. The movie wasn't Academy Award material, but it was the kind of film the public loved. It wasn't deep, or dreary, or violent, or politically relevant. It just made viewers smile, and it had a happy ending. The crime was solved, the bad guy was arrested, and everyone lived happily ever after. Crabtree was now back atop the heap of successful directors, and he knew his son-in-law's talents had helped get him there. It was the acting ability of Scowl and the charismatic talents of the incomparable Maria Barringer. Everyone fell in love with Maria as the English version of Nora Charles; she had been well worth all the trouble to get. Even Jason Trumbo had to admit he'd been "pleasantly surprised by Maria's interpretation of Nora," and *Time* magazine called Maria a "Nora Charles women in America could look up to." The movie was a resounding success.

The dreadful news didn't come until August 1984. I heard the story while watching the TV news. San Francisco police had found the dead body of Roger in an abandoned apartment building where he had died of a heroin overdose. I called Scowl, but Jen said he flew to San Francisco as soon as he got the news. I told her to have him call me when he returned, but I didn't expect him to call back anytime soon. In fact, I wouldn't have blamed him if he didn't call at all. I only wanted to extend my sympathies and ask if there was anything I could do to help. But he did call me back. He called the day after I had talked to Jen, and he said he wanted to meet for an interview, that he wanted to talk about Roger. I told him he might want to let a few weeks pass, but he insisted we get together as soon as possible.

I truly wish we were meeting under happier circumstances. I'm not sure where you want to begin this interview.

Go ahead and ask me a question.

Where were you when you heard the news?

I was sitting here in my living room. I was reading Herman Melville's *Moby-Dick* and drinking a cup of tea. It was Saturday morning, and the newspaper said it was going to be a sunny day. I was wearing nothing but a pair of shorts and an old T-shirt, and I had the French door open to let in some fresh air. This was the fourth time I'd tried to read Moby-Dick. Every time I picked up this book, I barely finished the first chapter. I don't know what it was about the book that made it so impossible to read. I don't know if it was the odd characters, the dialogue, the physical settings, or the time period, but it just didn't hold my interest. I'd put the book back on the shelf and grab something else. But this Saturday morning, I suddenly found myself entranced. I was curious to know what would happen. The book is a classic, isn't it? It ought to be worth my reading. Did you ever read this book?

I read it in college.

It's funny, I never did go to college. When I was a seventeen-year-old, I was singing rock 'n' roll with the boys in Trevor's garage, and by the time I was nineteen, I was rich and famous. There was never any need for me to attend college. Everything I've learned since high school, I've learned on my own. I'm not bragging about it. It's just the way it was.

I understand.

It's taken me a while to learn certain things.

What sort of things?

It seems to have taken me forever to get a handle on my place in the world. I'm not talking as in whether I should be a musician, or actor, or writer, but I'm talking about how I relate to other people. When I was growing up, everything was all about me. My parents dedicated every waking moment of their lives to me, their only son. I felt like a kid being groomed and educated to be a king. It was all about Scowl, about what his interests were, about what his talents were. I think I've told you before how I was raised, how my parents introduced me to every subject, how they nurtured me, how eager they were to see what sort of life I'd latch onto.

Yes, I remember talking about it.

When my father first heard me singing with the band in Trevor's garage, he sat me down that night at the kitchen table and said, "Son, I don't know much about singing or music and even less about rock 'n' roll, but I know you're going to be a star. I can tell by the way kids listen to you sing. I can tell by the way they react to your voice." And what my father said turned out to be right. I think he knew more about me than I knew about myself, and was it any wonder? His world revolved around me. I was the sun in his solar system, the center of his suburban universe. Mom and Dad both adored me, and never once did I feel unloved or disregarded. They were the best parents ever. When I spoke, they hung on my every word. I was overindulged, pampered, and spoiled. It's true that when Dad told me I'd be a star, I believed him. I had no reason to doubt him. After all, he was my dad.

What was it like when you first sang with the boys in Trevor's garage? How did it feel?

Music was everything, especially after that talk with my dad. In a way, he lit the fuse. I'd go to school each day and sit in class, daydreaming, thinking about going to Trevor's garage to practice. We'd start right after school and play until dinnertime. It was so exciting. We knew we were onto something big. But it's my parents I really need to tell you about. For better or worse, it was my parents who made the difference.

What do you mean for better or worse?

I'll get to that. Do you ever work in your yard? I don't do much yard work here at Dulcinea because we have a full-time gardener, but I do have my own flower box at the front of the house. This flower box belongs to me and me only. It's my little piece of God's earth. I buy plants for it, tend to them, and water them every day. It keeps me grounded. The planter is about two feet by five feet, and it's currently full of healthy hydrangeas. The plants were not always thriving. Several months ago, they were wilting and dying, and I figured it was because they were either getting too much sun or not enough water. I'd always heard that hydrangeas require a lot of water, so I watered the crap out of them. I hosed the soil morning, noon, and night, making sure the ground was always damp, but it seemed like the more I watered the soil, the worse the plants looked. Finally, I went to the nursery where I purchased the plants and asked the guy there what the deal was. He asked me what the symptoms were, and I explained the plants' leaves were turning yellow and often falling off, that the flowers were small and droopy.

What was the problem?

It turned out I was overwatering the plants. Can you believe it? It had nothing to do with them being dry or getting too much sun. Do you know what happens when you overwater hydrangeas? A fungus grows on the roots and disrupts the biology of the plants. The roots become brown and mushy, and eventually the whole plant just keels over and dies. Great Scott, what an idiot I had been! When I got home, I removed all the infected hydrangeas from my planter, and I cleaned out the soil. I planted new ones, and rather than watering them three times a day, I watered them carefully just once each morning. I made sure to keep the soil moist, but not soaking wet. Did you see all my hydrangeas when you came in through the front door? What did you think? They're thriving like there's no tomorrow. Plants need water to grow, and that's a fact of life. But sometimes withholding water is necessary to keep them from dying. Do you understand what I'm trying to say?

Not exactly.

I'm trying to say that my parents should have withheld some of their love and attention from me, that I was overwatered as a child.

That's a curious way of looking at it.

As an adult I've paid a terrible price. In fact, one could argue that I've never really had a chance to become a real adult. I'm often self-centered and conceited, like a bratty little kid, and I've never been the same kind of parent to my own sons that my parents were to me. I'm talking especially about Roger. That poor kid. What the heck was I thinking? Why didn't I reach out to him years ago? Now he's died alone and without me, all by himself in that filthy, abandoned apartment building. He passed away separated from those he loved, apart from those who loved him. At the very least, I should have been there to say goodbye. Roger was a victim, not just of me, but he was a victim of my parents' love for me. It's not that

Mom and Dad's hearts weren't in the right place, but they taught me that the most important person in the world was Scowl. I was raised to love and admire myself at the expense of everything and everyone else. The young girls screamed, and I knew they wanted me because I was worth it. Adults pandered to me because I was great. Money poured into my bank accounts because I deserved it. My interviews with you were popular because I was interesting, and the world wanted to know more about me. Everything was always all about Scowl. Even when I moved to San Francisco after Kennedy was shot, the move was all about me. It was all about me, me, me. I was thinking only about myself. I left my dear wife and child behind. Can you imagine that? I left them to fend for themselves, and for what? So that I could meditate and drop acid in a rundown house? It was all about Scowl and never about Audrey or Roger. I had learned at a very young age to consider myself as the most important person in the world. Through their devotion to me, my parents created a sort of monster. Thanks to them, and to me, Roger never had a real father. Thanks to all of us, Roger died alone. Lonely, defeated, and alone.

Are you angry with your parents?

No, of course not. They were good people, and they did what they thought was right. How can I expect them to have known what it's taken me forty-six years to learn, that the more attention you pile on your children, the worse parents they will be?

Isn't it true you reached out to Roger? Wasn't Bill's Guitar *an attempt for the two of you to finally get to know each other?*

Maybe it was, and maybe it wasn't. Maybe I wanted to be rewarded. Maybe I was just hoping others would see me as a good man. Or maybe I wanted Roger to assuage all the guilt I felt. It may have had nothing to do with loving him or truly caring for him. Lately I've been thinking that everything I ever said to you previously about Roger was a lie.

How old was Roger? I mean, when he died.

He was twenty-one. When they found him, he had only a few things in his pockets. There were three one-dollar bills and some change, and there was an expired driver's license. There was a tiny packet of heroin and a couple joints. In his back pocket was the folded-up Cherokee legend I gave him. I was surprised he hadn't thrown this away, and now it seemed like such an empty gesture on my part. I had given him a useless piece of paper that obviously did him no good. The police kept the heroin and marijuana but gave me the other personal effects. It broke my heart taking this stuff, and it seemed so pathetic. Twenty-one years living on this planet, and this was all he had to show for himself.

How's Audrey holding up?

About as well as can be expected.

Have you told her any of what you've told me today?

No, I haven't told her any of this.

Before we end this interview, is there anything else about Roger you'd like to day?

I told you I've been reading *Moby-Dick*. Yesterday I set the book down in my lap and fell asleep. I had the strangest dream. I imagined I was Captain Ahab, and my family and friends were the crew of the *Pequod*. The great whale was my passion, and I was in pursuit, ready to get him at any cost. I didn't care what happened to the crew, whether they were washed into the ocean or even killed. And I didn't care what damage was done to my ship. I only wanted to hunt down the elusive Moby-Dick once and for all. I pictured myself hobbling around on deck, shouting out orders like a madman, stumbling and tripping over my own whalebone prosthesis. Yes, Captain Ahab was a man I could identify with. I knew exactly what it was like to think only of one's self, to blindly put others in harm's way, and to endanger those you supposedly love. In this pursuit of the beast, I risked my son Roger, and the waves kicked up and splashed across the ship's deck, taking Roger with them. He was forever lost in the cold depths of the sea without a further word. He was gone, just like that. You asked if I spoke to Audrey about any of this, and I said no. But the truth is that there is nothing to say to her that I haven't already said. I've apologized many times for ignoring the boy, but the apologies are hollow. What was needed from me was decisive action, not now, but years ago. My chance to stand like a man and do something has come and gone. Now there's nothing left for me to do but lament the past and cry like a woman.

Night and Day

———— •◦• ————

S hortly after the Disneyland strike of 1984, Scowl decided to take Alex to the theme park. He asked Jen if she wanted to come along, but she opted to stay home. She would have liked to have gone, but she thought it would be good for them and Frank to enjoy a boy's day out. Alex was now seven, the perfect age for the park. It wasn't often that Scowl went out in public because he was still very popular, and people recognized him easily. Fans could be very annoying, staring at him, taking pictures of him, and asking him for his autograph. During the months preceding the trip, Scowl had been spending a lot of time indoors working on another book, and he'd grown long hair and a beard. All this hair provided a good disguise, but also to play it safe, he decided to bleach his hair blond and put on a large pair of sunglasses that covered half his face. Then, satisfied he wouldn't be recognized, Scowl had Frank drive him and Alex to Anaheim.

Frank had lost a lot of weight since Haight-Ashbury. He wasn't what you'd call thin, but he wasn't the giant mass of flesh that he once was. Don't get me wrong, Frank was still an imposing figure, well over six feet tall and weighing about two hundred-thirty pounds. Next to a man like Scowl, he appeared even bigger than he actually was, so he still made an excellent bodyguard. He had dedicated himself to keeping Scowl, Jen, and Alex safe, and in doing so, he'd become one of the family. He often dined with them, attended family holiday functions, and went with them on excursions. Frank had never married, and so he had no children. But he liked kids, and he especially liked Alex. The boy loved the big man and always called him his uncle. Frank often spent time with Alex at Dulcinea, teaching him to catch and throw a baseball, playing hide-and-seek, and playing basketball in the driveway. When Scowl told Frank they were going to Disneyland, Frank was elated since he'd never been there before. He was nearly fifty now, but he suddenly felt like a little kid. When they finally went, Frank had the time of his life. It was following this trip to Disneyland that Scowl invited me over for an interview. He said he wanted to talk about Disney. I came over and waited for Scowl on the sofa, talking to Frank while Scowl was in the shower. Frank told me a few things about the trip, about the rides they went on, all the food they ate, and what a great time they had.

Prior to my coming over, Scowl had been working on his book. We'd recently talked several times on the phone, but he hadn't told me anything about the book other than that he'd been working on it. The plot was a mystery to me. I always thought it was curious, the love-hate relationship Scowl had with writing, the way he complained about it and then spent so much time doing it. Neither of his previous books had been best sellers, and the *Bill's Guitar* story was an absolute flop when it was made into a movie. Yet he still had a passion for reading and writing that wouldn't let up. It was a little surprising, and Scowl was always so unpredictable, so that just when you thought you had a handle on what made him tick, he'd take an unexpected turn. This new book was such a turn. I really never expected him to start writing another novel. When he called me to meet, I was hoping we could discuss it because I wanted to know just what the heck the book was about.

Scowl was in a good place in light of Roger's recent death. I was impressed that Scowl was able to bounce back from the tragedy and move on with his life. I remembered when Claudia died, how hard he had taken the loss, and how long it took him to get over it. I'm guessing that a lot of his ability to deal with Roger's death came from having Jen at his side. She was still the light of his life, and I think her love and support meant the world to him. As I sat with Frank waiting for Scowl, Frank told me that Scowl had been spending a lot of time with Alex. He said they'd grown very close as father and son, and he said that Scowl was thrilled to be a dad. This fatherhood thing was new for Scowl, and I was glad to hear about it. When Scowl finally emerged, he was wearing a robe and his hair was wet from his shower. The hair was still blond, and to tell you the truth, it looked a little weird. Scowl went to the kitchen to brew some tea and then reappeared in the front room to sit with me. Frank got up and left the two of us alone.

How does it feel to be a blond?

I kind of like it. I did it to disguise myself at Disneyland, but now I'm growing kind of fond of it. What do you think?

It's different.

What do you think of the beard?

I haven't seen you with this much hair since San Francisco.

Jen doesn't like the beard. I told her I'd shave it when I'm done with my book.

How's the book coming?

It's coming.

Can you give us a clue what it's about?

No, I really can't.

Why all the mystery?

It's not that I want it to be a mystery. I just won't be ready to say anything to you about it until I'm done. I'm writing without an outline, and I've changed directions several times already. It's just kind of going where it's going. Great Scott, even I don't know what it's about, and I'm the one writing it.

When you called me for this interview, you said that you wanted to talk about Disneyland. You said it was very important. What's so important about Disneyland?

I just took Alex there. Did you know the last time I went was in 1955, the year they first opened? I think I was seventeen.

The park has changed a lot since then.

I suppose it has.

Did Alex enjoy it?

I think he had the time of his life, and so did Frank. Alex has always been a big Disney fan, and he loves Disney movies. His favorite movie growing up was *Bambi*. I can't tell you how many times he's watched that film. He knows every part by heart, every single line, every character, and every scene. I remember when he was younger, he'd wrap himself up in his favorite blanket, curl up on the sofa, and have us turn on the movie, and as soon as the movie was over, he'd tell us to rewind it and play it one more time. Have you watched *Bambi* recently? Do you know what it's about?

I remember bits and pieces. It's been a long time since I've watched it.

Bambi grows up with his mom. He's a white-tailed deer, and his father is the Great Prince of the Forest. Someday Bambi will mature and inherit his father's role. During his childhood, he makes friends with a skunk, rabbit, and a female fawn named Faline. All is going along just fine until the first winter, when his mother is shot and killed by a hunter. It is a horrible event, not the kind of thing you'd think was appropriate for little children. Seriously, killing Bambi's mother? What could be worse? Bambi finds himself distraught and alone, and the father takes his forlorn son home and looks after him, and when spring comes along, we discover Bambi has matured into a young stag. Bambi finds love with his childhood friend Faline. She is now a lovely doe, but pairing up with her is not so simple. Bambi has to fight another stag named Ronno to earn his right to Faline. He wins the battle, but as the story moves along, more problems come along. Bambi is separated from Faline by a wildfire. He survives the fire, as well as a frightening confrontation with dogs. It is one adrenaline rush after the other until the next thing you know you're at the end of the story. Bambi has been reunited with Faline and becomes the Great Prince of the Forest. He is proud, happy, and content, so I guess all's well that ends well. I've watched this movie several times with Alex, and I've observed the expressions on his face as he stares at the TV. It's remarkable the way he reacts to the story. When Bambi's mother is shot and killed, he's glued to the screen. Every time the mother dies, it's like he can't believe his eyes. He doesn't sob or cry out loud, but I can tell he's very upset. And he's equally affected by Bambi's fight with Ronno, and by the wildfire, and by the confrontation with the dogs. He's literally mesmerized by every tense moment. And it occurs to me this was the genius of Walt Disney, mixing joy and optimism with terror and heartbreak. It's masterful.

I take it you're a Bambi *fan?*

I'd rather see *Bambi* with Alex than watch most of the lame movies they're making these days. I think my son has excellent taste.

How are things between you and Alex?

God has given me a second chance at this fatherhood thing, and I'm taking it. I messed things up with Roger, and it ended tragically. But I think his death brought a whole new significance to my relationship with Alex. It has been like night and day. I know how bad things can be and how good they can be. I know the darkness and cold of night, as well as the light and warmth of day. And that's what life is all about, isn't it? The night gives meaning to the day, and the day gives meaning to the night. Right now, everything is clear and perfect and the sun is bright and shining. I wouldn't trade my current life for all the BMWs in LA. I'm on top of the world. I'm the Great Prince of the Forest. I have my son at my side, and I feel like I'm ready for anything.

Tell me about your trip to Disneyland. Did anyone there recognize you?

I had three people ask if I was Scowl. Each of them approached me carefully, like they were approaching a wild animal, and they said, "Are you Scowl?" I told them no, that I was often mistaken for him. They just stared at me sort of perplexed and then walked away. I'd have to say my disguise was pretty effective.

Which ride was Alex's favorite?

Without question it was the Matterhorn. I told Alex about the woman who died on the ride earlier this year. Do you remember her? She was thrown out of her car and landed in front of another. I told Alex we were going on a very dangerous ride, and I think this really got his attention. "Someone actually died?" he asked. Frank and I told him if he kept still in his seat and followed our instructions, he probably wouldn't have anything to worry about. Great Scott, you should've seen the look on his face. When we were done with the ride and climbed out of the car, Alex said it was the best ride he'd ever been on, and I think it had a lot to do with the story I told him about the woman who died. There's something about facing real danger that appeals to boys his age. He was like Bambi, with his life on the line. He was now confident and proud of himself, and I think he matured a whole year just by going on that silly ride.

Some critics have complained that Disneyland tries to manufacture happiness.

Some people will complain about anything. Why would anyone waste their time complaining about Disneyland? If you really want to complain about something, complain about alcoholism, child abuse, or war. Don't waste your time complaining about people taking some time off to have a little fun.

Can I ask you a personal question?

Sure, of course.

I heard it from a reliable source that you were going to AA meetings again. Is this true? Did you start drinking after Roger's death?

No, I didn't start drinking. But yes, I went to the meetings. Your source is correct about the meetings.

Did you think you might start drinking?

It wasn't that. I mean, I wasn't exactly craving a bottle of whiskey.

Then why go to the meetings?

I guess you can say AA is a way of life. It isn't just a thing you do to quit drinking. It provides you with a means to handle life's difficulties and to put faith in God. I find AA helps me to focus on God and to reach out to him. I suppose I could get the same thing out of going to church, but this way I don't have to listen to a lot of preaching.

I have another question. You probably have to pick your AA meetings carefully. Is being famous a nuisance?

Yes, at times it is, but at other times, it's a real blessing.

If you weren't a famous artist, what would you imagine yourself doing for a living?

That's a good question. I guess a lot of the pressure would be off, and people wouldn't expect so much out of me. I've thought about this question before, and I've never come up with much of an answer. But now that I've been to Disneyland, I think I have an answer. I might like to get a job doing something at the park. Maybe I'd be one of those people working at a souvenir shop, or a candy shop, or at the magic store. I think I'd really like working at the magic store, demonstrating the tricks to little wide-eyed kids, watching them stare in awe of the cheesy little illusions I can perform. You know, I've always liked to watch magic, the way it makes the impossible seem possible, the way it fills your heart with the hope that there's more to life than meets the eye. I think Disneyland would be a great place for a person like me to work. Just think about it. It has become a place where people from all over the world can come to be happy and enjoy themselves. Have you ever thought of all the diverse individuals the park draws in through its gates each day, people who otherwise don't even get along? Outside the walls of the park, they argue, fight, and resent one another. They tell lies about one another and stab one another in the back. Yet here they are at Disneyland, assembled with a single goal in mind—to smile and laugh. I think it would be a great life, working at Disneyland. I'd go home at the end of each day, feed the dog, eat dinner, kiss my wife, play with my kids, and maybe read a book before going to bed. Then I'd get up the next morning and go back to my job. I could definitely live like that.

Don't you think working at Disneyland would get old after a while? Don't you think you'd get tired of smiling all the time?

I guess there's no way of knowing until you've done it. Have you ever asked a Disneyland employee if he likes his job?

No, I haven't.

Neither have I.

THE SHOOTING

———— ◦•◦ ————

The shooting occurred January 12, 1985. It was just after three in the morning, and Frank was up late watching TV while Scowl was working on his book. Both Jen and Alex were sound asleep. An intruder named Dylan Clay climbed over the property line wall, made his way through the side yard, and then jimmied open one of the windows. Frank heard a creak from the window, and he went to investigate. He caught Dylan entering the house, so he called out for him to freeze. Rather than obey Frank, Dylan drew a handgun, aiming it toward Frank's head and mumbling something about his need to see Scowl right away. Frank tried to talk sense into the man, but rather than calm down, Dylan grew increasingly agitated. He told Frank to get Scowl and bring him into the room, or he'd let Frank have it. When Frank refused to get Scowl, Dylan grew irate and made good on his threat by shooting the gun. There was a loud explosion as the gun fired, and Frank fell to the floor holding his neck with both hands. Scowl heard the commotion and ran out of his study to the hallway near the kitchen to see what was going on. The man then aimed the gun at Scowl and demanded that he come into the kitchen and get down on his knees. My interview with Scowl at the hospital the following day describes all that happened next.

———— ⊗⊗⊗ ————

You've been through a lot. Are you sure you're ready to talk about this?
    Yes, I'd like to talk.
    What happened last night?
    I was working late in my study when I heard a loud gunshot. At first,

I wasn't sure what it was, and the last thing I suspected was a gun firing. I had no idea there was an intruder in the house.

What was the first thing you saw?

When I came through the hallway to the kitchen, Frank was on the floor, holding his neck with both hands, kicking his legs. He was obviously in a lot of pain. There was blood oozing from between his fingers, and he was moaning. I looked up and saw Dylan Clay standing several feet away. He was holding his gun and was now aiming the gun at me. He told me to come into the room and drop to my knees, and I did exactly as he said. He then began to rant. He was speaking loudly, almost shouting, and I was sure he was going to wake Jen and Alex. I didn't want them coming into the room and becoming a part of the situation. I was hoping the man would lower his voice, but he just kept going on and on.

What did he say?

He accused me of having sex with his wife and getting her pregnant. He said, "It was you who got Nancy pregnant. I know all about it. Don't try to convince me it wasn't you." When I asked who Nancy was, he told me how June had told him Nancy was pregnant. I then asked who June was, and he said she was Nancy's best friend. He said June lived across the street from them with Fred and also that Candice had confirmed the story. When I asked who Candice was, he said she was June's half-sister who lived over in Redondo Beach. None of this was making any sense to me, because I didn't know anything about any of the people he was naming. I told him I had no idea what he was talking about, and he said I was a liar. He said, "You're just like all the others. You ruin lives and think you can get away with it. You screw a man's wife and think it won't catch up to you. I'm here to make you pay for what you did to our family. You're going to pay." I was convinced the guy was out of his mind because nothing he was saying made a bit of sense, and when I told him to calm down, that I'd get to the bottom of things for him, he just grew angrier, like I was trying to stall him or lie to him. "What are we going to tell Evie?" he asked, and he asked it again over and over, as if there was no answer to the question. And I didn't have an answer. "Who's Evie?" I asked, and he said she was his eight-year-old daughter. "She's the victim in this mess you created, as if you cared. Why would you care who you hurt? What am I going to tell my daughter? What am I going to say to Evie?" As I pleaded with the gunman, trying to get him somewhere near to reality, I suddenly saw Jen appear in the hallway dressed in a nightgown. All the shouting had got her out of bed, and now she was standing there and wondering what was the heck was going on. I tried not to stare in her direction, hoping Dylan wouldn't notice that I'd seen her arrive. When he looked up for a moment to collect his thoughts, I motioned for Jen to leave the area before she was discovered. Jen hurried away to Alex's wing of the house, where she found him still sound asleep in his bed. She took him to the master bedroom, where she used the phone to call 911. During this time Dylan was still ranting, and I was still down on my knees. My arms and legs were shaking, for I was sure this lunatic was going to shoot me soon. Suddenly Luis appeared from the back door. Thank God for Luis.

Luis is your groundskeeper?

Yes, he'd heard the gunshot and all the shouting from his apartment over the garage, and he came to the house to see what was going on. Dylan didn't see Luis approaching from behind, and Luis crept up on him. Frank was still on the floor. He had stopped kicking his legs, but blood was now coming out of his mouth. It wasn't looking good for Frank. Then, in an instant, Luis tackled Dylan and the two of them hit the floor. Luis knocked the gun free, and he got Dylan in chokehold. With his legs wrapping up the rest of Dylan's body, he held him while I grabbed the gun. I knew Luis was an ex-Marine, but I never thought his hand-to-hand combat training would come in so handy. I got up from the floor and pointed the gun at Dylan, telling him to hold still. He looked at me, his eyes flashing with hatred, and he finally stopped resisting. His kept still for Luis, but he was still talking. "You're going to pay for what you did," he said. "I'll make you pay. Maybe not tonight, but I'll make you pay. Someday you're going to pay."

How was Frank?

Once Luis had Dylan under control, I kneeled beside Frank and yelled for Jen to get some towels. I honestly didn't know what to do. Blood was still oozing from the neck wound and dribbling from Frank's lips, and when Jen appeared with the towels, I wiped off some of the blood and pressed on the bullet hole to stop the bleeding. Finally, when the first responders arrived, Jen met them out in the driveway and brought them into the house. The next thing I knew the house was filled with uniformed paramedics and police officers. There must have been ten or twenty of them. Some attended to Frank, while the others handcuffed Dylan and took him outside to a patrol car. It was all such a blur, and none of it seemed real. Alex was now in the hallway crying and wanted to be with his uncle Frank, but Jen kept him by her side, away from the commotion. I was introduced to a detective who began to interrogate me and take notes. He was all business, and he kept asking me if I knew who Dylan was.

Had you ever seen Dylan before?

I've never seen him before. That's the weird thing. I had no idea who this guy was, and I had no idea why he shot Frank.

How's Frank doing?

The doctors say he'll be okay. They sewed him up. I guess the bullet just grazed his carotid artery, but they say if it had hit the artery, he might not have made it.

Have you talked to your detective today?

Yes, I have. He said he tried to get a hold of Nancy early this morning, to tell her what happened and get her to the station for questioning. But it's looking more and more like Dylan isn't even married. The detective told me he thinks Dylan made the entire story up about his wife, her friends, and the half-sister in Redondo Beach. I don't mean he made it up as in making up a lie, but rather that maybe he believed what he told me, but it just wasn't true.

Just another crazy fan?

Crazy, yes. But you know, I don't know if I'd call Dylan a fan. I think he genuinely hates me. I don't have the impression he's ever been a fan.

Has Frank's family been notified?

I think we're all the family Frank has.

He's lucky to be alive.

Can you imagine if that bullet hit his artery? To be honest, I don't know what we'd do without Frank. He's been at my side for so long, and he's been such a good friend to Jen and Alex. I can't tell you how many times I've told Frank he ought to carry a gun, but he won't do it. He says guns are just too much trouble, that they make things worse than they have to be, not better. But when I saw him lying there on the floor of my kitchen, bleeding from his neck and mouth, a thousand memories flew through my head. When something like this happens, it's funny the way your mind flashes back. As I was pressing down on Frank's wound with those bloody towels, I was thinking back to people, places, and things having to do with Frank, and I was suddenly way back in San Francisco. Did I ever tell you how I first met Frank?

No, I don't think so.

When I first moved to the city, I didn't know a soul. When I went out in the evenings to nightclubs, I went out by myself. There was one club called Perigee West I used to visit where they featured a lot of folk music and poetry readers. You don't see that these days, where poets would just stand up on stage and read their work to an audience. Those years were great, somewhere between the beatnik age of the fifties and the crazy hippie years of the sixties. There was something energizing in the air back then, like all this poetry and folk music was somehow going to make a difference in the world, like we were all on the cusp of something remarkable. I'd go to Perigee West, and for the most part people there would leave me alone. At times some of them would recognize me, but they were usually polite and kept to themselves, pretending not to notice who I was. Frank was working at the club as a bouncer, and he kept the crowds under control. So long as Frank was there, I seldom saw anyone get out of line, even if they'd had too much to drink, or were having a bad LSD trip, or were just having a bad night for whatever reason. Frank was gigantic back then, which you probably remember when you came to visit. Do you remember when you first saw Frank? No one wanted any part of the guy. He was over three hundred pounds, lifted weights in his spare time, and had arms as thick as oak tree branches. As years went by, his weight became more cumbersome, and we talked him into going on a diet for his health.

I remember the first time I met Frank. He made me show my driver's license. I remember thinking he was the largest man I'd ever met.

Yes, that was Frank. He made quite an impression on those who came to visit. Some people liked him, but others didn't like him at all because he was so protective. I remember before I even knew him, one night while I was at Perigee West, one of the patrons took to giving me a hard time. This guy had recognized me as Scowl and was singing one of my songs satirically, making fun of the lyrics. He had way too much to drink, and his voice was really loud. It was sort of funny at first, but then I realized the man wasn't trying to make me laugh. He was trying to coax me into a fight, and he was also working hard to impress his girlfriend. The girl seemed more embarrassed than she did impressed, but the guy was relentless. Finally, he came close and began poking at my chest. "You think you're so special?" he said. "You think you're too good for me? Let's see how good you are." This was when Frank stepped in. He walked up to me and asked, "Is this guy bothering you, Mr. Scowl?" Frank always called me Mr. Scowl back then. It took him years to drop the mister and just call me Scowl. Anyway, I told Frank the man in the club was indeed bothering me, and Frank then stood between us. He asked the man politely to leave, and the man grew angrier. He clenched his fist and made the mistake of throwing a punch at Frank's face. With one giant paw, Frank snatched the fist right out of midair and held it tightly. He squeezed the man's hand and told him it was time for him to leave. The harder he squeezed, the redder the man's face became. I don't think his face was turning red from anger so much as from the pain being inflicted by Frank. "Do we have an understanding?" Frank asked with one last squeeze. The man's eyes were now welling up with tears, and he nodded his head so that Frank would let go of him. He then grabbed his girlfriend, and they made their way to the exit door. "This isn't over," he said, turning around in the doorway. "You won't have this big goon to protect you everywhere you go." Then he walked out of the club with his girlfriend.

So what happened?

I stayed at the club until closing time, and when they were locking up, Frank told me he was going to walk me home. He said he didn't feel good about letting me walk home alone with that man possibly waiting for me in the dark. I accepted Frank's offer, and he walked me back to the house. I invited him in for a beer or marijuana, but he said he didn't drink or take drugs of any kind. I was able to coax him with food. I made us a couple hamburgers, and Frank and I talked for several hours in my kitchen, mostly about my music, my concerts, and some of the places I'd been to. I tried to bring up the subject of Frank's own background, but he said he didn't like talking about himself. So we continued talking only about me. Then it occurred to me that I could really use someone like Frank to guard the door. I was always getting curious fans and reporters knocking on the door and trying to get in. I didn't have many friends back then, but it seemed I had a lot of people who wanted to bother me. And I figured as the word got out that I lived at the address, things would only get worse. I told Frank I'd pay him twice what they were paying him at Perigee West and that all he'd have to do was protect my door. Without even thinking about it, he said yes.

Did Frank ever tell you about his past?

He's never has told me much of anything, and I haven't pried. I've always assumed that he wanted his history kept private for a reason. It didn't matter to me.

Aren't you even curious?

I guess I did used to wonder, but now I don't care. Frank has been at my side for twenty years, and I think I know all I need to know about the man. He is one of a kind, a true friend, and I'm glad he's now going to be okay.

CIRRHOSIS

It was in September 1985 that Tipper Gore, the wife of Senator Al Gore, gave her testimony before a congressional hearing to advocate warning labels on music albums. The point of these labels was to inform parents of offensive lyrics in the songs, the sort of lyrics that Gore believed were inappropriate for children. The music business was outraged, and lots of well-known artists spoke out. But Gore had a lot of support, and to help solidify her cause, she founded the Parents' Music Resources Center. It was now all over the news. John Denver, Dee Snider, Frank Zappa, and other artists spoke out against Gore's plans, criticizing them as an attempt to censor popular music. Zappa likened Tipper's plans "some sinister kind of toilet training program to housebreak composers and performers." Scowl, on the other hand, had nothing to say, and Scowl's silence didn't really surprise me. He'd told me before how much he hated political and social causes. But a month following the hearings, he called for an interview. He said he wasn't going to stand on the sidelines any longer, that he had to stand up and speak out about Gore and his fellow musicians. I knew Scowl pretty well, but I had no idea what he was up to.

You said wanted to talk about Tipper Gore. What did you want to say?

I wanted to say that Tipper is cirrhosis.

That's it?

Do you know much about cirrhosis?

Not really.

It results from abusing alcohol, and it has all sorts of delightful symptoms. Your face breaks out with little telltale spider veins, and your fingernails and toenails become ugly and discolored. Your bones ache and all your fingers get deformed. If you're a man, your breasts become much larger, and they get oddly rubbery around the nipples. Then you'll experience a loss of sex drive, infertility, and even testicular atrophy. And if this isn't bad enough, your liver gets swollen or shrunken, depending on the stage of the disease, and eventually it just fails to do its job. Cirrhosis is irreversible; in other words, once you've got it, you've got it for life. Unless you take steps to stop it from getting worse, it will kill you. It's a slow and pitiful way to die. No, there are several ways you can get this illness, but the most popular is by means of abusing alcohol. When you see someone who always has a drink in his hand, who's always ready to pour another, say a little prayer for his poor liver. It's a bleak picture to paint, I know, but it's also a fact of life. Have I lost you with all this? You're probably wondering what this talk about cirrhosis has to do with Tipper Gore. It's simple, for she *is* cirrhosis.

I don't understand.

Let me try to explain it another way. How many people do you know who smoke cigarettes?

Actually, quite a few.

Is it any secret that smoking cigarettes can cause lung cancer?

No, of course not.

Yet these people you know smoke anyway.

Yes, they do.

Then Tipper Gore is also lung cancer. She is lung cancer and cirrhosis both. She's a destructive and life-threatening disease, yet we can't seem to keep her at bay. Why do you suppose this is?

I still don't understand.

Gore found her calling with one of Prince's records. Do you know which Prince song prompted her to go on the warpath? It was "Darling Nikki." Have you ever listened to the words to this song?

No, I haven't.

There's a reference to masturbating in the song. It was more than she could take, the thought of her children walking around the house singing the song to themselves, singing about masturbating. How would you feel about your own young children walking around the house singing a song about masturbating? Would this bother you?

Probably.

Not to sound like I'm changing the subject, but do you like eating sunflower seeds?

Pardon me?

Do you like sunflower seeds—you know, salted and in the shell? You can buy them in cellophane bags at the gas station or grocery store.

No, I don't eat them.

I went on a sunflower seed binge last year, munching on the seeds practically everywhere I went. I was addicted to the darn things. The main problem with eating sunflower seeds comes down to disposing of the shells. There just doesn't seem to be any good way of dealing with them. I discovered the best place to eat the seeds was in my car, where I could flick the shells out the car window and be done with them. Did you know it's illegal to do this? I was pulled over by a police officer for flicking my shells out my window, and he explained to me that I was littering. "The fine for littering from a car window is eight hundred dollars," he said. "You've got to be kidding," I replied, and he proved he wasn't kidding by opening up his little ticket book and writing me a citation for littering. I couldn't believe the nerve of this guy. He was actually going to make me pay a fine for flicking a few sunflower seed shells out my car window. "I can't believe you're wasting time with this," I said. "Isn't there something more important you could be doing, like preventing murders or robberies? Why are we even spending time with this?" The cop politely listened to my objection, and he handed me my ticket. "Have a nice day," he said, and he walked back to his patrol car.

Did you fight the ticket?

I hired an attorney. He got the city to drop the matter, but retaining the attorney cost a couple thousand dollars. If I'd just paid the ticket, I would've saved twelve hundred bucks.

Do you still eat sunflower seeds?

Not anymore. They're too much trouble.

What does this have to do with Tipper Gore?

It has everything to do with her. Can you imagine what our streets would look like if littering wasn't against the law?

Then you agree with her?

I don't even like her, but I think she's what you get when you sell records to young people about masturbating. How old are your children?

They're sixteen and seventeen.

Do they always do what you say?

No, they don't.

My son Alex is now eight years old. Sometimes I feel like if I tell him not to stick his finger in an electrical socket, he'll wait until I leave the room and then stick his finger in the socket just to see what happens. Have you ever felt this way about your children?

Sure, at times.

Left to our own devices, adults aren't any better. We go to church every Sunday, and God teaches us to behave, but we can't help ourselves. We misbehave all the time. It's what makes us human. Misbehavior makes this world go around, and why do you suppose this is?

I don't know.

It's the proximity of consequences.

I'm not sure I follow you.

It's something my father taught me when I was a boy. "Don't be fooled by the proximity of consequences," he'd say, and it was great advice. But it was not always easy to follow. There's something about the way our brains are wired that makes the consequences of our actions always seem a hundred miles away, like they're always far off on the horizon, like they can only be seen with a pair of binoculars. But then you act out, and the next thing you know, the consequences are right in your face, nose to nose with you, whether you like them or not. We always act so surprised when it comes time to pay the piper. And this brings me to the subject of Tipper Gore. She is what you get when you poke your finger into an electrical socket. She's what you get when you drink too much or when you smoke cigarettes. She's what you get when you throw your trash out of your car window. And she's what you get when you sell records to children about masturbation. She is the consequence. Rock 'n' roll mailed this woman a formal invitation, and now she has arrived. She has her suitcase in hand and plans to spend the night. I can't think of a reason why anyone would be surprised about this visit. Rock 'n' roll should have seen this one coming a long time ago. Great Scott, did all these musicians really think no one was paying attention?

Now, I can't tell whether you agree with Tipper or not. Is she right? Or is she wrong?

She just is. And it's unfortunate.

Why is it unfortunate?

Because she's just a diversion. She's a tempest in a teapot. She's a ticket for throwing sunflower seed shells out a car window. Everyone is paying attention to her and her trivial objections while humankind's real obscenities go unnoticed.

The real obscenities?

What do you consider obscene?

I don't know.

I can tell you what I think is obscene. I think war, for example, is obscene. I think everything about war is grossly obscene. I don't care who you're fighting, or who you're rooting for, or what side you're writing a patriotic song for, the act of war is hideously wrong and obscene. Plain and simple, it's about the slaughter of human lives, about shooting bullets into bodies, about blowing people to bloody bits of flesh and bone. It's about killing by all means possible, about maiming and dismembering without a second thought. It's a nefarious and disgusting enterprise for all concerned, but don't you find our raw and morbid infatuation for war fascinating? Look at the way we strut in our military clothing, wearing ribbons and medals, our shiny swords dangling archaically at our hips. We stand up straight and salute one another as we pass, and we respect our superiors. There are captains, lieutenants, admirals, and other whatnots all designated by ceremonious stripes and stars. Our uniforms are clean and well-pressed, and our hair is cut and combed. We honor all this ritualistic hoopla just for the privilege of killing and maiming, just for the right to plunge a bayonet into another's beating heart, just for the thrill of shooting another man or woman between the eyes. Back in the late sixties, I ran into a friend who'd just returned from Vietnam. For every person he killed, he cut off an ear. He kept the ears on a looped rope he kept on his belt, and by the end of his tour he'd accumulated quite a collection. He told me his greatest disappointment during the war was not being allowed to bring the ears home, not being allowed to show them off to his friends. Can you imagine this? This kid was a good friend of mine. Before the war, he was a normal, healthy teenage boy who liked to ride his bicycle around town and play basketball at our public park. I think war turns us into monsters, into warriors, and there is nothing in this world as evil and awful as a warrior. A warrior stands for all that is wrong with us, all that is despicable, and all we should be ashamed of.

Don't you think some wars are justified?

Like I said, I'm not talking about which side you're on. Never mind that. I'm talking about the act of war itself. It's far more obscene than any of the lyrics in any music album. I think it's a shame.

A shame?

What rock 'n' roll has become. It's a farce.

How so?

It is supposedly on the edge, but it isn't at all. We expect it to be brutally honest and in your face. Yet what has rock actually become? While the world is riddled with injustices and true obscenities, rock 'n' roll is at war with the likes of Tipper Gore, clanging swords in public over its right to sing to our children about masturbation. It's a joke. The little boy was right. The emperor has no clothes.

THE POP SINGER

———— •◦• ————

J ust a few months following the Tipper Gore interview, a Hollywood
director named Lester Small sent out a press release announcing his
upcoming movie. Small had recently become popular with two hit movies,
Calling You and *The Other World*. Small's release was picked up by many
papers, including the *LA Times*, and I read about the movie in the Sunday
edition. The article said the movie was written by Jennifer Kruse, Scowl's
wife, and the leading man in the movie would be played by Scowl. The
name of this film was *The Pop Singer*, and the announcement took me
completely by surprise. Scowl had never mentioned this movie in any of
our recent conversations, and I called him to see if the news was true.
Scowl confirmed it, and he said they were to start filming in a few months.
When I asked Scowl why he never told me about it, he said he didn't want
to tell me anything until it was a done deal. I told him I had no idea that
Jennifer had been working on a screenplay, and he said she'd worked on
quite a few of them.

It turned out that Jennifer had been writing for the past several years,
bouncing her scripts off Scowl and her father. *The Pop Singer* was the first
that her father thought had real potential, and he passed the script along
to his friend Lester Small. I asked Crabtree later why he didn't direct the
movie himself, and he told me was busy with other projects. But more
importantly, he felt that Jennifer would get more out of the experience if
she worked with someone other than her father, someone like Lester Small.
I knew Jennifer always had a serious interest in film, and that before she
met Scowl, she planned to follow in her father's footsteps to become a
director. When she married Scowl and gave birth to Alex, she decided to
be a mother and wife instead. But writing was something she was able to
do while Alex was in school and while Scowl was out working. I was excited

for Jennifer and hoped this would work out for her. When I'd called Scowl about the story in the *LA Times,* I asked if he wanted to do an interview about the movie. He said it sounded like a good idea, thinking it would drum up interest in Jennifer's film. We met the following day at Dulcinea, and when I arrived, Jennifer and Scowl were both seated on the front room sofa. Jennifer said to me, "Can you believe this? They're actually going to make a film from my screenplay, and the leading man will be my own darling husband. I'm sure you two have a lot to talk about, so I'll leave you alone." Jennifer then picked up an empty glass from the coffee table and left Scowl and me to talk.

So your wife is now a screenwriter?

She's been working very hard at it.

Can you tell me something about the story?

It's called *The Pop Singer.* It's a work of fiction, but a lot of it is autobiographical. It's the story of a girl who marries a famous singer, and it's told from the perspective of the girl.

So it's about you and Jennifer?

It's about a couple named Carla and Tom and their son, Jacob. It is a family similar to ours, but not identical. Jen wrote four previous screenplays, but her father felt they all lacked insight. He told Jen to write about what she knew, and she came up with this topic. She poured her heart and soul into this project, and I think it shows. I think the public is going to fall in love with it.

What exactly happens in the story?

If I told you, it would take all the fun out of seeing the picture.

Who's going to play Carla?

Lester has several actresses in mind, but he hasn't decided on one yet. She'll be a new face, not someone the public is familiar with.

What's it like to be married to a writer?

I think I like it. It's great to see Jen working on something she's passionate about. I think she has a lot of talent.

Have you learned anything from her screenplay?

Yes, a lot. I've learned a great deal about Jen and me. For one thing, I've learned how our relationship has changed over the years. When we first met, we were focused solely on each other. Jen was the shining light of my life, and everything I did was for her. And everything she did was for me. I was so lucky to find her and so utterly blessed to be married to her. She was lovely, optimistic, and vibrant, and I found a superhuman-like strength in her youth. She made me feel fantabulous, my good man, and I believed I alone could make her happy. I truly believed all we needed was each other. I remember when we would kiss, the sun would burst from the heavens into a thousand colors, and when we made love, all the earth would shake and the universe would heave and tremble. I know this all sounds corny, but it's the only way I know to describe our first years together. We were a force to be reckoned with.

You were in love.

Yes, we were in love. But now things are different. I don't mean to say we're not still in love, I just think things are different. Anyone who's been married a while knows what I'm talking about. We love each other dearly, but it's a different kind of love.

I think I understand.

And of course, there's Alex.

What about Alex?

A child is a huge responsibility. Jen knew this, and she took on most of the duties. I wish I could say that I helped a lot, but what I contributed to the effort was minimal. It's not that I do nothing, but Jen is really the backbone of our parenting. For years she's put her own aspirations on the back burner to see that her child is properly taken care of. I think it's easy for a woman to lose herself this way. And in Jen's screenplay, this is Carla's dilemma. She doesn't want to stop being a good wife and mother, yet she also wants to be more, to be her own person.

Is there a resolution?

Yes, in a way.

But you're not going to tell us about it?

No, I'm not. Like I told you, if you want to know what happens, you'll have to go see the movie.

How do you feel about working for Lester Small? It's been quite a while since you worked for anyone other than Crabtree.

I'm looking forward to working for Lester. I've seen his recent movies, and I think he has a talent for getting the most out of his actors. It will be interesting to see how he treats Jen's story, being he's a man. Have you ever read *Man and Superman* by Bernard Shaw?

I read it some time ago.

Jennifer's theme is similar to Shaw's, but instead of focusing on a husband's freedom, the woman is the center of attention. Isn't it interesting how the shoe's now on the other foot? Will Lester will find this difficult to relate to? Perhaps he should get some women on his staff to help. A woman's insight would help.

That makes sense.

Don't you think it's odd how we accept men telling us women's stories? It's like Elizabethan times when women weren't allowed on stage, when males played all the women's roles. Women are such fascinating creatures. They should really have a louder voice. We would get so much more out of it. How many famous women movie directors can you think of who are working today?

Not many.

I can think of only a few.

Do you mind if I change the subject?

Sure, be my guest.

How are things coming on your book?

I'm still working on it.

The last time I asked you, you didn't feel like talking about it. Are you finally ready to reveal what the book is about?

I'm not sure I know, and I'm not sure I'm cut out for being an author. This project is really getting the best of me. Did you know I'm now forty-eight? Heck, I'm almost fifty. All my life I believed the older I got, the wiser and more mature I'd be. I thought all my life experiences would make me sage and knowing, the sort of person people would look up to, the sort of person who would have great and wise things to say. Yet sometimes it feels like just the opposite, like I'm actually regressing, like the older I get, the less I know. When I started this book, I wanted it to be special, a penultimate novel about everything I'd learned. I didn't write an outline, for I wanted the story to emerge organically from my life experiences. I wanted to write something amazing and inspirational. Now you're asking me about it, and you want to know what it's about. Heck, I don't even know if I know what it's about. I began with a plot in mind, but I've gone back and rewritten the story so many times that I don't even remember where it started. I thought I had so much to say, but now it seems like I'm speechless. You'd think I could just put it down and move on to something else, but it's become an obsession. I think about it all the time. I can't wait for afternoon to roll around so I can work on it again, reading what I've written, rewriting page after page, adding paragraphs and adding new chapters. I've already wrote over nine hundred pages, and I'm nowhere near the end. It's going to wind up being longer than *War and Peace,* and I honestly don't know if any of it will be worth reading.

The book sounds intriguing.

That's only because you haven't read any of it.

I heard you're writing some new songs for Lester's movie. Tell me about the songs. It'll be nice to hear some new music from you. Will you be releasing a new album?

Yes, I plan to cut a new album. I haven't released an album since Christmas four years ago. This one will be titled *The Pop Singer,* just like the film. It'll include some of the movie's songs and some others. I've got some good ideas, and I've scribbled them down on paper when not working on the book. There'll be some songs for Tom and Carla, but also a few that are specifically about Jen and me. I'd like to write some lyrics that show my love for my wife, that express the way I still feel for her. I think she deserves a few new songs written about her. I'd also like to include some songs about Alex. I don't want to leave Alex out. A child is truly a gift from God. Do you remember watching your own children when they were Alex's age, how much joy they brought you?

Yes, of course.

I always wondered if Alex would grow up to be like me, but he's turning out different than I ever expected. Do you know what he's interested in?

No, I don't

He's crazy about sports. He says he plans to become a professional athlete. He plays baseball, basketball, and football, and his bedroom walls are covered with posters of famous athletes. He collects pictures, autographs, and trading cards and practices at these games for hours and hours after school. Jen takes him to and from his games, and I go to a lot of them. He's quite gifted, and his coaches love him. You wouldn't believe how serious these competitions get, how important it is for the kids to win. There's a lot of pressure on the kids, but they seem to revel in it. I used to feel the same way about my singing and music, seeing it as a challenge and doing my best to live up to everyone's expectations. I think some kids like that pressure, and it brings out the best in them. I can still remember performing with our band in Trevor's garage while my parents were watching. They'd glance around at our audience to be sure everyone was enjoying what they heard. They were so happy. They were happy to see me doing something they knew I loved and even more happy to see others enjoying it. How many parents are able to do this, to watch their children pursue a dream? And this is the way it feels to watch Alex. He's so good at what he's doing. I don't know if this will translate to a future in professional sports, but for the time being, he believes that he's on the right track. He's letting nothing get in his way. I'd like to think I had something to do with his drive, that he got his fever to succeed from me.

He does sound determined.

Yes, he is.

Are you a typical sports parent?

What do you mean?

Do you scream and yell during his games?

Maybe a little. But I try to keep my emotions under control. To tell you the truth, I didn't participate much in sports when I was a boy, so I'm not really sure of a lot of what is going on. I like to bring Frank with me to help explain the rules. Frank's a big sports fan, and he knows a lot. Frank knows when to jump up and give me high fives. I get a kick out of that. It's also nice to have him by my side in case someone gets out of line.

Do the other parents bother you?

Sometimes they ask for autographs. I've had a couple of them ask to have their picture taken with me. It's been nothing we haven't been able to handle.

People in your area are probably used to seeing celebrities.

Yes, that helps.

BOOK BURNING

—•●•—

Production started on *The Pop Singer,* but I hadn't heard from Scowl. I did hear some things from others. I heard from a mutual friend that Lester Small was aggravated. I heard that Scowl was having difficulty concentrating, that he was forgetting his lines and stumbling over the ones he could remember. I also heard Scowl still hadn't written any of the songs he promised for the movie. This news was surprising, because during our last conversation, he seemed excited about working on the film. Then I heard from Jen. She said Scowl was driving her crazy, and she hoped that I could help. She wanted me to call and convince him to stop working on his book. The book had now become more than just a minor distraction. His book was taking over every aspect of his life, and he couldn't pull himself away from it. What was I supposed to say? Scowl was just Scowl. I couldn't remember him ever listening seriously to anything I had to say. He'd run ideas past me on occasion, and he'd listen to my questions and provide answers, but that was about the extent of our relationship. I was just Ralph, first and foremost a journalist, not someone who could tell him what to do. Nevertheless, I told Jennifer I'd give him a call.

I spent hours thinking about the call before I made it, how I would preface my advice, how exactly I would phrase my words, and what I would do when the whole thing blew up in my face. Yes, I was nervous. I was conspiring with his wife to stop him from working on one of his passions, and this kind of thing could have repercussions. My advice might make Scowl angry. He might get angry and call me a traitor. My words could even mean an end to our interviews, and I think I feared this the most. Just two days after Jennifer asked me to call Scowl, I phoned him at home. Jennifer answered the phone and handed the receiver over to her husband. I listened to Scowl's voice. "I know why you're calling," he said. "Jen told me what she asked you to do. Listen, why don't you just come over here to Dulcinea. There's no use doing this over the phone. You need to meet me at my fireplace." I had no idea what the fireplace had to do with writing his book, but I agreed to come. When I arrived at Dulcinea, it was freezing cold and pouring the rain. I parked my car in the driveway and ran to the porch, trying to keep dry. I rang the doorbell, and Frank answered. "He's in the front room," he said. I hung my wet jacket on the coatrack in the foyer, and I walked toward the front room. As I entered, there was a flash of lightning and the thunder boomed. It was like an eerie scene out of a movie, and after the lightning and thunder, there was nothing but the sound of rain pounding the roof and the crackle of logs burning in the fireplace. I saw there were no lights on in the room. There was only the yellow and orange flickering of firelight dancing on the walls, ceiling, and furnishings, and Scowl was seated on the floor near the fireplace hearth. In his hands he had a thick stack of papers. "Sit down beside me," he said. "We're going to take care of business."

"What are we going to do?" I asked. Scowl smiled and said, "Don't worry, you won't have to talk me out of the book. I've already come to an agreement with Jen. I'm done with it." I asked if that meant he was finally done writing the book, and Scowl chucked and said, "No, it will never be done. I mean it's done as in you and I are about to burn it all in this fire. I deleted all the computer files before you got here, and this paper manuscript is my only remaining copy. Page by page we're going to watch as this infernal book is consumed by flames until nothing is left but ashes. Then it'll be finished." I asked if he was sure he wanted to do this, and Scowl said, "Oh, yes, I'm very sure. It has to be done. I've asked God for the strength, and he's given it to me. Let's hurry before it wears off. Why don't you interview me while we're doing this?" I agreed to this idea, and the interview that was published three days later is the conversation I had with Scowl during the rest of our evening together, as we burned his book, all one thousand two hundred and eighty-six pages of it. I didn't have a recorder with me, so the interview was from memory.

⸻ ⚬⚬⚬ ⸻

The weather is perfect for this, isn't it? I couldn't have written a better setting. *They say it's going to rain all night.*

That's a good thing.

Why are we burning your book?

Do you know anything about Uncle Remus?

I've heard of him.

What do you know?

He was a fictional slave who would sit and tell tales to children. I think the stories were all published in a book, sort of like Aesop's Fables.

The stories were written up and published by a writer named Joel Chandler Harris. I did some reading on this subject last year. They were published as a book in 1881, and they were very popular at the time. Br'er Rabbit is often the protagonist of the tales, a likeable, troublemaking character. Also in the stories are Br'er Fox and Br'er Bear, who often oppose the rabbit. It's said the stories were passed down through generations of African Americans. Disney made a movie about them called *Song of the South*. Not long ago, especially during the civil rights movement of the sixties, Harris's work was criticized for its stereotypical portrayal of black slaves and for the use of old plantation dialect. But I think we've overcome that now, and his stories are regarded fondly as classics. Have you ever read an Uncle Remus story?

I may have.

Are you familiar with the Tar-Baby?

Yes, I am.

That was an Uncle Remus story. I've had more than forty different working titles for my book. One of the titles I was considering was *The California Tar-Baby*. I don't think I ever told you that.

No, you didn't.

Do you remember the tar-baby story? The fox builds a doll from a lump of tar, and he dresses it in a baby's clothing.

Yes, I sort of remember that.

He leaves the tar doll for the rabbit to find. When the rabbit comes across the doll, he says hello, but being just a lump of tar, the doll says nothing back. Offended by the doll's lack of manners, the rabbit takes a swing at it, and its fist sticks into the tar. As the story goes, the more the rabbit punches and struggles with the doll, the worse he becomes entangled in the sticky mass. With the rabbit now stuck to the doll, the fox flings the rabbit into the briar patch, where the rabbit is able to get free of the doll and escape. It's a good ending. It's good for me, anyway. This is what I'm doing here at the fireplace; I've been tossed into the briar patch, and page by burning page, I'm making my escape.

I'm not sure I understand.

In AA we recite something called the serenity prayer. We say, "God, grant me the serenity to accept the things I cannot change, the courage to change the things I can, and the wisdom to know the difference." You've probably heard this prayer before.

Yes, I have.

Would you agree that wisdom is a rare commodity?

I would agree with that.

Have you ever been addicted to anything?

I can't say I have.

I've been addicted to two things in my life, the first being alcohol and the second being this confounded book. Don't you think it's interesting that both addictions began with a family death? My drinking followed Claudia's death, and this book followed the passing of Roger. I learned a lot from my alcohol addiction, but mainly that turning to booze to drown sorrows only backfires in the worst way. I promised I'd never let that happen again, and when Roger died, I tried hard not to repeat my alcoholic behavior. I promised that instead that I would do something powerfully constructive in his memory, and I decided to write this book. It would be a great work, something I could dedicate to Roger on the opening page. This book was enormously important to me. It was something far beyond a bound and typeset piece of entertainment for my fans. It was meant to be my masterpiece. I would say what a million writers before me have tried to say, and I would sum everything up like no one before. My book would be published in every different language, and the world would read it in awe. I know it now sounds a little crazy now, but that's what I was thinking when I began writing. And I honestly felt I could do it. People loved me, didn't they? Didn't I have a finger on their pulse? Didn't even my biggest critics often praise my work? All I had to do was set my mind to it and write it.

What was the book about?

It was about everything.

I mean what was the plot?

There were plots and subplots, and there were plots within the subplots. Just keeping the plots all straight kept me up at nights.

Did you have a main character?

Yes, his name was Arnold Simon.

Isn't that your given name?

It's my first and middle names.

So is the main character you?

Not me exactly. He's more like an alter ego. But the story was written in the first person, so I guess you could say it was me. You asked me for the story's plot, and I wish I could tell you more. It would help if I told you how the story starts, but it has no beginning. I would give you a rundown of the characters, but there are just too many to list. I really attempted to stay on task with this project, but every time I tried to get a handle on what was going on, things would suddenly split and veer in a multitude of different directions. Each day I'd begin afresh, giving it another shot. I'd sit down in front of my computer screen and pull up the story file, and I'd go steadfastly to work. It would always be exciting. There was this amazing feeling I'd get when I'd begin, something I'd compare to the euphoria of a first drink, or snorting a line of coke, or taking a hit from a hash pipe. It was a feeling of intense optimism, knowing that everything was going to be okay, that I was on the right track, that all the pieces to this puzzle were going to fall neatly in place. Then it would happen.

What would happen?

The euphoria would come crashing down, giving way to panic and frustration. I'd find myself frantically reading and rereading all I wrote, writing over again, cutting and pasting paragraphs and sentences, looking for new words in my thesaurus. I'd do this for hours straight, pausing only for dinner. Even during dinner I'd pretend to be listening to Jen and Alex, while actually I was concentrating on my book. I'd carry my dirty dishes to the kitchen sink and then go back to my study. I'd stay up late until the early hours of the morning, and by the time I finally went to bed, I'd be thoroughly exhausted and befuddled. As the days, weeks, and months passed, this obsession became worse. It was incredible. I was hooked on writing the book, locking myself in my study every single day like a mad scientist in his laboratory. Then along came Jennifer's movie. I was being forced to shave my beard and go to work with Lester, yet what did I actually spend my time doing? I brought my laptop to the movie set and spent all my free time working on the book. Every time I fired up the laptop, I had this burst of optimism and enthusiasm, like I did at home, like I was on the verge of pulling everything together. And again, I would fail. Lester was getting angry, and others on the set were growing impatient. I was botching my role in Jennifer's movie, and I knew it. Do you know what they say about insanity? They say it's doing the same thing over and over and expecting different results. According to that definition, I guess I was insane. I was addicted to writing this ridiculous book, this masterpiece, this bizarrely complicated conglomeration of words, paragraphs, and pages. And I needed help. And that's when Jen called you.

I had no idea.

There was nothing you could have done. I had to hit rock bottom.

You hit rock bottom?

Lester gave me an ultimatum yesterday. He said it was either the book or the movie. I made my decision with Jen just a few hours ago, and I chose the movie. And so here we now are, sticking papers into the fireplace. I really needed to stop the writing. I needed to put an end to the entire life-consuming affair, and I'm feeling better with each page we burn.

Aren't you disappointed?

I'd be lying if I said I wasn't. No one likes to be a failure, and I set out to do something that I'm apparently incapable of doing. But it's like Clint Eastwood said, "A man has got to know his limitations." Do you remember which movie that's from?

No, I don't.

It's from *Magnum Force*. Eastwood plays the infamous Dirty Harry Callahan. It's a classic movie line, one of the best. Did you see the movie?

I never saw it.

Are you a movie fan?

I like a good film.

What do you think of movies? I mean, how do you think they'll go down in history? I don't mean as in our current history, but as in history a long time from now, way into the future. Books have survived the ages, haven't they? They're timeless, simple, and don't require sophisticated technology to be enjoyed. You simply write the book, and a person can open it up and read. It's really as simple as that. In order to see a movie, you need electricity, and then you need a video cassette, or DVD, or film reels, and you need some sort of TV or movie projector and screen to see it. So will movies really survive the test of time? What do you think?

I've never really thought about it.

I've always thought the simpler the medium, the longer it will last.

I suppose that makes sense.

They say a picture is worth a thousand words, thus the popularity of the movie. But take Harry Callahan's famous line. I say a good sentence is worth a thousand pictures. Which do you think it is?

I guess I prefer the words.

That's because you're a writer. You understand the clean beauty of words, of one man sitting down in a room and typing, of another man reading. It's so simple and yet so wonderfully complex. With mere words a writer can take his reader to worlds he's never dreamed of and places he'll never see. The reader can be the world's greatest lover, most beautiful woman, or richest industrialist. He can climb the highest mountain, trek the driest deserts, and traverse the stormiest seas. In a single well-written sentence, the author can summon up a lesson that it took a lifetime for him to learn. There are no limits to the potential of a book. It's deceivingly simple, yet I think it's the most powerful means of communication ever put into play. It's louder than any public address system and more colorful than any rainbow. When I was a teenager, I didn't care much for books. I thought reading was a bother. Books had too many words and took too long to take in, but as I grew up, I developed a love and respect for books. I think I now admire authors more than I admire anyone. It's not that I don't love and respect other artists; I just think writing is incomparably special. It's taxing and time-consuming. It requires the utmost patience, intelligence, and skill. It's a venture best tackled by the best of the best. Many try their hand at it, but truly great books are far and few between. I ought to know.

Do you think you'll try writing another book, maybe after a few years have passed?

No, never.

A Broken Nose

———•———

When *The Pop Singer* was about to be released to theaters, Jennifer was a nervous wreck. Lester Small was certain they were sitting on a hit, but there was no way of knowing until the public saw it. In the meantime, Scowl's album with the same title was put on the market, and it was being well-received. The song "My Two Sons" was the most popular, and it got the most radio time. The song was about Roger and Alex, about how Scowl had worked his way through the tragedy of Roger's passing and was finally making things right through his love for Alex. It was a very touching song, but in my opinion, what drew people to it was the fact that it was based on a true story. People liked true stories, and they like happy endings. The song had both components. The only person who expressed a dislike for the song was Audrey, who was quoted as saying it was "too little, too late." I felt her criticism was unfair, given that Audrey had never encouraged Scowl to spend any time with Roger. She barely allowed the boy to act in *Bill's Guitar.* I think she was bitter about how the whole movie thing went down, but in my opinion, what happened wasn't Scowl's fault.

In the meantime, Scowl was spending a lot of time with Alex, especially now that he was done with his book and Jennifer's movie. Scowl went out of his way to learn more about sports, hoping it would bring him closer to Alex. He went to the store and purchased a stack of books on sports, and he took time out of each day to watch the news and talk shows on ESPN. He brought Alex with him to several Laker games, where they sat courtside along with other wealthy ticket holders, and he promised to take him to Dodger games when the season started. But most importantly he went to Alex's own games. Alex was leaning toward baseball as his favorite sport, and it was during one of his baseball games that the media got hold of the big story. Frank and Scowl were involved in a fistfight with the umpire, a coach, and the coach's wife. When the story first broke, I thought it might just come and go like any other lame story, but it got worse with each passing day. There were conflicting eyewitness accounts of what had happened. Everyone had an opinion on the matter, and the event was blown all out of proportion. It made national TV news and was discussed by psychologists on a couple popular daytime talk shows. I met with Scowl to discuss the fiasco, and he still had a black eye and a bandage on his chin. He was smiling when I met him, which was a good sign.

That's quite a shiner.

Don't let them fool you. Baseball is more dangerous that it looks.

Apparently so. Any injuries other than what I see?

No, this is the extent of it.

How's Frank holding up? He met me at the door, but he seemed unusually quiet.

He'll be fine.

Are you going to tell me what happened?

Do you remember when you and I talked about Roger and his acting performance in *Bill's Guitar?*

Yes, I remember.

Do you recall what I had to say about fathers loving their children, about how they were probably biased, how they saw what they wanted to see? Maybe I just wanted to see things a certain way. I'm still not sure exactly what happened at that game. I mean, I remember everything about the fight, but I'm still not sure how it started. Well, I take that back. I know how it started, but I'm not sure what I saw. I stood my ground, and I guess that's what counts. Am I making any sense?

Not really.

Several weeks ago, I watched *Bill's Guitar again* for the first time in years. Now, I wasn't feeling sorry for myself or yearning for something I couldn't have; I just wanted to see some moving images of my son. When you lose someone, there's this fear that you'll forget what your loved one looked like and sounded like. The movie brings those memories back to me, and watching it was a real eye-opener. To this day I still don't see what all the fuss was about. Sure, Roger's acting wasn't superlative, but it also wasn't nearly as bad as some people said. In fact, there were some scenes that were pretty darn good. The question that still haunts me is why was everyone so cruel to my son? Why were they so willing to accept me, yet so unwilling to accept Roger? I still don't understand what happened when we filmed that movie. Did I love the boy so much that I couldn't see what a bad actor he was, or was everyone just out to get him?

I thought we were going to talk about the fight at Alex's baseball game.

Yes, that's exactly what I'm talking about. No one ever mentions Roger when they talk about the fight. But in order to understand the fight, you have to understand what happened to Roger.

I don't understand.

You know, I've watched a lot of Alex's ballgames, and I swore I'd never find myself in this position. I've seen other parents make fools of themselves. When I think of what happened, I think of Henry, for example. For a brief time, Henry's son, Clay, was on one of Alex's teams, and Henry's story is important. Clay couldn't play baseball to save his life, and everyone knew the kid was bad. All his teammates groaned every time he was put into a game. When he swung the bat, you'd swear he was blind as Helen Keller, and when he threw the ball, there was no telling where it would go. One evening Alex's team was playing against a crosstown rival, and Alex's team was holding its own. One of the reasons they were doing so well was that the coach kept Clay on the bench, but toward the end of the game, his father had seen enough. Eight innings had gone by, and Clay was still just watching, and Henry got up and walked to the dugout. He jabbed his finger into the coach's chest and demanded his boy be put into the game. I couldn't hear much, but I did hear Henry say, "My boy's as good as any other player on this team." I really felt for the guy. He was the only person there who didn't see what a terrible player his son was. Words were said, and finally Henry walked to his son, took him by the hand, and pulled him out of the dugout and off the field. Everyone just sat in the stands silently. That was the last I ever saw of Henry or his son, Clay.

Are you saying Alex had to sit on the bench? Was that the cause of the fight?

No, of course not. Alex is one of the best players. I think you're missing my point. I wasn't telling you about a player. I was telling you about his dad.

But tell me about the fight.

Okay, I'll tell you. It wasn't a particularly important game. I mean, it was important to the boys, but it wasn't a playoff game or anything like that. It was the bottom of the ninth inning, and Alex's team was ahead by one run. There were two outs, and the other team was at bat. They had a runner on third. Their batter swung at a fastball and knocked a line drive into center field. Fortunately, Alex was there to get the ball. The ball rolled right into Alex's mitt. Meanwhile, the boy at third base ran toward home. Then the most amazing thing happened. Alex threw the ball toward the catcher. It was like a rifle shot, and it went right into the catcher's mitt. The catcher tagged the runner out, and the game should have been over. Alex's team should have won, but the umpire said that the runner was safe, and the game was now tied. "You've got to be kidding me," I shouted. "Are you fucking blind?"

That's what you said?

I don't ordinarily cuss, but the word just blurted out of my mouth. The umpire gave me a look, like I should've known better than to cuss in front of a lot of children. Then I said, "You're out of your mind. The boy was out by a mile. What game are you looking at?" As I was yelling, I found myself walking onto the field. I was headed for the umpire at home plate. He was standing with his hands on his hips, preparing himself for my arrival. "The boy was safe," he said. I could tell he didn't plan to be bullied by one angry parent, even if that parent was as famous as Scowl. When I arrived at home plate, the ump and I stood face-to-face. "My son just made the throw of his life, and you're not going to give him credit for it? Do you have a problem with my boy? Do you have a problem with me?" The umpire replied, "I do have a problem with you being out on the field. Go back to your seat." By now the coach from the other team had come from the dugout, and he was standing beside the umpire. He too had his hands on his hips, and he backed up the umpire. "Why don't you sit down?" the coach said. "The call was made. The runner was safe." Now our coach decided to join the fracas, and he stood beside me. He tried to grab me and lead me back to the stands, but I pulled my arm away from him. "I want the call changed. You're robbing my son of his out. It was a great throw, and the runner was out by a mile." Our coach put his hand on my shoulder and said, "The boy was safe. The ump is just doing his job." He was trying to calm me down, trying to get me to leave the field and sit back down. Then it happened.

What happened?

I shoved the umpire. I pushed him so hard he nearly fell over. "What's your problem?" the other coach said, and he pushed me back on behalf of the umpire. During this pushing, my mind drifted back to Roger. I was thinking of his performance in that movie and the way he had been treated.

Why were you thinking about Roger?

It just seemed so unfair. Both of my boys were doing their best, yet these crazy adults wanted to steal their thunder. What did my boys ever do to deserve this sort of treatment? Yes, I was thinking of Roger, how he took his acting in *Bill's Guitar* so seriously. He spent hours with his acting coach, and he knew all his lines. When Joseph made a suggestion, he followed it, and when the cameras were rolling, he did his best. I was so proud of him back then. So why did the critics and public turn on him? And why was this umpire now turning on Alex? It was like a conspiracy. I wasn't going to stand for it, not a second time, and I wasn't going to let this idiotic umpire steal this moment from my son without putting up a fight. I drew my arm back, clenched my fist, and with all my might, I threw a punch at the umpire's face. I felt my fist land square against his nose. I could feel the cartilage buckle under the impact, but when I opened my eyes, I realized I had done something horrible. I hadn't hit the umpire at all. The wife of the other team's coach had come out from the dugout to join the argument, and unbeknownst to me, she had positioned herself in front of me. I hadn't seen her, or I would never have thrown the punch. But the wife was now holding her nose, her eyes filled with tears and blood streaming from between her fingers. For a moment I just stared at her, and then there was a sharp pain at the right side of my head. I was reeling backward. The coach from the other team had hit me in the ear. Our coach lunged at him before he could throw another punch, and the next thing I knew we were all fighting. None of us were very good at it. We must have looked ridiculous. Frank then appeared on the field. In a matter of seconds, he put a rapid end to the fight. I don't know exactly what he did, but when he was done, both coaches and the wife were on the ground, and I was being held in Frank's arms. "Let's go," he said to me. "Let's go to the car." That's when Frank, Alex, and I left the game.

And that was the end of it?

That's exactly what happened.

I heard the other coach has hired an attorney.

I turns out I broke his wife's nose, and Frank fractured the man's wrist when he intervened. They're going to want some money from us.

What are you going to do?

I told my attorney to do whatever it takes to make the idiots go away.

Did you offer any apologies?

I'll apologize to the coaches and the coach's wife, but I won't apologize to that umpire. My boy made a great throw, and he should've received credit for it. Am I just a father seeing only what he wants to see? I don't know, perhaps I am. It's not like it was a professional game where instant replay would tell us what really happened, so I guess we'll never really know. But Alex is my son, and I have to take his side. Does this make sense to you? Do you understand what I'm trying to say?

I think so.

A man should never have to apologize for being a father.

THE BIG CANVASS

D espite Scowl's objections, the head honcho at the baseball league told
him he would have to apologize to the umpire if he wanted to attend
any more games, and Scowl finally made the apology. He told me later he
couldn't imagine being banned from his son's games. "This would've been
a huge disappointment for Alex," he said. "He counts on me to be there."
Fortunately, there were no more incidents, and Scowl behaved himself at
the games. Meanwhile, *The Pop Singer* was finally released to the theaters.
The movie wasn't a smash hit, but lots of people liked it so that it was
turning a healthy profit. Scowl and Jen threw a huge party at Dulcinea to
celebrate the movie's success, and all sorts of people were invited. Honest
to God, the guest list read like a who's who in Hollywood. I had been
asked to come as well, and I'd never rubbed elbows with so many film
celebrities in a single evening. Toward the end of the party, Scowl took me
aside. "You're probably wondering what my next project is going to be," he
said, and I told him I was indeed curious. "Come with me," he said. "I'll
show you what I'm up to." He led me through the house to his large ten-car
garage. Half of the garage had been cordoned off, and on one of the walls
was a gigantic blank canvass. In front of the canvass stood several fold-up
card tables, many tubes of oil paint, jars half-filled with turpentine, paint
brushes, a pile of rags, and everything else he would require. "I'm back in
the painting racket," Scowl said. "Can you guess what I'm going to paint?"
I told Scowl I had no idea, and he laughed. He then said, "I'm going to
put a year on canvass. One year, and that will be the extent of it. One year
out of the life of Scowl." As usual he told me enough to make me curious,
but not enough to know what the heck he was talking about. "It'll be like
nothing you've ever seen," he said. "I think we ought to do an interview

about it. In fact, I think we should do one right here and now." I didn't have my recorder with me, so I asked him to get me some paper and a pen.

———— ⌘ ————

I'm looking at a large blank canvas.

Like a newborn baby.

I suppose that's one way of looking at it.

Do you remember seeing your own newborn children? Do you remember the way it felt to hold them in your arms for the first time, to look into their curious eyes? Infants are such amazing little creatures, so devoid of history, so utterly empty, having no baggage of any kind. They make you feel so worldly and experienced, and you're ready to teach them and fill their minds with all you know.

Yes, I remember that feeling.

That's how I feel about this canvas.

Do you have enough paint here to cover a canvas this size?

If I run out of paint, I'll go to the art store and buy more. If I run short on brushes, I'll go to the store and buy more of those. If I run out of rags, I'll tear up more of my old T-shirts. The only limit I'm placing on the project is my time. I'm giving myself exactly one year to paint this thing, and I won't work on it a solitary day longer. Twelve months from now I'll invite you back to see what I've accomplished. Do you know what the title of this painting is? Can you guess? I'm calling it *A Year in the Life.* This isn't just a working title. This will be the final title of the completed painting.

What are you going to paint?

A year of my life.

Isn't that a little self-indulgent?

My fans will love it.

Yes, I suppose they will.

Just look at this canvas, big and square and empty. Right now, it's a clean slate. Like I said, it's like a newborn baby. There's not a speck of anything on it, not a droplet of milk, not a smudge of applesauce. Can you smell it from where you're standing? It smells like an infant, like a warm bowl of oatmeal. A year from now it will reek of oil paints and turpentine. It will be an extravaganza, a full-scale masterpiece of colors, brushstrokes, shadows, and textures. And it will have so much to say. It will stand on its own two feet like it's ready to walk right out of the garage and shout out to the world. Great Scott, it will be alive!

It sounds like a tall order.

Yes, it does.

What was the name of that art teacher you used before, when you painted all those portraits?

That was Cynthia.

Are you going to have Cynthia help you?

No, I'm doing this on my own.

Are you sure that's wise?

I won't need her. I know exactly what I want to do, and I know how I'm going to do it. I'll begin right now, with the month of August.

What will you paint for August?

For one thing, I can paint my outings with Alex to his Dodger baseball games. Have you been to Dodger Stadium for a game? Have you ever eaten a Dodger Dog on a warm summer night? Do you know what it's like to see a player hit a home run out of the park, to hear the crack of the bat, to yell at the top of your lungs and hear thousands of fans yelling with you? And there's the organ music? There's no better place than Dodger Stadium to hear organ music. It's even better than a church. It's hard to believe I lived all these years without going to Dodger baseball games. I didn't know what I was missing. Alex opened my eyes to his world. I helped open his eyes, and now he's opened mine. How would you translate this into an oil painting if you were me? It's a daunting task, but certainly it won't be impossible. All I require is a little inspiration, and I have plenty. Take me out to the ballgame, right? Buy me some peanuts and Cracker Jack.

So August is about baseball?

And much more.

Such as?

August is the sweet aroma of our citrus trees and the singing birds at Dulcinea. It's the desultory barking of our neighbor's guard dogs early in the morning. It's going to a movie on a Saturday evening. Maybe we'll go see *The Pop Singer* again. We've seen it in the theaters so many times over the past month that I've lost count. Jen likes to observe to the audience's reactions to her script. She can't get enough of this. This party we're having tonight is in her honor. I mean, Lester directed the film, and I played the main character, and hundreds of others took part in its production. But without Jen's screenplay, the movie wouldn't exist. She created it, and it's the sole product of her talent and imagination. Every morning I wake up in August, I thank God I met her, that she became my wife, and that she gave birth to Alex. Heck, I'm just beginning with this month. There's so much more. Do you see why I need such a large canvas? There are so many things to cover, and now I'm wondering if the canvas I bought will even be big enough. What do you think? Should I get a larger canvas? Compared to what it has to hold, it now seems like the size of a postage stamp.

When do you plan on starting all this?

Let's start right now. I mean now as we're standing here. With this paint and this brush, I'll smudge two gray spots here at the center of the canvas. These two spots will represent you and me. We're standing in the middle of this empty canvas like two pioneers standing in the Mohave Desert. We're hoping for a freak summer rainfall, waiting for the parched land to come to life. And so now my work has started.

So it has.

This smudge is you and the other is me.

Okay.

Do you believe in God?

Yes, of course.

We're all supposed to live our lives per God's will, right? Did you ever wonder why God doesn't just come right out and tell us what to do? I mean, when you pray and ask God a question, why doesn't he just answer it? Why is his will always so hard to decipher?

I've never really thought about it.

Don't you think it's curious how some people believe that God gives them signs? Some event will happen in their lives, and they'll interpret it as a sign from God, as if God would take the trouble to rearrange reality for their benefit. Can you imagine the effort it would require to arrange reality in such a way as to provide such signs for everyone? How would you keep track of it all? How would you keep one person's sign from altering another's? And how would you know for sure that a sign is actually a sign, as opposed to just a random event? You know, the more I think about it, the less likely I think it is that God uses such signs as a means of communication. Signs are way too nebulous and way too easy to misinterpret. So what do I think? I think if God really wanted to communicate with us, he'd just come out and talk to us. He'd come out and say, "Joe, you do this," and "Henry, you do that." Don't you think that would make a lot more sense?

I suppose so.

But he doesn't do that, does he?

Some people say he talks to them.

And we write them off as nuts, don't we?

I suppose we do.

If some guy told you God came out and told him to do something, wouldn't you say he was either making it up or not playing with a full deck?

You're right, of course.

My guess is that God doesn't want to talk to us. He doesn't want to talk to us and therefore he doesn't. I truly believe that. I think he wants us to figure things out for ourselves. I think long ago, God said to himself, "I did a decent job when I created human beings. I gave each of them a brain and a heart, and if they can't all figure out how to get along and do the right things, then nothing I come out and tell them is going change their lives." You want to know what else I think? I think no one really needs a Bible, minister, pope, or holy miracle to see what's right and what is wrong. I think the answers are all inside of us, always accessible, within our hearts and minds as God created them. I think if you follow your God-given conscience and stay on the straight and narrow, love your neighbors, behave yourself, and keep a civil tongue, you'll automatically be travelling on the right path.

What does this have to do with your painting?

Nothing.

Then why did you bring it up?

Because it interests me, and I thought we were done talking about the painting.

DYLAN'S STORY

———— ·•· ————

I n November 1987, I got a call from Scowl about Dylan Clay, the intruder who broke into Dulcinea and shot Frank in the neck. Scowl said he met with Nathan Clay, Dylan's father, and that he now wanted to do a phone interview with me concerning the man and his son. Nathan had approached Scowl, wanting to explain what had happened and hoping to apologize for the trouble his son had caused. Nathan had nothing to say to the press (or anyone else) after Dylan hung himself and died in his jail cell two years ago. As you may remember, there was never a trial. To tell you the truth, I was a little surprised that Scowl met with Nathan. Frank meant the world to Scowl, and Scowl was furious about what had happened. Shooting Frank was unforgiveable. It wasn't like the situation with Lynette, where a house had been burned down. "A burned house can be rebuilt," he told me. "But we could've lost Frank for good." Somehow Nathan convinced Scowl to meet him at Dulcinea. Nathan drove down from Northern California, and when he arrived, Frank showed him into the house. Nathan sat beside Scowl on the front room sofa, and Scowl then listened patiently as Nathan told his son's story. Just a few days later, Scowl wanted me to interview him so that he could make Dylan's story public and recount what Nathan had told him.

———— ∞∞∞ ————

I understand you met with Nathan Clay.
    We met just a few days ago. He came to me with his heart in his hands. He was a very nice guy. He was not at all what I expected.
    What did you learn?
    Nathan told me Dylan's story.

What did he tell you?

He began by describing Dylan's childhood. He told me what a bright boy Dylan was, how he always got high grades in school. Nathan said he was like any other red-blooded American boy. There were no red flags. There was no cause to be worried. He got in trouble every now and again, like boys his age are inclined to do. But it was nothing to be concerned about. When he was in high school, he planned to go to college, and he wanted to become a doctor. Nathan is a doctor, and Dylan wanted to follow in his footsteps. "He was such a wonderful young man," Nathan told me. "We felt blessed to have him as our son." Nathan told me he used to look up at the sky at night with his wife, and they would count their lucky stars. He told me they had heard about parents having difficult children, but it was never that way with Dylan. Never in a million years did Nathan or his wife ever suspect Dylan's life would take the turn that it did. I told Nathan that I could relate. I was referring, of course, to Roger. I didn't live with Roger when he was younger, but I always imagined that he was a good kid like Dylan. Audrey always told me how great he was, and I had no reason to doubt her. As I listened to Nathan's story, I actually felt a little like crying.

Did you cry?

No, I didn't. I listened as the man went on. He told me about Dylan's last year in high school, about how much he was looking forward to college. He told me how they checked out schools all over the country, trying to find the ideal college for Dylan. They finally decided on UC Berkeley, and to play it safe, they picked several others in case Berkeley didn't accept him. Then they sent out the applications and waited for responses. When Berkeley sent its letter of acceptance, Dylan was ecstatic. It was time to celebrate, and the family went out to dinner at Dylan's favorite restaurant in San Francisco. Nathan said he was thrilled to see his son so happy, and this brought back a lot of memories for me. I remembered feeling that same way about Roger when he found out he'd be in a movie. I was so darn proud of him, just as Nathan was proud of Dylan. For sure, a father's pride is a very special thing. There's no other feeling in the world like it. When you feel this sort of pride, you have the sensation you're soaring like an eagle, soaring right out of your feathers.

So what happened?

When fall came, Dylan packed and moved to Berkeley. Everything was going fine at first. Dylan signed up for classes, and he made new friends. He studied hard during the week and went to parties on the weekends. He called home once a week to let his parents know how he was doing, and sometimes he'd send letters and photos. Then during the second half of his freshman year, he began to act strange.

What did he do?

Nathan said at first it didn't seem like a big deal. There were just some little things Dylan would say and do. Then Dylan complained the cooks at the dormitory cafeteria were trying to poison him, that he was now eating at local restaurants. Nathan thought Dylan was just joking around at first, making up the story about being poisoned as a ruse to squeeze more money out of his parents to dine out. A couple months after this food issue, Dylan began to talk about Nancy. Nancy Petersen was a girl who Dylan dated in high school, a girl he had a crush on. The girl didn't feel the same way about Dylan, and a romance never did materialize. But now Dylan was talking about Nancy as if she had changed her mind about him, as if she was now his steady girlfriend. He spoke as if the two of them were seeing each other on weekends and talking on the phone every night. Nathan figured there was something wrong, because he knew Nancy Petersen's father, and her father told Nathan that Nancy was going to Boston College. She hadn't been to California for months, and she'd never mentioned talking to Dylan. "We thought maybe we just misunderstood Dylan," Nathan said. So he and his wife ignored the matter and pretended everything was normal. Then spring came, and Dylan came home to visit. Now his behavior was stranger than ever. For no reason at all, he'd fall to the floor and start doing push-ups. He said he needed to stay fit, that he had to be in good physical shape to defend himself. He didn't say who he was worried about or why, but obviously, he was concerned about someone harming him. Then his eating habits changed. He wouldn't eat breakfast or dinner and had very little for lunch. He was jogging through the neighborhood four times a day to improve his conditioning. He began losing a lot of weight, and his clothes were now all too big for him. When Nathan tried to speak to Dylan about these things, he said it was like talking to a brick wall. He would try to make eye contact with the boy, but Dylan seemed like he was off on another planet. "We thought the problem might be drugs," Nathan said. "So we asked him if he'd been taking any drugs, and he vehemently denied it." Dylan was so adamant that Nathan figured he was telling the truth. Yet after Dylan returned to school, things got even worse. When Nathan and his wife talked with Dylan on the phone, he told them he'd soon be in jail. It was very alarming. He'd say, "I'm going to jail," and then he'd hang up the phone abruptly. The situation with Dylan reminded me of Roger when he ran off, the way he wouldn't communicate with us, the way he'd say strange and troubling things. This was when he was in San Francisco, strung out on heroin. I've always wished that I had done more to help Roger during those months. I was a failure as a father. If I'd made more of an effort to help, Roger might be alive to today. I should've put my foot down.

What happened to Dylan?

It turned out he was right about going to jail. One afternoon after his geography class, he went to the local police station and threatened several of the officers. He tried to kick and punch them, and when they attempted to restrain him, he reached for one of their guns. Nathan said he talked to the cops after the incident, and they said Dylan seemed like he had some serious problems. Then Nathan drove to San Francisco to see his boy, to get him out of jail, but the cops said he was too unstable. They wouldn't release him to Nathan. Instead, they transported him to a hospital for observation, and shortly after that Nathan got the news. The doctors at the hospital had done several interviews with the boy and felt he was suffering from schizophrenia. "It all just happened so fast," Nathan told me. "One day he was our little boy, flying kites and playing baseball, and the next thing we knew he was locked up in a fucking mental hospital. It was so unbelievable." As I watched Nathan tell this story, I could tell the man was still suffering.

So what happened to Dylan?

They transferred him to another hospital and treated him for his illness. They were able to stabilize him with medications, and eventually he went home with his parents. He lived in their house in Marin, and he stayed there for seven years. Nathan said the boy spent most of his time watching TV and playing video games. He wasn't rational or dependable enough to hold down a job. "Those were seven long and depressing years," Nathan told me. "It pitted my wife and me against each other. We both felt like we'd been robbed, and often we were blaming each other." Dylan was their only child. When he was a young boy, he was the light of their lives, but now he was schizophrenic parasite taking up space in their home, watching TV and eating their food. It was awful, listening to this story, and Nathan began to weep. I went to the powder room to get a box of tissues. "I'm sorry," he said. "I just wanted to tell you Dylan's story. I'm not trying to make you feel sorry for me. I just wanted you to know what happened. I felt it was important for you to know."

What did you say to him?

I told him not to worry about it. I told him I knew what it was like to lose a son.

How did Dylan end up in Southern California?

He left his parents' house without any warning. He didn't take anything with him, leaving with nothing but the clothes on his back. That was the last time Nathan and his wife heard anything about him until the shooting at my house. They had filed a missing person report right after Dylan left, and when Dylan was arrested for the shooting, the cops contacted them and told them they had their son. It turned out that Dylan had been holding down a job near to Brentwood as a janitor, and he was living in a small apartment. His parents were surprised he'd been able to survive as long as he did. I have no idea why I became a part of his delusion. Maybe he just saw me on TV or read about me in the paper. He never was a fan, and the cops said he didn't own any of my records or DVDs. It's so weird being famous. If I was just an ordinary guy on the street, I would never have met Dylan. I would never have known that he existed, yet because I'm famous, I'm now linked to him. He nearly killed Frank, and he wanted to kill me. Like it or not, he became an intimate and very scary part of my life.

What else did Nathan have to say?

He came to apologize. After hearing the story, I told him there was no need to. I told him I had been very angry about the event, but that I'd learned a lot from his story. It's funny how that works out, isn't it? You have all this pent-up hatred inside of you, yet it can be instantly and perfectly disarmed once you hear the truth. The Bible says the truth shall set you free, and this is so true. When Nathan got up to leave, I realized I should've had Frank sit in on our conversation since it was Frank who took a bullet to his neck. He should've heard Dylan's story. As I showed Nathan to the door, I called Frank over. I said, "This is the father of Dylan Clay," and Frank just shook his hand. He smiled and said he already knew who he was. Frank said there were no hard feelings. That's one thing about Frank I've always liked, that he never held grudges or felt a need to seek revenge. So I guess it was really me who needed to hear about Dylan. When Nathan left, I sat and thought about Roger. I used to send him birthday cards when he was a kid. That was all I did for many years. I could've done so much more.

Are you still blaming yourself for Roger's death?

Yes, I suppose I am.

TICK, TICK, TICK

—•—

B etween 1987 and 1988, Scowl worked diligently on his big painting. He called me several times, but he wouldn't let me view the painting until it was done. Meanwhile, in the national news, Colonel Ollie North testified in the Iran-Contra hearings, and evangelist Jimmy Swaggart begged the world for forgiveness after soliciting a prostitute. The eighties weren't exactly a decade of exciting news, not like the sixties or seventies. I think the eighties were the big-hair-and-Japanese-car colored calm that came after the storms. Reagan was our president. He chopped wood on his ranch, and his wife redecorated the White House. When it came time for me to view Scowl's painting, Yellowstone National Park was ablaze. There were twelve fires, eating up 88,000 acres, but even the fires were seen in a positive light. Experts said that the fires were actually good for the forests. As these fires raged, I received a call from Scowl. He said he was done with his painting, and since I was there when he dabbed the first gray dots onto the big canvass, he wanted me to be the first to see the finished work. I told him I'd be there, and I hurried to Dulcinea. I found Scowl sitting on a large and overstuffed chair in his garage, admiring his work. I looked at the painting, and I was stunned. I'd never seen anything like it. It was alive, intricate, colorful, and bold. It was for the most part an abstract painting, but I recognized certain shapes, as if they were coming from some psychedelic fog. There were crazy silhouettes of tall trees, animals, phone poles, clouds, and a slew of other things—or were there? Every object seemed to morph into another. The colorful dribbles and globs of paint seemed to be moving across the canvass, yet they held perfectly still. I felt like I could walk right into the painting at any point, at any time. And it seemed to be inviting me in. It seemed to be calling my name. "It's amazing," I said, and Scowl smiled.

"It's my masterpiece."

∞∞∞

What does it all mean?

Pick any spot.

How?

Put your finger on any location on the painting, and I'll tell you what it means.

Okay, how about this?

Ah, funny you should pick that. That's from August of last year. That's right after our interview when I showed you the blank canvass. That's when I was just starting the painting. I got a call from Andy Black. Do you know who Andy Black is? He's the son of the well-known Southern California real estate tycoon David Black, and he bought nearly half of my forty-two portraits years ago. Do you remember when I painted those? I heard he recently sold most of them for a tidy profit, keeping three or four of them that he liked. He's a big art lover and a big fan of me. He read our interview about the blank canvass in the *LA Times*, and he called to make an offer on my painting, sight unseen. I told him he should wait until I was done with the painting, but he insisted on buying it right away. He offered me a ridiculous sum of money. Can you imagine that? I'd barely even started to paint, and already he wanted to own the painting. It seemed crazy at the time, but I think he was actually very shrewd. I think now that I'm done, the painting will fetch more than he bought it for. But never mind that. I sold the painting to Andy because I liked him, although there were a few strings attached.

What kind of strings?

I made him agree to loan the painting to the Museum of Contemporary Art in Los Angeles for five years, and he also had to agree not to resell the painting while it was on display. I previously talked to MOCA, and they said they wanted my painting. In a few weeks, this masterpiece will be hanging on the walls with the likes of Warhol, Miro, Lichtenstein, and Pollock.

I'm impressed.

It'll be good for the museum. My painting should draw a lot of new visitors. I think that's why they want it, because I'm so popular and because my work will draw some new people to the museum. If you'd like to meet Andy, let me know, and I'll set up a meeting. I tell you, he's a real character. Everywhere he goes, he's always got two beautiful girls with him, one on each arm. He's like Hugh Hefner without the pipe and smoking jacket. His knowledge of art is very impressive. Ask him about any period or about any artist, and he'll rattle off facts like a college art professor on amphetamines. He's entirely self-taught, and I don't think he's ever attended a day of college. His father wanted him to go to UCLA, but Andy told him he had other plans. I think his dad is now proud of him. He's an art connoisseur and a shrewd businessman, and I'll bet he makes twice as much money on his art deals as his old man ever did with real estate. They say Andy's fantabulous art collection is worth over a hundred million dollars. While my stuff is a drop in the bucket, I'm glad he's shown an interest in it. Having a guy like Andy interested in my work gives my work a lot of credibility. This art world isn't like music or movies, where you need to entertain the masses. The art world is about just impressing a select few of buyers and experts.

Can I pick a different spot?

Point away.

How about this? What's happening here?

Now you're in the month of September. Jen and I are at her parents' house for dinner. Joseph invited us over along with Lester Small and his wife. We're done eating dinner, and the men are seated around the table while the women are in the front room talking. Lester and Joseph are drinking whiskey while I have a cup of coffee, and Lester and Joseph both have had a little too much to drink. They are having a friendly argument over who's the homeliest actress ever to grace the silver screen. I have to admit it is funny watching these two successful directors talk about leading ladies with such disrespect. Joseph leaves the table for a moment and then he comes back with three big cigars. He hands them out to Lester and me, and we light them up. As the room quickly turns hazy with cigar smoke, the argument continues, and Lester makes his case for Katherine Hepburn. "She had to be the scrawniest, prickliest bag of bones ever," he says. "Do you remember her in *African Queen?* Every time Bogart glanced in her direction, he looked like he was going to retch. Do you remember that? He looked like he'd just seen the head of Medusa. I don't know how he made it through the entire film without turning to stone."

Joseph laughs and says, "It's true that Kate wasn't much to look at, but she was nothing compared to Jean Harlow in *Public Enemy.* Have you ever seen such an overrated, so-called bombshell? Never mind that her acting in that movie was awful, she looked like a dopey, fat-faced girl who'd been playing dress up with her friends in her mother's closet. And she looked like she was drunk when she put on her makeup. Do you remember those ridiculous eyes? She looked like if she smiled, they'd shatter to pieces and fall right out of their sockets. I swear to Christ, I've never seen such a mess. Cagney should've stuck with Joan Blondell." Joseph stops talking to sip his whiskey, and Lester flicks an ash from his cigar into the ashtray. He says, "Still, the all-time award for ugly has to go to Joan Crawford. She has to be the ugliest lead actress ever. I've seen all her films, and each time I see her, she seems to get uglier. I mean, it's scary. Those black caterpillar eyebrows of hers give me the creeps. You know what I think she looked like? She looked like a character in a Three Stooges reel, like one of those Neanderthal, unibrow ghouls limping from room to room, chasing after the boys."

Joseph and Lester both break out laughing. Joseph then reaches for the whiskey bottle and refills their glasses. I'm puffing on my cigar, wishing I could pour myself a drink and get drunk with them. I'm glad I no longer drink, but there are times I wish I could, and this is one of those times.

How about this spot? What am I pointing at now?

You're on April 1 of this year.

What's going on here?

In order to understand April 1, you need to move your finger to the left, to March 23.

Okay, how's this?

Yes, that's perfect. That was the day of the earthquake. Do you remember the earthquake we had earlier this year?

Yes, I do.

It wasn't big enough to cause a lot of damage, but it did shake things up. Jen and I were both away from home when the quake hit. Jen was doing some shopping in Beverly Hills, and I was in Santa Monica at the annual Goodman Car Auction. Have you ever been to the Goodman Car Auction? They have some amazing automobiles. On the day of the earthquake, they were auctioning a 1936 Cadillac Series 60 Touring Sedan that once belonged to W. C. Fields. The car was all original, right down to its 332 flathead V8 and double spare tires. It was a rich, dark-green color and had the most incredible gray tweed upholstery. But just the fact that it had been owned by W. C. Fields was enough for me. If I bought this car, I could drive around in a genuine piece of Hollywood history. When the car came up, I jumped into the action, and I ended up in a bidding war against some clown who wanted the car as much as me. I always get into bidding wars at these darn auctions. It never fails. We kept raising the price until I finally won. I hate to tell you what I finally paid.

This was the day of the earthquake?

I bought the car late that morning, and the earthquake hit in the afternoon. The auction was on the ground floor of the Stratford Arms Hotel, and everyone ran out of the building when things started shaking. The auction stopped, and no one knew what to do. Then slowly, everyone came back into the building. They restarted the auction an hour later. Anyway, I couldn't pick up the car until evening, so Frank and I came up with a great idea. We decided we'd go to Dulcinea and play a prank on Jen. We went into the house, where we made a mess of things, making it look like the earthquake had shaken the house more than it actually had. We moved pictures on the walls so they were crooked, and we tipped over lamps and vases. We took some books and knickknacks off the shelves and placed them on the floor. When we were done, we drove back to the auction to get my car. When we returned home, Jen was at the front door waiting for us. Jeez, she was wide-eyed and out of breath. "Come inside, quick!" she exclaimed. "You're not going to believe this! You guys won't believe it!" Frank and I entered the house, and Jen showed us everything we'd done, thinking it was all from the earthquake. Too funny, right? I burst out laughing, and Jen asked me what was so funny. When I told her what Frank and I had done, she rolled her eyes, and I think she was a little angry. Jen never was a big fan of practical jokes.

Did she like the car?

Oh, yes. We showed her the car. The next day, we took the car for a spin around Brentwood. "How do you know for sure it was owned by W. C. Fields?" she asked, and I told her I had all the paperwork, that there wasn't any question about it. I'd always wanted to own something like this, especially something that belonged to W. C. Fields. Then it happened.

What happened?

Fast forward to April 1. Move your finger to where you started. There you'll see the car. But this time there's trouble.

What sort of trouble?

On that morning, I had my breakfast, and then I stepped outside to get the morning paper. When I looked toward the garage, the door was wide open and the Cadillac was gone. I couldn't believe my eyes, and I looked toward the gates to the property, and they too were wide open. Someone had broken into the grounds during the middle of the night and stolen my car! I ran into the house and told Jen. I was really upset. "Someone took my Caddy!" I exclaimed. "It's gone!" I ran to get Frank. "Someone stole the Cadillac," I told him. Frank was in his bathrobe, but he ran outside to check out the evidence. "Call the police," Frank said, and I ran back into the house to call the cops. Just as I was about to dial the number, Jen started laughing. "Why are you laughing?" I asked. Jesus, I guess I should've known. It was after all April 1. Jen had taken the car out of the garage in the middle of the night and parked it down the street, making it look like someone had made off with it. It was her joke on me, her way of getting even for our earthquake prank.

Sound like she got you good.

Yes, she got me good. I fell for it, hook, line, and sinker. I felt like an idiot.

Where is the car now? I don't see it here in the garage.

I sold it.

You sold it?

It kept breaking down. Great Scott, what a piece of junk. Every time I took it out, I'd wind up having it towed it to the repair shop.

So what's going on at this spot? It looks like a Christmas tree.

Yes, that's exactly what it is. You're pointing to our Christmas tree from last year. Jen and her parents are sitting in the front room, and I'm in the kitchen making a pot of coffee. Alex is still asleep in his room. Frank is outside walking the grounds, checking things out. How old are your kids now?

Carter is twenty, and Pamela is nineteen.

Alex is now eleven. He's still a boy, mind you, but he isn't a little kid anymore. With your kids being as old as they are, you should know what I'm talking about when I say Christmas is no longer the same. As you can see, I'm pouring water into the coffee maker, thinking about how different things are. I'm remembering how Alex used to be the first one up every Christmas morning, how he'd rush downstairs to see what Santa brought, how he'd then come to our bedroom and jump all over our bed to wake us up. Do you remember those days? Wasn't it that way with Carter and Pamela? For some reason, last Christmas it all hit home. We didn't leave out any cookies and milk for Santa Claus, and there were fewer presents under the tree. The front room was calm Christmas morning, just the low voices of sleepy adults drinking coffee, rubbing their eyes, and waiting for Alex to wake up. Since when do the parents wake up before their kids on Christmas morning? It seemed sad to me that Alex was no longer an energetic, toy-crazy boy. And it made me want to have more children, just so I could enjoy Christmas with them, but at fifty I'd be too old. I don't want to be wrangling wild teenagers when I was in my sixties. Do you know if Roger were still alive, he'd now be twenty-six? He'd be old enough to be married with children, and I might actually be a grandfather. Can you imagine having grandchildren running around Dulcinea during the Christmas holidays? I don't like to dwell on things that might have been, but this Christmas made me a little morose, thinking about Roger and some of the things that might have been. That's what I'm thinking about while making coffee in the kitchen. That's what I've tried to depict in the painting, that desire we have in our hearts to turn back the hands of time and make our lives a little different. I would love having grandchildren.

Children can be a great source of joy.

The more, the merrier, right. It took me a long time to learn that.

This painting should come with a manual.

I thought about that, but it would kill the mystery. I think all great art is mysterious. I'm not just talking about paintings. I'm talking about music, books, movies, and all other forms of artistic expression. The more you spell out in black and white for your audience, the less interesting it is.

Is there anything you want people to take away from this painting?

There is, and I didn't even realize what is was until I was done with it. I started it, and did it, and then sat down and looked at it. And only then did I understand what the point was.

And what was the point?

The point was that there's no time like the present. The here and now is everything. It's the whole enchilada. It's the whole ball of wax.

I don't get it.

Think about it. It was one year, and it came and it went. When I started the painting, I had no idea what it would look like, and now that I'm done, it's just a memory. But while I was painting it, well, that's what counted. Each day, each hour, each minute. Time, priceless time. A little red paint here, a little blue there, a little orange on top of that. Tick, tick, tick.

THE JAYWALKER

———— •●• ————

Two years passed since I spoke with Scowl or did any kind of an interview with him. I was busy with other projects, and I assumed Scowl was doing okay. He hadn't been in the news since he unveiled his painting to the public, and he seemed to be living a quiet and private life. He hadn't released any new albums, starred in any hit movies, or written any books. Then came the New Year of 1991, when Scowl brought the year in with a resounding bang. It was not a good bang. Honestly, I was shocked when I heard the news. It was early in the morning while Scowl was on his way home from a New Year's party. A homeless man decided to jaywalk across Sunset Boulevard; he was stumbling across the street without bothering to look for oncoming traffic. The man staggered in front of Scowl's car. Scowl stomped on the brakes, but it was too late. Before he had come to a stop, he plowed right into the man and sent him head over heels toward the side of the road. The man wasn't killed, but he hit his head on the curb and was badly injured. When the police arrived at the scene, they noticed Scowl was slurring his words, and they asked him to take a field sobriety test. When Scowl failed the test, he was asked to blow into a breathalyzer. He blew twice the legal limit, and the cops arrested him.

I was truly surprised to hear Scowl had been drinking. I thought he'd licked his drinking problem years ago. Only once during our recent interviews did he express even the slightest desire drink again. It was when he told me about his dinner with Crabtree and Lester Small, when he casually said he wished he could drink with them. Had this been a warning sign? Should I have seen this coming? I knew so little about alcoholism that I really had no idea. All I knew was that my friend was now in serious trouble, so I called a couple days after the incident to see what was going on. Frank answered the phone and said it wasn't a good time to talk to Scowl. He said he'd tell him that I called, but he told me not to expect a prompt call back. "I'm sure he'll want to talk to you eventually," Frank said. "But right now, he needs to sort things out. And we need to get him sober." I thanked Frank for his honesty and hung up the phone. Then for weeks I waited for Scowl to call.

In the meantime, I read in the paper that Scowl was scheduled to appear in court. After several meetings with the DA, Scowl's attorney was able to help Scowl avoid jail, striking a deal whereby Scowl agreed to plead guilty to drunk driving, pay a small fortune in fines, and do a lot of charity work. He was also required to complete a one-month rehab program, so Scowl went to the Betty Ford Center up in Rancho Mirage. It was a week after he was released that he finally called me. I was surprised at how happy and upbeat he sounded. He was lively and optimistic. He asked how soon we could do an interview, and I told him I'd meet as soon as possible. So we got together at Dulcinea a couple days later. Scowl was seated on the sofa when I arrived, strumming his guitar and humming a song I didn't recognize, and when he saw me, he jumped up to shake my hand.

You've been through a lot.

Yes, I have.

I suppose you want to talk about it?

I want to tell you everything.

Let's start at the beginning. Why in the world did you decide to drink again? And why would you drink and drive?

I guess those are the two questions my fans want me to answer, and I've been thinking about it a lot. I even picked up my old copy of *Aesop's Fables*, a book my father gave me as a boy. I thought I might be able to find a tidy and appropriate fable that related to my situation. Have you read any of *Aesop's Fables*?

I read some of them when I was a kid.

There's one about a man and a snake. You probably don't remember it.

No, I don't.

It caught my attention. There's a man who lives in a cottage with his family, and there's a snake who lives nearby in a hole. One day the snake slithers out of its hole inside the cottage, where it bites the man's infant son. The little boy dies, and the father wants to kill the snake. He grabs an axe and waits at the hole for the snake to come out, and when the snake appears, the man swings the axe. His swing is wild and reckless, and instead of beheading the snake, he chops off the end of the snake's tail. A day or so passes, and afraid that the snake will seek revenge, the man places some bread in the hole as a peace offering. Much to the man's surprise, the snake pokes his head out of the hole and says, "There can be no peace between us, for whenever I see you, I shall remember the loss of my tail, and whenever you see me, you will recall the death of your son." Do you know what the moral is?

No, what is it?

It's that one never truly forgets his injuries in the presence of he who caused the injury. Do you think this is true?

It makes sense. But what does this have to do with you drinking?

I think the human mind is an odd and perplexing organ, and I believe it can play tricks on us. Do you remember I told you a few years ago how we should be able to rely on our own internal sense of right and wrong? I told you that I believed God expects us to do this?

Yes, I remember something like that.

I think I was wrong. In fact, I know I was wrong. The human mind is far too flawed and unreliable. That's why we have churches. That's why we have the Bible, and that's why we have groups like AA. I started drinking again about six months ago. I've been drinking in secret during those months. Great Scott, what was I thinking? Did I think I could be friends with the snake? I think that I did. I think we often ignore reality and look to our enemies for friendship. We know what they've done in the past, and we know what we've done in response. But for some crazy reason, we often see them as being harmless, even as being good. We're as dumb as cats. Do you have any cats?

We have two cats and a dog.

Do you have coyotes where you live?

I haven't seen any.

Every so often we get coyotes at Dulcinea. They come from the nearby hills, and they are very brazen. They walk right onto the grounds like they own the place. Sometimes they eat the old fruit that's fallen from our trees, and sometimes they hunt our rabbits. They also go after our cats. We have four cats living on the grounds. They're usually inside the house, but sometimes they go outside. Usually the cats run away when they see a coyote, climbing up a tree or coming back into the house, but several years ago I found one of our cats face-to-face with a coyote in the yard. The cat's name was Missy, and she was a two-year-old calico. She wasn't hissing or arching her back or showing any signs that she was threatened. Missy just stood there staring at her enemy about three feet away. I think Missy knew instinctively that the coyote was trouble, but for some reason she wanted to make friends with it. She stepped closer to the coyote so that they were eye to eye, and they touched noses. It was as if she thought she could defy the cruel laws of nature. At this point I tried to interfere, clapping my hands and shouting to break them up, but neither animal would budge. They stood there and held their ground. Then, in a sudden outburst, the coyote bit down on the cat's back, and Missy went berserk, clawing at the coyote's face and screaming in pain. The coyote let loose of the cat for a moment and then it bit down again. Missy fought for her life, a struggle that only lasted for several seconds. When she broke loose from the coyote's mouth, she ran into the house through the open patio door. I clapped my hands and shouted again, and this time the coyote ran away. I then went into the house to check on Missy. She was a mess. She had tooth punctures, a few lacerations, and coyote slobber all over her back, and I had to take her to the vet. After an hour of surgery, she came home with us to recover. Until very recently, I had no idea why she approached the coyote, but now I think I get it. I think I truly understand.

You said you were drinking secretly. How did you do this without anyone noticing?

Alcoholics are clever.

Didn't Jen smell it on your breath?

I ate a lot of peanut butter. Peanut butter is an excellent masking agent.

Didn't she think it was strange you were suddenly so interested in eating peanut butter?

She never said anything.

Where did you get your booze?

From the liquor store like everyone else.

I mean, how did you get it without either Jen or Frank noticing? And how did you hide it?

Let's just say there were times during which I could make my runs to the liquor store without being noticed. I kept my stash hidden in the garage in a box full of old tax returns. There was just enough room in the box to hold a couple of quart bottles.

Was the car accident the first time you were caught drinking?

No, Jen caught me several weeks before.

Why didn't she stop you then?

No one but God can stop an alcoholic from drinking. I love Jen, and I listen to her, but she didn't stand a chance.

How did she catch you?

I was careless. Or maybe I wanted to get caught. I don't know for sure. One night while I was working late in my music studio while Jen was asleep, I brought a bottle of vodka in with me. I got pretty hammered that night and forgot to put the empty bottle in the trash before I went to bed. Jen walked past the studio the next morning and noticed the bottle. Later she asked me about it, and I confessed. "I just wanted to see what it was like," I told her. "It's nothing for you to worry about. I didn't like it, and I won't do it again." Hell, I was lying through my teeth. Jen didn't have any experience with alcoholics and didn't know any better. If she'd had more experience, she would've known that I was full of it.

Was that the only time she caught you prior to the accident?

That was the only time.

It didn't work out well for you. Your drinking, I mean.

No, it didn't work out well at all.

Nor did it help that man crossing the street.

No, it didn't help him either.

I understand his family has tried to contact you. Have you heard anything from them?

They've tried to call me several times, but my lawyer has told me not to talk to them. I'm following his advice. It's the hardest thing about being an alcoholic, coming to terms with the harm you've caused others. In fact, I'd say this is one of the hardest things about life itself, coming to such terms. You don't have to be an alcoholic to hurt other people. But as an alcoholic, it's worse.

Tell me something about the Betty Ford Center. Were there any other celebrities there?

Yes, there were a few.

Who were they?

I can't tell you. They make us sign an agreement to keep quiet.

What's it like there? What do they do?

There were a lot of lectures, assignments, and group therapy sessions. That's really about it. There isn't anything magic about rehab. The one thing I didn't like was their attempt to link my drinking to Roger's death. They insisted my drinking might be a latent response to losing Roger, but I knew better. An alcoholic doesn't need a reason to drink. An alcoholic may come up with excuses when you ask him why he's drinking, but the real reason he drinks is simple. He drinks to drink. He drinks because he likes the way it makes him feel. There really isn't any more to it than that. The sooner one realizes this, the sooner he can get sober. Giving excuses only delays the recovery process and prolongs the misery. This isn't a professional opinion. It's just my opinion, but I think I'm right.

You said earlier that only God can stop an alcoholic from drinking. Can you explain this? And how does one enlist the support of God?

God is all-powerful. And he doesn't make mistakes. Once you understand this, everything else falls in place. I don't know how else to explain it. Put your faith in yourself, and you're sure to lose. But put your faith in God, and you'll win.

I'm still curious about the victim of your accident. Why have you been advised not to talk to his family? Don't you at least want to apologize?

They've recently threatened legal action. My attorney wants me to keep my mouth closed until their anticipated suit is settled. Just like anyone else, I have obligation to protect myself.

Are you going to AA meetings again?

Yes, twice a week.

What will you do the next time you have the urge to drink?

Like a smart cat, I'll run up a tree or back into the house. I'm really not interested in another brawl with the beast. They like to call it a disease, but I like to call it a beast. I think my description is more accurate.

What do you have to say to your critics who complain that you're just another disappointing and irresponsible celebrity? Are you aware that you've made a lot of people very angry?

I'm aware of the anger. And I don't blame anyone for it. But yes, I do also have something to say. He who is without sin, right? And Jesus said, "Neither do I condemn thee; go and sin no more." That's right out of the Bible. I'm sorry for what I did, but please don't expect me to be perfect. I'm a singer, an actor, a writer, an artist, and a generally good person. If you're expecting me to be more than that, you're going to be disappointed, just as you'd be disappointed with anyone for whom you set unrealistic standards.

LIGHTNING STRIKES

————— •❖• —————

I n June 1991, I read an article in the *LA Times* about a man who was struck by lightning and killed at the US Open in Minnesota. He was standing near a tree by the eleventh tee during a thunderstorm. The victim's name was William Fadell, and he was only twenty-seven. He died of cardiac arrest. There were about forty thousand spectators that day, and the storm was upon them quickly. So what were the odds? I did some research on the subject and learned that the odds of the average person in the United States getting hit by lightning are about a million to one. Scowl read the same story, and he called me a couple days later to talk about it. He thought it would make a good subject for an interview. I wasn't sure what any of this had to do with him, but I agreed to the interview. He wanted to meet at a shopping center in Riverside, at an Italian restaurant in the center called Angelo's. We sat at a table in the back of the restaurant. The waitress brought out bread, mineral water, and some antipasto.

————— ⊗⊗⊗ —————

So you read the story of William Fadell.
Yes, I did.
Was there something you wanted to say?
Actually, I'd like to tell you a story about a friend of mine. He was a kid I met in high school, and his name was Herbert Lane. I've never told you his story. Herbert and I first met on the school bus. One day, we wound up sitting next to each other; he was by the window, and I was on the aisle minding my own business when Oliver Farr approached me. Oliver was a bully. He was a fat, porcine kid who was always picking on smaller kids like me, making our lives miserable. He usually had other boys with him,

and today he was accompanied by Todd Hill and Ricky Miller. As Oliver came down the aisle with his buddies, I tried to avoid eye contact, but he singled me out. "Well, if it isn't little Arnie Kruse," he said. "Did anyone ever tell you that you're really ugly. Someone ought to wipe that ridiculous sneer off your face. Should I be the one to it? Maybe I ought to do it right now." Oliver then slapped my cheek. Then he did it a second time, but even harder. I was embarrassed and frightened, and I had no idea what to do. I didn't know how far Oliver planned to take this confrontation, and I prayed he would just go away. Then Oliver slapped me a third time, and this time it really hurt. At this point Herbert, who had so far remained silent, reached over and grabbed Oliver's hand. "That's enough," he said. "Leave the kid alone." Herbert wasn't someone to be messed with. He was strong, tough, and self-confident, and best of all he was a member of the school wrestling team. No way Oliver would tangle with Herbert.

"Is this runt a friend of yours?" Oliver asked, laughing.

Herbert let go of Oliver's hand and said, "Yes, he's a friend of mine. Leave him alone or I'll let you have it."

Oliver stared at us for a moment and then he backed off. "He's all yours," Oliver said. He walked on to find a place to sit.

My face throbbed, but I was glad that Herbert had interfered. "Thanks," I said to him, and he told me not to worry about it. He said as long as Oliver thought I was his friend, he'd leave me alone. And he was right. That was the last time Oliver Farr bothered me. He had crossed me off his list.

Did you and Herbert become friends?

From that day forward, every day after school I made it a point to sit next to Herbert on the bus. At first it was awkward because we weren't really friends, but then we began to talk. Herbert asked me what I did with my time, and I told him I was into music. I told him I sang and wrote my own songs. This was early in my junior year. Toward the end of that year, I had joined the boys in Trevor's garage, and I invited Herbert to come hear us play. He came, listened, and then told me that our music was good and that I should stick with it. I appreciated his encouragement. We were now officially friends. Later, after the boys and I became famous, I made it a point to stay in touch with Herbert. We'd get together when I wasn't touring, and I'd tell him my stories about the people I'd met and the fantabulous places we played at. He'd listen with great interest. Sometimes we'd talk for hours about where we were going with our lives. Herbert's future was always so clear to him. He wanted to be a builder like his uncle. His uncle was a contractor, and Herbert admired the man. Herbert said that someday he'd be building projects all over Southern California. "I'll be the guy who puts it all together," he said. "I'll figure out how to turn an architect's pencil lines into real structures. You can hand me a roll of plans, and I'll turn your dreams into a reality." You should've seen Herbert's face when he spoke about his future. He was so optimistic. And I wished the best for him. I was sure he was going to be a success.

So how did things go for Herbert?

When he graduated from high school, Herbert got a job with a builder in Pasadena. This lasted several years, and he learned a lot. Then he quit his job and immediately got his contractor's license. He started his own construction company using money he borrowed from his dad, and he began by doing house remodels. He told me it was difficult work, putting up with picky housewives and their stingy husbands, but he stuck with it. He built up an excellent reputation. At the same time that he was working on these small jobs, he was also submitting bids on larger projects to a couple of local real estate developers. I remember the day he landed this first big job and how excited he was. It was great, and he couldn't wait to give me the news. He was chosen to build a shopping center, the shopping center we're sitting in now.

He built this place?

I'll get to that. He didn't exactly build it. Let's just say he started it. I remember when he called me with the news that his bid was accepted, and I'd never heard him sounding so happy. He soon broke ground, and he began with the site grading. Then it happened three days later. When I heard about what happened, I couldn't believe my ears.

What happened?

Herbert was run over by one of the tractors. Somehow he was in the wrong place at the wrong time, and one of the giant tractors backed over him. He didn't stand a chance. His foot got caught under the massive wheel, and it rolled right over him, from his foot to the top of his head. It was a horrible tragedy. He was flattened, his bones completely crushed and his guts oozing out from his sides. One of the guys who witnessed the event told the newspaper that it was like seeing someone stomp on a tube of toothpaste.

That's an awful story.

What do you suppose God had in mind?

What do you mean?

He has plans for each of us, doesn't he? What did he have in mind when he took Herbert's life? God doesn't make any mistakes, not ever, so there's got to be a good reason for everything he does. What do you suppose his plan was with Herbert? And why did he have him die such a horrible death?

I don't know.

When I saw the story of this fellow Fadell getting hit by lightning, I thought immediately of Herbert. I thought of how suddenly death came for these two men, right out of the blue. I felt awful about the guy on the golf course, and I thought of Fadell's family and friends and how they must be grieving. It seemed so pointless and arbitrary, the way these two men died—one struck by a bolt of lightning and the other run over by a tractor. Were their deaths really a part of God's divine plan? Did God take careful aim to strike the men dead on purpose? I really had no idea what God was thinking. They say God works in mysterious ways, and they must be right, because for the life of me, I can't figure out what he had in mind.

You'll go crazy if you try to understand everything that happens in life.

You're probably right.

Are you afraid of death?

Yes, I'm afraid of death. I'm not afraid of dying, but I'm afraid of death.

What does that mean?

It means I'm not afraid of the actual act of dying. I'm not afraid of having a heart attack, or getting hit by a car, or getting run over by a tractor. We all have to die somehow, and there's no sense fretting over how it's going to happen.

Then what are you afraid of?

I'm afraid of no longer being alive. There are still so many things I want to do.

Such as?

Great Scott, I don't even know where to begin. But I'll tell you the first thing that comes to mind. I want to watch Alex grow up. There's nothing in the world like watching your child grow from and infant to an adult. It's the miracle of all miracles, the joy of all joys. It's full of pain, love, laughter, and fear, but you wouldn't trade the experience for anything. It's the greatest show on earth. I can't even imagine what things would be like without Alex in our lives. He's opened our eyes. He makes us laugh, and he makes us cry. He's grown before our very eyes from a blanket-wrapped bundle of joy into a remarkable fourteen-year-old boy. It's hard to believe, but very soon he'll be a man. And I want to see it all. I want to see him graduate from high school, go to college, get married, and have children of his own. I want to see it. I don't want to miss a single frame.

What else do you want to do before you die?

I want to record the ultimate song. Do you get what I mean when I say ultimate? I'm talking about a song that sums up all my life experiences. I feel I've learned so much during the years I've been alive, and there is so much I'd like to share with my fans. I'd like to write a masterpiece. Do you think this is even possible? I tried something like this with that last book I attempted, and I failed miserably. But perhaps I can find success with a song. There's no question that I'm much better at writing music than I am at writing books. Songwriting is such an amazing medium—there's so much you can do with a few words and a good melody. I know it sounds crazy, but I'd really like to give this a shot.

Anything else you'd like to do?

I can think of a lot of things. I'd like to see Jen sell another screenplay. In fact, I'd like to see her sell a hundred of them. I'd like to see her name rolling in movie credits. I'd like to see her dad direct one of his daughter's screenplays. And I'd like to act in a few more movies myself. I love acting, and I wish I did more of it. You know what else I'd like to do? I'd like to see the Grand Canyon. I've been to Paris, Athens, London, Rome, and a hundred other places, but I've never been to the Grand Canyon. Isn't it one of the Seven Wonders of the World? I'd like to take Jen and Alex there on a family vacation, where we could to on nature hikes and take loads of pictures. And speaking of Jen, I'd like to watch *Gone with the Wind* with her one more time. We can make a bowl of buttered popcorn and curl up in the movie room with a big blanket. It's her favorite film. I can't count the number of times we've seen it together, but I'd like to do it again. I can also think of some things I'd like to try. Have you ever gone fishing? I've never been fishing, not once in my entire life. Maybe Alex and Jen would join me. Or maybe Frank would like to come. I've always wanted to go fly fishing in the High Sierras. I'd like to breathe the fresh mountain air and stand in the middle of streams under giant cumulous clouds and deep blue skies. We'll have our trusty fishing rods, and we'll cast long, artistic loops of line and haul in buckets of shiny trout. And I've also always wanted to ride a horse. I'd like to saddle up on a healthy steed and gallop through a wide-open field of grass and wildflowers. And I'd like to learn to cook. Can you imagine me cooking in the kitchen? I don't mean as in heating up a couple frozen chicken pot pies, but as in preparing a whole meal from scratch. I'd wear a chef's hat and apron, and I'd chop, dice, and sauté like a pro. I could go to the farmers market and pick out all the best ingredients, and I could outfit our kitchen with all the best pots, pans, and utensils. And I'd also like to learn how to play chess. I know even less about chess than I do about cooking. I can't play the game worth a darn. Even Frank can beat me with his eyes closed, and he hardly ever plays. He knows as much about chess as I do. I'd like to be thought of as an excellent chess player. I care about what people think of me. I always have. You know, I'd also like to be thought of as generous. I've never been that free with my money. I'm at a point in my life where I'd like to give something back to the world, and I was recently thinking of starting a foundation. I would name it after my mom, who was always very giving of her time. I was thinking this foundation could give out a ton of great college scholarships to poor and disadvantaged kids. I know what it's like to miss out on a college education, and I think my foundation could do a lot of good. If I really sit here and think about it, I could probably come up with a hundred other things I'd like to do before I die. Some of them may seem frivolous. Some may seem vain, but they're all very important to me. I guess what I'm saying is that I'm not ready to call it a day. I'm not done living. Not by a long shot.

And yet you'll have no say in the matter.

You're right, I'll have no say. When it comes time, God will take me when he's ready. He'll toss down a hot lightning bolt or run me over with a tractor as he sees fit.

And you're okay with that?

Do I have a choice?

I suppose not.

I used to ask why. I asked why William Fadell was struck dead by lightning? Why was Herbert run over by a tractor? Why, why, why? Then I realized it wasn't really my place to be asking why. Each of us is given life as a gift from God. It's an outright gift. We don't earn it, or deserve it, and we're not entitled to it. It simply comes our way, and when the jig is up, we have no right to demand an explanation. God has his reasons, and that's all we need to know. All we can do in the meantime is show our appreciation for what has been given to us and live our lives to the fullest. And you know what? That should be enough.

The Hollywood Bowl

S cowl wasn't kidding about the scholarship foundation. He started working on the organization shortly after our interview, and two years later it was a fully functioning charity. In July 1993 Scowl was scheduled to give a benefit concert at the Hollywood Bowl. It was a concert that sold out in three days. Scowl hadn't given a live performance for years, and I was surprised at the public interest. All the proceeds from the concert would go to his foundation. There were rumors that Richard from the old band would be making an appearance, and there were rumors about Chuck Berry, Phil Everly, and George Jones showing up. Scowl would neither confirm nor deny any of these rumors. I met with Scowl three days prior to the evening of the concert to conduct an interview for the *LA Times*. The fact that Scowl was giving a live performance for the first time in so many years was big news, and the editor thought readers would want to know what he had to say. When I arrived at Dulcinea, Frank said Scowl was in his recording studio working on the songs he'd be playing in the concert, putting some last-minute touches on the arrangements. Frank led me to the studio. When we got there, Scowl removed his headphones, and we walked to the backyard patio where we could talk in private.

So how do you feel?

I'm excited.

Are you ready to give a live concert?

I'm more than ready. My body is humming. The hairs are standing on the back of my neck. My mind is going a million miles a minute.

Your old performances are legendary, but these are different times. Do you still have what it takes to electrify a live audience?

Jen asked me the same question. I suppose I could boast and answer yes, but instead I'll tell you exactly what I told Jen. I'll recount another story from my book of *Aesop's Fables.* Are you familiar with the story about the boasting traveler?

No, I'm not.

There was once a man who had traveled far and wide, and he liked to boast to others about the amazing and heroic feats he performed while in these faraway places. Among other things, he bragged that while in Rhodes, he leapt for a distance that no man has ever been able to match. He said there were many witnesses to the feat, but that these witnesses all lived in Rhodes. He said, "I would bring them forth to testify to the truth, but they live too far away." One of the bystanders said, "If all this is true, there is no need for witnesses. Pretend we are all in Rhodes now, and leap for us."

I don't get it.

I'm about to leap for you. Screw Rhodes. I'll do it for you here and now at the Hollywood Bowl. What's your next question?

Are you nervous?

No, I wouldn't really say I'm nervous. Perhaps I'm a little manic. Okay, I'm a lot manic. This concert means a lot to me.

What songs are you going to play?

A lot of old numbers, plus some new compositions I've never played in public. I'm not going to be shy about it. I think the new songs will knock a lot of socks off.

Are the rumors true about Richard making a guest appearance?

I'm not saying one way or the other. He's been invited, but I don't know if he'll show.

What about George Jones and the others?

You'll just have to wait and see. Are you going to be there?

I'll be there with my wife and kids.

You won't be disappointed.

How much money do you think you'll raise?

I think I'll raise enough to send a lot of good kids to college. That's the whole point, right?

There are many who say the money you raise could be better spent, as in fighting world hunger and disease. They say entire populations are dying and suffering while you're diverting much needed charitable cash toward the college educations of a few kids.

No matter what you do, there will always be critics. They don't interest me. I've never taken my critics very seriously.

That's all you have to say?

Can we talk about something else?

What would you like to talk about?

I'd like to talk about the state of our country. I'd like to talk about the dumbing down of America. I read a magazine article about this topic just the other day. Do you know where the term dumbing down originated?

No, not exactly.

It comes from the 1930s, when movie screenplay writers would revise their scripts so that their stories would appeal to those of little education or intelligence. They would oversimplify plots, themes, and characterizations to the point of absurdity. It was a conscious effort to make movies palpable to the general public. Rather than try to raise the intellectual levels of their audiences, they'd dumb down their movies. It still goes on today. In fact, it may be worse today than ever. And it's no longer just a film industry ploy. It's become the *modus operandi* for anyone who has to deal with the public. Have you noticed? It's much easier to dumb things down than to educate or improve levels of public awareness.

Can you give me an example?

Sure, I can, and I will. When Clinton was faced with questions during the last presidential campaign about him smoking marijuana, he told the press that he didn't inhale. This is exactly what I'm talking about. Everyone knows this was an inane lie, yet everyone was willing to accept it and look the other way. Rather than have a meaningful discussion of the use of marijuana by young people, and rather than appealing to the public's ability to think deeply about a real topic, Clinton concocted this bizarre fib to fend off his detractors and calm his supporters. I mean really, his answer couldn't have been more childish. Either he personally had no faith in the public's desire to think through an issue, or some cynic on his staff talked him into making the statement, but either way the result was the same.

You think this problem is pervasive?

Yes, it's pervasive. That's a good word for it. And I see it getting worse before it's going to get better, before people wake up and demand to be challenged, before they begin using their brains as God intended them to be used. Right now, the public is complicit. They're as much to blame for Clinton's lie as Clinton himself. There's culpability all the way around. Now, if you don't mind, I'd like to change the subject again.

It's your interview.

I'd like to talk about the arts. I'd like to talk about the predicament.

What predicament?

I think today's artists are caught in a pickle. At one time they were rolling along just fine, but now they've got their cars stuck in a muddy rut. They're rocking back and forth, gunning their engines, spinning their tires, but I don't think they know how to break free.

I'm not sure I get what you mean.

Shouldn't art have heart?

Yes, I think so.

So where's the heart? Great art should do more than just be a pleasure to the eye and ear. It should do more than make us feel warm and fuzzy. It should pound and shout to the world with all that's vital, alive, and relevant. It should pump hot blood into the veins and arteries of our lives. And its energy should be contagious. So, I ask you, where are all the artists?

You once told me you thought Rockwell, Dali, and Picasso were great artists.

And they're all dead.

Surely you admire someone that's living.

I admire myself. Let me ask you something. Do you like pasta?

Yes, it's okay.

Do you know what pasta is made of?

I think I do.

It's made of unleavened dough, most commonly of wheat flour mixed with water. Other flours can be used, and eggs are often used instead of water. The dough is formed into various shapes and cooked. As you know, all these shapes have their own special names. There's linguini, spaghetti, penne, and a load of other varieties, but all of them are cooked dough. You can call them whatever names you want, but they're still just pasta. I think this aptly describes art in America. This is the state of our music, painting, sculpture, and architecture. We are living in a world of pasta.

I don't follow you.

There is no heart. We're just mixing up all the same ingredients into different sizes and shapes. We label our efforts by a hundred different names, but when you boil it down, it's just another pan of pasta. Is this now making sense to you? I mean, we tap our fingers to our music. We read horror, romance, and science fiction novels. We mix colors and paint canvasses with realist, surrealist, and impressionist images. Everything we do has a name, a genre or style we can recognize. We feel like we're sitting at this terrific banquet of creativity, when we're really just feasting on pasta.

And Scowl is different?

Yes, I'm different. I'm not linguini, spaghetti, or penne. So what am I? Am I a musician, writer, actor, or painter? Am I rock, country, or popular? Am I a serious actor or a comic? The answer is right before your eyes. Quite simply, I am Scowl. Now I need to change the subject one last time.

Okay, go ahead.

Have you ever sat in my backyard? On one of my benches.

I don't think I have.

Luis does a wonderful job keeping things up, don't you think?

Yes, it's very nice.

He works on the grounds eight hours a day, five days a week. It's an endless chore. There's always something for him to do. Last year I was in San Francisco. Have you ever driven over the Golden Gate Bridge?

Yes, a few times.

Have you ever noticed the painters?

Not really.

The last time I drove over the bridge, I noticed all the painters. They were hanging from cables and struts, and I got to wondering how often they actually painted the bridge. When I returned to my hotel, I asked the concierge how often they painted. She said she thought it might be every seven years, but she didn't know for sure. She said she'd find out for me, and that night she called my room with an answer. She said they never stopped work, that as soon as they got done painting one section, another part would need to be painted. In other words, it was a never-ending job. It's like the grounds here at Dulcinea. The work goes on and on. I had

243

breakfast here this morning with Jen, and I got to looking around at all Luis's hard work, and I got to thinking about my upcoming concert at the Hollywood Bowl. I asked Jen, "Do you know how long I've been preparing for this concert?"

Jen thought for a moment, and she said, "Hasn't it been a few months?"

I laughed and said, "It's been fifty-five years. I've been preparing for this performance my entire life."

If you've been preparing for fifty-five years, no wonder you're not nervous.

No, I'm not nervous at all. In fact, I can hardly wait. I'm truly looking forward to standing onstage, to playing my music, to watching the crowd's faces and then listening to them cheer. There's nothing like giving a live performance, having your efforts instantly recognized by thousands of human beings. It's intoxicating, and it literally rings in your ears. It's a power trip. It's an undeniable rush of euphoria. It's been so many years since I've done this, but I can remember exactly how it feels. It's something I've missed. I can't wait to grab my guitar and step up to the microphone. I can't wait to strum the guitar. I can't wait to sing. This is why God put me on this earth.

THE SNODGRASS MUFF

———— •●• ————

S cowl's gig at the Hollywood Bowl was a huge success. The audience loved hearing his old hits, and the new songs were well received. The concert also resulted in a call to Scowl from Bobby Breen the following day. He had been in the audience that night. Bobby said he wanted to get back together with Scowl for a new project. He said he wanted to help produce a Las Vegas show that would run nightly at one of the resorts. His idea was to create a show that featured not only Scowl and his most popular music, but an opening monologue, readings from some of his books, and some scenes from Scowl's movies acted out on stage. He even thought of projecting some of Scowl's paintings over the stage and having Scowl explain them to the audience. It would be a grab-bag retrospective of what Bobby referred to as Scowl's "eclectic and amazing life." Scowl called me and asked for my opinion. He said, "I'd like to work with Bobby again. It's been so many years, and it might be a lot of fun. But I'm not sure I'm ready for doing any kind of retrospective. I'm not a young man anymore, but I also don't feel all that old. I'm still doing some new things, still writing the last chapters of my life. I'm just not sure it's time for me to be looking backward and talking about the good old days." I told Scowl Bobby was up there in years, now pushing seventy, and probably now saw things a little differently. He was probably growing nostalgic, and so a retrospective made more sense to him. I told Scowl if he really didn't want to do the show, he should tell Bobby the truth. "Maybe you can tell him it's something you'd consider doing ten years from now. It sounds like a great idea. It just doesn't sound like you're ready for it." So Scowl called Bobby. I don't know what Scowl told him, but I learned the project wasn't shoved up in the attic. Bobby called me the following week to get copies of all our interviews dating back all thirty-six years so he could use bits and pieces of them in the show. I asked Bobby if Scowl had given him a green light on the project, and he said Scowl told him to "get the ball rolling."

In November 1993 Scowl was ready to release a new album featuring the songs he played at the benefit concert. One of the songs, "Sorrowful Fred," had already been released as a single and done quite well. The title of the album was to be *Watching the Clock,* another one of the new songs played at the concert. I've always been amazed at Scowl's longevity, how he's managed to stay relevant for all these years. He seemed to be able not only to keep all his old fans, but he attracted many new ones along the way. The research done by Scowl's record label showed that the main demographic for Scowl's fans were young as well as old. It wasn't at all unusual to hear Scowl's music on the radio playing right alongside the current artists, and he fit right in. When it came time to release the album, Scowl called me for another promotional interview. He wanted the interview to be published in *Billboard* or *Rolling Stone,* which I didn't think would be a problem. When Scowl called me, I agreed to meet him at Dulcinea the following day. I arrived at the house, and Frank, Jennifer, and Alex met me at the door. I hadn't seen Alex for a long while. Wow, had he ever grown! He had to be a foot taller than Scowl, and I figured he must have got his height from the Crabtree side of the family. I asked Alex how old he was, and he told me he was now sixteen. That morning, he was driving Jennifer and Frank to one of his ballgames. "So now you're driving a car," I said. "That's very cool." Great Scott, it was just yesterday that Scowl was taking the boy to his first ballgames. My own children were now in their mid-twenties, and I was sixty-two, supposedly just a breath away from my golden years. My life seemed to have gone by so fast. Like so many others my age, I was asking myself, where did all the time go? Zoom, and the next thing you know you're in your sixties. "We'll have the house all to ourselves," Scowl said. He had arrived at the front door behind his family. The two of us walked into the house while the others left for the ballgame. Scowl had brewed some tea as usual. He asked me if I wanted some, and I said no. I've never been much for tea, either hot or iced. Scowl couldn't seem to get this through his head.

<hr />

So tell me about your new album.

It's one of the best I've done.

Tell me about the title song, "Watching the Clock." What can you tell us about this song?

Do you remember much of high school?

I remember a fair amount.

Did you have a favorite class?

I liked my English class. I always liked reading and writing. I guess you could say English was my favorite class.

For me, without question, it was my sophomore year art class. Great Scott, how I loved that class! I took other art classes in high school, but my sophomore class was the best. Our teacher's name was Miss Conklin. Since I was only sixteen at the time, she seemed much older than she was. In retrospect she was quite young, probably in her late twenties or early thirties. She was very attractive. She had a very sweet face; long, sandy-blonde hair; and a figure like Sophia Loren. She always wore her hair in a braid to keep it clear of her work. When she wasn't on her feet checking up on us, she was always busy at the head of the class spinning a hunk of clay on her pottery wheel or working on one of her paintings. She always wore an apron over her dress to protect it. When she lectured, her eyes would dance and her voice would sing. I mean, she wasn't actually singing, but she may as well have been. She had such a wonderful voice. And I can remember the way she smelled, like wet clay and turpentine.

Did you have a crush on her?

I may have. Looking back now, I probably did. What red-blooded boy wouldn't? But, honestly, I wasn't so much attracted to her good looks as I was to her class. I was in love with that art class. I loved everything about it. I loved applying paint to canvasses, cutting out pictures for collages, dipping strips of newspaper and molding them to my paper-mache creations. I liked all the paste, paint, charcoals, pencils, brushes, and sheets of paper. I liked the way you were allowed to talk to others while you did your work, and I reveled in that feeling of accomplishment I'd have when I was done with a project. I was sure to be complimented by Miss Conklin and the other kids. I had a real talent for art, and I knew what I was doing. I had a natural and good sense for shape, balance, and composition. I understood colors, light, and shadows. I belonged in that art class like a bee belongs on a flower. I was also keenly aware of the classroom clock, and this brings me to the title of the song. A clock hung above the classroom exit door, and I had the oddest obsession with the clock, watching it, ignoring it, then watching it again. If I looked at it long enough, I'd swear I could get the second hand to slow down. I'd get it to creep around the numbers, extending every second. The problem was that if I didn't watch the clock, my time in the class would go by too fast, and this hour-long class would seem like five minutes. It didn't seem fair that the one class I truly loved would jet by so quickly.

So the clock is an allegory.

Yes, that's what I was trying to say when I wrote the song, that the more we love what we're doing, the faster time seems to pass.

I understand your hit single "Sorrowful Fred" will also be featured on the album. Can you tell us who this song is about? I've heard some say it's about Fred Martinez, a boy who lived on your street in Arcadia when you were growing up. Is this true?

No, the song is not about Freddie Martinez. In fact, I barely remember anything about Freddie Martinez, and I'm sorry the rumor ever got started. I understand reporters have been pestering Freddie about the song. They ought to leave him alone. The song is actually about Fred Snodgrass, who was born in Ventura and went on to play big league baseball. He was a center fielder for the New York Giants back in the early 1900s. I learned about Snodgrass when Alex and I were reading a book called *The Glory of Their Times*. I bought the book for Alex when he was younger, and we read it together. It's a collection of classic baseball tales compiled by a guy named Lawrence Ritter. One of the stories in the book is about Fred Snodgrass, about how this otherwise talented young player dropped a routine fly ball in the tenth inning of a deciding World Series game. The error has gone down in history as one of the all-time great screwups in major league baseball, and it was called the Snodgrass Muff. He never lived it down. When he died in 1974, the headline of his obituary in the *New York Times* said, "Fred Snodgrass, 86, Dead, Ball Player Muffed 1912 Fly." My song is about how cruel the world can be to those who happen to make mistakes. I had Roger in mind when I wrote the song, thinking about how no one will let go of his performance in *Bill's Guitar*. Did you know that to this day people still make fun of Roger's acting? I saw a news show the other day that said *Bill's Guitar* has a cult following. People invite one another over to their houses for beer and popcorn to watch the movie, laughing at their TVs like they might laugh at dumb Ed Wood movie, like they laugh at *Plan 9 from Outer Space.* It makes me kind of sick to my stomach. Did you know Bella Lugosi made that movie when he was addicted to painkillers and desperate for work? It was a tragedy. It was sad and pathetic, and there was really nothing funny about the situation. Yet there seems to be this morbid glee people drum up when they see others at the lowest points of their lives. I've never understood why people feel act like this. I don't remember ever doing this myself, laughing at another's misfortune. I'm not saying I'm so much better than other people. I just don't remember ever doing it.

Freddie Martinez will probably be glad you've cleared this matter up.

Yes, he probably will.

Will "Porky and Slim" be included on the album? You got such a good reaction to this song from the audience at the concert. Some people say this was your best song, and I'd like to get your thoughts on it. It's been analyzed extensively by critics.

Yes, "Porky and Slim" will be on the album, but I'm not familiar with what the critics have been saying. I try to ignore them.

Many of them are saying you were promoting interracial marriages. They believe you were saying that despite all the progress we've made over recent years, that interracial marriages are still frowned upon. Most performers shy away from these kinds of issues. What prompted you to tackle such a touchy subject?

Actually, the song wasn't meant to have any sort of social significance at all. It was just meant to be funny. It's about a fat boy who marries a skinny girl. I was just trying to make people laugh. There's nothing wrong with having a good laugh, is there? It's one of my favorite tracks on the album for the simple reason that it does make me laugh. I've heard it a hundred times, and it still tickles me when I listen to it.

I know a lot of your fans are looking forward to this album. It's been a while since you've released anything new.

They won't be disappointed.

Now that you're done with the record, what's next for Scowl? What new projects do you have coming up?

I'll be working on a movie with Joseph and Jen. The screenplay was written by Jen, and Joseph will be director and producer. This'll probably be Joseph's last movie before he retires.

When did this all happen?

We decided to start the movie just a few months ago. Jen finished the screenplay last year, and she's been tweaking and revising it with her father. They want me to act in it, and I agreed to do it.

So it's a family affair.

Yes, a family affair. And I think the movie has real potential.

What's the name of the movie?

It's called *The Doctor's Sons.*

Can you tell me what it's about?

It's similar to *East of Eden,* except in this story the father is a successful medical doctor and his wife still lives with him. There are two opposing sons, just as in *East of Eden.* The good son follows his father's footsteps and becomes a doctor, practicing in the same hospital as his dad, while the bad son is the manager of a disreputable topless nightclub. Both boys fight for the father's love. Joseph wants me to play the father, but he hasn't decided on who'll play the sons. He'd like the wife to be played by Maria Barringer, taking advantage of the chemistry we had in *The Thin Man.* I have no idea whether Maria will take on the role, but I think she'd be perfect. I've read Jen's screenplay over and over, and I think it's a winner. It's the best writing she's done. The dialogue is fast-moving and profound, and I really like all the surprising twists and turns in the plot. And you can't go wrong with this good son versus bad son theme. Straight out of the Bible. Cain and Abel, you know.

Does it have a happy ending?

Yes, it has a happy ending. You'll smile from ear to ear. It is very satisfying.

I remember how you used to insist on happy endings. Do you still believe they're important?

Yes, I definitely do.

Do you know what Orson Welles had to say about happy endings?

No, I don't.

He said whether you have a happy ending depends on where you end the story.

I love that. I'll remember that. Good old Orson Welles, right?

The Project of Projects

———— •●• ————

E arly in the morning, in January 1994, those of us who lived in Southern California were rattled from our beds by the Northridge Earthquake. They say fifty-seven people died and over eight thousand were injured. With all the toppled buildings and freeway overpasses, it went down on the books as one of the costliest natural disasters in US history. Dulcinea fared well, suffering only minor cracks in the stucco and some broken bottles and dishes that fell from the shelves. Amazingly, my own house made it through completely unscathed. The earthquake was important news for a while, but it was nothing compared to the truly big story that year. In June, Nicole Brown Simpson and Ronald Goldman were found murdered outside of Brown's condominium. Just a few days following this grisly murder, O. J. Simpson was pursued by police in his famous low-speed chase through our freeways in his white Ford Bronco. He wound up at his home in Brentwood. I remember Scowl telling me, "This is not what we need in Brentwood, a thousand nosey onlookers, carloads of uniformed cops, and prying news reporters with their damn video cameras. I hope this circus ends soon." The circus, as Scowl described it, would not end until late the next year, when Simpson was found not guilty at the end of his long and infamous trial. The reading of the verdict was watched on TV by half of the US population. It was one of the most watched events in television history. Scowl was quiet during the trial, but he decided to speak up after the verdict was read. He called me for an interview so we could discuss the outcome of the trial. He said he also wanted to talk about his most recent project, a venture he described as the "project of projects." It sounded crucial and intriguing, and I wanted to learn more. Rather than meet in Brentwood, we met at a sushi restaurant in West LA. I began the interview by asking the first and most obvious question on people's minds that year.

∽

So what did you think of the Simpson trial?

Like they say, it was the trial of the century. No one could keep their eyes off it, and everyone now has an opinion.

What did you think of the verdict?

I thought it was befitting.

Did you think Simpson was innocent?

I said I thought the verdict was befitting, my good man. I didn't say I thought Simpson was innocent.

What's the difference?

Did you ever read *To Kill a Mockingbird?*

Yes, some time ago.

Do you remember the character Tom Robinson? If you remember the story of Tom, then you'll understand the true significance of the Simpson trial. Guilt and innocence? Heck, they have nothing to do with the Simpson verdict. The verdict was a payback, an act of God. God was teaching the world a lesson. Do you believe in God?

Yes, you've asked me that before.

When the Northridge Earthquake hit, they called it an act of God. Do you think earthquakes are acts of God, or aren't they actually just random acts of nature? Do you really think God would take time out of his busy schedule to cause death, injury, and property destruction for no good reason? I think people have a warped perception of what God does and doesn't do. God gets blamed for way too many things that he has nothing to do with. When God get a bug up his butt to interfere with our lives, it's for a good reason. Believe me, he doesn't make it rain just so we'll get wet and catch colds. He doesn't strike a tree with lightning just so he can break a branch or cause a fire, and he doesn't shake up the earth just to create mayhem. When God interferes with our lives, he does so with a purpose in mind. He is trying to teach us. He's trying to show us the way.

You said the Simpson verdict was an act of God. Do you really believe this?

How many Tom Robinsons in this country do you suppose have been wrongfully tried and convicted of serious crimes? And I'm not just talking about the past. I'm talking about today, during modern times. I'd say there are more than a man can count.

So you think God is getting even?

No, I think he's trying to teach us.

Is God a teacher?

Perhaps more than anything else, yes, I think he's a teacher. What else would you call him? Don't we always turn to him for answers? Don't we constantly seek guidance from him?

What do you say to those who are calling this verdict a travesty and a miscarriage of justice?

I'd say they're right.

What do you have to say about your father-in-law's comments on the trial?

What exactly did Joseph say?

He said he should never have allowed The Doctor's Sons *to be released during the trial. He said all the public cared about was the trial and that the movie didn't stand a chance. The last thing the public wanted taking up their entertainment time was a Hollywood movie.*

I'm not sure I agree with that.

What do you disagree with?

The box-office receipts for *The Doctor's Sons* were disappointing, but I don't think great movies always draw big crowds. And there were some big hits this year. There was *Apollo 13* and *Die Hard*. They both did well. Did you happen to see our film?

Yes, I did.

What did you think of it?

I thought it was quite good.

So did I. You know, sometimes good movies just don't translate to big profits.

Do you really think this will be Crabtree's last picture?

Yes, I think it will. He told me he was getting out of the business, and although his health is good and his mind is sharp, I honestly don't think he has the energy for another project. He told me he plans to write his memoirs instead. He's had an interesting life, and I think he's already sold the idea to a publisher. It should make for interesting reading.

And what have you been working on? What's this new project Scowl has up his sleeve?

I've decided to work with Bobby on his Las Vegas idea. We've been spending a lot of time trying to get something going.

I thought you said you were too young for a retrospective.

Yes, I remember saying that. But I've thought a lot about it since then, and the more I've mulled it over, the more sense I think it makes. I'm almost sixty, and I have to be honest with myself. I'm not getting any younger. My hair is thin and gray, and my body is weaker. I don't mean I'm frail, but I'd have a hard time doing even half the old dance moves I used to do. My ability to perform is waning each day. And I look so different. I stare at my face in the mirror when I get up in the morning, and I don't see the same young Scowl that used to look back at me. There are crow's feet and wrinkles, and the irises of my eyes are no longer a deep and crystalline brown. They are a dull, deadwood hue. My beard bristle is snow white, and there are fuzzy little telltale hairs inside my ears. Even my eyebrows are bushier, and my teeth have yellowed over time, like old elephant ivory. I have to face these facts, that I'm practically a senior citizen now. If ever there was a time to do a show like Bobby has in mind, now is probably the right time. Besides, I think a show in Las Vegas could be a lot of fun. I'd thrive on all the action, the musical slot machines, the clattering dice and jingling coins, the perpetual beat of music from nightclubs. I can see my name in lights. And I can see myself on stage, soaking up the applause from my fans. It would be like the Hollywood Bowl on LSD. Two shows a night, six nights a week, every show about me, Scowl.

Is Jennifer behind you on this?

Yes, she's been very supportive.

Tell me more about the actual show.

Bobby and I have just scratched the surface, so there isn't much to say right now. It's a lot like starting a book. When's the last time you wrote one of your books? Do you remember the day you began your last book, all the ideas you had swimming inside your head? Do you remember all the things you wanted to say and all the stories you wanted to tell? Do you remember having ideas for certain chapters, for certain paragraphs, even for certain words? You'd jot down notes on scraps of paper, on napkins, on any pieces of paper available. You then collect them all and enter them into your computer, hoping to incorporate each and every one of them into your work. Then you begin. You sit down in front of your computer. You close the window blinds and lock the door. You struggle to type the very first sentence. You'd look at it, maybe revise it, or just leave it be. But yes, it's the first sentence, the opening salvo of your creation, and for a minute you'd sit back and savor the sight of it, a single solitary sentence on your computer monitor. That's precisely where Bobby and I are right now, on that first page, on that first sentence. We have a whole galaxy of ideas, but only one sentence has been typed, and we're trying to figure out how on earth we're ever going to get fifty-seven years of a man's life distilled down to a ninety-minute Las Vegas show. It's exhilarating. It's inspiring. It's a rush! But it's also inexplicable.

How long do you think this will all take?

I have no idea.

Have you been in touch with any of the resorts in Vegas? What venues are you considering?

I'm leaving all that up to Bobby.

It sounds like a lot of work.

Yes, it is. But when Bobby and I are done putting this together, we'll have something my fans will flock to see. Great Scott, I think we'll have created one of the most jaw-dropping, fantabulous shows in Vegas, and we'll make Wayne Newton and Elvis look like amateurs.

EDGAR BRYCE WINSLOW

———— ·•· ————

I t was devastating news. I remember precisely where I was when I heard. I was in my study on a Saturday afternoon. It was now the spring of 1996, and I was working on a book I had recently started about several of the great rock 'n' roll guitarists of the twentieth century. The phone rang while I was starting a chapter about Stevie Ray Vaughan. Ordinarily I would let Julia pick up the phone, but she was out shopping. It was Jennifer calling. I don't ordinarily get calls from Jennifer, and at first I thought there was some problem with Scowl. Jennifer's voice was stressed as though she'd just been crying. She then told me the news, that Frank had been killed. I asked her what happened, and she said he'd gone to the local drugstore to pick up some aspirin, when the store was held up by two men wearing ski masks. Both the men were armed, and Frank was standing in line with his aspirin. As one man accosted the clerk at the counter, the other kept the customers at bay with his gun aimed at them. Witnesses said the man with the gun on the people in line suddenly threatened to shoot a black kid. They said held his gun to the boy's head, shouting racial slurs and promising to pull the trigger. Concerned for the boy's life, Frank attacked the man and went for his gun. "It was just like Frank to think he could be a hero," Jennifer said. "If he'd just kept in line, none of this would've happened." Frank and the man fell to the floor, struggling for the weapon as the people in line watched in horror. The man with the clerk then swung his gun toward Frank and fired. The bullet went into Frank's back and into his heart. Frank slumped over. The man on the floor got out from under Frank, and the two men fled the scene, leaving Frank writhing in a pool of blood. The man behind the counter called 911 and asked for an ambulance, but it was of no use. Frank's wound was fatal.

You never expect news like this. I asked Jennifer how Scowl was taking it, and she said he was extremely upset. She said Scowl had asked her to call me, that he wanted me to know what happened. But she also said Scowl was in no condition to talk about it, that he'd probably call me later. I thanked Jennifer for the call, and as I hung up, my thoughts went back to my interview with Scowl about the guy who was struck by lightning five years ago, and about how Scowl's buddy had been run over by that tractor. Life was so precarious, wasn't it? One minute you're at a store buying a bottle aspirin, and the next minute you're lying on the floor with a bullet in your heart. It was hard to fathom that Frank was actually gone. He seemed like the kind of guy who'd outlive all of us. Now, thanks to some nut wearing a ski mask, he was gone. I didn't hear from Scowl for months, and when I talked to him, he was still a little depressed. He said he wanted to do an interview to discuss Frank, and he said there were things about him the public needed to know. I didn't know what he was talking about, but we agreed to meet at Dulcinea later that week. "Are you sure you're ready?" I asked, and Scowl said he was more than ready. "I need to put his death behind me, and in order to do so, I need to put a few things to rest. I need to tell you what I've recently learned about Frank's past."

Where were you when you got the news?

I was in my recording studio working on the opening for the Vegas show. I was trying to decide which songs we should use during the first minutes. Bobby had been over earlier in the morning, and we decided to create a medley. I was alone when I got the call. A police officer told me his name and then told me he found my phone number written down in Frank's wallet. The cop said Frank had just been killed in an armed robbery.

How did that make you feel?

My knees felt weak, and I sat down. The only thing going through my mind was that this can't be happening. I mean, it just didn't seem real. I knew it was happening, but it didn't seem real.

Do the police have any leads?

They have no idea who the men were. They have video from the surveillance cameras, but the men both wore ski masks and nondescript clothing. There were no helpful clues, and the men are still at large.

You said there were things about Frank that the public needed to know. What are they exactly?

I need to tell Frank's story. I knew very little of Frank's past until recently. His personal history before we met in San Francisco was always a mystery. Years ago, out of curiosity, I hired a private detective to look into Frank's past. I gave him Frank's name, driver's license, and social security number, but even after weeks of work, the detective came up with nothing. It was so strange. It was as though before he came to San Francisco, he didn't exist. I never did ask him to explain. I figured if there was anything he wanted to talk about, he'd bring it up on his own. Then along comes this murder. His sister saw a photo of Frank in the *National Enquirer* that was published in an article about the holdup, and she contacted me. I flew her to California to meet with Jen and me, and she told us all about Frank's life in Chicago before he moved out west.

What exactly did she tell you?

It turned out Frank wasn't really Frank at all. His name was Edgar Bryce Winslow, born and raised in Chicago. His sister told me he barely made it through high school and that he never went to college. She said he wasn't dumb, that he just didn't care for school. When he was out of high school, he got a job as a finisher for a concrete company where he made a decent wage, enough to move out of his parents' house and rent a small apartment. He then met a girl named Alice Parker, and Alice became the love of his life. Alice worked at a local car dealership, and after a year of dating, Frank finally asked Alice to move in with him, and Alice agreed to it. After a few months, Frank asked Alice to marry him, and she said yes. According to Frank's sister, everything went fine after the wedding. Frank was promoted to the role of foreman, and Alice was still working as receptionist at the same car dealership. Everything was going fine, that is, until Alice met Felix Nelson.

Who was Felix Nelson?

Felix was one of the car salesmen at the dealership. He was married, but he developed a liking for Alice. One thing led to another, and the next thing Alice knew she was tangled up in an affair with this man. They would go to Alice and Frank's apartment during their lunch hours and make love while Frank was at work. This went on for months without incident. Finally, Alice came to her senses, and she tried to end the relationship with Felix. In the meantime, Frank's sister caught on to what was happening after she saw Felix and Alice leaving the apartment in the middle of the day, but she was afraid to tell Frank about it. Instead she went to Alice. Alice told her she'd been trying to end the affair, but that Felix wouldn't listen to her. Frank's sister then went to Felix, and she tried to talk him into leaving Alice alone. She threatened to tell Frank about everything, and Felix responding by saying it would be fine with him, that maybe everyone would be better off knowing, that maybe this would finally force Alice to choose him over her husband. Then things came to a head in the worst way.

What happened?

Alice had been begging Felix to leave her alone, and Felix finally told Alice he would leave her if she'd spend just one more afternoon with him. He told her to call in sick for work and said he'd meet at the apartment. He said if after an afternoon of lovemaking she still wanted to call things off, he would agree to it. Alice went along with the plan, and she called in sick the next day. Prior to coming to the apartment, Felix called Frank anonymously and told him to come home after lunch. He figured if Frank saw him in bed with his wife, their marriage would be over, and he would have Alice to himself. When Frank arrived, he found Alice and Felix in bed, and he went berserk. Alice tried to calm him down, but he was out of control. He jumped to the nightstand where he kept a loaded revolver for protection, and in a matter of just a few seconds he emptied the gun into his wife and her lover. The sister showed me the newspaper article about the event. There were shots of Alice and Felix and a grisly photo of the bloodstained bed.

Did they die?

Neither of them died, but they were both in critical condition for weeks. The police wanted to arrest Frank for attempted murder, and Frank ran to his sister's house out of desperation. He told her what he'd done, and she tried to talk him into turning himself in. But instead he fled, and that was the last time anyone in Chicago saw him. He emptied his savings and checking accounts and ran off to California, where he was able to create a new life in San Francisco. He got a new California driver's license and a social security card under a fictitious name. He kept a low profile, working in various bars as a bouncer, and then he worked for me.

Frank never told me any of this during all the years I knew him. But now that I know, a lot of things make sense, such as why Frank always refused to carry a gun, and why he didn't want to be photographed, and why he never dated women. It's funny, but I would never have known any of this had the *National Enquirer* not published his photo. I would still have been completely in the dark.

Would you have taken him in if you'd known he had such a violent temper?

You know, I've never seen Frank lose his temper. I've never even seen him raise his voice. I've seen him handle others who were out of control, but I've never seen Frank get out of line. I think he was crazy in love with this girl Alice, and I think that kind of love can make men do wild things. Love can be a very powerful motive. I don't blame Frank for any of what happened, and I certainly would never have asked him to leave Dulcinea. He's been one of our family for years. We loved him, all of us did. Alex, Jen, and I miss him terribly. I don't care what others may have to say about his past, I will always see him as one of the finest men I ever met. He was a giant man with a giant-size heart.

I haven't read anything about this story in the papers.

We've kept it quiet until now. I wanted to be the one to break the news, just like we've done all my other news revelations over the years. I wanted to be sure the full story was told without any crazy sensationalism, and his sister agreed with me. She promised to keep quiet about her brother until after our interview. I think she was happy to learn Frank had found a home with us. She thanked Jen and me for taking such good care of her brother, but Jen told him it had been Frank who had been taking care of us. God, I really miss Frank. Dulcinea just isn't the same without him.

A Halloween Party

---·●·---

I stayed in touch with Scowl during the months following the interview about Frank's death. He didn't call me, not once, but I called him several times. I was worried about him becoming depressed and drinking again, and I thought I could be helpful. He probably needed someone to talk to, someone other than his family. During these months Scowl had suspended work on the Las Vegas project with Bobby; in fact, he didn't seem interested in working on any projects at all. He was reading a lot and watching old movies on TV, trying to keep his mind off the fact that he'd just lost one of his closest friends. Then came Halloween of 1996. As if Scowl didn't already have enough bad news for the year, Alex was arrested for drunk driving. He was on the way home from a Halloween party down in Newport Beach. Alex was still living at Dulcinea at the time and commuting to USC. He was on the college baseball team, and one of his teammates had thrown the party. Alex went dressed as Babe Ruth, putting on an old Yankees uniform and stuffing the belly of the shirt with a pillow. The article in the newspaper made it very clear what had happened, telling readers that the nineteen-year-old son of Scowl had been arrested for driving over the legal limit. The newspaper stirred the pot by asking its readers, "Like father, like son?" Of course, they dug up all the details of Scowl's own drunk driving arrest, and they did their sworn duty as a purveyor of relevant news by reminding the public about how Scowl had run into a homeless man on Sunset Boulevard, nearly killing him. I thought I'd get a call from Scowl about all of this, and I did. I expected Scowl to be upset about his son's arrest, but our interview surprised me. He was in a remarkably good mood.

I guess when it rains it pours.

It can sometimes seem that way. But I'm glad Alex decided to drink and drive.

You're glad?

Yes, I'm glad. You need to understand what happened. Alex went to the party with some friends. Jen and I knew about the party, and we knew the kids would be drinking. It was a college party, for crying out loud. That's what college kids do. The plan was for Alex to spend the night at his friend's house so he wouldn't have to drive home. He never intended to get in a car that night. But he got into an argument with the boy who was throwing the party, and he decided to come home rather than stay. He left the house at a little before two and was pulled over on his way home. No, he shouldn't have been driving. He knows that. So what happened? His car was impounded, and he was taken to the Orange County Jail. At the jail he was allowed a phone call, and when he called us it was four o'clock. Jen answered our phone, and she gave me the news. He needed a ride home from the jail. We decided it would be best for Jen to pick Alex up since my presence might cause a scene. Alex was released at five-thirty, and Jen had him at Dulcinea just before seven. Alex had sobered up, but I could tell he was tired. I decided not to talk to him until after he had some sleep. I wanted us to have a meaningful conversation.

So did you talk?

Yes, we did.

What did you talk about?

I told him about a kid I knew in high school. When I was in high school, there was a boy named Tracy Newman who reminded me of Alex. No, Tracy's father wasn't a star, but he did own a big lumberyard in Arcadia. The Newman family lived in a big house in the expensive end of town. Tracy's dad bought him his own car for his sixteenth birthday, a brand-new, bright-red Chevy Bel Air. Like Alex, Tracy was tall, good-looking, and athletic. And like Alex, he had so many things going for him. My parents didn't have much money during those years, and they couldn't afford to buy me a car. I would borrow Dad's car on occasion, but for the most part, I got around town on my bike. I told Alex that one night while I was riding my bike with Richard and Trevor, there were suddenly police and ambulance sirens screaming from every direction.

We decided to follow them to their destination. They finally came to a stop, and so did we. And there at the side of the road was Tracy's brand-new Chevy, its front-end wrapped around a large oak tree at the corner of a busy intersection. Steam was spraying from the crushed radiator, and the radio was still blaring. There were empty beer cans littered all over the road, and there was a girl's purse on the sidewalk. But sitting in the middle of the street was something I would never forget. It was about forty feet from the car, on its bloody side. It was Tracy Newman's head, severed from his shoulders by the windshield during the collision. It must have bounced off the hood and rolled into the road. It sat there in the middle of the street with the strangest expression on its face, its eyes wide open and a very weird grimace on its face. It took months to get that horrible, bloody image out of my mind. One of the cops covered the head with a blanket, and eventually they picked it up and carried it away. Two other kids also died in that accident that night. There was Tracy's girlfriend, Denise Harwood, and Denise's best friend, Joan Vincent.

So what did Alex say?

Nothing really. Then I continued. I described some of my own experiences with alcohol, how I became addicted, how I nearly killed that poor guy crossing the street. I told him some other things about my drinking, things that few people know about. Then I told him about AA meetings, and I explained why I still go to them and the constant effort it takes on my part for me to stay sober. Was I getting through to him? I don't know if I was. I then explained how research has shown that alcoholism is most likely hereditary and how he was flirting with disaster every time he took a drink.

But you don't know if he was listening?

He was listening. But I'm not sure if I was getting through to him.

You started this interview saying you were glad Alex drank and drove.

I am glad.

But why?

It was a knock on my head.

I still don't understand.

For months I've been moping around and feeling sorry for myself. I haven't been on my game. Not at all. And I haven't been paying attention to Jen or Alex. Frank's sad death really sent me into a tailspin. But this all changed with Alex's drunk driving arrest. It was like coming out of an amnesia.

An amnesia?

Do you remember those old movies where someone would get knocked in the head and lose their memory? They'd try to recall who they were. Then, wham, later in the story, they'd be hit on the head again, and suddenly they would remember everything. That's exactly what happened to me. One big bop on the head, and I suddenly remembered that I was a father. It was like I was hearing the voice of God. "Scowl," the voice was saying. "Your son needs you. Your wife needs you. Get off your pitiful butt and take care of business."

ARE YOU CRAZY?

———— •◦• ————

S cowl was soon back on track, now working with Bobby on the Vegas show. They sent out press releases to whet the public's appetite. They consequently received bags full of letters from fans who wanted to know when they could see the show, and realizing how eager his fans were, Scowl and Bobby stepped things up. They began working day and night, usually in Scowl's studio. Once they had the basics down, Bobby went to Vegas and worked on finding a venue. Several popular resorts were interested, but Scowl decided on the Mirage. Six months later they were ready to fill seats and raise the curtain. The show sold out in hours, and Scowl sent me four tickets for the opening night. I brought my wife and kids with me, and we were amazed at the number of celebrities in the audience. When the lights dimmed and the music began, the audience went berserk. The show went on for ninety minutes, and it was remarkable how many facets of Scowl's life they'd been able to pack into a single night. It was everything a great show should be, mesmerizing from start to finish. There were no slow or boring moments. If I were asked to give you one word to describe the entire extravaganza, the word would be Scowl's word, fantabulous. I realize I may be biased since I'm Scowl's friend, but in my opinion this show was the best thing going on the Strip. And it was a huge success with his fans. When the curtain dropped at the end of each show, the audiences were giving Scowl standing ovations that seemed to last forever. On the night that I went, I listened to people talking as they left the auditorium. They were all raving about Scowl and how much they enjoyed their evening. I was so proud of Scowl. He had truly pulled this thing off. I didn't get to visit with him backstage that night, but we had arranged to meet in his hotel suite the next morning. When I arrived at the suite, I found him seated with a cup of tea at a large grand piano.

———— ∞∞∞ ————

Are you writing another song?

No, I'm just fooling around. I'm glad to see you could make it. What do you think of this place? It comes with this piano. Imagine that. A hotel suite with its own piano. Pretty wild, isn't it?

This place is huge. You could drive an eighteen-wheeler through here.

I have a view of the entire Strip. You should see it when the sun goes down. I'm staying here four nights out of the week. I spend the rest of my time at Dulcinea with Alex and Jen.

How does Jen feel about all this?

I think she's on board. She doesn't like me being gone, but she's glad I'm doing what I love. So what did you think of the show last night?

I thought it was outstanding. And apparently so did everyone else. I think you have an honest-to-God hit on your hands.

That's what Bobby says.

What did you want to talk about this morning?

I wanted to talk to you about Alex. I also wanted to talk about the foundation. I wanted to talk about both. I also wanted to talk about Susan Strasberg. Did you hear the news about her?

I heard she died.

She was my same age, almost exactly. Our birthdays were only six days apart. I understand that she had breast cancer. You know, Claudia died of breast cancer.

Yes, I remember.

Did you know before I even got together with Trevor and the boys, Susan was already making a name for herself? She was in the movie *Picnic*. Did you see that movie when it came out? It starred William Holden and Kim Novak. It was a big hit, and it was nominated for six Academy Awards. I think it won two of them. Susan was only sixteen when they hired her to act in that film, and when she turned eighteen, she was on Broadway starring as Anne Frank. She was nominated for a Tony and became the youngest actress on Broadway ever to have her name in lights. She appeared on the cover of *Life*, just like I did. Susan was her own kind of sensation. I never did meet her, but I always imagined us to be kindred spirits, the way we both achieved so much early on in our lives, the way we were nearly the same age. I'm sorry we never met, and I was sad to hear she passed. Great Scott, she was only sixty when she died. I remember when

I was young, sixty seemed so old, but now sixty seems like only thirty. Heck, I'm her age, and just look at me. I have my own Las Vegas show. I'm sixty, and I'm still as relevant as the day I first appeared on the *Ed Sullivan Show*. Do you mind if I change the subject? When was the last time we discussed my foundation?

I don't think we've talked about it since your benefit concert at the Bowl.

Do you know since that night, we've helped hundreds of boys and girls with their college tuitions? It's a very successful enterprise. President Clinton even used it as an example in one of his recent speeches about education. Did you know a percentage of the money I'm making from this Las Vegas show is going to the foundation? My fans should know every ticket they buy is helping someone somewhere to get a good education.

That's good to know.

Do you remember Lester Small?

Yes, I remember Small.

He called me last year with the name of a girl he felt would be a good candidate for a scholarship. Her name was Becky O'Doul, and her parents ran a dry-cleaning business in Hawthorne. Becky was interested in film, and she made a documentary all by herself about the treatment of elderly people in assisted living facilities. The film was shown on PBS. That's how Lester came to notice her. She's not even eighteen, and already her work is being shown on TV. Lester said Becky had been admitted to USC's film school, but her family didn't have enough money to pay the tuition. They'd tried several scholarship programs, but none of them panned out. Lester thought my foundation might be able to help her. I told him I couldn't use my name to pull any strings, but that I would have someone contact her family. Well, Becky applied and was granted a full scholarship a month later. Lester was elated, and he invited all of us over to his house to celebrate. Becky's parents came with Becky. Jen and Alex came with me. Alex didn't want to come, but I thought it would be nice for Becky to have someone her age to talk to. Great Scott, who would've guessed?

Guessed what?

Our son fell in love that night. Do you believe in love at first sight? From the second their eyes met to the time everyone was leaving, Alex was absolutely head over heels enthralled with the girl. It was hilarious. And was it any wonder? She was drop-dead gorgeous. She had long auburn hair and clover green eyes, the sort of Irish eyes that turn you to butter. She was trim, but not skinny, and she was about six inches shorter than Alex, the perfect height. She seemed to take an immediate liking to our son, laughing at his jokes and listening attentively when he spoke. When we were done with dinner, the adults retired to the front room while Alex and Becky went outside to sit and talk in the garden. When we drove home that night, Jen asked Alex if he a good time, and Alex looked her in the eye and said, "I'm going to marry that girl. Maybe not right away, but give me a couple years. In about two years from now, I'm going to ask her to marry me. And I know exactly what she's going to say. She's going to say yes." Jen and I both laughed.

Are the two of them still together?

Whenever they're not in class, they're with each other doing something. They're joined at the hip. I'd be lying if I said Becky hasn't been a great influence on our son. He's now less interested in baseball, but maybe it's a good thing. I mean, he seems to be interested in growing up. He declared a business major at school, and he got a part-time job. He's much more mature and is beginning to plan his life. It will be interesting to see what he decides to do when he gets out of college. A business degree is good for about anything. My guess? I think I know what he's planning. I think he intends on getting into the movie business. I think he plans to use everything he's learned at USC to finance and produce Becky's films. That's my guess. I think they'll be a team.

Do you think she has talent?

Lester thinks the world of her.

But what do you think?

I think an opinion from me would be biased.

Did you read Jason Trumbo's review of your show?

It's out already?

It was in this morning's LA Times.

What did he say?

He called it the best show in Vegas. He said there's never been anything like it on the Strip, and he suggested that everyone should see it, kids as well as adults.

Wow, that's quite a compliment, especially coming from Trumbo.

I thought you'd like it. All the other critics will probably fall in line. It looks like you're going to be performing this show for a while. Are you going to have the energy for it?

How old are you?

I'm sixty-eight.

Are you still working?

Yes, you know I am. I have another book coming out in June. It's about the influence of punk rock on country western music.

Is it going to be your last book?

Not if I can help it.

I think people in our society make a huge mistake when they reach their sixties. For some reason, they feel obligated to retire. Don't you notice that? Unless your mind and body are literally falling apart, you should stay active as long as possible. You should stay on your toes and keep swinging your fists. Why throw in the towel just when you're hitting your stride? Why waste precious time puttering around the house and yard and hitting golf balls into little holes? When I compare myself now to what I was when I was younger, it's pitiful. I don't mean I'm pitiful now; I mean I was pitiful way back then. When I was young, I was an idiot. I thought I knew a lot, but I really knew next to nothing. Having and stronger body and a head full of thick hair doesn't make you more adept at life. If anything, it puts you at a big disadvantage. Older people should be reveling in all their experience and throwing themselves into their work like they never have before. Being a senior citizen should be something we all look forward to. We should be proud to be seniors. What on earth is wrong with being a senior? Since when did the word senior become synonymous with being a doddering old nobody who wears his pants higher? To be a senior should mean that you're at the top of your game, king of the hill, and sharp as a brass tack. Some people are looking at my Vegas show as if it's my goodbye-to-the-world performance before I hang everything up, when it's actually just the beginning of the rest of my life. There are so many things I still have left to do. When people tell me, "If only I was twenty years younger," I look at them and say, "Are you crazy? Are you out of your mind? Who in the heck wants to be twenty years younger?" I wouldn't give up my thin hair, wrinkles, or tired old bones for anything on earth. I like being my age.

THE WEDDING TOAST

I n January 2001, George W. Bush took over as our new US president. The Florida vote count was a complete fiasco, and we all suddenly became experts on voting machines and chads. It was all anyone talked about. It was worse than Chinese water torture.

I have no idea who Scowl voted for in that election. In all his years of public life, he never endorsed any one particular candidate. Well, that is, except for JFK. But Kennedy was a lot different, wasn't he? He wasn't anything at all like the grab bags of freaks and fools we're asked to choose from today. I wouldn't say Scowl was vehemently against celebrities endorsing politicians. He just felt it was appropriate for him to keep his own opinions private. Shortly after Bush was inaugurated, Scowl called me for an interview. He was in Las Vegas and asked if I could drive over and meet him in his hotel suite. He said he had an announcement to make, and he didn't want to wait until he was back in California. I'd been busy with a book project, spending a lot of time writing as usual. The way I saw it, the drive to Vegas would do me good. It would be nice to get out of the house and roll across the wide-open desert. It would give me a chance to clear my head.

It's about a four-hour drive from my house, and I used some of my driving time to reminisce. I thought about all the crazy things that had happened during the forty-three years Scowl and I were friends. I thought about all the interviews, the untimely deaths, the great successes, and even some of the flops. I thought back to our very first interview in 1957. I remembered all the nutty screaming girls, all the excitement, and the surprising limo ride to Scowl's hotel. Scowl never did tell me why he picked me out from that crowd of reporters. And I still don't know the reason. As I drove up the Cajon Pass, my thoughts rolled backward to something Scowl told me years ago. I remember what he said word for word. He said, "God snaps his fingers and sets the wheels in motion. Your life is no accident. He has a plan for each of us, and you shouldn't waste your time wondering about his motives and asking why. Never, never ask why. Always ask how. That's the key to a fulfilling life."

When I arrived in Vegas, it was noon, and I stopped at a café in the Mirage for a bite to eat. I then played the slots until it was time for our meeting, and when it was time, I took the elevator up to Scowl's suite. And there he was. He was ready for me, seated on one of the sofas with a cup of tea in his hand. He was both pleasant and energetic and told me to sit beside him. It'd been almost two years since I last met with him, and I swear he hadn't aged a single day. He'd been doing two shows a night, four days a week, and it hadn't taken any toll on him at all. If anything, he was more cheerful and energetic than ever. Performing for live audiences had rejuvenated him. I heard through the grapevine that he had signed with the Mirage for another two years. When I first heard this, I thought he was a little crazy. But now that I saw him in person, I understood. He may have been sixty-three, but he was in his element, doing what he loved. More than anything else, he'd always been a performer. It was how he started his career, and it was how he was concluding it. As usual, I put my voice recorder on the coffee table and pressed the record button. It was just like old times. I had no idea this was going to be our last interview.

∞

How was your drive?

It was nice to get out of the house. I liked driving through the desert. Some people feel desolation in the desert, but I find it inspiring.

I have something to announce to the world. It's very important to me. But before I tell you what's on my mind, I want to tell you a story. The story is about a friend of mine. Maybe you remember him. Years ago, I told you about a kid named Mike, the boy who lived across the street from us in Arcadia. He and I snuck out at night to steal the cash box from the movie theater.

Yes, I remember the story.

Well, I never told you what became of Mike. His story is important. The day after the theft, Mike and I met at his house while his parents were gone. He had stashed the stolen cash box behind a bag of fertilizer in their garage. He wanted to split the cash with me, but my conscience got the best of me, and I told him I didn't want the money. In fact, I said we ought to return it. But Mike insisted that we keep it and divide it. "We earned it," Mike said, as if we both had been working at legitimate jobs. I argued with him, telling him we didn't earn anything, but Mike wouldn't listen. He insisted again we keep the box and split the cash. "Listen," I said. "You can keep it all. I don't care. But I don't want anything to do with it." Mike said that suited him fine, so long as I agreed to keep my mouth shut. I promised I wouldn't tell a soul, and I never did. But that was the end of our friendship. We hung out a few times after that, but that was all. We soon drifted apart. And for Mike, his life sadly went downhill from that day forward.

What do you mean it went downhill?

The movie theater theft was just a beginning for him. After we parted ways, he began hanging out with Roscoe and Oscar Hamilton, two brothers who lived a couple blocks away. Soon the three of them began to spend their nights burglarizing homes and businesses. Oscar was only twelve, but Roscoe was sixteen. The boys were clever, and for two or three years they eluded the police. They stole a lot of cash and jewelry. They kept their stolen goods hidden in an abandoned factory building just outside of town. I know all of this because the details were in a newspaper article my mom gave me. Mike was arrested shortly after he turned eighteen. "This could've been you," my mom said. "You were once such good friends with this boy. It's such a shame. I wonder what's going to happen to him."

What did happen to him?

Since Mike was eighteen, he was tried as an adult. So was Roscoe, but Oscar was tried as a juvenile. They were accused for twenty-six burglaries, most of them in Arcadia. The jewelry they kept was the key to solving the crimes, since it was identifiable and could be tied to the specific complaints. Everyone was amazed at how long the boys got away with their illegal activities. They were caught while trying to rob a downtown furniture store where a policeman happened to see their flashlights dancing against the walls inside the store. The officer pulled up to the curb and entered through the storefront door, which had been jimmied open by the boys. When the cop told the boys to freeze, they took off running. They went out the rear door and into the back alley. Mike and Roscoe got away, but Oscar tripped and hit his head on the corner of a metal dumpster. He was dazed but not unconscious. But the fall had been enough to slow him down for the officer. He was cuffed and stuffed into the back of the police car. The cop took Oscar down to the station, and they interrogated the boy until he confessed to everything. According to the article in the newspaper, he gave up the names of his accomplices and revealed their hiding place. The police picked up the other two boys, and when they searched the old factory, they found the stolen cash and jewelry. They now had the evidence they would need. After the trial, Mike and Roscoe went to jail, and Oscar went to a juvenile detention center. This was big news in Arcadia, and Mike's family was totally humiliated. They wanted nothing to do with their criminal son and did nothing to defend him. They refused to visit after he was locked up. They wouldn't answer his letters. As far as they were concerned, Mike was no longer their son. After about a year, my mom stepped in.

What'd she do?

She tried talking to Mike's parents, hoping to patch up things with their son. But she got nowhere with them. Then she began visiting Mike herself, and she wrote him letters. She talked to him a lot about God, and she told him if he repented, that God would forgive him and improve his life. My mom could be very convincing when it came to matters of faith. You know, a lot of my own faith comes directly from my mother.

Why would your mom go out of her way to help this boy? He sounds like such a rotten kid.

You have to understand my mom. In fact, you have to understand both of my parents. For them, life is all about decency. My parents didn't hate others just because they did a few bad things or even a lot of bad things. They were very decent people. They believed no matter what that people were inherently good. People might go astray, but they still deserved our kindness, because like the rest of us, they were God's children. Further, Mike was once a friend of our family's, and Mom didn't think it was right to abandon a friend.

So what finally happened to Mike?

He was released from prison after serving all of his sentence. He then worked at a job for several months, but grew tired of the low pay. He got a hold of a handgun, and he used it to rob a liquor store. He held his gun on the clerk and demanded the money, and the clerk reached into a drawer. But rather than pull out cash, the clerk pulled out his own gun and shot Mike in the shoulder. Mike then shot at the clerk twice, missing him but hitting the booze bottles behind him. He then ran away. The police found him in a hospital two hours later where he was trying to talk a nurse into removing the bullet from his shoulder. All my mom's work with Mike was for nothing. I asked Mom about this, and I remember what she said. She said, "He's a human being, and he needs to be loved. I'm not going to give up on him." It was kind of unbelievable.

Did Mike go back to prison?

Yes, they gave him a long sentence for armed robbery and attempted murder.

Did your mom stay in touch with him?

Yes, she did, until she passed away.

Do you keep in contact with him now?

No, I don't. I don't know where he is.

Do you think your mom's words and actions inspired you to pay visits to Lynette Ann Bauer after she burned down your house?

Yes, I think my mom had a lot to do with my visits to Lynette.

Do you still see Lynette?

A couple times a year.

Why did you tell me Mike's story?

Because I think it's important.

Why is it so important?

There's a huge gap between the actions of people who call themselves Christians and the precepts they claim to believe in. People don't practice what they hear preached. We're supposed to be forgiving, aren't we? Yet let's be honest here. We seem so perversely unwilling to forgive. I think in Mike's case, my mother's forgiveness was a good thing, but what Mike really needed was to be forgiven by his parents. It probably would've meant the world to him. Why couldn't his parents love him? Why is it so hard for some of us to forgive, especially when it comes to our own flesh and blood? What is it about forgiveness that makes it feel so wrong and unnatural? We so easily revert to anger, vengeance, and hate. Why does it feel so wrong to be good? Do you have a good answer for this?

Not really.

Never forget, a little love and forgiveness can go a long, long way.

Do you think Mike wouldn't have held up that liquor store if his parents had forgiven him?

I guess we'll never know.

You said earlier that you brought me here to make an announcement.

Yes, I did. It concerns Alex.

Did something happen to him?

In a manner of speaking, yes. Becky and Alex have decided to get married. The wedding will be held this summer.

So Alex was true to his word.

Yes, he was.

What kind of wedding will it be?

We're going to hold both the ceremony and reception at Dulcinea. Everyone we know will be invited. It will be a huge affair. We want to get these kids started off on the right foot.

Will you allow photographers?

Yes, we'll allow a few. My fans will be curious to know what's happening.

Have you set an actual date?

Not yet. It'll be sometime this summer. Jen and Becky's family have yet to come up with a date.

Are you nervous?

At first, I was a little nervous about having to give a toast to the bride and groom. I'd never made a wedding toast before, and I wanted to be sure I would say just the right things. So what do you say? What do you say to two starry-eyed newlyweds who are so deeply in love? I figure I could reel off some old clichés, giving them some obvious bits of advice that lead them in the right direction. But I thought about it, and now I figure the best thing I could do is to tell it like it is. I want to say something real. I want to say something that actually makes sense, that'll be inspirational and useful no matter where they go. So I've come up with something, and if they think my words are as profound as I believe they are, maybe someday they can raise a champagne glass and pass them down to their own children.

So what is your toast?

I'll say, "Alex and Becky, here's what I have to say to you. Here's my humble advice for a successful marriage. In fact, here's my advice for a successful life. I thought long and hard about what to say to you today. I could tell you to always be honest with each other. But doesn't that kind of go without saying? Everyone is going to tell you the same thing. I could also tell you to love each other, but I don't foresee you having any problem with that. I don't think you need any coaching here. Clearly your love is strong. I think you've loved each other from the first night you met. I could also tell you not to keep secrets. This is such good advice. Secrets are like poison, but doesn't that go with the honesty advice? If you're honest with each other, you won't keep secrets. No, I don't think that's the advice I want to give. I guess I could also tell you to be patient. Don't expect more than the other is capable of giving or doing. This is also probably good advice, but it's still not what I want to say. No, what I really want to say can be expressed in a single, marvelous word. And that word is forgiveness. I have lived a long time, and I have learned that this word is worth more than all the diamonds, rubies, and gold you can stuff into your pockets. Forgiveness is what it's all about. Forgiveness is everything. As you travel through life, you're going to discover that hurt will be as much a part of your daily routine as each breath you take. Every day, you're going to hurt others, and they're going to hurt you. And you're going to hurt each other. And you're also going to hurt yourselves. There's no way to avoid it. And it can't be ignored. It can't be swept under the rug or put up in the attic. But if you can learn to forgive, you will hold the magic key. If you can learn to forgive others and learn to forgive yourselves, you will live glorious and loving lives. I mean, you will truly live. And you will love in ways you never felt possible. You'll soar over mountains, valleys, seas, and forests like eagles in the clouds. The world will be yours for the taking. God will be your sure partner, and life will be your friend."

I like it.

Not bad, eh?

EPILOGUE

O n the morning of June 2, 2001, I woke up and had breakfast with Julia. I had two eggs over easy and a slice of whole wheat toast with butter and raspberry jelly. I had a small glass of orange juice and a cup of coffee. Julia asked me if I wanted any bacon, but I said no. Julia and I talked about our daughter, Pamela, and her plans to have a baby. We thought it was about time, since she was now thirty-two and her biological clock was ticking. Julia and I then agreed it was hard to believe that our children were now in their thirties. Time seemed to have had gone by so fast. I'm in the habit of doing something you might find strange. Or maybe not. On important days in my life, I write down all that happened during day so that I'll have a record of it, so that I'll never forget any of the details. That's how I know so much about my breakfast on June 2. I wrote down everything that happened that day. I'm not going to bore you by recounting every little detail I recorded. Right now, I just want to convey that the day moved along like any other. Julia went off to her job, and I stepped into my den to work on my latest project. I was writing an article for *Rolling Stone* about Chrissie Hynde and the Pretenders. I wrote until noon and then made a pastrami sandwich for lunch. I went back to work. Julia came home at five, and we ate dinner. We watched a little TV after dinner and climbed into our bed to read. I got the call from Joseph at a little before midnight. The call alarmed me since we don't usually get many late at night calls. Joseph's voice sounded ominously grave. I knew something must have happened to Scowl, and Joseph got right to the point.

"Scowl is gone," he said. I knew what he was saying, but I didn't want to believe it. I asked him what he meant, and he said, "He's dead. He's no longer with us." When I asked what happened, Joseph told me Scowl had a massive heart attack shortly after his show in Vegas and passed away in his dressing room. They called 911, and paramedics came and worked on him. They thought they had him out of the woods, and then his heart stopped. It just stopped beating. Jennifer was out of her mind, and she asked her father to call me. She was in Vegas with Scowl when it happened. She was unable to speak with anyone. She wanted me to come to the Mirage as soon as possible to act as their family spokesman. She told her dad that I was the only person qualified to talk to the press about her husband. I didn't look forward to this task, but I agreed to do it. I drove to Las Vegas that night, and the next morning, I was meeting with reporters at the Mirage, facing a cluster of microphones. I told them Scowl had died from natural causes, from a heart attack, but that the Clark County Coroner was performing an autopsy. I don't know why they insisted on the autopsy. I knew they wouldn't find drugs or alcohol in Scowl's system. There were rumors and a lot of speculation, but it was the sort of nonsense that always occurs when someone famous drops dead out of the blue.

Later that morning I sat in my hotel room and watched CNN on the TV. They were talking about a Hamas suicide bomber who had killed twenty-one people the day before at a disco in Tel Aviv. Then they ran a story about Scowl and showed the video of me standing in front of all those darn microphones. I looked ridiculous. I was a writer, not a PR man. They ran clips of Scowl's past performances and scenes from his movies. They even showed a brief segment of Andy Black showing off some of Scowl's paintings. They had statements from Bobby Breen, Richard, and Trevor. Some other celebrities chimed in about the loss. I don't drink, as a rule, but I poured myself a glass of Scotch from one of those little bottles in the minibar. I then received a call from Jennifer, and she wanted me to come up to Scowl's suite. She said there was something she had to give me. I had no idea what she was talking about, but I agreed to come up. I set down my half-finished glass of whiskey and left my room. As I walked toward the elevators, I had the strangest sensation that Scowl's entire life was flashing before my eyes. I felt like crying. I thought about the evening after the concert when we first met, right up until the last interview when he'd announced Alex's engagement. He was going to miss the wedding. I hoped Jennifer and Alex wouldn't postpone it. That would be the last thing Scowl would want.

When I arrived at Scowl's suite, Jennifer was at the door to greet me.

Her eyes were horribly red and swollen from crying, and she gave me a hug when I entered. She then stepped to the desk in the corner of the room and picked up a small piece of folded paper. She handed the paper to me and said, "Scowl asked for a pen and paper right before he died. He wrote this note. He asked that we give it to you, and he said you would know what it meant." I took the piece of paper and unfolded it. Then I read the writing. The penmanship was shaky, as though written by a dying man. The note said simply, "Orson Welles was right." Below the sentence Scowl had drawn a smiley face.

"What does it mean?" Jennifer asked. I handed the paper back to her. "It means everything is good," I said. "Everything is just as it ought to be. It means your husband got his happy ending."

Printed and bound by PG in the USA